Fall & Fly

by Polly Meek

Copyright © 2023 Polly Meek
All rights reserved

First published in Great Britain in 2023 by Kindle Direct Publishing.

Copyright © Polly Meek 2023

The right of Polly Meek to be identified as the Author of the Work has been asserted by her in accordance with the Copyright, Designs and Patents Act 1988.

All rights reserved. No part of this publication may be reproduced, stored in a retrieval system, or transmitted, in any form or by any means without prior written permission of the publisher, nor be otherwise circulated in any form of binding or cover other than that in which it is published and without a similar condition being imposed on the subsequent purchaser.

All characters in this publication are fictitious and any resemblance to real persons, living or dead, is purely coincidental.

ISBN: 979-8-37395-698-7

For Gary, my co-pilot in life.
With love Px

1. Sky Bar

Romilly West tugged up the zip of her insulated jacket, and deep-breathed San Francisco's surprisingly clean air – the antidote to her long-haul flight and un-openable hotel room windows. Standing just beyond The Beaumont's ornate glass canopy, she had positioned herself upwind of some late-night smokers, and a discrete distance from where a dubiously dressed woman applied lipstick. Same scene, different city. Hoping to catch a glimpse of the stars above downtown's soaring glass and metal, Romilly tipped her chin upwards. A comparison with Barcelona, or even Nairobi came to mind. She smiled to herself, ever grateful for her career. Nothing rivalled a cruising-altitude night-sky from the cockpit.

Back through the swish revolving doors, Romilly checked her phone while waiting at the bank of art-deco elevators. Nine forty-five pm locally, five forty-five am back in the UK. A glass of wine in the hotel bar would see her through to eleven pm and on to bed. Any pilot would say the same: set yourself up for a solid sleep on the first night of layover.

A windswept, elderly couple approached from the marble-pillared foyer.

'Evening, ma'am, surprisingly blowy for fall,' said the man, nodding politely as they came to a stop beside her.

'Chilly, too.' Somehow, Romilly sounded extra-British when she was away. 'Have you had a pleasant evening?'

'Yes, we're returning from a delicious dim sum dinner in Chinatown – it's only five blocks from here. Been swept most the way back, mind you,' the woman replied, adjusting her grey bob.

The man chuckled. 'My wife would sooner endure the weather than ride one of the city's driverless taxi cabs.'

'I completely agree with you.'

The furthest elevator dinged its arrival. Once its passengers had emptied, the man gestured for Romilly to enter first, while crooking a practiced arm for his wife.

'Which floor?' said Romilly, stepping inside. Confronted by her own dishevelled hair in the three-sixty-degree mirrors, she hastily raked her fingers through its lengths.

'Fourteen, please,' the couple replied in unison, then smiled at each other.

Romilly pressed the vintage-styled buttons marked '14 – Rooms' and '22 – Sky Bar'.

Within seconds, their rapid ascent muffled the elevator's chaotic piped jazz. For Romilly, air pressure fluctuation was a routine occurrence, easily relieved by a deep swallow. The couple performed exaggerated yawns and raised hands in synch to cover their mouths.

'Goodnight,' Romilly said as they exited on their floor.

'And to you,' they chimed. The man kissed his wife on the head as they walked away, then murmured something in her ear.

The view narrowed, leaving Romilly staring at an infinite mirror tunnel of other Romillys. She reminded one and all, that life was simpler when she relied solely on herself. No one to distract her from striving for goals, or to ask questions about a past she'd worked hard to forget. Hard-earned lessons of fair-weather relationships were reinforced daily, by stopping the version of herself that allowed hurt to happen. Now her life was flying and her father, nothing more. Forwards was the only way to face, alone the best option. In commitment to that resolve, she pulled out her phone again and added a note to her list of places to explore while on her thirty-five-hour layover. Dim-sum-for-one sounded perfect.

On floor twenty-two, Romilly strolled into diffused, amber lighting, headed for Sky Bar's semi-circular, polished wood bar. The space afforded uninterrupted triple-aspect views across the glittering Bay of San Francisco. She paused for a few seconds to admire the panorama, but, for the second time in a matter of minutes, appreciated the privileges of her decade-long career.

Just three hours earlier, passengers and crew aboard Sterling Air's outbound from Heathrow had witnessed a striking sunset vista of the Golden Gate Bridge, Alcatraz Island, and the Bay Bridge as they banked into the final approach for San Francisco International Airport. Were it not for the absolute concentration Romilly had needed to coax the Boeing 777 along a crosswind into a fluid, centre-line landing, she might have asked the second officer to take some photographs on her phone. Her dad could have enjoyed them – perhaps a reminder of routes he'd flown, back in the day.

The low mumble of conversation from a dozen candlelit customers at perimeter tables-for-two mingled pleasantly with a lounge pianist tinkling away. Romilly slid onto a high-backed stool at one end of the bar.

'What can I get you, ma'am?' a varsity-esque bartender asked, who seemed barely old enough to drink.

Perhaps it was her approaching four-o ticking in her subconscious, or merely a game she'd use to occupy herself, but her current inclination when meeting people was to size up their age. 'A glass of dry white, please – whatever you'd recommend.'

'Our chardonnays are very popular.' He selected a bottle from the chiller behind him and tilted its label towards her. 'This is from the Hornbrook Estate, Napa Valley.'

'I'm guessing that's one of the local wineries?'

'Sonoma is an hour away, Napa another hour or two beyond, depending on the vineyard. Worth a visit any time, but my folks head there often at this time of year, just for the autumn colours. I'm sure they'd recommend it.'

At least he hadn't said 'my mom'. She cleared her throat and nodded approval of his wine suggestion. 'That would be great. A large glass, please.'

The only other customer at the bar was sitting opposite at the other end of the semi-circle. Possibly a local, wearing a hoody and cradling a tumbler of something caramel coloured. She recognised his contained posture as suggesting contentment with his own company. Or at least that he was intent on it. Salt-and-pepper flecks, glinting at his temples through dark hair in the bar lights, pegged him at mid-forties. Her hand lifted to the sides of her own hair. Being a mousey blonde had finally proven advantageous, disguising as it did the odd grey. Nature's highlights, her mum used to say.

The bartender placed a half-full tulip glass onto a branded drinks doily. 'On a tab?'

'On my room, please. One second …' She pulled her card key from the back pocket of her jeans. 'One-two-oh-five. Thank you …'

'Carter, ma'am. No problem. Enjoy.'

Romilly closed her eyes as the first sip of cool wine slipped down. Delicious. And well-deserved. Opening her eyes, she permitted herself a congratulatory smile. No matter how many hours of simulator training a pilot underwent, touching down at a destination for the first time in real life was always something special. With its spectacular approach, and renowned watery surrounds lapping at the peripheries, San Francisco International hadn't disappointed. Despite the tricky winds, Senior Captain Alistair Blair had shown faith in her ability to hand-fly the landing. She was still on a bit of a high from managing to keep it so smooth.

The man opposite her stared in her direction. Romilly's polite nod of acknowledgement, however, was not reciprocated, so she watched Carter for a moment or two as he wiped down his preparation area and replaced an optic. Seeking her phone again, the bastion of any solo drinker, she opened her vintage Louis Vuitton shoulder bag, a second-hand gift she'd bought herself after gaining her wings. Since then, shouldering a mortgage while still repaying her flight-training loans meant that luxury anything – even at second-hand prices – was out of reach. After all, wasn't she sitting here in supermarket-brand jeans and a four-year-old blazer from a sale at Next?

Relieved at not having missed any messages, Romilly double-checked the eight-hour time difference to home, before tapping out a text to her dad. Her recent opportunity to bid for this eight-week block of Californian long-haul would require an absence from home of three consecutive nights each week, but it was the most efficient way of racking up the hours needed to apply for captaincy. She had an ambitious goal and meant to achieve it.

Peering through her lashes, Romilly realised that the man in the hoody was still staring at her. His dark eyes barely even blinked. She knew the drill; a simple switching of seats would most likely resolve the issue. Romilly hitched her bag onto her shoulder.

'All okay?' said Carter, motioning at her glass.

'Yes, but I may move to another stool.'

'The screen's bothering you?' Carter frowned, pointing a remote control above her head. 'It's definitely on mute.'

Romilly twisted round and up to see a TV screen suspended from the ceiling directly above her head, currently playing a local news channel called KPR.

'No, it's fine, I'll, er, just move up a couple of places anyway.'

Once re-settled, she busied herself with scrolling through her phone, avoiding eye contact with anyone, especially the man who probably hadn't been watching her at all.

Several minutes later, an overpowering combination of perfume and cigarettes caught Romilly's attention before the woman emitting it leaned across the bar, seeking Carter's attention. A couple of years his senior, maybe.

'What time does this bar close, please?' the woman said.

'Two am, ma'am, not for three hours or so. Can I get you something?'

'Vodka orange highball, lots of ice.' The woman eased long, bare legs shod with knock-off studded Valentinos onto a stool, then opened an obviously fake Gucci bag. In her travels, Romilly often saw designer 'bargains' for sale on blankets at local markets. It was always the gold metal hardware that gave them away.

'Coming up.'

'Quiet this evening, usually find pilots away from home in here, I heard,' said the woman, drumming weapon-grade fingernails on the bar.

'Not always,' said Carter, with admirable discretion. 'On a tab?'

The woman shook her head, delved into her bag, and passed him a twenty-dollar bill. Her presence wasn't particularly surprising. Copenhagen, Cork, Cape Town – it didn't matter where. How pilots spent their downtime while away on layover was their own business. Some wanted to 'play'; others were social with their crews. Ones like Romilly mostly avoided complications and distractions. She wasn't a nun, occasionally joining her crew for nights out. As it happened, the friendliest cabin manager she'd ever worked with, Steph, from today's flight had persuaded her to host a happy-hour gathering there at Sky Bar for crew cocktails tomorrow evening. As was sometimes the case, cabin crew were put up in less glamorous accommodation, usually devoid of bars with roof-top views.

Pilots who rolled up at hotel bars in uniform were either too exhausted to first check into their rooms, or were deliberately touting for attention – but both were almost certainly breaking their airline's protocols. A case in point had just exited the elevator and was wandering towards the bar, flight case still in hand. Romilly couldn't identify his uniform – perhaps a regional airline.

'Bourbon on the rocks, sir,' the man drawled at Carter, leaning his arm onto the bar, flashing the three stripes of first officer ranking on his jacket sleeve. Thirty or so, thirty-five at a push.

'We have a West Coast special, the St George?'

'I'd prefer a Henman Texas if you have it.'

'Yes, sir, we do, coming right up.'

'Much obliged.'

The woman next to Romilly adjusted her pose. 'That's what I like to see – a man who knows what he wants after a busy day keeping his passengers safe,' she purred.

Romilly rolled her eyes, and briefly caught a similar action in the eyes of the man in the hoody, who still stared at the TV screen. She pulled out her electronic reader and settled into the next chapter of a mediocre thriller.

The pilot was almost through his second bourbon when the woman, now glued to his side, purported very indiscreetly to 'love it when pilots lose control' and 'tip over the edge when they gave in to what they need most'. Draining the last of their glasses in haste, the pair then stumbled towards the lift.

Romilly finished the last of her wine and placed her empty glass nearer to Carter. 'Thank you, that was a good choice. I'm afraid I don't have any cash yet to tip you with. Are you here tomorrow evening?'

'Yes, ma'am, most evenings – keeps me afloat through my final year across The Bay.'

'You're at Berkley? What are you studying?'

'Business Management, ma'am.'

'Well done, you, and please call me Romilly. I know it's the American respect thing, but I feel old when I'm called "ma'am".'

'I'll try to remember.'

The man in the hoody stood up, slid a dollar bill beneath his empty glass, and nodded subtly at Romilly. She returned a polite smile before he headed to the elevators.

'Thanks. See you again, sir,' Carter called, tucking the cash into his waistcoat pocket.

The man raised his hand in acknowledgement.

'If my airline books my layover at the same hotel each week, I'll be here regularly over the next month or so, maybe longer,' Romilly said.

'Which airline are you with?'

'Sterling Air – you know us?'

'Of course, you're big in England, aren't you? A couple-thousand pilots, if I remember correctly from my travel and tourism seminars. It's a wonder you guys ever have the same crews twice. They often put up their cockpit folk here.'

Romilly felt a swell of pride that her airline featured in one of Berkley's seminars, and smiled to herself.

'Good to know. And the other pilot? I didn't recognise which airline he was from?'

'The uniformed guy, you mean? Haven't seen him before. If he was wearing a cargo carrier's tie,

FedEx or UPS – they aren't usually on long layovers like you international passenger airlines. Don't hang here much.'

Cargo. Romilly shuddered. That explained a lot.

'I'm planning on doing the tourist thing to make the most of the city for my eight-week block. I've got a list here, pulled together some research. Mind if I ask your opinion?' She scrolled through her phone. Bartenders and concierges usually gave excellent insider recommendations, helping to home in on the priorities.

'Sure, but avoid Fisherman's Wharf for starters. We do way better than that, like the cable cars, streetcars, bridges, and parks. See Alcatraz, but forget the so-called scary night-tour – it's ridiculous. Also, go across Golden Gate into Sausalito and the Bay Bridge to Berkley – they're all worth your time, I reckon.'

'I'll need to lock into this route for the next few blocks for all that,' she said with a smile, 'but thank you. Any tips on where to eat would also be good.'

Carter talked animatedly of the city's sour dough origins and its history of local fish tacos. He was elaborating on what he meant by 'San Franciscan soul food' when Romilly's eyelids grew impossibly heavy.

'Sorry, that's me for the night. At least I'm tired enough to sleep. Trying to avoid jet lag if I can, because I've only two nights here before the Wednesday inbound.'

'Sure thing. I'll have a restaurant list for you for tomorrow evening.'

Romilly couldn't avoid catching sight of herself inside the elevator once again. A rawness seemed to have replaced the whites of her eyes. She examined them closely, checking for dreaded 'pink-eye', the condition that would ground a pilot until healed. No, she decided, it was just the hour – probably eight am back in the UK. As the doors opened at her floor, she faltered, surprised by two people waiting to get in. One was the woman from the bar, with eyes glistening merrily, and one side of her top ridden up, revealing a lacy black bra. Beside her was not the cargo pilot, but the man in the hoody.

'Thanks, baby, you're the best,' she slurred at him, tripping past Romilly into the elevator.

The man followed her in, avoiding eye contact.

Romilly shook her head. In anyone's time zone, that was fast work.

2. Painted Ladies

Only the late hour saved Nathan Reed from slamming his hotel room door, but it sure as hell deserved to be. He slumped onto one of the two king-sized beds, exhausted, yet pricking with frustration. Whether real or imagined, a lingering stench of cheap perfume forced him to his feet and over to the windows. Great, there were no handles. He notched up the aircon and headed for the shower.

Inside the walk-in enclosure, he waited for the steam to relax him. For the first time since the painfully messy situation back home, he'd entertained the prospect of feeling attracted to someone. Minding his own business in the Sky Bar, his attention had been caught by the naturally beautiful woman drinking opposite him, who'd seemed content in her own company. Or at least intent on it. Fortunately, she'd sat below the television screen, so he could study her covertly.

Instinct told him she might also fly: her cursory survey of what to a regular person must be a breathtaking view; economical with her movement; red-rimmed eyes, perhaps from having battled the same crosswinds he'd engaged with twenty-four hours earlier; and spatially aware when slipping onto the bar stool, without even looking at it. But it was her humorous eye-roll, and confident but gracious chatter with the barman that told him she might also have been interesting to talk to. A fellow Brit, no less. He hadn't been able to fully make out her name when she'd introduced herself to the bartender – though it had sounded like 'Milly', a name he'd more likely associate with a newly qualified member of cabin crew twenty-five years his junior. It was academic now – after the look on her face when she'd seen him at the lift with that … 'girl'. He was a bad bet, anyway. Probably did the woman a favour. After making a couple of calls back home, he slipped into bed, intent on drawing a line under the whole situation. This time tomorrow, he'd be halfway across the Atlantic.

Lying awake in the pitch black, his mind played tug of war with sleep versus sensual, slow-motion images of the woman in the bar closing her eyes as she tasted her first sip of wine and smiled to herself. Maybe if he saw her around the hotel tomorrow, she might listen when he relayed what had happened. But honestly, who would believe that after a quick walk around the block before bed, when exiting the elevator on the eighth floor for his room, he'd found the girl wandering around? That she had tottered after him, claiming she could 'help him relax'? He had of course said he wasn't interested, but then, to his horror, she'd said 'Look at this real quick' and whipped her top off, right there in the hotel corridor, and proceeded to drape herself over him. Desperate to avoid manhandling her, or for inquisitive hotel guests to begin appearing from their doors, he'd somehow persuaded her to put the top back on. Escorting her to reception had seemed the right thing to do.

Just as sleep seemed within grasp, his phone pinged. That's what came of never switching it off. The airline had placed him on early alert of tomorrow's inbound to Heathrow being cancelled, due to significant mechanical work underway. Obviously planes had to be safe, but delays and cancellations were a crew scheduling headache. Nathan spared a thought for Customer Services who might have to reassign or bump three hundred unhappy passengers from tomorrow's flight.

By morning, the cancellation had been confirmed, and he was to await instruction from Crew Services for his repositioning from tomorrow onwards. Compared with certain East-Asian destinations, there were worse places to be delayed in than San Francisco. Though devoid of quality sleep, Nathan maintained his usual routine for acclimation to new time zones. Like yesterday, he coaxed straining calves and jarred knees through ten kilometres' worth of San Francisco's foggy and notoriously brutal hills. Today, forty-six felt more like fifty-six. The apparent ease with which the local elderly carted bags of shopping up and down their steep roads put him to shame.

After a shower and a bagel 'n eggs breakfast, Nathan packed his camera bag, hoping for some shots of Golden Gate Bridge from its nearside bank. If only he'd taken some shots yesterday, when the air was clear. Feeling doubtful, he sought the advice of the concierge down in reception, asking if the fog would lift by lunchtime.

'I probably wouldn't rely on it today, sir. "Old Carl", that's our famous fog, sets in for longer periods the further into fall we go. Might be better tomorrow, though.'

Nathan nodded at the burgundy-uniformed man, knowing it might be aircraft mechanics and Crew

Services, not just the weather that would impact the likelihood of his taking photos tomorrow. 'I'll leave the camera here today, then.'

'If you get yourself up higher, say to Alamo Square Park, you may be lucky. I've seen some amazing shots of the city's rooftops above the cloud-line. Bit of a hike up there, but I noticed you coming back from a run earlier. There are rows of coloured houses alongside the park, too – we call them "The Painted Ladies". If you've got a decent zoom in that bag, the struts of the Bay Bridge sometimes poke up behind them in the distance.'

'Thanks … Bill,' Nathan said, eyeing the man's name badge. Concierges and bartenders – always his first port-of-call for advice in a new city.

'You're welcome, Sir. But do yourself a favour, take care of your bag up there.'

'Yes, I noticed there are homeless everywhere. Worst I've seen it, even in Asia.'

'After New York, we're the most expensive city to live in. Forces some desperate folk into petty crime.'

'Understood. See you later.'

Photography had been a saviour these past few years. As a creative outlet and providing a purpose to explore places while on layover it was an excellent hobby – more than that even, as he had lately achieved modest success by uploading architectural shots to a photo-sharing website. Losing himself for hours while digitally editing – whether in a hotel room or back in the UK – also offered relief from torturing himself over his shortcomings and the part they played in a fractured home life.

Finally, after lugging his camera bag full of lenses, filters, and a lightweight folding tripod up a foggy, three-mile route, Nathan emerged into brilliant sunshine at the entry pillars of Alamo Square Park. He followed a path over the brow of a hill, passing benches of homeless people who gazed into bottles, or slept.

Shielding his eyes, he stared out at the azure sky and a myriad of spires and turrets that pierced the floating fog blanket. Furthest away lay the faint arcs of the Bay Bridge's suspension cables; in the foreground, buildings, slate roofs supported by ornate wooden gables, and varied pastel-coloured facades caught his attention. Unable to resist any longer, he took up a position on the hilltop grass between other photographers and tourists.

Nathan had just begun clicking when his phone pinged. He sighed, never truly off-duty. Apparently, crews were being merged; he would be reassigned shortly. This wasn't the first time, wouldn't be the last. Mechanical failures and a myriad of other disruptors were out of his hands. While he acknowledged the message, a pair of teenage lads, in grungy, head-to-toe black, entered the periphery of his vision. They weaved between where people were sat, surveying belongings, ignoring the view. Nathan threaded an arm through the strap of his camera bag and returned to his phone.

Taking a break from landscape architectural frames, he switched his wide-angle lens for his telephoto and began to scan nearby surroundings through the viewfinder. Zooming back and forth from rows of birds on nearby telegraph wires, to a clump of buttercups beside him, his attention was snagged momentarily by a woman sitting with her face in her hands, elbows on knees. Her ponytail blew in the breeze as she shifted to hug her legs and stare at the grass. He flicked his camera away to estimate the distance — two hundred feet or less, maybe. Refocussing, he'd been about to heed his inner chastisement at the invasion of her privacy when the same two shifty teenagers joined the frame. In haste, he checked the area around her and saw she had a bag lying on the grass. The lads separated and circled out wide. Shit. No, this was nothing to do with him; he should mind his own business. Then the woman tilted her face briefly towards the sky, revealing her identity.

'Fuck sakes ...' he muttered and, with a withering side-helping of *what the hell am I doing?*, bundled everything haphazardly into his bag, tucked it under his arm, and jogged towards her. He'd better think of something, and fast.

3. Alamo

Romilly blotted her eyes with the sleeve of her fleece and tried to pull herself together. Rueing the absence of her pilot sunglasses, she squinted at the iced-top view of the Bay from Alamo Park. Bill, The Beaumont's concierge, had suggested she walk there, perhaps astute in recognising her need for a distraction, though of course he couldn't have known that all-time favourite, Robbie Williams had let her down earlier. Even a high-volume 'Rock DJ' pulsing through her headphones as she pounded the hotel treadmill hadn't shaken her concern at not having heard from her dad overnight.

'No news is good news' was not an adage she subscribed to, especially when it came to her father. In the years since her mother had passed, he had declined rapidly; now his seventy-eight years hung on him like oversized overalls. In an effort to inject some joy into his life, when she couldn't visit, she would message him every day from wherever she was in the world, and he would reply. Yesterday's photographs of the airport that she'd sent him had gone unanswered, driving her niggling concern. Episodes of his confusion during the year had been attributed by his GP to winter viruses, old age, and even too much whisky. But Romilly trusted her own instincts, and they were waving caution flags.

Before leaving for the hike up to Alamo, she'd rung her dad's number, knowing it was around four pm in the UK. He would most likely be at his flat in the luxury retirement complex he'd downsized to after selling their large-gardened family home in the suburbs. There had been no answer. While packing a drink into her holdall, she pulled up the contact details of Benita Gonzalez, his friendly carer, who was contracted to visit every day, and requested an update on today's visit. If Romilly hadn't received a response from her by the time she reached Alamo, she would telephone.

Alamo Square Park enjoyed a micro-weather system that reminded Romilly of the hilltops of Spain's Costa Blanca. An oasis of sunshine and smiling faces, if you didn't count the ruddy-faced homeless who probably sought it out just for warmth. She had just added 'find a cash machine' to her reminder app, when a text arrived from her dad, saying he was glad she was having a nice holiday, and hoped Jess and Maria were also enjoying themselves. He would see them all soon, he said. Romilly stared at the screen, re-reading the words. Jess and Maria were long-since forgotten school friends, and the last time she'd been on holiday with them was to Weymouth with the Girl Guides in 1990. Finding a quiet spot on some grass, she had dialled his number immediately. He picked up.

'Dad? It's me.'

'Joan?'

Romilly tried to disguise the crack in her voice. 'No, Dad, it's Romilly. Were you napping?'

'No, I'm watching television.'

'I wasn't sure from your text whether you're feeling all right. I'm calling from San Francisco, flew in yesterday on the triple seven?'

'Oh yes, I'm a bit tired, should have waited before sending you a text. How is Fog City?'

'Living up to its legend.'

'It always did,' he chuckled. 'Sometimes I had to land without visible runway lights until the very last seconds.'

'I flew in with someone who knows you, Senior Captain Alistair Blair. I hadn't worked alongside him before. He's only part-time now, and was on his way home here after a weekend in London. He let me do the honours with a manual landing.'

'Did he? That was good of him. And how was it? Usually, a wicked westerly gusting across the South Bay channel, if I remember correctly.'

'Smooth as you like.' She giggled, referencing one of his frequent sayings when she'd been learning to fly. 'Anyway, he passes on his regards to you.'

'An excellent aviator – knew he'd go far.'

Romilly swallowed, pained by the certain knowledge that her dad didn't think the same of her. 'How are you feeling, Dad?'

'Oh, I'm safe … But I'd better go – *Bargain Hunt* is starting.'

'Okay,' she said, barely reassured by their conversation. 'I'll be over on Friday morning.'

'That's wonderful! How I've missed you, Joanie. Romilly will be so happy to see you too. Bye-bye for now, my love.' The line went dead.

There was no denying it – even allowing for his early evening weariness, some form of memory problem was afoot. She pulled up a search engine on her phone and started to investigate the subject. After reading some grim first-hand accounts of devastated relatives and delving into medical explanations, she dropped her head into her hands, engulfed with dread. If he was to suffer with something with rapid onset, what would his quality of life be like? Romilly's impetus to achieve captaincy cranked up another gear; she couldn't accept the prospect of him never seeing her wearing that fourth stripe. Of him never truly feeling proud.

A plan. That's what she needed. She would talk it through with the GP again. Maybe Benita, with her caregiver background, had some ideas. Romilly had just glanced up at an intricate lattice of vapour jet trails that made her think of home, when she noticed a man jogging towards her and waving in her direction. She swivelled to see if there was someone beyond her responding to the man, but nobody seemed to acknowledge him. A large bag bounced clumsily on his hip, and at about fifty feet away, he started calling out to her.

'There you are! I've been looking for you,' he said, uncomfortably familiar.

Trusting her escalating heartrate, Romilly grappled for her bag, and set off quickly in the opposite direction. Seconds later, he fell into step beside her.

'Look, I'm sorry,' she started, 'I don't know who you think I am, but—'

'It's all right but keep walking calmly. Those two lads behind you were eyeing up your bag,' he said quickly.

'What? Well, there's nothing valuable inside – my phone's in my hand …' Romilly turned and saw two shifty-looking youths disappear over the hill.

'A thousand pounds' worth of Louis Vuitton would serve their purposes well enough,' he said, gesturing at her shoulder.

'Who are you?' she said, switching focus from her previous problem, but slowing her pace slightly. Somewhere in the back of her mind, she had clocked his British accent, standing down her personal alert warning a notch or two.

'I was over there taking pictures, and noticed them scouting for easy prey. Thought I'd better warn you, as you seemed … distracted. You're at the same hotel as me, The Beaumont. I recognise you from The Sky Bar, last night – even if it was in happier circumstances.'

Romilly blinked, trying to process what had just happened. 'Hold on, so you're the man in the elevator with that … *woman*?' she said, with no attempt to disguise her opinion of him.

'Well, yes, but I was only—'

'No, honestly, I can live without hearing the sordid details. Thank you for tipping me off about those guys, I appreciate it. Help-a-fellow-Brit and all that, but I was just about to head back to the hotel,' she said, then stalled at an unfamiliar fork in the path. She was excellent at navigating invisible air corridors, vectors, and complex taxiways at international airports, but grassy-pathed parks, not so much.

'Do you mind some company, then? I was going back soon anyway.'

'I suppose …' she said, feeling awkward, but he'd done something chivalrous, after all.

'It's this way,' he said, indicating they should take the right-hand fork. 'Passes some colourful houses that are worth seeing, apparently. The concierge recommended them.'

She stood down another notch. 'Oh, right, yes, to me, too. It's a row of Victorian houses from the 1800s – that's mainly why I came up here.'

'They're called The Painted Ladies.'

'Ha! Should be perfect for you and your tarty friend with her fake handbag then,' she threw over her shoulder and strode on ahead. Lord only knew where the antagonistic attitude was coming from. Perhaps it was fuelled by jetlag?

He caught up with her again. 'Look, I don't know you, and you don't know what actually happened with me last night, but I suspect that comment is probably beneath you.'

'Suspect away. Who you do what with is none of my business.'

'Not that I'm defending her, but do you think she's in a position to justify a few thousand pounds on a real Gucci then?'

'You'd know more about her finances than me.'

The man stopped in his tracks. 'For Chrissakes. Forget it. Maybe you should make your own way back.' He veered off to a nearby bench and began sorting through his bag. From its higgledy-piggledy state, it looked to Romilly like he had packed it in a hurry. He carefully repositioned each item, re-strapping it into its correct compartment. It must have risked damage, when he'd run to warn her.

'I know what I saw,' she said more quietly, but even as the words left her mouth, doubts were forming, adding to the mêlée of worries about her dad and a general feeling discombobulation.

'Yeah? Not more assumptions coming, are there, by any chance?'

It was too late; she simply couldn't stop herself. 'Pilot for main course, bonus random from the bar for afters.'

'Jesus! That's not …' Dark eyebrows shot up as he continued the reorganisation of his bag. The frustration on his face told her that maybe she'd gone too far.

'Look, if I'm wrong—'

'You are. It's down the track to the left, follow the signs towards the Bay.'

4. Hattrick

'Sorry. I'm really not myself today.' Romilly slid onto one end of the bench and pressed the heels of her palms into her eye sockets for a moment, desperate to reset. God, she was tired. When she removed them, the man was sitting on the other end of the bench, studying her.

'There's more to last night than what you saw … but I think I know what I'm seeing now,' he said gently.

'And what's that?'

'Someone away from home, perhaps used to being in control, is feeling upset about something – lashing out. Maybe could use a friend.'

Romilly turned her head away from him and bit her lip at his intuitive bullseye. 'Don't.'

'Just stop a minute. Breathe.' The man took slow breaths in and out.

She shook her head.

'Breathe.'

He waited for her to gather herself. 'Look, there's an ice cream stall over there. Want one?'

Romilly eyed the vendor and its short queue of customers, conceding an ice cream might actually be just what she needed. 'I suppose some cream and sugar wouldn't hurt. It's three miles back to the hotel.'

'My thoughts exactly. Come on,' he said, leading the way. 'My name is Nathan, by the way.'

'Romilly.'

'Pretty name.'

She froze. 'It's just an ice cream. And I'm paying my own way.'

'Handing over a ten-dollar bill isn't going to break the bank.'

'Let's not talk cash transactions, shall we?'

Nathan sighed. 'Right, that's enough. When we've got our ice cream, we're going to sit over on that grass. If you want, you can talk about what's upsetting you, but whether I pay for yours or not, the least you might do is to hear me out.' His furrowed brow spoke of an injured party, the upturned corner of his mouth a plea to listen.

'All right.'

'Good.'

Romilly ordered a strawberry cornet, and Nathan chose pale-green pistachio and dark chocolate. She made up for the regret at not having chosen something more sophisticated by paying for both.

'Thank you,' he said. 'I graciously accept.' A half-smile gave way to folds of attractive crinkles at the corner of his eyes. She ignored a ridiculous squirm of desire in her stomach and gestured at a patch of grass that offered them better access to both the distant view and The Painted Ladies. For a few minutes, they sat in comfortable silence. He didn't push, or pry – reasons she usually avoided letting people too close. Unaccustomed to sharing, she surprised herself by taking a deep breath and telling him, 'It's my dad. I'm worried he's suffering with some type of dementia.' There, she'd said it out loud to someone. Romilly gauged his reaction, warily bracing herself for a series of questions she didn't want to have to consider.

Nodding, eyes holding hers, he seemed to digest the information along with his ice cream.

She filled the silence. 'And just as I've routed onto a block of long-haul flights, he seems to be worsening ... And up there on the hill I had a conversation with him that upset me.' Now she couldn't put the sodding lid back on.

Nathan angled his head and stopped eating. 'Tell me about that if you want to.'

'He was confusing me with my mother, which wouldn't be so bad if she hadn't died five years ago.' A tributary of pink cream dribbled down the cornet and onto her hand.

'Eat,' Nathan urged. He waited for her to stem the melting. 'So ...you're a pilot?'

'Mmhmm.'

'And your dad mistook your voice for your mother's. Was he lucid at all in the conversation?'

'Yes, he's a retired pilot himself and recalled landing in fog here.'

Nathan flicked his eyes from the view and back to her face. 'He lives alone?'

'Yes, but there's a lovely carer called Benita who goes in every day. I've contacted her – she's going to check in on him, but I'm keen to see him for myself as soon as I'm home.'

'And he didn't seem otherwise unwell? He's eating?'

'Yes, I think so. He said, "I'm safe", which doesn't actually refer to security; it's—'

'I know the "I'm safe" acronym.'

'You do?'

'Illness, Medication, Stress, Alcohol, Fatigue, Emotions. The pilot's personal health checklist before every flight.'

'So … you also fly?'

'Yep. Hattrick.' His lips curved into a conspiratorial grin.

Romilly rapidly reassessed her first, and second, impressions of him. 'You're with British Airways, I take it?'

'Unfortunately not. No, with Sterling, usually Far East Asia sectors, though. Needed a change, and thought I'd test California by initially covering sickness on the routes. You?'

'My dad flew for BA, but I've been working Sterling's Europe and Africa routes, mainly. This is also my first Californian one.'

'Explains why we're at the same hotel for layover then. And now I know why you had that self-satisfied smile on your face last night at the bar.'

'I did? You do?' She could feel her cheeks beginning to flush.

'You landed in a hellish crosswind, didn't you?' He paused while she nodded. 'Totally get it. Twenty-four hours before you, I was in crab landing right until the final fifty feet or so.' He arched his hand to demonstrate the severe angle of his sideways approach manoeuvre. 'But let's not get off track with work talk. I'm sorry about your dad. For what it's worth, I have an aunt with Alzheimer's, and I know my mother and my cousin struggled to get her to the GP for diagnosis for months, because she denied anything was wrong. The key thing was to keep a log, so maybe you could ask the carer to keep track too. With my aunt, there were some basic tests and after that she was referred for medication and eventually relocation. It depends on what his doctor thinks it's necessary.'

Romilly could swear she felt the moment heaviness left her shoulders. 'Thank you, that actually is a real help.'

'You're welcome. How's your ice cream?'

'Delicious,' she murmured. 'Yours?'

'This is a great combination. Want to try some?'

'How?'

'Lick it, swipe your finger in it – either's fine.' His tongue darted from full lips to scoop another mouthful, his strong jaw twitching as he swallowed. He tilted his cone towards her, and raised a questioning brow.

She hesitated, searching his face to second guess any ulterior motive behind eyes that held hers. Nestled in his cupid's bow, a few dark hairs seemed to have evaded his most recent shave. For a mad nanosecond, she wanted to touch it. Her pulse rate was jumpy – and not solely from sugar overload. 'I can't tell if you're joking.'

'I wasn't,' he said, offering his cone even nearer. She scooped her little finger along the edge and tasted it.

'Oh, that's amazing,' she groaned.

Nathan was observing her reaction closely. His laboured blink and slowly parting lips suggested she wasn't alone in experiencing an unexpected chemical rush that had nothing to do with artificial colourings.

'Want to try some strawberry? Not that it's as good as yours …'

He cleared his throat. 'I'm actually allergic to strawberries.'

'What? Why didn't you say! There might have been some on my finger?'

'I doubt that micro-amount has very much real strawberry in it, but if I start turning pink and become dotted with white hives, it's time for some antihistamine. Nothing major.'

'Wait, so … much like an actual strawberry, then.'

'Unfortunately.'

Romilly smirked and propped herself back onto an elbow, people watching. Wasn't it amazing how thirty minutes had improved her morning? 'Can't believe how clear the air is.'

'I was in Los Angeles a fortnight ago – overheard someone saying it was the most air-polluted city in the States. Amazing that it's only an hour's flight away.'

'Must be the geography here – the steep hills and coast maybe?'

'And the high number of electric vehicles.'

'Mmm.' She nodded, taking in the spectacular view. 'It's been a surprise, really wasn't expecting it.'

'Me either.'

'All right then. Tell me what happened.'

He cocked an eyebrow. 'Apparently I was five – ended up in A&E after overindulging at a "pick your own".'

'No, I meant with that woman last n—'

'I know what you meant,' said Nathan, with a playful grin. 'But do you mind if I take some pictures of the houses while we talk? Missed my chance in yesterday's weather; this may be the best we'll get today.'

'Go ahead. Looks like you've got all the gear.' She pulled out her phone. 'My pictures will be ridiculous by comparison.'

'Smartphone cameras have lots of tools to help you – a grid for framing the shot for a start.'

'Where's that?' With her free hand, she opened the camera function on her phone, keen to locate the tool.

Nathan leaned over and pressed a combination of options on her screen, making a system of yellow lines overlay the image. The familiar scent of the hotel's shower gel mingling with his freshly earned sweat fought for Romilly's attention as he explained 'the rule of thirds'. Something about keeping the sky in the top third, the houses in the middle, and, the foreground, was it, in the bottom?

'Thanks, I'll give it a try when I've finished this,' she mumbled and continued to manage the rivulets of her fast-melting cone.

'Actually, could you hold my cone a second? I've just had an idea for a photograph.' Nathan held out his ice cream, struggling to fix his complicated-looking camera onto a short tripod with one hand.

She took it from him. As their fingers brushed, somewhere in a crevice of her brain logged *nice hands*.

'You see the pink house and the green one a few houses further up the hill? Would you hold the two cones underneath the right colours? Might be a fun shot.'

'Like this?' she said, focusing on the task literally in hand.

'Perfect.' He clicked in rapid-fire, then checked his pictures back in a display panel. 'A bit lower … Great … Thanks.' Nathan nodded as he took his cone back. 'Who knew Victorian houses could look like this? They're so brown at home.'

'From the research I read for San Francisco, I expected something more like a Disney interpretation, but they're pretty, aren't they? Those towards the end of the street are Edwardian. See? They're slightly different.'

'How so?' he said, pausing the final demolition of his cone.

'They're wider and have more windows. Front gardens, too. Plus, there's the obvious date on the gable on the end one, 1908. So that was in Edward the VII's reign.'

He was smiling at her.

'What?'

'Nothing, I enjoy photographing buildings, but you seem to know about architectural history.'

'Well, yes, a bit. Long story short, before getting my wings, I worked at the British Museum for a while. So much there, you can't help but absorb some of it. Anyway, how are you getting on with your photos?' She had become adept at skirting over past issues, and careful not to reveal more about herself than she wanted.

'I've taken enough. Do you want to go? We could walk back or go to the cable car stop and take a ride back down to the hotel. I'll share the details of what definitely didn't happen last night if you tell me what you know about other historical places in the city that seem worth a visit.'

Romilly breathed a sigh of relief at avoiding anything too personal. 'That works for me. Riding a cable car is on my list.'

'Great,' he said, repacking his bag, 'but do me a favour – let's avoid work talk at the moment. We're off duty.'

'Fair enough.'

5. Wings

Hangry. He'd learnt the word from a cabin manager recently, when one of her team was losing patience with some overbearing business class passengers during an interminable delay at Singapore Changi. Ice cream had been the answer, apparently, courtesy of a raided food cart in the galley. Up at Alamo yesterday with Romilly, Nathan had surmised that ice cream might help her replace lost energy after the uphill hike, and relieve her low spirits. Maybe take the edge off her mild hostility. Thankfully, it had. But then there was the chemistry. When she'd sampled his ice cream, the fullness of her lower lip sucking her finger had clenched at his insides, inciting a sudden craving to taste her, pistachio, chocolate, and all.

They had enjoyed chatting with the cable car operative who had proudly showed how he connected the traditional wooden car onto San Francisco's below-ground cable system. Romilly had grinned widely from their open-air bench seats as they were whisked downhill, which had made him smile, too. Arriving back at The Beaumont, Nathan had been about to forgo his intention of avoiding complications by suggesting a late lunch, when she'd frowned at her phone and said news from home meant she needed to go. Repeating her thanks for his intervention with the bag thieves, she'd apologised again for misjudging him and her near miss in turning him into an allergenic strawberry. There had been something innately sexy about the way her lips had formed a smirk.

Just before heading for the lifts, she'd awkwardly mentioned that her crew would be gathering for five pm cocktails in The Sky Bar. She had attempted to conceal rampant blushing by checking her watch, and had casually added that 'anyone could come along'. That his own clear thinking was momentarily thrown might have explained why she hadn't noticed that he should have already left for the airport and that afternoon's flight.

Fortunately, Nathan had reacted noncommittally as she'd disappeared behind the lift doors, because his own phone had brought notification from Crew Services of staffing changes. He and some of the cancelled cabin crew from today's withdrawn flight would be rostered onto tomorrow's – the remainder and those being displaced would have their layovers involuntarily extended for another thirty hours. Some would be happy about that, he expected, but others angry. He checked the roster for the flight and noticed Romilly's name was missing. Trying not to overthink his motives as being anything other than helpful in getting her home to visit her dad, he dialled the administrators at Crew Services. Having jumped onto flights at the last minute to help them out too many times to count, a small favour like that was an acceptable ask.

All things considered, he'd given The Sky Bar a miss.

In his hotel room the following morning, Nathan gave up on the homogeny of hotel cable channels, and picked up his camera. After editing, some of the pictures from yesterday would be good enough to upload to the website he sold through. The ice cream shot he'd taken with Romilly definitely had potential.

He began packing his flight cases, shined his shoes, and flint-rolled his jacket. His hadn't been some glib compliment – Romilly was a pretty name, but the woman herself intrigued him. Conversation had flowed easily – architecture, weather patterns, and homelessness to name but a few topics, and he had successfully avoided work talk. She was endearing, interesting, and impressive in equal measures.

He straightened his trousers in the press and hung them to cool, ready to change into shortly.

Understanding the demand for focus and control that flying necessitated, it must have been difficult for Romilly to have shown her vulnerability at the park. He didn't doubt she'd faced assumptions over her abilities through flight school, due to her sex, and in all likelihood throughout the subsequent years she'd been flying. It shouldn't be the case, but it was still a man's world, and she probably had to keep proving she belonged in it. That took inner strength. Resilience. Commitment. She was probably reading through her flight briefing information right now, just as he himself had already done.

Citing heritage and authority, Sterling were one of several airlines still to require flight crew to wear hats. After changing into his uniform, Nathan settled the peaked hat on his head, checked the room one last time, and headed for the elevators.

'I hope you've enjoyed your stay with us,' one of The Beaumont's receptionists said to him down at the main desk. Though her extra-wide smile seemed excessive for a check-out procedure, he wasn't blind to the fact that his uniform had magnetic qualities. Sometimes women stared – and sometimes men – but he'd remind himself they didn't know him.

'Yes, thank you. Very good, perhaps I'll be back soon.'

Nathan wheeled his cases towards the gathering of navy blue-and-red suited cabin crew, immaculate in their attire and grooming, and busied himself with learning the names of those he hadn't previously met on Sunday's outbound. Just as he'd finished speaking with the affable cabin manager, Steph, about the boarding procedure, a woman's voice behind him cleared.

'Captain J.P. Reed?'

He turned around. Christ, Romilly wore her uniform well.

'So, Nathan is short for …' She was staring at the fourth stripe on his jacket sleeves and the brocade around the peak of his hat. To her credit, she barely blinked.

'Jonathan.'

'And you are …'

'Your captain, yes.'

Without losing composure, she offered a tight smile. 'May I speak with you privately for a moment, Captain Reed?'

'Of course, but it's Nathan, please.' He gestured towards the sofas nearer the central foyer. Once there, she opted to stand.

'You said you were a pilot,' came her hushed, yet accusatory opener.

'I am a pilot.' He flicked the golden wings on his jacket.

She raised her eyebrows. 'We're in uniform and on Company time, so I'll resist saying what I'm thinking, in the expectation of professional behaviour.'

'You think I'm not going to be professional?'

'I don't know.' She flicked the wings on her own jacket in exaggerated imitation.

He stifled a smile. From the way she then narrowed her eyes, that was the wrong thing to have done.

'So, yesterday's "let's avoid work talk, we're off duty" was to deliberately mislead me?'

He held up a defensive hand. 'Not maliciously, I just didn't want to spoil the—'

'And how's that working out for you now, Captain?'

She took a deep breath and strode back to the group. Well, this was going to be an interesting flight.

'Pre-flight checks complete,' said Nathan, from the left-hand seat in the cockpit.

'Checks complete,' confirmed Romilly, beside him on the right. Her cheeks were wind-whipped from performing the outside walk-around safety checks beneath the wings and of the engine, fuselage, and wheels.

'I'll take us up, then Second Officer Stevens will relieve you after three hours for your break. After that, he'll cover mine. When I'm back, I'll decide whether it's you or me who takes the landing at Heathrow.'

Without looking at him, Romilly maintained a steely focus on the cockpit dials. 'Roger.'

Other than for their briefing and technical procedures, she hadn't spoken to him since their spat in the hotel lobby. To ensure he wasn't about to fly across the Atlantic with an angry or distracted pilot, he tapped her sleeve and looked her directly in the eye. In silence, to avoid the black box that recorded conversation and all procedures taken, he waggled a questioning thumbs-up. Second Officer Stevens would arrive shortly to take his position in the fold-down jump seat for take-off. If necessary, Nathan was prepared to move him to her seat.

Romilly nodded, defiantly turning the same query on him. He returned his own confirmation. When it was time to fly, he could be relied on to compartmentalise and pack emotions into a box. Unpacking them once home, not so much. Was she the same?

A three-rap knock on the cockpit door preceded Second Officer Steven's arrival, followed by Steph, who poked her head in.

'First passengers are just boarding, Captain,' Steph said.

He nodded, and shifted out of his seat. 'Thank you.'

'Where are you going?' said Romilly.

'Checks are all complete. I want to be visible when the passengers board.'

'Whatever strokes your ego, Captain Reed.'

He sighed. 'Assumptions, First Officer West, assumptions.'

6. Checks. Reality Checks.

At forty thousand feet, somewhere over Colorado, Romilly climbed through the crew quarters hatch beside the cockpit door, toed off her shoes, and crawled into an empty rest bunk. Flying was a thrilling and responsible career, but switching off the heightened levels of focus it demanded didn't always come easily. She closed her eyes, waiting for her mind to quieten, to chase a couple of hours' sleep.

Nathan. She'd ably avoided any personal thoughts while working with him on the flight deck, but now she replayed all their conversations. She stared at the underside of the bunk above, seeing his face at Alamo, remembering his smell. Then she reran his sensitive handling of the triple seven's yoke as they took off and his strong wrist, bearing tufts of dark hair, when he'd eased the engines' throttle levers. For pity's sake, she told herself, this was not like her at all. Get it together; he's just another colleague. Friendly, and with a gorgeous smile, but a colleague, all the same. The hatch door opened, startling her.

'Hi, Romilly,' said Steph, wriggling through the limited headroom in her red-and-navy skirt. 'Mind if I take this one?' She indicated to the bunk on the opposite side.

'No, go ahead.'

'Drinks were fun yesterday – shame you didn't stay longer,' Steph said, picking up an abandoned fashion magazine from another bunk before squeezing herself into hers.

'It's a bit different when you've got to fly the plane following afternoon, otherwise I might have been tempted. How's service been so far?'

'Mostly smooth. Must say, having Captain Reed there to deflect any nonsense from the twenty-four-hours delayed passengers as they boarded made a big difference. You know what delays do for people's disposition, not to mention their alcohol consumption. I wish more captains had the forethought to personally reinforce the airline's non-tolerance of cabin crew abuse like that.'

Romilly did a double take. 'But … there weren't any issues?'

'He spoke to a group of rowdy guys, and then to a couple whose child was panicking about flying and needed reassurance. He had me fetch one of the model airplanes we sell – said he square up later.'

Strike two for making incorrect assumptions. What was the saying? Once is a mistake; twice is a coincidence? Since she didn't believe in coincidences, another apology seemed to be in order.

'Where are you scheduled after this?' said Steph, rubbing her feet.

'Four days off, then back on this route. Have that shift pattern locked for seven more weeks. I may collect some extra hours with some emergency cover short hauls in between. Tenerife, maybe. Good for out-and-backs in a day.'

'Yep, Christmas is coming – we can all do with the money,' Steph said, absently flicking through pages of glossily photographed fashion.

'I don't know how you do it, being on your feet for so much of it.'

'This is nothing compared to when I was hairdressing. You never get long breaks like these; only time I saw the inside of a magazine was peering over a client's shoulder.'

'How long have you been cabin crew?'

'Eleven years, but I keep my hand in with cut and colour. Want to open my own salon once I've travelled in this job.'

'Nice plan.' Even without knowing anything of Steph's technical ability, Romilly imagined Steph would be a popular hairdresser.

'Everyone's got to have a dream. What's yours?'

'To become a captain as soon as possible.' Sudden emotion choked at Romilly's throat, so she forced out a yawn. 'I ought to try for some sleep, sorry.'

'Of course, I'll just plug in to a podcast. Sweet dreams.'

'Thanks, Steph.' Romilly rolled away from her, and lay staring at the fuselage wall.

As Nathan settled back into his seat after his allotted rest break, Romilly updated him about the non-eventful cruising portion of the flight and the early weather forecast she'd obtained from radar in preparation for landing at Heathrow in a little over two hours' time.

'Did you rest well?' she said, warming up conversation. Her plan was to make a straightforward apology so as to avoid any further awkwardness. They both had important jobs to do.

'Yes, thank you,' he said and smiled at her, though a slight squint of his eyes suggested otherwise.

She held his eye contact, formulating the words of her apology, ruing the ever-present cockpit voice recorder. He tilted his head, somehow locking into her interior struggle. Their eyes would soon be hidden by the dark aviators necessary for meeting the dawn horizon, but right at that moment, his pupils were blotting his chocolate-brown irises at the exact rate a tingling warmth spread through her chest. In seconds, the atmosphere in the cockpit had shifted.

'Listen, I …' she began.

Maintaining his gaze, Nathan tapped a finger to his lips and shook his head.

She cleared her throat and nodded. 'I'm … on this route for the next seven weeks. I don't want to make any *assumptions*, but San Francisco seemed like a *decent* place after all. I was *sorry* that my layover wasn't longer.'

He hesitated for a few seconds, scanning her face. 'Like you, I hadn't expected to find it so … interesting there,' he said, a new husk to his voice. 'On my break, I learned that the captain's seat is available on this routing for the rest of the block. Crew Services used a part-time captain on your outbound?'

His contagious smile pulsed a frisson of chemistry through Romilly, catching her off-guard. 'They did. Are you considering it?'

Nathan nodded, then looked away, staring into the expanse of mauve sky. His lips pursed on a long exhale.

'I'll take this landing,' he said, a minute later.

'Roger,' Romilly croaked. Though she could land the plane without issue, he was a captain making a solid decision.

Last to leave the plane after completing arrivals checks and paperwork, Romilly and Nathan dragged their flight cases towards the pick-up point for aircrew shuttle van transfers from the satellite terminal to passport control in the main building.

'Steph mentioned how helpful it was that you'd been visible to passengers when they boarded,' Romilly offered, breaking the silence.

'I've had enough of cabin crew taking abuse over the years. It seems to diffuse things during boarding when captains are visible. Remember that when you're one.'

'It may be a while.' She glanced at him, wondering what he thought of her – professionally speaking, of course. But perhaps non-professionally, too?

'You'll get there.'

'Look, I'm sorry what I said about your ego,' she mumbled.

'Doesn't mean I don't have one.'

He pointed at a Sterling shuttle van in the distance at the pick-up point, whose driver had just started its engine, so they sped up a little.

Romilly inhaled deeply. 'Ah, the special smell of Heathrow and aviation fuel after your inbound.'

'A day's delay and somehow it's even sweeter.'

'Of course, you would have been here twenty-four hours ago if it weren't for the faulty plane.'

'Monday's outbound pilots must have really crunched the gears.'

Romilly chuckled. 'Sorry, I rode the clutch for five thousand miles.'

Nathan laughed. 'Noted.'

'Actually, I'll admit to fretting for a while yesterday because Crew Services initially placed me on extended layover, which would have caused a delay in being able to see my dad. But obviously they had messed up, because a few minutes later I received new advice that I was back to my first officer seat on this one.'

Nathan carried on walking. His lack of reaction aroused her suspicion.

'Wait. Did you know that had happened?' she said, pointing at him.

'Yes, captains see the crew list before anyone else.'

She stopped walking. 'Did you intervene?'

'Romilly—' He turned to face her, but didn't meet her eyes.

'Did you?'

'It wasn't entirely altruistic, but yes, I knew it was important to you to get back. Keep walking. It'll be a twenty-minute wait for the next lift.'

She swallowed, processing his words as they continued on. 'That was … Thank you, that means a lot.'

Just in time, they clambered into the last two spaces inside the van, squashed onto a lengthways bench seat. Was he as hyperaware as her that their adjacent arms and legs were touching? Even through their uniforms, his body warmth began to seep into hers.

Opposite them sat Steph, whose eyes swivelled between the two of them while she clutched a bag full of duty-free. A tiny smirk curled on her lips.

'Where are you headed now, Captain Reed?' Steph asked casually.

'Home for four days. Then, if I can lock it in, back out to San Francisco on Monday and on this route for the next seven weeks.'

'Interesting. You're not tempted to take some short-haul overtime – an out-and-back to Tenerife or something?'

Romilly flicked a cautionary glance at Steph.

'No, feet on the ground. You?' said Nathan, apparently oblivious.

'Girls' long weekend ahead, then I'm back on this route for the remainder of the block.'

'Glad to hear I could have such an excellent team.' He pulled out his phone, causing his leg to press even harder against Romilly's.

Steph continued talking about the crew's mooted plans to ride on San Francisco's pleasure ferries the following week, but Romilly's ears were pounding with anticipation at the prospect of sharing more than just flying hours with Nathan. Where these feelings were coming from, she had no idea.

'Done,' he said, 'Confirmed for the next seven weeks.'

Steph winked at her. Romilly smiled and shook her head.

'Terminal 3,' the driver announced, prompting them all to decant into the building, headed for the dedicated airline staff channel at passport control.

Along the transits and walkways, Nathan acknowledged passing captains from other airlines. Very few were women. Romilly nodded at any accompanying first officers; at least those saw a higher percentage.

Nathan motioned that she should go before him as they reached the front of the queue.

'Got a car here?' he asked, catching up with her the other side.

'Yes. In long-term 4. You?' she said, zipping her passport back inside her shoulder bag.

'Also in four. May as well walk together.'

'Okay, but via caffeine-to-go from Costa?' she said, gesturing ahead at the coffee shop.

'Definitely. Far to drive?'

'Kingston – an hour at this time of day. You?'

'Battersea – sometimes forty minutes, sometimes four hours.' He shook his head.

'London traffic,' they said in unison and smiled.

For a Thursday lunchtime, Terminal 3's Arrivals Hall was moderately busy with the usual hubbub of reuniting friends and families and pre-booked drivers holding the name cards of their pick-ups. The scene never failed to lift Romilly's spirits. She turned to share the feeling with Nathan, but he was staring wide-eyed into the distance. Jetlag. It might be noon in the UK, but their bodies thought it was five am Pacific Standard Time.

'It's always good to be home. Expect you're looking forward to some downtime?' she asked.

Nathan turned to reply, an unreadable expression swiping across his face. 'I'm …' In a blur of activity, people ahead of them parted, making way for an overcome young girl who was barrelling towards them, and an attractive dark-haired woman giving chase. Romilly turned to see who the child was destined to reunite with behind them, but the child didn't pass.

'Daddy!' the girl cried, circling arms around what must be her father's legs.

'Nora?'

Nathan picked up the girl and squeezed her to his chest, her jumble of dark curls obscuring his face. The woman, who finally caught up, smiled and breathlessly announced, 'Surprise!'

Muscle memory propelled Romilly's feet forwards. Hopefully they would take her to the correct car park on autopilot.

7. Brace

Nathan smelt ripe banana and flowery shampoo when he scooped the most beautiful five-year-old in the world into his arms. 'And what are you doing here, young lady?'

'I've done you a picture, Maria's got it.' She sniffed.

'Has she indeed? Well, let's have a look.' Nathan shifted his tearful daughter onto one hip. In all the trips he'd returned from, she'd never been upset like this. For her sake, Nathan masked his concern, and his frustration with her new nanny for dragging her out to the airport, especially on a school day. He smiled as he took in the primary-coloured painting and waited for Nora to explain it.

'It's your 'partment with me in it when I come to stay. See, all the windows and no garden. That's the river.'

Nathan studied the representation of the modern, Thames-side apartment he'd been staying in since he and Liz had called time on their seven-year relationship at the beginning of the year. 'That's wonderful. And who are these people in the window? Are they your friends?'

'No. Only my dolls, so we can play when I come.'

'So they are. And there's Oinky Pig. When we're home later we can have a tea party.'

'Yeah!' Thankfully, Nora brightened and wriggled from his grasp. Once on the ground, she slipped her hand into his. 'Can we go now?'

'Just give Daddy a minute.'

'Okay.'

'How did you get here, Maria?' he asked in a low voice.

She beamed at him with innate Latina confidence. 'By train, to surprise. School closed two days. Ees good idea, no?' She held up Nora's usual weekend-stay rucksack. 'You no have come to house now, can go your place direct, yes?'

'Yes, but some warning would have been better. I thought I was collecting her tomorrow dinner time.' What the hell was Liz playing at? She could have told him Nora's prep school was closed. And frankly, for its astronomical term fees, Queen Elizabeth Preparatory School should be open every day of the year.

'Daddy, come *on*!'

The sticky warmth of his daughter's small hand in his was something videocalls couldn't convey.

'I see how excited she is, though. Is she otherwise all right, Maria?' he said softly.

'Two times to your place each month is long to wait, I think.'

It was long for him too. 'Lucky I keep the spare booster seat for her in the boot of my car. Come on, I'll pick up another strong coffee en-route to the car park.' Nathan opened the parking app on his phone. Sunday morning seemed a very long time ago. 'Car Park 4, Level 4b,' he read aloud.

Car Park 4. Romilly. He scanned the crowd, but she was gone.

With Nora safely buckled in next to Maria on the back seats of his Mercedes, Nathan wound his way through the multi-storey's one-way system towards the exit. An older, black sports hatch at one of the exit barriers was causing a bottleneck. Probably lost their ticket. His attention spiked when he saw Romilly get out of the car and fumble through her jacket pockets. The car behind her sounded their horn. She glared but continued checking. Nathan admired her restraint; wearing an airline's uniform required a certain level of conduct that he'd rued many a time. Romilly pulled her shoulder bag out of the car, rested it on her bonnet, and began raking through its contents. Enough.

'Maria, I'm just pulling over here for a moment. Wait with Nora, please,' he said, steering into a lay-by.

Nathan hot-footed over to Romilly's car, not quite sure what he would say. 'Hello, Ma'am, what seems to be the problem?' he drawled, trying the humorous track. God, he sounded ridiculous.

Apparently sharing his opinion, she scowled and carried on searching.

'There's a button on the payment screen for lost tickets if that's the problem. At the bottom on the right. See? I've used it before. You have to estimate your length of stay.'

She stopped raking through her bag and stared at him, eyes burning. At first look, they bore a tirade of abuse; then, he saw something worse. Hurt. Damn. Was she waiting for him to explain about Nora, or mentally calculating the length of her parking stay? Since the latter option required a shorter conversation, he totted up the hours he'd been parked.

'Mine's about a hundred and twelve, so, deducting twenty-four hours for your later flight ...' he offered.

She took a deep breath and turned her attention to the payment screen, tapping in a number, then swiping her payment card. The barrier jerked into life. She flung her bag onto the back seat and slid into her own.

Say something, man. 'Let me expl—'

The door slammed, and within seconds she screeched off into the wet autumn afternoon, tyres slipping as she ratcheted through the gears.

Dear God, he hoped she didn't fly like that.

The motorway crawled along at fifty miles per hour, thanks to its ever-present roadworks. Nathan followed a filthy aggregates lorry as if on one long, auto-piloted conveyer belt. Nora was dozing, thumb in her mouth with what sounded like *Peppa Pig* playing on the video tablet, lying abandoned on her lap.

With another hour of traffic ahead of him, he debated whether he should try to contact Romilly before Monday and offer context to what she had seen at the airport. No doubt she'd made all kinds of assumptions, only one of which was likely to be correct. With no guarantee she'd listen to him, he could probably distil his message to three sentences: *'Have a five-year-old daughter. Split from her mother ten months ago. Pilots make awful partners.'* The last point lingered – maybe he should just close down this attraction and warn her off. She deserved someone who brought joy to what he suspected might be a deliberately solitary world, not someone who complicated it. And imagine how disastrous a two-pilot household would be.

'Mr Reed!' screamed Maria. 'Alerta!'

Nathan braked hard, narrowly avoiding the nose of his car wedging beneath the rear axle of the lorry who had stopped just as quickly. Instinct flicked his eyes to the rear mirror in time to see a pick-up truck's bull-bars rapidly eating up his view.

'Brace!' he shouted, reaching his left arm behind the passenger seat to protect the sleeping Nora. A crunching impact to his rear bumper lurched the car forwards and hurled Nora's tablet towards him, striking him on his brow before clattering onto the dashboard. Everything ground to a halt.

'Are you all right, Maria? Is Nora okay?'

'Yes, yes, I am good. Nora ees sleeping.'

'Wake her up. Check her. Quickly.' Nathan held his breath as his daughter's heavy eyelids fluttered opened on Maria's gentle rousing.

'Are we there yet, Daddy?' she said dozily.

'Not yet, sweetie. Soon.'

The lorry driver, and an outdoorsy-looking man from the pick-up, approached.

Nathan wound down his window.

'You all okay in there?' said the man in a 'Ben's Tree Surgery' fleece.

'Yes, you both all right?'

'Idiot youngsters cut in front of me,' said the lorry driver, shaking his head. 'Had to emergency brake. Wrecked his go-faster bodywork on the central reservation barrier, but no one's hurt. Police are on their way.'

'Thanks to the bars on my truck, there's no damage to mine,' said the other man. 'But I knocked your rear bumper off, mate. Pop yer boot – I'll sling it in. Otherwise, you're drivable, I reckon.'

Nathan hit the button for the automatic boot opener. 'Thanks. Then I'd get back in your vehicles – there's no hard shoulder in these roadworks. It's dangerous standing so near to the traffic.'

'Will do,' said the lorry driver, 'But I'll get everyone's details quickly first.' He passed Nathan's car to speak with the pick-up driver, who was already loading the bumper.

Nathan swiped at some moisture near his eye, leaving a smear of blood on his hands. The sun visor's vanity mirror revealed a short but deep gash on the outer corner of his right eyebrow. He sighed to himself. Just great.

'Maria we'll need to get ourselves checked out at the walk-in centre once we are back. Then, as long as you're okay, I'll drop you at the station.'

'Si, Mr Reed. Ah, oh nooo, Mr Reed … Miss Daniels is calling me – what shall I say?'

'I'll speak to her,' Nathan said, reaching his hand out for her phone. The last thing he wanted was for Liz to overreact and add the incident to the ammunition he suspected she was gathering to fight for full custody of Nora.

Partners of pilots need to be content with who they are, he'd discovered. Able to enjoy having their own space, with ability to resolve problems when they were alone. Towards the end of their relationship, Liz had seemed incapable of managing any domestic situation without distress, making him feel sorry – and guilty when he was away. He'd once been handed an urgent message on landing in Kuala Lumpur, about a fire alarm battery in their garage.

'Hi, it's me, before you say anything, Maria's here. I've answered because we had a minor incident on the motorway on the way home. A few vehicles involved in a shunt, none of our faults. We'll get ourselves to the medical centre, but I think we're all fine. Nora was sleeping.'

Nathan waited for the hysterics, but nothing came.

'Liz?'

'You were fit to drive her, I take it?'

'You know I wouldn't risk Nora's safety. I wasn't exactly expecting Maria and her at the airport, but … hold on, you don't sound surprised that I've got her. Did you know they were coming to meet me?'

'You should have called me; we would have come if you were too tired to drive.'

'*We*, who?'

'Mark has a new BMW.'

'I thought his name was Wayne?'

'That was before,' she said, matter-of-factly.

Nathan held his tongue, but it was hard to keep up with who Liz was seeing – and, more importantly, who Nora was meeting.

He'd been determined to keep things civil with Liz, if for nothing else than to show Nora that he'd treat her mother with respect. In their first few months together, Liz hadn't minded the travel perks, enjoying trips to places like Singapore and Bangkok among others. What she had soon minded was that, when he returned home, he needed a small amount of space to readjust to home life, shake off jet lag, and come down off the responsibilities he carried at work before meeting expectations to be wined and dined.

'And Mark is?'

'The owner of an insurance company.'

'Right, well I appreciate the offer, but there is no need. It's under control.' Now his head was beginning to thump.

'So, you'll return Nora after six pm on Sunday? We won't be in before that – Mark is taking me up to the Bicester Designer Shopping Outlet.'

Nathan steadied his voice, wondering what clothes she could possibly need. Liz could set up her own store with the amount of designer goods and handbags in her walk-in wardrobe. 'Yes, and I'll text again later once we're back at the apartment, just to confirm all is well.'

'Fine.' The call ended.

After dinner, and with Nora fast asleep, Nathan was sorely tempted to pour a generous whisky to dull the throb of six angry stitches in his eyebrow. Instead, he tidied up after the 'best tea party ever' held on the living room rug. To the exquisite sound of his daughter's squeals, he'd channelled the best of Sterling's cabin crew by tucking a tea towel over his arm and politely offering each of her dolls, Teddy, and of course Oinky Pig, a pretend drink of 'tea or coffee' on a tray, using 'real cups and plates'.

Finally, sitting on the sofa in the quiet, he had the opportunity to take stock of the past forty-eight hours. A jumble of emotions, borne of frustration with flight delays and shift changes, the joy of Nora's hugs at the airport, and the fallout from the motorway prang all lay in one box, fighting for rank and release. In another box – a new box – lay the feeling that he might have met someone interesting, in Romilly. His experience with Liz had dented the confidence required to carry it safely, so he mentally marked it 'handle with care', but kept it in sight.

8. Lift

'Tea?' said Romilly when she arrived at her father's warden-assisted retirement flat first thing on Friday morning. Per usual, the place smelled of milky porridge and newspapers, signalling that Benita had already visited to take care of breakfast.

'Yes, please,' he replied, following her into the kitchenette.

He seemed more like his old self today, pleased to see her and keen to chat about the sport he wanted to watch over the coming weekend. She shook the tea canister, finding it and his cupboards frustratingly empty of teabags. How had Benita missed that? Fortunately, Romilly still had her coat on.

'I'll just nip to the corner shop first. See if there's some fruitcake for us to have with it, bit of a treat.'

'Lovely.' He returned to his recliner armchair, contentedly humming something indecipherable.

Romilly took the opportunity to discretely check his fridge for any other items he might need. Inside was a bottle of milk, and a lonely stack of pre-ordered ready meals. Not wildly dissimilar to her own fridge.

'Won't be long,' she called from his hallway, opening his front door.

'Okay. Oh, Joan?'

Romilly froze. 'Yes?'

'Could you see if there are any crumpets – we like those, don't we?'

'I'll try.'

Romilly dragged herself around the convenience store, debating whether her father had enough toiletries, then biscuits, then fruit – anything to put off having to go through the pain of yet another explanation of who she was, on her return. At the section stocking goods for hot drinks, a man slightly younger than herself reached in front of her.

'Excuse me, just need ...' he said, taking a jar of coffee.

His wedding ring caught her eye and instantly she thought of Nathan. Some married men didn't wear rings – not that she was after one. And she was certainly not a homewrecker. She'd tossed and turned throughout the night, thinking about it, only finding sleep after acknowledging her part – that she'd stupidly let her resolve slip, begun to let someone in. Hadn't she learned that the only man she could rely on was her father? Even if he was sometimes confused as to who precisely she was. And who she knew doubted she'd make captain ...

Romilly added a box of PG Tips to her basket and joined the queue for the till, resolving to redouble her efforts at work. Nathan was just another colleague, nothing more.

'I'm back.' Letting herself in to her father's flat, she slipped off her shoes. After laying her coat on the back of her father's sofa, she braced herself for an emotional pummelling.

'I managed to get some Dundee cake and a packet of crumpets.'

'Romilly? I wasn't expecting to see you!' Her father hastily stood up and beckoned her to his outstretch arms before folding them around her. Taken by surprise, she pressed her cheek to his chest and sighed, desperate to commit the father-daughter feeling to memory.

'Yes, it's me. I love you, Dad,' she croaked.

'I know you do, darling. I love you, too. Come on, let's have some of that cake with a pot of tea, shall we?'

'I'll do it – you sit down.' Romilly swiped at her childish tears and busied herself in the kitchenette. While waiting for the kettle to boil, an urgent enquiry from Crew Services pinged on her phone, seeking a pilot for an out-and-back to Lanzarote the following afternoon. She poked her head into the living room and smiled at her father, who was contentedly studying his local newspaper. Promising herself an early night, after an afternoon with him, she messaged back, accepting the job.

A few minutes later, she rested a tray carrying a cosied teapot, mugs, and slices of cake on the coffee table. 'Here we are, Dad,' she said and handed him a plate. 'There's three of everything because Benita will be here again any minute.'

He peered over his newspaper, at her, then dropped it into his lap. 'Joan? Where have you been? When did your hair grow that long?' he said, screwing his eyes at her.

'It's me, Dad – Romilly. I'm grown up now. I know that I look like Mum used to.'

Distressing confusion contorted his face. 'Who are you? Where's Mum?'

Romilly took a deep breath, hoping as always that presenting the simple truth was for the best. 'Mum died, five years ago … She was very brave.'

'No!' he crumpled, ageing before Romilly's eyes as he once again processed news of the terrible reality. She braced herself for the situation turning more challenging.

'You're lying.'

'Dad, I'm not, I'm sorry.'

'Get out. You're not Joan and you're not Romilly. Leave.'

'Dad, please.'

'In that case, I'm leaving, going to look for my Joanie.' He levered himself up and headed out of the room, into the hallway.

Romilly almost wept at the sound of Benita's voice greeting him, and watched with gratitude as the woman gently ushered him back into the living room, towards his easy chair.

'Charlie, let's see if we can find a programme you like, shall we?' Benita said, switching on the television.

'Same as before,' Romilly whispered to her, 'But he is trying to leave.'

Benita smiled kindly at her and nodded, murmuring, 'Don't worry, I'll contact Dr Woods – she's coming here to see a few of the folk later this afternoon. See if we can get something to calm him. She's aware. We are keeping a record of these memory issues now, and I'll update her.'

'Thank you.' Never had two words meant so much. Romilly didn't know what she or her father would do without Benita.

'Here we are, *Gardener's World* – you like that one, don't you? I've bought some of that decaffeinated tea we talked about, so you should sleep a bit better. Let's make you a cup.' Benita shrugged out of her coat, then turned towards Romilly. 'You know, it may be best if you leave us to it.'

'But he might improve after this programme, or a nap, maybe?'

'Perhaps, but why don't you come back tomorrow for a bit? I'll be here – you can give me a ring before you set out, if you like.'

Romilly's shoulders slumped. 'I'm working tomorrow, but I'm back in the country on Sunday, and then, as you know, I'm away for four days again. That will be my routine for the next seven weeks, before I'm rostered off for rest week. You know that when I'm on the ground I always have my phone with me. Do you think it would be possible for me to speak to Dr Woods today after you've seen her?'

'I'll let her know.'

'I appreciate everything you're doing, Benita, truly.' Romilly crouched next to her dad. 'I'll be back on Sunday,' she said to him. 'Love you.'

He stared at her vacantly.

Benita patted his shoulder and he grasped at her hand.

Romilly strolled through Heathrow's Terminal 4 on Monday morning, ahead of her afternoon outbound to San Francisco, harnessing the energy from the thrum of activity. A difficult Friday with her father, and a visit to him yesterday when he'd spent most of the time asleep, had proven draining. She passed a young family saying their farewells and again thought of Nathan, reuniting with his family. It was simple – from here on in, she would keep her relationship with him as she did with any other senior colleague – formal, respectful, non-personal. By the end of this block, she would be nearer the tally required to submit an application to the list of approved pilots awaiting captaincy positions. That's what mattered.

Romilly's resolution was tested the moment she entered the crew room. Nathan's uniform accentuated the breadth of his shoulders, its silver-trimmed navy blue playing off his dark features and glints in his hair. He and Steph were the only two yet to have arrived, and were laughing about something.

'Hi Steph, Captain Reed, good weekends?' Romilly adopted a professional smile and parked her flight bags at the furthest seat, ignoring the flicker of surprise on Nathan's face at her formality.

'Brill, we went to a silent disco up the top of The Shard. Unbelievable views, and the DJs played the best tunes,' said Steph, alternating quizzical glances between Romilly and Nathan.

'Sounds … quiet, then. And you, Captain Reed? Some quality time back with your family I hope?' she said, in a casual, rhetorical manner, that necessitated only the briefest eye contact.

Nathan studied his shoes before lifting his focus in a way that made her feel they were suddenly alone. 'With Nora, my daughter, yes, thank you. I was expecting to have her this weekend, but not Thursday and Friday. I hadn't known the school was closed – nor that her nanny would bring her to the airport. Yesterday I returned Nora to her mother.'

'Her nanny … So …'

'Just popping over to Pret, be five minutes,' said Steph, closing the door behind her.

'Perhaps you have some questions?' he said. 'I know I would.'

'I don't need an explanation of your personal life.' The obvious lie wedged in Romilly's throat.

'All right, but just so we're clear, her mother and I have been separated since New Year. Nora lives with her, except for every other weekend when I have her,' he said, then paused, awaiting her response.

Romilly kept checking the door, hoping that another crew member would arrive at any moment, curtailing the conversation. 'Your arrangements with your wife are not my busine—'

'*Not* my wife – we never married. At least having been a "lousy partner" seems marginally less of a failure than a "lousy husband".'

Romilly hesitated, surprised by the chink in his confident uniform revealing itself. 'Well … again, not my—'

'Business. Yes, I hear you.' He sighed. 'So, how was your weekend? Did you see your dad?'

On the back foot after Nathan's explanations, and surprised that he'd remembered to ask about her dad, Romilly reassessed so fast that she forgot to filter. 'Hard. Actually, harder than that, he was barely lucid. Fortunately, his carer arrived – you remember I mentioned her?'

'Yes, Benita, isn't it?'

'Right, yes,' she stammered, before jabbering on. 'And I transported sun-seekers to and from Lanzarote on Saturday, but there was a two-hour delay at Arrecife with refuelling for the inbound. I walked around the terminal building in sunglasses for a bit, but it wasn't exactly Playa Blanca, you know?'

'Yes, I've lost count of the times people seemed to marvel at my good fortune at flying to Australia via Thailand. Three hours sweltering in uniform at Don Mueang Airport in Bangkok is no fun. And sorry, that's tough with your dad.'

'It may be about to get tougher. His GP telephoned to explain about new medication and the likely next steps for him. Dad's current flat is only warden assisted, so he may well need something more … I don't know …' She gulped. How did Nathan draw all this out of her?

'Comfortable?' he said gently.

'Exactly. Anyway, how is the route looking – anything over the Atlantic likely to give us any problems?' To give herself an excuse to regroup, she walked over to her flight case.

After unzipping some lip-balm from a side pocket, she realised that Nathan had followed her. As she turned, she saw that he had just curved an arm towards her shoulders when the door began to open. As he snatched it back, she was shocked to find that she had already tilted towards him.

'Let me know if there's anything I can do, please,' he said quietly.

'Thank you. I'll see how he is on Friday, I guess.' It shocked Romilly how much she really could have done with that hug.

'It'll be okay,' he mouthed.

She nodded again and attempted a smile. His, in return, gave her an instant lift.

9. Positive Climb

'Hi, folks,' said a younger, blond-haired man, walking into the room, wearing the double stripes of a second officer. He swivelled his flight case into position next to Romilly's and came over to where she and Nathan were talking.

'Max Krüger.' He shook Nathan's hand, then hers. 'Read to rock 'n roll?'

'Once we've touched down safely in San Francisco, maybe. Jonathan Reed.' She and Nathan held a bemused moment of eye contact.

'Romilly West, good to meet you. Been with us long?' Boyish good looks, and the taut shirt of a dedicated gymgoer pegged him as having yet to reach thirty.

'Four years in January, mainly puddle-jumping 737s across the Nordics and Northern Europe. Moved to transatlantic cover work a few months ago after getting my type-rating licence for the 777. Hoping for a first-officer seat soon.' He grinned, winking at Romilly.

'I'll watch my back, then.' She smiled, admiring his ambition.

His response was delivered with a good-natured laugh. 'Think I'll be watching yours from the jump seat, mostly, but I'm looking forward to seeing San Francisco – never been. Do you have any regular cabin crew on this route? It might be fun to organise something as a group while we're there?'

'Yes, we have an excellent cabin manager and several of her team are regulars,' said Nathan. The door opened, and Steph returned, right on cue. 'This is her actually. Steph, come and meet Max Krüger.'

'Hello, Stephanie Hoffman, call me Steph.'

Max's eyes widened. 'A pleasure …'

'Okay, then, Romilly, Max, let's have a seat at the table, run through the briefing. Looks like we're on track for the scheduled departure.'

On her way to the flight-deck while pre-boarding was underway, Romilly passed Max chatting animatedly in the front galley with Steph and two enraptured-looking cabin crew. Romilly entered the flight deck, removed her high-visibility jacket, and took her place in the right-hand seat, next to Nathan. 'Ground checks complete.'

'Checks complete,' he acknowledged and smiled at her. 'Windy out there?'

'A tad.' She smoothed her hair back. 'It's all right for you guys with short hair,' she said, flicking her fingers at his, then squinted. 'Jesus, what's that?'

'The eyebrow? Nothing, a nick.' He waved his hand as if the row of stitches were of no issue.

'Big nick.'

'Not compared to my cousin's.'

Romilly frowned. 'Why, what happened to you both?'

'He messaged me yesterday with a picture of blood-stained staples in his head, thanks to a second row's boot at Saturday's rugby match. Has to wear a scrum cap for the next month, much to his disgust.'

She was none the wiser. 'But you weren't playing rugby, you had Nora?'

He smiled.

'Yes, I try to listen too.' She said, casting him a side-smile.

'Touché. No, he and I weren't together – it's just a coincidence. Dan is a professional player. I do still play actually, just socially, for a veterans team. Thursday night training, occasional Saturday morning matches, local opposition, quite tame stuff. Anyway, as you rightly remember, I had Nora, so I wasn't playing. Got these courtesy of her flying video tablet during a motorway shunt on the way home on Thursday from the airport,' he said, then raised his hand, 'and yes, before you ask, apart from these stitches, we're all okay. The car's unfortunately feared less well and is currently at the repair shop.'

'Does it hurt?' It certainly looked like it might, being right on the corner of his browbone.

'No, not now.' He pointed at the black box voice recorder somewhere beneath their controls. 'Obviously, in full disclosure I logged the incident with HR and relayed details of these stitches and the formal all clear from the health centre's concussion check afterwards.'

'Well, I'm glad you're all okay,' she said, then mouthed 'sorry'. She'd forgotten about the head injury policy; it was just as well Nathan had not.

He acknowledged her with one of his warm smiles that she couldn't help but return. 'Let's commence standard checks.' Nathan started to guide them through the usual procedures.

Max appeared and took his place in the jump seat. 'Steph says all good for passenger boarding if you are.'

'Thanks.' Nathan switched his headset channel to the cabin PA, 'Cabin Crew boarding to commence, thank you.'

'Our slot is in thirty minutes,' Romilly confirmed. 'Should be pushing back from the stand in fifteen.'

'Roger that,' said Nathan. 'Want to do the honours today?'

'Yes, thank you.' She continued to check, log, and re-read the panel of instruments around and above her, all the while remaining alert to the ground crew below and the constant communication in her ears between the air traffic control tower and other aircraft in the vicinity.

Twenty minutes later, Romilly had taxied the plane to runway 21 left, ready for take-off. 'It's the Airbus ahead, then us,' she reconfirmed, watching the impressive quad-engine plane gather speed and eventually begin to rotate upwards. One day, maybe. As she clicked her shoulder harness into place, adrenaline begun to build. For her, this was the best part of flying.

'Cleared for take-off,' said Nathan, after they had received clearance from tower.

'Roger.' Romilly placed her left hand on the throttle and, per Airline procedure, Nathan hovered his right hand near hers, in case he was needed to take over. With her other hand on the yoke, she eased the plane's engines into action. Attuned to their distinctive sounds, and continuously monitoring the instrument readings, she eased the plane into motion. After a few seconds, they were thundering down the runway.

'Eighty knots,' Nathan advised.

'Cross checks.'

'Hold.'

'Roger,' she acknowledged, waiting for the necessary momentum, and his command so she could activate take-off.

'Rotate.'

The nose lifted as Romilly pulled the yoke towards her, angling the plane into a steep incline to rapidly gain height.

'Positive climb,' said Nathan.

'Positive climb checks. Gear up.'

On her command, Nathan flipped the switches to retract the wheels.

She waited for the cadence of landing mechanics beneath her feet to quieten, then for visual confirmation from the relevant cockpit indicator lights to extinguish. 'Gear up.'

Into the sky they soared one thousand feet, three thousand, banking left, still climbing. Through the clouds into the blue. Exhilaration in its purest form.

'Engage autopilot.'

'Autopilot engaged, check,' she confirmed and removed her hands from the controls. It was only then that she noticed Nathan subtly nodding at her. He got it. Understood the thrill. That incomparable, addictive rush for which there were almost no words.

'Okay, Max, you can head to crew quarters if you want,' said Nathan.

'Roger, see you both in three hours.'

'Tell me to mind my own business, but what's up with you and Captain Clooney, then?' Steph murmured conspiratorially across the flight bunks during their rest break.

'Nothing, and you can't call him that! What makes you ask?' She concentrated on smoothing out a ragged fingernail to detract from the whoosh of sudden blushing.

'Observations. One minute you're behaving formally and all "Captain Reed", the next, it's like there's no one else in the room with you two. Plus, Max might have mentioned something about sexual tension in the cockpit,' said Steph, grinning like the proverbial Cheshire Cat.

Romilly couldn't help but chuckle. 'What? I think our amiable new second officer might have his sights rather focused on sexual tension with someone from cabin crew for layover.'

'Yes, his name is on some of the girls' lips already. He's attractive, I'll give him that, and has a puppy-like thirst for life. Pity he's not three or four years older.'

'If you say so.' Romilly kept thoughts about the way Max spoke admiringly to Steph, to herself.

'Still, though, you and Captain Reed are of similar age and you're both single, aren't you?' Clearly, Steph wasn't about to let the subject drop; curiously, Romilly didn't altogether mind.

'He's older than me, and anyway, my life is full.'

'Not that much older, I don't think, and I know I'm not alone in seeing he's very easy on the eye. He's perfect for you.'

'We're just colleagues, nothing more.'

'I see,' Steph said, giving Romilly a strange look. 'Okay, tell me about your full life, then.'

Romilly sighed. 'Well, work mostly, and also my dad is poorly. Might have to move him into a specialist care home shortly.'

'Sorry to hear that. But apart from work and your dad, how's your social life?'

'Minimal so that I can fly as much as possible,' said Romilly, aiming to emphasise the practicalities of achieving her goal.

'What? Work is part of life – we work to live, not the other way around.'

'I love my job.'

'And most of the time I love my job, too. Doesn't stop me going out with the girls, hoping to meet someone who might treat me decently, and I try to make plans to celebrate special events and stuff. So, for example, when's your next birthday?'

Romilly groaned. 'Soon. The big four-oh is looming.'

'You're joking? When?' Steph cocked an eyebrow.

'The sixteenth,' she said, already predicting what Steph's response might be.

Steph immediately scrolled up her phone. 'That's three weeks' time … We're going to be in San Francisco then! Let's at least have drinks on our arrival night. Ooh, tell you what, I'll give you a free cut and colour the weekend before – that can be my gift.'

Romilly was taken aback. 'Why, do I need one?'

'Nothing major – a trim, a little shaping, some lighter pieces to frame your face. Don't be offended but my guess is you haven't changed up the style in a few years.'

Romilly nodded, defensively sliding her sensible ponytail through her fingers. Truthfully, it was decades.

'That's … well, let me think about all that. I need to rest now, and probably so do you.'

'Okay, but if you switch on your Bluetooth, I'll Airdrop my contact details, for when you've decided what time we could meet that weekend before your birthday.'

There it was – the hand of friendship, rare and genuine. Before she could talk herself out of it, or allow memories of friends who'd let her down to deflect from Steph's warm openness, Romilly followed her instincts. Utilising the airline's popular inflight WiFi, and her phone's Bluetooth, she reciprocated.

Steph grinned, rapping her fingers along her phone case. 'Thanks. You've got me thinking now.'

'Rest!' said Romilly and rolled over onto her side.

Captain Clooney had asked her to take the landing at San Francisco and she wanted to feel refreshed. Captain Reed, she admonished herself.

10. Navigation

By nine pm local time, Nathan was halfway down a light beer at the Sky Bar when Romilly arrived from one of the elevators, closely followed by Max, then several of their flight's cabin crew, including Steph, who had walked the four blocks from The Excelsior.

'Drinks on me,' Nathan announced, giving bartender Carter a nod. Air crew had deceptively gruelling jobs that they somehow performed with smiles on their faces, shift after shift. R&R during their layover was critical.

Carter jumped into action, preparing the requested glasses of local spicy margaritas for everyone except Romilly, who opted for a classy Napa Chardonnay.

'Cheers, to a smooth outbound,' Nathan offered as the group raised their glasses, clinking in weary but spirited camaraderie.

The group eased into comfortable banter, sharing anecdotes, and suggesting ideas for a group outing in the morning. Beside him, a distracted Romilly checked her phone every few minutes.

'Perhaps set it to vibrate?' Nathan suggested quietly, opening the flap of his jacket to reveal that he'd tucked his own phone in a pocket that would reverberate against his chest to alert him to new messages. She blinked a nod of thanks and slipped hers into her trouser pocket.

'I've got a great idea for us all tomorrow,' Max announced, draining the last of his cocktail. 'There's a cycle hire place two blocks from here. What do we think about attempting the Golden Gate Bridge?'

'Yes! Sounds fantastic, the views will be amazing. We'd better go easy tonight, though. It might be a bit energetic,' said Steph.

'There's a long but scenic drag to get up onto the bridge, but apparently once you're up, it's fairly easy going. On the other side, there are pedal-free hills all the way down to a coastal resort called Sausalito, where we can grab some lunch by a marina. We wouldn't have to cycle back – there are passenger ferries that take bikes. They sail right past Alcatraz Island and into Pier 39, which isn't far from the cycle hire shop.'

Other than Steph's enthusiasm, Nathan sensed his crew's reluctance. It was one of those moments to lead by example. 'All right, I'm in. Great idea, Max.' One by one, all except for Romilly confirmed they'd join in. It surprised him how much he minded the thought she'd be missing.

'Live a bit, come on,' Steph levelled at her.

'I'd be constantly bringing up the rear,' said Romilly. 'Don't think I've been on a bike since I was ten; I don't even use the air bikes in the gym.'

'It's not a race. Come on, it won't be the same without you,' Nathan said, hoping his casual encouragement might reassure her.

Romilly exchanged looks with Steph and blushed. 'Okay.'

'Fantastic, I'll book the bikes now then. Ten o'clock?' said Max, already on his phone.

Carter interrupted the conversation. 'Best make it eleven, guys. You can't see much from the bridge before then if it's foggy. Most days it's the case, some days worse.'

'Thanks, eleven it is then," said Max, "Meet downstairs in the lobby at ten forty-five?' Everyone nodded. 'Right, who's for another round?' Nathan had to smile. His second officer was clearly in his element.

'Not me,' said Romilly. 'Once I finish this, there's a bath and bed with my name on it.'

'Me neither, I have a video-call,' Nathan admitted.

The others sunk their drinks and headed noisily for the lift, allegedly bound for the cabin crew's hotel.

Nathan shook his head. 'Think there might be some green faces on the ride tomorrow.'

'They're all younger, they'll be fine,' said Carter, innocently polishing some glasses.

'Hey! I might be the wrong side of forty-five, but I can still cycle a couple of miles, thank you.'

'It's twelve miles, sir, but apologies.' Carter backed away, unsuccessfully trying to conceal a grin.

'What? No one mentioned *twelve* miles,' Romilly said.

'You'll be fine. I'll keep you company, even if we have to walk up the steep parts.' He really didn't want her to back out.

Romilly cocked her head at him. 'I bet you're a great dad.'

'That's a nice thing to say. Think I might be failing, but I try. And I wasn't thinking paternally when I offered to keep you company, even if some people think I do look ten years older than you.' He glared good-naturedly at Carter, who raised his hands humorously as if being aimed at.

'Nathan, I'm not as young as you think – no doubt Steph will blab, if she hasn't already, but it's my fortieth in three weeks' time.'

'Really? Are we going to be here for that?'

'Yes, and she wants to organise something.'

From the way she stared at her empty glass, she didn't seem convinced.

'You don't have to do anything you don't want to, but for what it's worth, I also think that it's important to mark the big ones.'

Romilly nodded.

'You don't look your age, if you don't mind my saying,' said Carter, bobbing his head into their conversation again.

'All right, back off, buddy.' Nathan waggled his hand, laughing. Somehow the words had just slipped out. Romilly's pale eyes questioned his implication, and rightly so. God, but that colour under the amber lights was stunning.

'Sooo?' she said.

'Yeah … I …' A punch of arousal had kicked when her mouth held the 'O'. But no, this wasn't what he wanted, nor what she deserved. They were colleagues. He was her captain. His home life was complicated. He stood up, desperate to draw a line under the heated moment. 'I ought to make a move.'

'Watch out, Captain, Carter doesn't want to *witness when pilots lose control*' she said in mock sincerity, then seemed immediately shocked with herself. 'Sorry, obviously something in the air tonight, or else it's my wine talking … That was a reference to the other—'

'I know it was. He shouldn't see us *tipping over the edge as we give in to what we need most,* either.'

Carter's eyes switched between the two of them. 'You jokers.'

Now Romilly stood up. 'On that note, or should I say dollar bill, I'd better go. See you in the morning. And thank you, Carter.'

'Goodnight,' he and Carter said at once.

Nathan barely blinked as she sauntered towards the lift. Despite all the reasons why he shouldn't, if she looked back at him, he couldn't guarantee he wouldn't follow. She didn't.

'Daddy's going on a bike ride tomorrow,' said Nathan, thirty minutes later, alone in his hotel room.

'You haven't got a bike.' Nora's puzzled expression on Nathan's screen made him smile.

'It's okay – there's a special shop here to borrow them from.'

'With stabilisers?'

'No, but I might be a bit wobbly, just like you were when you were learning.' He grinned, miming almost falling off his chair.

Nora giggled.

'Off to school soon. I wonder what you'll be doing today?'

'I've got a tummy ache.' The way she suddenly avoided looking at him aroused his suspicion.

'Oh no, have you told Mummy?'

'She says I have to go to school.'

'Well, if she thinks that's best, but tell a teacher if you feel poorly.' Parenting, he'd learned early on, necessitated uniformity in approach from himself and Liz – now more than ever.

'Mmm.'

'Maybe you'll be doing some painting today.'

'I'll do one of you on a bike!' she said, rallying.

'There you go, and if not, there's always time when you're home afterwards isn't there?'

'I suppose.'

'Nathan, Nora needs to get ready, she's not in her school clothes yet,' Liz said, walking into the room behind Nora.

'Okay, princess, speak to you tomorrow.' He blew her a kiss and watched her leave the room before speaking quietly to Liz.

'Nora mentioned a tummy ache?'

'It's trending. Featured a few times last week, too. Think she'd rather be home, playing with her dolls.'

It had been a long day, so Nathan mindfully tempered his frustration at why Liz hadn't mentioned the issue. 'Do you know what's behind that? She loved school last year.'

'Not sure, she hasn't mentioned anything specific.'

'Not to me either. But I'll let you know if she does.'

'Got to go – she'll be late. Where are you again?' she muttered, already walking out of the room.

'San Francisco.'

'Nice for some.' Liz cast him an all-too-familiar look of resentment, then ended the videocall.

Nathan sighed, staring at the blank screen. Keeping things civil was challenging when it only went in one direction.

Word of the Golden Gate cycle had apparently spread to other members of the crew, as Nathan discovered more than half of them assembled in reception the following morning. Before he'd greeted them, Bill, the concierge, beckoned him over.

'Sir, you should take weather gear for the bridge, it can get very wet and blowy up there. Forecast is for sun by lunchtime over the other side in Marin County – it'll feel much hotter there.'

'Just like home then – pack for everything,' Nathan chuckled.

'Yes, sir, exactly.'

Nathan relayed the advice to the crew, who between them reckoned that they had sufficient protective clothing. Romilly arrived last, looking toned in black workout leggings, and a matching windproof jacket, her hair dangling in a damp-darkened plait between her shoulder blades.

'Morning, all,' she said, nodding at everyone in turn, Nathan last, and not quite meeting his eye. Perhaps their banter at the bar last night had been on her mind, too.

'Great, that's everyone,' said Max, clapping his hands and leading the group through the revolving doors.

The cycle hire shop equipped them all with hybrid road-mountain bikes, helmets, and bike locks, and a helpful young woman used a large wall-map to brief them on the best route. After five minutes of level road cycling, the crew snaked onto a dedicated path, headed towards a marina, berthed with hundreds of boats.

Nathan trailed at the back of the group with Steph and Romilly, chatting while they pedalled along the smooth bike trail. Max double-backed from leading, beaming a look of exasperation. 'Come on, you three, this is the flattest part.' He circled round to pull into line beside Steph.

'Keen on the water?' Nathan asked them all as they pedalled in a row.

'Are you kidding? Who doesn't love boats like those? Not that I've never been on one. Would need to find myself a millionaire first,' Steph said with a laugh.

'They're yachts,' said Max dismissively, 'and the bigger vessels there are Viva superyachts. Don't be fooled, though, not all millionaires would treat you as you'd hope.'

The rest of the group exchanged glances.

'Well, I can take them or leave them, to be honest, my heart's in the air, not on the water,' said Romilly.

'Same,' said Nathan, selecting a lower gear so as to ease the strain on his legs, 'though I'd never say no to lunch on a yacht like that.'

'Me neither, but there's something about flying, having control of an airplane, the thrust and lift, the exhilaration. Nothing has ever come close to that.'

Not for the first time, Nathan found himself wondering about her sex life.

'Come on, slow coach,' Max baited Steph, then darted off like an excitable teen.

'Right!' Steph shifted her own gears, and within a minute, the two of them were far ahead of Nathan and Romilly, who pedalled on sedately, admiring the scenery.

'Wow, look that!' Romilly marvelled. 'Must be The Palace of Fine Arts over there with the enormous dome. I've read about that, it was built for the 1915 Pacific Exposition. It's on my list to visit.'

'Next time, we'll go and see what's there,' said Nathan, not convinced at what he meant by 'we'.

'Not sure the rest of the group would be interested, though.'

Was she saying something beyond words? He couldn't be sure. 'Perfect place for some photography.'

'It would be.' She pedalled on, craning her neck to take in the architecture for as long as possible.

The thought of spending time together with her offered undeniable appeal, but whatever he'd just suggested, or she had agreed to, was suddenly overtaken by the demands of the narrowing and rapidly steepening route.

'There's no getting out of this now.' He puffed, switching to an even lower gear, swooping in behind her and increasing his thigh-burning pedal speed. Far ahead of him and disappearing into some thin fog was an indistinguishable couple pushing their bikes.

'I can't,' Romilly panted. 'Sorry.' She swung her leg over the saddle and began to push her bike. From the frustrated shake of her head, she seemed disappointed with herself.

'Fine by me.' He dismounted and walked his bike beside her.

'Better switch our lights on – the fog is getting worse. I can't see much ahead of us.' She flicked the switches, and he followed suit.

'Not quite Boeing standard,' he said.

She chuckled and then groaned. 'My calves! I'm obviously doing the wrong circuits in the gym.'

'Nearly there. I think it's a shallow run-up to the bridge after this.'

'Hope you're right, need to keep something in the tank to get across the bridge.'

He paused, attempting to establish his bearings, but the increasingly dense fog clouded their every direction. 'Unless they're waiting for us, somewhere up ahead, I think we've lost the rest of the group,' he said, gasping for air.

'Wouldn't you kill for a radar?' She laughed. 'Keep going or turn back?'

'Forecast over the other side is supposed to be sunny, but the bridge might not be up to much.'

'Keep going, then?'

'Roger that. Hopefully we're almost up.'

11. Lost Sense

They'd been nowhere near it. Hairpin after brutal hairpin, the road led them ever higher, ever deeper into a thick bank of fog.

'Might be regretting I didn't overrule you and turn us back,' Nathan said, lungs screaming.

'I can hear traffic – the slip way that the woman in the cycle shop mentioned must be around the next corner. Keep going.'

Finally, they drew parallel with vehicle fog-lights of passing lorries and cars making their way onto the bridge. Somewhere ahead lay the famous, red-painted girders, but they might as well have been on Battersea Bridge, for all he could see of them.

Beside him, Romilly reached for her backpack and removed her water bottle, making him realise that he'd stupidly forgotten his. And he was absolutely gasping.

'You don't have one?' She somehow read his mind and offered hers to him.

He shook his head, still catching his breath.

'Don't be daft,' she said, nudging it into his hand.

If he wasn't so dry mouthed, he might have thought more about the fact her own mouth had just used it. Still, out of courtesy, he unscrewed the lid and gratefully swallowed a small amount straight from the bottle. 'Thanks. Can't believe I forgot mine. Usually better prepared.'

'Pilot characteristic 101, prepared for everything. Don't worry, there are shops in Sausalito.' She winked at him and cocked her mouth into a cheeky smile. His heart rate was only just settling from the steep climb; now it was picking up again.

He zipped up his jacket against the sudden drop in temperature. 'Ready for the bridge?'

'Not that I can see a thing, but yes.'

'Tighten your helmet,' he said, tilting his bike towards hers, and without thinking, slipped his fingers under her chin. Romilly's eyes fixed on his as he adjusted her buckle, his fingertips meeting soft skin, flushed warm from exertion. Before he could stop himself, he brushed his thumb across her cheek. She blinked slowly and leaned her face into his touch.

'Great place to stop, you dipsticks!' a cyclist yelled, grazing past Nathan's arm, and only narrowly avoiding a crash into them.

'Sorry,' Nathan called as the guy disappeared ahead of them.

'We'd better get going,' said Romilly, clearing her throat. 'Shall I lead? We can swap in the middle if you like. Remember there's a pull-in viewpoint? Not that we'll have anything to see.'

He nodded, before finding his voice. 'I'm right behind you.'

The towers of the suspension bridge were reportedly seven hundred feet above the water. Nathan could barely make out even the supporting struts of red iron as he passed right beside them, let alone anything below. He pedalled as close behind Romilly as possible, so as not to confuse her rear light with others', supremely grateful for both the waist-height railing on the left that separated cyclists from vehicles, and for the higher, red metal grid barriers on the right that marked the edge of the bridge.

Ten minutes later, Romilly pulled into the viewpoint area and steered her bike to a corner. He guided his next to hers and peered out, hoping to see something of San Francisco Bay in the distance, but it was just like flying through storm cloud. Suddenly, she clasped the front of his jacket, pulled him towards her, and kissed him, softly at first, then a little harder. The rhythmic rumble of traffic crossing the sectioned tarmac behind them faded, replaced by the escalating pulse in his ears.

She withdrew, bringing a finger to her lips. 'Sorry, really don't know why I did that.'

'Christ, Romilly,' he murmured, winding a hand around the back of her neck, and drawing her back to him. Other words, especially sensible, cautionary ones, refused to form into anything coherent. Wrapped in the secretive blanket of fog, all he heard was his own moan as their lips reconnected, and their tongues explored.

'What are we doing?' she said, eventually pulling away to catch her breath.

It was as if he were flying blind, without instruments to navigate, both exhilarating and uncertain. 'I don't know. But it feels good.' He'd somehow known it would.

Romilly grabbed her water bottle again and swallowed rapidly. 'Here.' She passed it to him.

Unscrewing the spout seemed pointless now. When he gave it back, her huge eyes stared up at him, windows that revealed the same appetite for more that he himself was experiencing. Her lips parted slightly causing another lick of heat to flash through him. 'Keep looking at me like that and we'll never get off the bridge.' He groaned.

'All right,' she croaked, 'we'd better go. Your turn to lead the way – hard to believe it, but sunny Sausalito is waiting for us somewhere over the other side.'

Nathan forced his pedals along the second half of the bridge's path, the gradual decline easing the effort required. Before long they were freewheeling, winding down the roads into the town. Once out of the fog, they were at last able to appreciate the scenic rocky views. He tried to take it in, but the lingering taste of Romilly trumped all other senses.

The rest of the crew had already locked up their bikes in the storage pen that Max had pre-booked, and were milling around, waiting.

'Sometime today, you two. At last, right, everyone ready for lunch?' said Max, twisting his phone in various directions, ready to navigate their route.

'Definitely,' said Steph, 'I think we're all a bit deflated after the bridge. It was a bit disappointing to be honest.'

Nathan didn't dare look at Romilly.

Within an hour, Sausalito was indeed bathed in cloudless sunshine, as if on an entirely different planet. Nathan's sports wrap sunglasses saved others from knowing he couldn't tear his eyes away from Romilly. If she was experiencing anything like the same throb of attraction as him, well, she was doing a good job of disguising it.

The crew spread out on a grassy area beside the water, devouring much-needed fish and chips, milkshakes and beer. Afterwards, they broke off into smaller groups to tour the clapperboard, upmarket town. Romilly agreed to browse the shops with Steph and a few others; meanwhile Nathan and two others of the crew visited a local photography exhibition. He tried to focus on the technical and creative skills that each exhibitor had demonstrated, but all he was really doing was counting down the minutes until the group reunited at the bike pen for the ferry.

'How was it?' Romilly asked him as they pushed their bikes along the queue for the three o'clock crossing.

Full of pictures of her, he wanted to say. 'Interesting. The shops?'

'Also *interesting*.' She blinked at him innocently, then wheeled her bike onto the ferry's boarding ramp. He followed suit, and once they'd locked their bikes, the group climbed the stairs to the outdoor deck of the heavily rocking boat. Romilly accepted his hand as they struggled towards seats on rows of long benches. About to release her fingers, he squeezed them. She ran her thumb across the back of his, then they parted touch. Sitting side by side on the bench, they gazed out at the water. His hand felt strangely empty.

Max strolled over to them, his balance apparently untroubled by the pitching. 'We're all thinking of drinks at the Sky Bar at six, then dinner at an Italian in Battery district. Interested?'

'Sounds good,' said Romilly, with quick grin, then immediately fiddled with something on her jacket's zip.

'Count me in,' Nathan added. Hopefully he had sounded nonchalant.

The route passed alongside Alcatraz Island and its famous prison buildings. Nathan marvelled at the iconic water towers and clicked some shots on his phone with the bridge in the background. He tapped Romilly's leg to point out a tour group arriving at the Island's dock. She signalled a thumbs-up. Another location to explore, but as a group, or just with him? With luck, they would have a chance to talk at the restaurant, later.

Back at the hotel lobby with Max and Romilly, after returning their bikes to the hire shop, Nathan acknowledged Bill, and thanked him for his earlier advice.

'Shit!' Romilly muttered, beside him, 'I've got four missed calls from Dad's wardens, and a voicemail from Benita.'

'Hope everything is all right?'

'I don't know! This is because I still had my phone on vibrate. I knew that was a stupid idea.'

Nathan bristled.

'Oh my god,' she breathed, listening to her phone.

'What's happened? Anything I can do?'

'No, I can handle it. Shouldn't have allowed myself to be … distracted.' She waved an accusatory hand in his general direction, then strode off towards the bank of elevators.

Max shot him a look of confusion. 'Excuse me a second, Max,' he muttered before jogging after her.

She was frowning at the elevator floor indicators. 'Hey,' he said, 'Don't be like that.'

'Stop! Just … leave it.' She jabbed at the already lit call button, and without a second glance in his direction, stepped into the first elevator to arrive.

Showering after a day that had culminated in an eleven-flight frustration-busting stair climb to avoid having to explain himself to Max, or riding the elevator with Romilly, Nathan nonetheless debated whether he should call her. The fact he didn't know her room number or have her mobile wasn't his main concern – switchboard could transfer his call room to room, after all. It was more that she probably needed space to regain control of things, have room to work through her thoughts. If his own mind was anything to go by, their kiss on the bridge could hardly have helped her state of mind. On balance, he chose to wait the hour before he would see her at The Sky Bar.

Nathan immediately regretted the decision, when overhearing Steph at the bar tell others that Romilly had a headache and would be giving the evening a miss. He pulled her to one side. 'Did she say anything else?'

'About?'

'Things at home, maybe,' he tested, without breaking Romilly's trust.

Steph hesitated, looking him directly in the eye. 'As it's you, I'll tell you what she told me – that her father had somehow gone missing from where he lives, but eventually was picked up by a police car a mile away and brought home. I'm not sure of the details or what's wrong with him, but she must be worried – not that she'd admit it. She doesn't open up much. I couldn't persuade her to come out with us, even for a bit.' Nathan chewed on his lip. Romilly had begun to open up to him, though. Trusted him. 'Thank you, I appreciate your sharing that with me. I ... don't suppose you'd also share her number?'

'Tempting, believe me, but I shouldn't.'

'Quite right, you're being a good friend. Everyone needs those.' He smiled, then turned to walk away.

'But ... you know, I think she'll be okay. She was saying how quiet it was up on the fourteenth floor, especially with her room being located right at the end of the corridor.' Steph flashed her eyes, then returned her attention to the rest of the group.

Romilly answered the door. Grey joggers, grey hoodie, grey face. Even her blue eyes seemed to have dulled their intensity. Perhaps she had been expecting room service, but her body language when she saw him shrieked of 'wary'.

'I'm not coming tonight, I've got a—'

'Headache. I heard. Sorry about that. You're missed. Wondered if I should bring some pizza back for you from the Italian later?'

'Why would you do that when there's room service? I can call down for some perfectly well myself.'

Nathan took an extra breath. 'You don't have to do everything yourself. Was the news from home bad?'

'Sorry. Yes,' she said swiping a hand across her forehead.

'Do you want to talk about it?'

'No, I'm waiting for a call from my dad's GP, then I just want to go to sleep, get to the airport tomorrow, and fly home.' Understandably worried but frustratingly stubborn, she seemed to him in need of a hug. He lingered, debating whether he should, but she pulled her hoody up tighter around her neck and stepped backwards. Words, he decided, would have to suffice.

'There are at least twenty hours before we collect in the lobby tomorrow lunchtime. If you need a friend before then, you can ring me on the room to room. I'm in 1101. Won't be late back from the restaurant. See you in the lobby tomorrow.'

Romilly acknowledged him with a tight nod.

'See you in the lobby, then.' She closed the door on him.

He was fifty feet along the corridor when her door handle clunked open, and she called out to him.

'Nathan?'

She was leaning out of the doorway.

'Yes?'

'Thank you.'

'You'll be okay?'

With a faint smile, she nodded, then disappeared behind her door.

12. Tug

Having lain in the darkness for almost two hours, Romilly could make out most of the detail on the triple-shaded light fitting above her head. Worry, guilt, and confusing, pent-up emotions allied to attack her vital need to sleep. She checked off the solutions to some of her main items of concern: Dr Woods had reassured her that her dad was comfortable; Benita would be making extended visits; and the wardens at his retirement complex confirmed they would be extra vigilant at the entry doors. Even so, Romilly checked her phone again, paranoid that she'd miss another call.

Soothing one set of worries simply made room for others to swell. Steph had encouraged Romilly to live a little, so she had. But what had happened with Nathan on the bridge wasn't Steph's fault. Whether he knew it or not, since they'd met he had been pressing buttons that had long been stuck. Nonetheless, she'd been as surprised as him by the surge of desire that saw her kiss him. It was as if she simply *had* to. Until she'd checked her phone, when they had arrived back at the hotel, all Romilly had kept in mind was the way he'd made her want to discover more, feel more. Now her face flamed hot at how she'd lashed out Nathan out for having missed those important calls. In the heat of the moment, her behaviour might have been understandable, but it was not excusable. And he'd still bothered to ask if she was all right after all that.

Romilly clicked the bedside light on and sat up. Trying not to talk herself out of it, she picked up the handset on the room's telephone and dialled 1101.

'Hello, Nathan Reed,' came his croaky voice in her ear.

Maybe calling him was foolish; it might just make things worse. She should turn off the light and try again to get some sleep.

'Romilly, is that you?'

'Yes. Did I wake you? she replied, screwing her eyes tight.

'No, I've just video-called home, now I'm reading.'

Why did she feel so nervous? 'Anything interesting?'

'Researching the Pacific Exposition in case I'm in the vicinity of The Palace of Fine Arts sometime in the next six weeks.'

'Oh … Was the restaurant good tonight?'

'Really great – a couple of young guys using organic produce from Napa. The pasta was superb.'

'Sounds like I missed out there.'

'It'll still be here next time.'

Romilly exhaled, feeling lighter. 'I'm sorry, I don't know what came over me earlier. I really shouldn't have behaved like that.'

'Well, as long as you're talking about what happened after discovering your phone messages, and not us kissing on the bridge, then, apology accepted,' he said, gently.

'I am. It's just that my dad somehow slipped past the wardens, and no one had noticed until Benita arrived. Can you believe? Anything could have happened to him. I don't know why I took it out on you.'

'I know why. Fear.'

'Fear?'

'I lost Nora once at her pre-prep summer fete, completely panicked when I couldn't see her. I remember lashing out at everyone, and was even cross with her when I found her initially – she'd only bent down to pet a friend's family dog. All kinds of scenarios flashed through my mind.'

'That must have been awful. You're right. The thing is, I have no siblings, no aunts, or uncles. I need to be there.'

'We are A-type personalities, aren't we as pilots? Responsible, in charge, capable. We know the procedures for flying, and practise in the simulators for all manner of emergencies. But life outside of the cockpit can be messy, and events happen that can spin you off track, make you cautious and uncertain – and I'm speaking from experience. But you'll get through it, especially if you ask for help.'

'I'm usually fine, but the truth is, there isn't anyone …' she said, throat rapidly thickening with unshed tears. It was no use, all she could do was to give in to them. She dropped the handset onto the bed and sobbed into a pillow. She'd never felt further from home than right at that moment. After blowing her nose, she picked up the phone again, half-expecting Nathan to have hung up. 'Hello?'

'Still here,' he said quietly. 'How do you feel now?'

'A little better. Sleepy.'

'Good, I'll see you in the lobby tomorrow lunchtime. Then we'll be home before you know it.'

Standing handsome in their Sterling uniforms, Nathan and Max were discussing something when Romilly arrived in the lobby for the shuttle transportation to the airport. Several of the cabin crew seemed to be lamenting sore backsides from the previous day's expedition. Steph pulled her to one side.

'Are you doing okay today?' she asked with a frown. 'You look a little puffy, if you don't mind my saying.'

'I'll be all right – got a solid eight hours in.'

'Glad to hear that. You've eaten?' Steph rummaged in her bag and produced a cereal bar.

Romilly's chest warmed at the kindness. 'Yes, don't worry. But I appreciate the offer.'

'Captain was worried about you last night. Asked me for your mobile number, but I wouldn't give it.'

'He caught up with me, somehow knew my room number.'

'Hmm, funny that.' Steph made a comedic shrug.

'Funny.'

'Morning Steph, Romilly,' said Nathan, coming over with Max in tow. 'Looks like we'll have a better view of the Bay on take-off today. For the first time since we've been here, there's only light cloud and no fog bank.' Nathan's natural enthusiasm was like sunshine, warm and relaxing. Exactly what the crew needed, ahead of a long shift.

'Typical, isn't it? A shame we couldn't go up on the bridge again today,' said Steph.

'It is. I'd definitely try that again next time.' Nathan glanced at Romilly and smiled.

Romilly diverted her gaze towards the floor. The sunshine felt a little hotter.

'Crew van's here, sir,' Bill called from the lobby door.

Max had just taken his place on the jump seat behind Romilly, ready for push back, when the cabin intercom pinged. 'Captain, contact Cabin Manager, please. Captain, Cabin Manager, thank you.'

Eager to get flying, but detecting a problem in Steph's tone, Romilly groaned. With all checks complete and passengers settled, they were ready for control tower's imminent permission to leave their stand.

Nathan called through to the cabin's phone, switching his conversation to the flight-deck's speaker. 'Steph, everything okay?'

'No, a passenger has just realised he's left the medication he needs for the journey in his bag.'

Nathan's shoulders sagged. 'Tell me the bag's not in the hold.'

'I'm afraid it is.'

'Roger that. I'll contact the ramp agent, stand by.' Nathan switched channels to request that the stairs urgently be reconnected, and for the ground handlers to return to the hold doors, ready to search the names on over three hundred passengers' suitcases for the relevant one.

Romilly tried not to show her dismay. Airports of this size probably handled more than a thousand departures a day; this passenger could mean Sterling might miss their take-off slot.

'Back in a minute,' said Nathan, clutching his high-viz waistcoat. Before she could say that Steph would let him know once the bag was in the cabin, he'd gone.

Romilly used the spare moments to double-check her instruments and checklists of procedures. As with the outbound flight, Nathan had once again decided she would pilot the plane for take-off.

'I don't believe it!' said Max, a few moments later.

Romilly turned to see him peering through the side windshield.

'He's only down there waiting for the bag. Literally never seen a captain do that before,' said Max, shaking his head.

Romilly watched Nathan curtail a conversation with someone from ground crew when a black suitcase was passed in his direction. The ramp agents and ground crew retreated and, two minutes later, a slightly ruffled-looking Nathan reappeared in the cockpit.

'I think we're just within our slot tolerance,' he said and, quickly replacing his headset, he addressed the team via the cabin PA. 'Cabin crew arm all doors, cross-check, and report.'

Within a minute, Steph had confirmed all was secure, and double-checked that the cabin was ready for departure.

'Tower, Sterling 299 ready for push-back,' he said, back to full composure.

'Sterling 299 push-back confirmed,' Tower confirmed into the flight-deck's headsets.

'Good effort, Cap,' said Max. 'The crew owe you one at the Sky Bar next week.'

Nathan raised his hand in acknowledgement.

Though what Romilly really wanted to do was to hug him, she instead mouthed a 'thank you'. No one wanted a delay, but she suspected his efforts lay in part to her concern at getting home in time to meet with her dad's doctor tomorrow afternoon, or at the very least to visit her dad during waking-hours.

Nathan acknowledged her with a brief smile before focusing on the hand signals of aircraft marshals on the ground.

The jolt of the tug connecting to the plane quashed the last of her emotions, and professional mode concentrated solely on the sequence of the push-back procedure. For the next fifteen hours, their only focus would be on flying.

13. Wine (Talkin')

Romilly and Nathan were bringing up the rear of the crew as they walked towards the crew transit to the main terminal at Heathrow.

'I just wanted to say thank you, for everything. I won't forget it,' said Romilly, trying not to shout, despite their noisy surroundings.

'That sounds a bit final. We're back here for the outbound in four days' time, and that will only be week three of eight.'

Monday suddenly seemed a long time away.

Nathan frowned at her. 'Apart from seeing your dad, what are your plans?'

'For the first time in months, I've not made myself available for last-minute hops to bolster my flying hours. I needed to keep tomorrow, Saturday, and Sunday clear to view some care homes, unless my dad's doctor diagnoses something unexpectedly better at this afternoon's meeting. How about you? Surely a great deal more exciting than mine?

'I only have Nora on alternate weekends,' he said, rubbing the back of his neck.

'I'm sorry, that must be hard.'

'It kills me,' he muttered, the rawness of his response showing her what being a father meant to him.

Romilly wished they weren't in company. 'So, what will you do instead?'

He took a deep breath and sighed. 'Keep busy. There's rugby training tonight – we've got a friendly match on Saturday. Tomorrow night, a friend of a friend is opening a small restaurant-come-wine bar, and I've said I might go along – they know I like my food. Apart from that, could go to the gym, tidy up the balcony on the apartment, edit some photographs. Sunday, I'm up in Bedford, for lunch at my parents. Last time I was there, I picked up some of my old vinyl records going back as far as sixth form. My ancient record player's broken, so maybe I'll investigate buying a new one.'

'That all sounds … so full …' Romilly's voice trailed off. The comparison to her own weekend couldn't have been starker. That's what her life should be like. She sensed him studying her face, so pulled together a suitable question to deflect. 'What records have you got?'

'Some eighties rock – U2 and Queen. There are a few jazz albums, which my dad got me into. What do you like?'

'I'm embarrassed to tell you, now that I know what you listen to.'

He chuckled. 'If you're about to confess you're a hip-hop fan, I won't believe you.'

'Very funny. I do like U2 and Queen, and sometimes switch to Brit-pop, though I can't say I'll *ever* understand jazz. My heart belonged to Take That, and Robbie Williams specifically. I still rely on his tracks to get me pumped for the treadmill.'

'Good to know.' Nathan nodded to himself, though she couldn't be sure what he was actually thinking. 'I had Take That aboard a few years back – they were flying between their Asian Tour Gigs. Your chap had left them by then, of course. Had them up onto the flight deck for photos once we'd landed. They all wanted to sit in the pilot seat. Nice guys.'

'My professionalism might have slipped by requesting a fan-girl selfie.' She'd once flown Jeremy Clarkson to Cape Town. No danger of having wanted a selfie with him.

'Oh, I got a picture – if you're *very* nice to me, I'll show it to you some time.'

His easy smile spread to her own face. 'Well, it sounds like your weekend is all set.'

'It is, but … here.' He discretely pointed his phone in her direction. 'I've just airdropped you my details. If you need to talk, or catch up, whatever, that's how to get hold of me.'

Romilly heard her phone buzz. Uncertainty at whether to drop her details back in return was temporarily suspended by the arrival of the crew van and their need to hurry to catch up with the rest of the team at the pick-up point. 'Thank you,' she breathed as they trotted along, wondering whether he meant what he'd said or was just being kind.

'It's there to be used,' he replied.

Was she that transparent?

They all clambered in, some with more energy than others. 'Off to a fancy spa weekend for a friend's hen do at a health resort in Kent. Can't wait,' Steph was saying.

'Whereabouts?' said Max.

'Canterbury, I think. Why – thinking of turning up in your uniform?' Steph grinned.

'No … just asking,' Max mumbled, then turned to Nathan. 'It's been great flying with you. Might see if there's bidding open for second officer on this route again soon.'

'Several of this crew is scheduled for the next six weeks. The jump seat position usually varies, but it would be good to have you with us for the remainder of the block,' said Nathan.

'Thanks. I'll log in later, see if I can persuade Crew Services.'

Nathan nodded.

Romilly also nodded, admiring aspects of Nathan's character. She wouldn't put it past him to intervene on Max's behalf.

By Saturday evening, Romilly's emotions were all over the place. For someone used to control, it proved exhausting. On Thursday, after freshening up at home after the flight, she had met with Dr Woods and Benita at her dad's flat. Though he had recognised her, she'd been shocked at his doziness. Dr Woods had explained that it was on account of his increased level of medication. With an official diagnosis of vascular dementia, it was agreed that specialist accommodation should be sought as soon as possible, and in the meantime to increase carer support.

'You've had an opportunity to look through some of the links to local options that my secretary sent you?' Dr Woods had said.

Romilly had nodded. 'I'm seeing three over the next two days. I suppose I'll need to make arrangements to sell this place in the meantime.'

'They aren't cheap, the dementia care homes.'

'My dad has funds, but I need to get hold of his accountant, then I suppose the bank, and the solicitor

… estate agents …' The realisation of what would be involved had weighed on her already-tired body.

Dr Woods checked her watch, then began packing her notes into a large day bag. 'If you need anything further from me, do contact my office. There's a lot of guidance on charity websites, and the Council's Social Services teams can help to point you in the right direction. I'm here again on Monday visiting some other residents, so perhaps we'll see each other then.'

Romilly had stood up to see the woman out.

'Don't forget to look after yourself,' Dr Woods had said, resting a hand on Romilly's shoulder.

'Thank you, Dr Woods. I will. There's a ready meal with my name on it at home, but I'll just sit with Dad some more before I go.'

After two hours, Romilly had left the flight magazines she'd picked up at the airport on his coffee table and promised her lethargic father that she would return over the weekend. He had barely seemed to register that she was leaving.

At the first care home viewing, yesterday afternoon, she had been unprepared for the brutal reality of seeing incapacitated residents being fed, cared for, and spoken to as if they were children. The prevailing smell had reminded her of aircraft toilets, mingled with school canteens. A large television blared in one of the communal lounges, with rows of vacant shells of people faced towards a Disney film. She had been trying to visualise her dad sitting there, his memories of flying all over the world reduced to watching a flying elephant join a circus, when a resident had yelped from the back row of chairs.

'Dumbo's crying!' a man had said, and pointed at the television, while a carer had gently reassured him. Romilly had put the resident at fifty, maybe fifty-five.

The second place, that she'd seen earlier today, had been little different. Pummelled by the serious prospect of needing to choose somewhere for her dad, let alone getting her head around how soon he might deteriorate and become like the residents she'd seen, had led to a much-needed opening of a bottle of wine. Half a bottle in, abandoning the dubious joy of a ready-meal paella, she'd ordered a pizza. With Dr Wood's advice on her shoulder, at the last minute she'd included a salad.

Waiting for her food to arrive, she opened her laptop and clicked through several advice pages on how to choose care homes. Contradictory and utterly overwhelming information swam before her eyes. She wished she could discuss it with someone who understood, or at least had family with dementia. Hold on – Nathan's aunt! Hadn't he said she was now cared for in a specialist home? Romilly stared at her phone for the longest time, debating whether to ring or to send a message. He was probably still out at after his rugby match, but this seemed a legitimate reason to contact him. Deciding a voice message might be best, but feeling suddenly apprehensive, she attempted a practice run.

'Hi, it's me, just calling to say hi …' No, now she'd said hi twice. She deleted it and tried again.

'It's Romilly, give me a call if you have a minute, not urgent, not important, it's—' No, that all sounded cold and negative. Another attempt deleted. She should just say what she really meant. She inhaled a steadying breath.

'Hi, it's me. Hope you're okay. Could do with your advice about selecting specialist care homes. You mentioned that your aunt was living in one, I think. Anyway, thanks for everything the last few days. And … Oh, for pity's sake, Romilly, why can't you just say what you really think? … Like, you're a really good kisser, Nathan, in case I didn't say so at the time. Really, *really* good, and truthfully, I wasn't sure my lips still worked. I'm so glad they do, but I'm not sure yet about the rest of me, though maybe we'll … Oh for goodness sake … I can't say all that, I sound ridiculous …'

The doorbell rang – food at last. Romilly dropped the phone onto the sofa and took ownership of a gloriously greasy-looking box and a carton of green salad from the delivery driver.

Moments later, having put the salad in the fridge and installed the box beside her on the sofa, she picked up her phone again. Immediate nausea kicked in. No … No, no, no, no … How had the voice message sent itself? She played it back and cringed. Looking up 'How to retrieve a voice message' revealed that, well, basically you couldn't. Perhaps she should record another one, apologising for the first? No, that might draw even more attention to it. Well, if he didn't contact her, she'd just have to brazen it out when she saw him at work on Monday. Somehow.

14. Loud and Clear

Nathan reversed his insurance-rental car into a parking space outside The Bedford CodFather, deeply regretting having synched his phone to its speaker system and having just played aloud a voice message from an unknown number.

'Well, son. She sounds lovely.'

Unbeknown to Romilly, she had influenced Nathan's decision to surprise his parents by driving up that evening, instead of the following lunchtime, in an effort to extend quality time spent with them. You never knew what the future held. Now, with his mother in the car, who 'hadn't cooked for three', and insisted on buying him a fish supper, he knew exactly what the immediate future looked like. He braced himself for the inevitable inquisition.

'I know you – she wouldn't be cabin crew,' she said, opening her campaign.

'Is that a question?'

'No, excepting Liz, I just notice you've always liked natural-looking girls.'

'She's a pilot.' It was best to offer *something,* or she wouldn't stop.

'Interesting. What's her name?'

'Mum …'

'Fine, I won't pry.' She sat quietly, keeping her seatbelt on. He almost laughed – she'd used the tactic of waiting for him to fill the silence since he was a boy, to extract what she needed, and here he was, still unable to withstand it.

'Romilly, but that's the only thing I'm saying.'

'Romilly, what a lovely name.'

His mind's eye pictured Romilly on the ferry, hair blowing. 'It is. Suits her.'

'Does it?' His mother's eyes bore into the side of his head.

He sighed. 'Yes, though she's not only … Well, she's interesting, too. But we're just friends. You know how I've fucked up.'

'Language, Jonathan.'

'Sorry. I'm keeping it light. We're just enjoying each other's company, nothing serious.'

'Well, she certainly seems happy with your company.'

'Enough. Let's go.'

Nathan resisted further interrogation while they waited for his order to be prepared. But his mother had always been tenacious.

'I'm hoping you don't resort to this sort of food too often. Women don't find a spare tyre round middle-aged men attractive, you know.'

'Mum.'

'Just saying,' she said, lifting her hands.

'You forget that I run regularly. And that for most of the last five years, I had a home gym in the garage.'

'You were never in it, though, were you? Spent most of your time in the shops with Liz, buying her stuff.'

Yes, unfortunately. 'Not to begin with.'

'For a very short time, but the shine of living with a pilot soon wore off. She wasn't one to cope with your erratic timings and you being out of contact for hours at a time, especially once Nora came along.'

'That's my doing, not hers. It isn't easy living with someone who always has a clean uniform and overnight bag packed in the boot of his car, ready to abandon her at a moment's notice.' Nathan stifled his frustration at the numerous times he and his mother had discussed this exact subject.

'Still, now she's off with someone else.'

Nathan smiled at the girl in a hairnet behind the counter as she handed over a paper-wrapped parcel. 'Yes, Mum, and I'm not, so please can we just get this home. It's almost ten o clock.'

'Dad will probably be asleep – was back from a driving job very early this morning. Tomorrow I'm cooking roast lamb, your favourite. I remember how tiring it gets, eating out all the time while you're away.'

He gave her shoulders a quick hug. 'Thanks.'

'And how's my gorgeous granddaughter?'

'Mostly okay, although she's started saying she's got tummy ache, which Liz thinks is to avoid school.'

'Could be. The jump from Reception which, let's face is it mostly play-based learning, to Year 1, when they are learning to read, write, and count may be a factor, but so could a number of things. I remember you didn't want to go in once because you were convinced that your PE bag had gone "missing", and you thought you'd be unable to play sports or perhaps get in trouble. Of course, it was found on another boy's cloakroom peg, but it was a big deal at the time.'

'All I can do is keep an eye on her.' Trivial or otherwise, if whatever troubled his daughter wasn't resolved by its own means soon, he would need to take action.

'Usually there are the odd clues, just stay tuned. You still speak to her most days?'

'Apart from when I'm in the air. At the very least I send her some photos or a short video.'

'You're doing the best you can, then,' she assured him, patting his sleeve.

Why didn't it feel that way?

An hour later, sitting alone in the living room when the house was quiet, Nathan allowed his thoughts to return to Romilly. It hurt to imagine the miserable time she was having with her dad, and not having a family home to return to like this. Aiming for something to make her smile, he sent her an upbeat voice message.

'This is the Golden Gate Kissing Service, following up after your trial appointment. We hear from your feedback you were satisfied with your first experience, so one of our operators will call you tomorrow morning to discuss further.'

He left it until ten o'clock on Sunday morning to call, ensconcing himself in the car with some coffee while his mother was getting ready to go out with him.

'Hi, it's me – are you free to catch up?'

'Just ironing my shirts for tomorrow, then I'm visiting another care home in an hour.'

'Ugh, ironing. That joy awaits me when I get home,' he said, taking a sip of coffee to relieve his sudden dry mouth.

'Sounds like you're in the car – are you on your way to your parents?'

She remembered. 'Actually, I came up last night instead. Wasn't as tired as I'd expected to be, and the rugby friendly was cancelled due to sickness. I'm taking

Mum to the garden centre in a bit; she has a long list of plants she's planned for the balcony at the apartment. I thought I'd try you first.' Was he gabbling?

'They're both well?'

'They are, thank you, but tell me how your dad is.'

She yawned. 'Sorry. Saw him Thursday, Friday morning, and yesterday.'

'He recognised you?'

'At times, I think. He didn't confuse me with Mum, at least.'

'I notice that you don't mention her much,' he said gently. He couldn't imagine losing his own.

'She was a nurse – worked long hours, but was the soul of the home, and loved cooking. Everybody adored her. She left a gigantic hole in mine and Dad's lives.' Not for the first time, Nathan felt Romilly's emotion as if it were his own. His arms ached to comfort her.

'I'm sorry. She would have got on well with my mum. You should see the pile of food she's prepared for lunch – there're only the three of us.'

'Ah, but home-cooked food, though. A pilot's dream.'

For a crazy moment, he wondered about the logistics of getting her there in time for lunch, but remembered she had the appointment. 'I'm very lucky. How did you get on visiting the care homes?'

'It was all right, I suppose.'

'It's me you're talking to.'

She paused, as if weighing up whether to trust him.

'It can't have been easy?'

'Okay, it was awful.' She sighed.

He waited, giving her space to open up. God, he had turned into his mother. Silence. Unfortunately, he suspected she might have reverted to internalising mode. 'And?'

'And nothing.'

'Romilly.'

'Okay! And now I'm really scared about my dad's future. I tried to explain it to him, but he doesn't understand about moving to somewhere like that. I'll have another attempt this afternoon. His new medication should stabilise soon, which may see him more receptive to a discussion. It's going to confuse him horribly to move somewhere new without warning.'

'That must be really tough for you. I can ask Mum about her sister, my aunt Laura. See if there were any lessons learned when the time came to move her to specialist care.'

'Thanks. That would really help. And just before you go … About my voice message – I hadn't actually meant to send that version.'

'What version did you mean to send?'

'Something … less.' Her voice petered out.

'That would have been a shame.' His mother came out of the house and started to double lock the front door, then paused to check through her handbag as if she had forgotten something, in the way she always did. How frightening it must be to lose your memory. Romilly had gone quiet, again. 'Are you still there?'

'What are we doing?' she said faintly. 'I think it's friendship, but then maybe … I don't know.'

'Nor do I, but do we have to define it?'

'I can't go around kissing my superiors and expect it not to affect things.'

'Well, as long as there aren't others, you'll be fine. And anyway, I kissed you back. Willingly, as you might have noticed. Come on, we're pilots – we can focus on certain things while we postpone thinking about others. Compartmentalise,' he said, knowing the advice was also directed at himself.

'Keep it professional in front of others, you mean.'

'Yes, but unprofessional anywhere else you feel the urge – bridges, historic exposition sites, former prisons.' She burst into laughter.

He loved hearing it. 'Got to go, sorry, shrubbery calls.'

'Have fun.'

For the rest of the day, Romilly had never been far from Nathan's thoughts. Driving back to London later that evening, a back seat full of exotic potted plants for his balcony, he rang her again.

'Twice in one day, people will talk,' she said, but instantly he recognised a false joviality to her tone.

'On my way home. Thought I'd check in, see how it went today,' he said, trying to sound casual, despite having counted the hours since their earlier call.

'Dad was better; the care home was worse.'

'Mixed then. Is that water I can hear? You're washing up?'

'No, I'm in the bath.'

His mind raced, imagining bubbles floating over her slender limbs. Her hair might be curling at her temples like he'd seen on their bike ride. He cleared his throat. 'Never really been one for baths. Take too long.'

'That's the point, to slow down and relax. Enjoy the bubbles, light a candle or two, you know?'

'I'm visualising it as you speak.' Jesus, he was kidding himself to think this was solely friendship. Imagine how blue her eyes must look against flushed pink cheeks.

'Nathan?'

'Er, yep, just joining the motorway, sorry.'

'Right, I suppose I'd better let you drive home safe.'

'Or we could keep talking.' He sensed that she wanted the company. And he couldn't remember a woman ever having quite this effect on him.

'I'd like that ... Tell me more about your childhood. Did you always live in Bedford?'

'No, just outside, in a village called Stagsden. When I went to university, my parents wanted a fresh challenge and bought the old post office in Bedford as a restoration project. That's been the family home ever since. Dad still does some part-time driving work, mainly to get away from Mum's list of jobs for him in the house and garden, I suspect.'

Over the following hour, they covered school memories, experiences of flight-school, and more. He was beginning to learn what made Romilly West tick – and whether she realised it or not, almost all roads led back to her dad. He hoped Nora would always adore him as much, though not experience the pressure Romilly seemed to be under.

'Hold on, I'm just topping up the hot. My skin is going all goosey,' said her echoey voice.

Nathan felt himself tighten. 'Do me a favour, try not to splash too much.'

'What, like this?' Trickling water and her teasing laugh bounced around the car.

'That's plain cruel.' he protested, over her seriously sexy chuckle.

'Honestly, you should try a bath. I rely on them if I'm struggling and need to be extra kind to myself.'

It saddened him to have confirmed by her own words what he'd already suspected. 'You can always call me instead, if you feel like that, from the bath or anywhere.'

'I can manage.'

'Yes, that may be, but there's life beyond merely managing.'

'Not for everyone.' He heard her yawn.

'I'll let you go now.'

'Yes, parts of me are looking rather shrivelled.'

He moaned.

'See you in the crew room at lunchtime,' she said with a laugh.

'Sleep well, till tomorrow.' He disconnected the call, feeling rather flushed. Tomorrow would not come quickly enough.

15. Aerophobia

'First Officer West contact Cabin Manager. First Officer West, Cabin Manager, thank you.'

'What's up, Steph?' said Romilly, flicking on the flight deck's loudspeaker and hoping that there wouldn't be a reason for a delay in boarding passengers.

'Ramp agent has just radioed to say there's an exceedingly nervous flier in the departure lounge waiting until last to board, apparently on the verge of panic. Can you be available once she's seated, if needed? Some pilot reassurance may be good. Her mother thinks she'll respond better to a woman.'

Nathan – who, perhaps in guarding the privacy of their burgeoning friendship with obvious professionalism, had barely widened conversation beyond procedural checks and limited small talk – nodded his consent.

'Of course, knock on the door if you think I can help, Steph.'

'Thanks. If so, it'll be in five minutes. We've almost finished boarding rows thirty to forty-two. She'll be seated in H25, aisle seat.'

'Understood.'

'Aerophobia,' Nathan muttered. 'I wish passengers realised how carefully the flight deck works to keep everything safe. Too many disaster movies out there scaring the crap out of people.'

'I know, although the passenger might suffer with anxiety more generally.'

With a thin smile, he nodded again. 'That's true.'

Max Krüger arrived to take his place on the jump seat. Those of the crew who had flown the route the previous week were pleased to see his return as second officer for the remainder of the block, bringing his infectious cheer and camaraderie to the group.

'Think a few of us might hike to Twin Peaks tomorrow. Fancy it, either of you?' he said, eyebrows up as he awaited a response.

Romilly tilted her head to Nathan, whose body language read as tightly coiled. Maybe keeping things professional was taking more out of him than expected. That, or he was having second thoughts about their private plans to tour The Palace of Fine Arts.

'I'll see, if not this time, then perhaps the following week,' she said.

'Ah, but if the rumour is true, then it's your special birthday next week – don't think there will be time for a trek on that layover,' Max said with a grin.

'Steph mentioned something to you, by any chance?'

'Yep. Heart of gold, that one.' Yes, glad he had noticed.

A knock on the cockpit door preceded the woman in question poking her head in. 'Got a minute for that passenger?' she asked.

'Sure,' said Romilly, disconnecting her headset and following Steph to where a young teen was wringing her hands.

'This is Katie Williams,' said Steph, as if introducing a friend.

Romilly crouched down. 'Hello, Katie. I'm one of the pilots, Romilly West. Just thought I'd come and reassure you that you're in safe hands. Is there anything you'd like to ask me about the flight?'

'I'm afraid about the take off and the landing; the middle bit, hopefully I'll just eat and watch a film. It's the not knowing whether everything's normal, if the wings are working properly, all that,' the girl stammered, picking at the cuff of her sweater.

'Well, we have a long checklist of procedures to follow even before passengers board the plane. I personally have walked around the wheels and engine, and seen the flaps working.' Romilly gave Katie her most reassuring smile.

'You look young to be a pilot.'

'I think you've just made my day. But it took me three years of training for these first two officer stripes, and another two for the third one. All in, I have more than ten years' experience flying passenger airliners, and our captain has even more. You're in safe hands.'

'What if something goes wrong?' The girl stared out of the window.

'All pilots are trained for emergencies; we practise and are tested in simulators at least twice a year to keep our licences for each of the different types of aircraft we fly. My latest test was six weeks ago. Would it help if you could see the wings or wheels?'

'How could I?' She turned her attention to Romilly's face and frowned.

'Well, on this aircraft, the 777, we have exterior cameras fixed to key moving parts of the plane, so that we on the flight deck have constant sight of them. On one of the channels on your screen in front of you, there's an option to switch to outside camera view, which shows the wheels, the wings, and my favourite view, from the nose of the plane – not dissimilar to the one we pilots have.'

The girl nodded. 'It might help.'

'Is there anything else I can reassure you about before I go? We're almost ready to depart?'

'Have you flown to San Francisco before?'

'This time last week I was doing exactly the same thing, and the week before that too.'

'Okay. Thank you.'

Steph leaned in. 'Thank you, First Officer West, we'll let you get back.'

'No problem at all.' Romilly nodded and headed along the aisle to the sound of Steph calmly showing the passenger how to select Channel 8 for the camera view.

For once, the usually sombre October skies of Heathrow were replaced by brilliantly crisp but gusty conditions that necessitated sunglasses, even as they waited on the runway for final permission from the tower for take-off. Within minutes, Nathan had flown them up high above West London, engaged autopilot, and Max had retreated to the crew quarters to rest, ahead of his cover hours.

'Good job through that wind shear,' she said, impressed with his natural ability to manage the plane through a sudden gust.

'Thanks.'

Conversation tailed off, and Romilly suspected that either he was concerned about their privacy with the black box recorder or was more conserving energy. After her return from break, she noticed he hadn't eaten much of his meal, but then airline food was very hit and miss. She went on to push something that was meant to resemble chicken curry around the food tray, before mostly eating the rice.

As they entered San Franciscan airspace, a static-filled radio request arrived from traffic control. 'Sterling 298 be advised, First Officer is randomly selected by FAA for drug testing on arrival. Please follow the usual channels and remain on site until all clear is given.'

'Confirm First Officer random drug testing, Sterling 298,' said Nathan.

Romilly groaned. That would hold her up for at least forty minutes, and she would miss the crew shuttle van to the hotel. Had she even seen where the taxi rank was located at San Francisco Airport?

'I'll accompany you if you'd like,' said Nathan, focusing on the instrument panel.

'Thanks, I was just thinkin—'

'I know.'

She smiled at him, but he didn't seem to notice.

After a landing that Romilly kept as soft as possible for her passengers, and especially thinking of Katie Williams, she and Nathan headed through passport control, customs, then into the FAA screening centre. After she'd been administered with oral swabs and been breathalysed, they had hung around the corridor outside for almost an hour, waiting for officials to give her the all-clear to leave. While there, she had usefully caught up on messages from Benita, accountants, and lawyers. Nathan, meanwhile had barely said a word, making her feel guilty – after all, she was a grown woman and perfectly capable of making her own way to the hotel.

By the time their taxi pulled up to The Beaumont, it was almost nine pm. Nathan passed the driver his credit card and huskily confirmed that he needed a receipt for expenses. At eighty dollars, she was relieved to hear it, but not so much the rasp in his voice.

She studied his face. 'There weren't any strawberries in the afternoon snack tray, were there?' she asked. 'You're sounding throaty.'

'No, don't worry.'

'Good to know – hopefully I'll never see that.'

'Feels worse than it looks, as you can imagine,' he said, shuddering.

'You're cold? It's quite mild here compared to home.' She had almost asked the driver if they could crank down the windows.

He nodded, walking alongside her as they approached the reception desk. 'A bit.'

'Welcome back, Captain Reed, Ms West. You're aware your airline has changed the layover room formats from this week and going forward?'

Nathan shook his head. 'I'm not – what do you mean?'

Romilly cast him a side-look at his unusually curt manner with the receptionist.

'It's more economical for them to use our multi-bedroomed suites. They have booked a two-bedroomed one, and a double room for this stay.'

Nathan flipped up the collar of his jacket and pulled the lapels across his tie. 'Which are we in?'

The receptionist typed on her touchscreen. 'Mr Krüger has checked into the double room, so, as you're last to arrive, you'll be sharing Bay Suite, on floor eighteen.'

'How is that configured?' said Romilly, without missing a beat, nor looking at Nathan.

The woman tapped her screen and nodded to herself. 'Separate bedrooms with en-suites, a shared living room and a small kitchen area.'

'Fine,' said Nathan, clearing his throat and holding out his hand for the card key.

'I'm sorry, there's nothing else available?' Romilly added, trying to compensate for Nathan's paucity of manners. She'd also have a word with Max when she saw him.

'Unfortunately not, but it's on the Bay side, and enjoys the best views.'

Romilly peered out of the suite's windows, enchanted by twinkling suspension bridge lights reflected in the Bay's glossy, ebony water. She mentally promised herself to take some shots of it for her dad, and of the sprawling campus of Berkley University glistening on the distant shore. But first, as ever, she would unpack her cases – she just couldn't relax until clothes were hung and she'd unwound in a long shower. Even when she was staying somewhere for a single night, she would install her book, chargers and personal items bedside her bed.

'I'll take this room, if that's all right,' she said to Nathan, indicating the first on the left and dragging her flight case across a tasteful rug.

'Whichever you want.' He sat down on the sofa and bent over to remove his shoes.

After her shower and exchanging her uniform for a comfortable T-shirt and joggers, Romilly left her bedroom in search of bottled water. As always, it was important to rehydrate after the flight.

Nathan hadn't moved from the sofa.

'Want some water?' she called out from the kitchenette, relieved to discover that the small fridge had a stock of bottles on its shelves. 'Nathan?'

She peered round the corner into the living room. He'd slumped back against the sofa, eyes closed and jacket still on. Taking a bottle over to the table beside the sofa, she nudged his arm. 'Hey, it's boiling in here – how can you stand wearing your jacket? Did you not hear me asking if you want water?' He didn't stir. She crouched down, only then noticing that his face was flushed and sweaty. She touched a hand to his face, and he flinched. 'You're burning up! Nathan, come on, take this off.'

The movement of her pulling at his jacket roused him, but he gripped its collar. 'F-freezing.'

'It's not, you have a temperature. For God's sake, why didn't you tell me you were feeling this ill?'

'C-cross.'

'Yes, I am cross. Hold on, I'll open the windows.' After two steps towards them, she deviated instead for the room thermostat. 'Forgot, the stupid things don't open.' She flipped the cap off his bottled water. 'Here, have a few sips of this.'

Water slopped out of the bottle as soon as he gripped it.

'All right, let me have it back a sec.' She took a long gulp from the bottle and returned it to him. 'Try now. Actually, hold on, you need paracetamol. I've got some in my bag, wait there.'

'Not … going …' he rasped.

Whilst Romilly retrieved the pack, she debated whether to call for medical help.

'Here, take two of these. Shall I ask for a doctor?' She placed two tablets into his palm and watched him shudder as he swallowed them.

'No. Sleep.'

If it came to it, the hotel probably had medical assistance on call, Romilly told herself. In the meantime, sleep might be the best thing for him. She scooted his flight bag into his bedroom.

'Can you make it to your room?'

Nathan nodded and slowly stood up, grabbing at the arm of the sofa to steady himself. She took the opportunity to tug his jacket off. He'd only managed two shaky steps, before she needed to position herself under one of his arms to help.

After he'd flopped heavily onto his bed, she mentally worked through what she knew about fever relief. 'Undo your shirt and tie. You're still too hot,' she said.

He shook his head and within seconds passed out. Without overanalysing, she removed his tie. Only when releasing the first few buttons of his shirt, which revealed sweat-darkened hair at the base of his throat, then along the top of his chest, did the intimacy of what she was doing cause her to pause. In the semi-darkness, she studied his glistening face and the shadow of growth along his jaw. Handsome, even as sick as he was.

'You'll be okay, I'm just outside.'

She left him to sleep but kept the door open so she could hear him, and so he could enjoy the view of Bay Bridge lit up when he awoke.

16. O_2

Nathan's woozy head and heavy limbs pinned him flat, like acceleration g-force. Somewhere from a past experience, a memory flashed the warning that these symptoms might signal something important. No, not important – critical. For his crew, for his passengers, his plane.

With great effort, he pushed himself upright and tried to take stock amid dizziness. Was he flying? No first officer to his right, no second officer behind him. Where were the control dials, the thrust levers, and his yoke? Blurred vision struggled with incomprehensible rows of distant lights in the sky beyond the cockpit window. Were they landing strobes at the airport's runway? Spatial disorientation – another symptom of hypoxia he had experienced in the altitude chamber for oxygen starvation at the training base. Was this a rapid decompression session? Both sweating and shivering, he gulped deep breaths into his lungs, willing oxygen to the tissues of his body. He was going to lose consciousness.

17. F-fine

Sufficiently worried, Romilly had abandoned her usual pre-sleep routine of some outdoors fresh air and settled onto the living room sofa, ordering two rounds of club sandwiches from room service, and flicking through the local offering of Monday night's cable television. Heightened awareness of Nathan made it difficult to concentrate on anything.

An hour later, she'd checked on him after hearing him moan something undecipherable. Worryingly, his sweating seemed worse and his temperature even higher, partly, she suspected, because he'd wrapped himself in the bed cover. She laid one dampened face flannel from his en-suite over his forehead and used another to blot across his neck and face.

'Palace … picnic … p-p,' he whispered, wracked with shivers.

'It's all right – we'll go there another time. A tepid shower might help you feel better, if you can manage it?'

He shook his head.

'Right, we'll just open these then.' She undid a few more of his shirt's buttons, trying not to study the hazy path of hair.

He moaned and winced. 'Not how I th-thought it would be.'

'What do you mean?'

'Y-you taking my uniform off …' he mumbled, staring at her, glassy-eyed.

Romilly froze. She hadn't been the only one with that dream then. 'Well, let's just park that thought for the moment. I think you need to be seen by a doctor. You're really sick, Nathan.'

'Don't. F-fine.'

Insubordination be dammed. 'Back in a minute.'

Staff at the reception desk were as efficient as she had expected from a quality hotel, sending up paracetamol, ibuprofen, and fever relief gel packs for Nathan's overheating forehead. The doctor on call would visit within two hours, they'd said. Mercifully, it turned out to be only forty-five minutes later when a firm knock sounded on the door shortly after one am.

'You've caught yourself an unpleasant flu virus, son,' the portly doctor declared, propping rimless glasses up his nose after examining Nathan's mouth and chest. 'Your throat's also a bit streppy – that can be viral, and part of the flu, and sometimes it can be bacterial, for which I can leave you some strong antibiotics if you'd like. Of course if it's viral, they won't have any effect.'

Nathan uttered a weak 'okay'.

'Not surprised – you aircrew folk all sharing the same air in a metal tube of with hundreds of passengers for a dozen hours.'

'I'm told the air is passed through HEPA filters. That supposedly reduces bacteria and viruses by ninety-nine per cent,' Romilly said, trotting out the company line perhaps a little defensively. This wasn't the first time she'd heard the health perils of aircraft 'incubators'.

'All due respect, ma'am, doesn't seem that way now, does it? Anyhow, mostly they're short and sharp these nasty viruses. We're fond here of a method called the "ache and bake", meaning you let your body's high temperature burn off the virus faster by resisting painkillers. You'll recover quicker, but it's uncomfortable, I won't lie. Alternatively, relieve your fever with paracetamol and ibuprofen, but it'll just prolong things.'

Nathan nodded his understanding, sinking back into his pillows. He turned his head listlessly towards the doctor. 'I can fly home Wednesday?'

'In two days' time? That's up to your recovery, son. How long have you felt unwell?'

Nathan's brows knitted. 'Not sure.'

'Did you have symptoms back in England?'

'Of course not,' Romilly cut in. 'He absolutely wouldn't have flown if he'd felt unwell.'

Nathan managed a small smile in her direction.

She positioned herself closer to his face. 'Don't try and estimate the time – think where we were when you first felt sick?' she said, wracking her brain to recall how well he had seemed along different points of their journey.

'Maybe Greenland?'

Romilly made a quick calculation. 'Okay, that's about twelve hours ago.' Tempting as it was, there seemed little to be gained in being angry with Nathan for not having said something earlier. At least, not until he was well again.

'Wednesday is possible, I guess. Might peak tonight through until morning. You're not coughing, so that's something, but as well as not wanting to infect others, you'll need to be strong enough to cope with that long journey in two days' time. You're only fit to fly once you've beaten your fever. Just rest and drink plenty of clear fluids, and you'll start to feel a whole lot better.' The doctor packed his stethoscope away and left his contact details with Romilly to organise payment.

'Here, take two of these antibiotics; the others are ibuprofen if you want them.' Romilly held out the four tablets in one hand, a glass of water in the other.

'Thank you. Really sorry. Tired,' Nathan slurred.

She wasn't sorry that he swallowed them all without debate. Despite the doctor's rhyming recommendation to forego fever relief, she just wanted Nathan to feel better, and sleep.

'There's nothing to be sorry for, just rest. If you want something to eat, there's a sandwich in the fridge.'

'You have it,' he said, eyelids shuttering. Within seconds, he'd fallen asleep again.

On the sofa, utilising pillows, and the duvet from her room, she set herself up with direct line of sight of Nathan, into his room. Appetite gone, she abandoned the club sandwiches, in favour of setting the timer on her phone for his next doses. Making herself as comfortable as possible, she flicked through *San Francisco Monthly,* the first in a stack of coffee-table fodder, and tried not to glance at him more than once a minute.

At nine am and two further doses later, Romilly answered the suite door, this time to breakfast room service. Coffee had never been more welcome when her night had featured fractured sofa-dozes, the intermittent freshening up of Nathan's flannels, and helping him with paracetamol, antibiotics and ibuprofen. She had just picked up one of the continental pastries when a groan rumbled from Nathan's room.

To her astonishment, he was inching himself towards the edge of the bed. 'I'm okay, just need …' He pointed to his en-suite.

'You'll be all right in there?'

'Got to be,' he said and winked.

Some humour was intact, at least. While Nathan was in the en-suite, Romilly straightened his bed, but the sheets were damp and stale. When he came out, he still moved slowly, but seemed to have splashed water on his face and hair.

'Maybe you should sleep in my bed – the sheets are fresh, she added hastily. I'll ask housekeeping to change yours later.'

He cast eyes around his room, stopping on the view to the living-room sofa. 'You didn't sleep there? God, I'm sorry.'

'It's fine. Come on, I'll grab another bottle of water for you at the fridge – keep hydrated.'

'Don't want you to be sick,' he said, weaving slightly as he shuffled alongside her.

'I have my mum's solid constitution, and anyway, I had my flu jab last month, didn't you?'

He shook his head slowly. 'Two weeks' time.'

'Great, well your new antibodies can have a wild dance party with the vaccine.'

'Tom's the dancer, not me. Think I got this from the boys.'

As they walked slowly to her room, she could tell he was trying not to lean too much on her, but still, it was an effort to support him. 'That's it, lie down. So your friends are sick?'

He crinkled his face in apparent confusion at her question. 'Rugby club, bad flu going around.'

'Oh, I see. Well, you'll be back tackling in the mud again in no time. Tom's one of the players?'

'Cousin. Dancer in the West End.'

'Right, so light feet run in the family then, with your professional rugby player cousin too?'

'You remembered.' A sweet, fleeting smile passed over his face.

She nodded. 'You mentioned him after you cut your eyebrow. Do you want a hot drink as well as water?'

'Tea?'

'Coming up. White without, isn't it? Curtains closed?'

Another smile curved his mouth. 'Er, yes, and open, need to kick this jetlag. Doctor said I should be okay to fly with you tomorrow.'

'He didn't say that exactly, and I noticed you were ambiguous in what you asked him.'

Nathan settled himself into her bed, tilting his drawn face towards the window's sky view. The way he gazed at it drew empathy; for pilots, being at the controls of an airliner is their happy place.

'Please don't tell me you're thinking you might be in the cockpit? You'd fail at least three of the "I'm Safe"s at the moment – illness, medication, fatigue. Even as a passenger, you might not be flying anywhere tomorrow, probably not until Thursday at the earliest. Please rest. I'm just going to make a couple of calls.'

His shoulders slumped, battle lost. 'Better call me in sick then.'

'That was going to be one of them.'

An hour later, Romilly's timer beeped. Picking up the packet of paracetamol she knocked on her bedroom door.

'I'm awake,' he said, propping himself up.

'You're looking a little better. Maybe the temperature's more under control, at least. Do you still want some paracetamol?'

'I'll try without it now, but I definitely need a shower.' He swung his legs over the bed, stood up, swayed ominously, and slumped back onto the mattress.

Romilly rushed forwards. 'Let me help you. Go more slowly. At least have some water first.'

'Wait, just give me a second.' He stepped gingerly towards the door, then seemed to change his mind. 'Maybe I could use your en-suite here?' he said, gripping onto the frame.

'Of course. I'll be out here if you need me. Maybe leave the door ajar?'

'Roger that.'

Romilly listened intently for the sound of anything untoward, but fifteen minutes later, Nathan emerged in a steamy haze, smelling of her coconut shampoo, stubble untouched, and a towel knotted around his waist. She swallowed slowly.

'Managed it. Just need clothes.' he said, leaving a trail of damp footprints on the carpet as he stepped towards the bed.

'I'll get your case, hold on,' she said, desperate for an escape from feeling appalled at wanting to do bad things with a sick person.

'Here it is.'

He took the handle from her, keeping one hand on his towel.

Despite her best effort, her eyes were magnetised to his chest. Clearly, that task hadn't helped. Greater distance and a longer distraction were necessary. 'Erm, I was thinking of hitting the hotel gym for an hour or so. You'll be okay?'

'Yes. Go easy, doubt you've slept much.'

God, she was staring at his chest again. 'There's water there. I'll be back in time for your next antibiotics.'

'Something to look forward to.'

She retrieved her gym-wear from a drawer and left him to dress in private. A woman had her limits.

18. Alliteration

Romilly reduced the temperature in the gym shower to the coolest she could withstand. Her reluctant limbs had made heavy weather of the treadmill, but they were not to blame for how she was feeling. The steam room during her post-circuit session hadn't been faulty, nor did she have a fever. The heat was solely in her mind, because in truth she hadn't expected a man in his forties to look so … hot. Maybe it was fortunate genetics; perhaps it was his regular runs, but those toned shoulders and defined arms were just … And his chest, well. Internal heat began to pool lower, so she turned down the shower control another notch.

After stopping by the foyer's take-out café for a couple of filled baguettes for lunch, and back in the suite, Romilly found Nathan asleep, in her bed. His next dose was due, so she opened some fresh water and bent down to rouse him.

'Nathan, it's time for your antibiotics,' she said gently, admiring his thick black lashes. If only her blonde ones didn't need mascara to look as good. Her fingers itched to soothe the fresh pink scar at the corner of his eyebrow, but she settled for tapping the nearest forearm that poked through the sleeve of his white T-shirt. What he was wearing beneath the bedclothes she couldn't tell.

Slowly, his eyelids fluttered open. 'Hi,' he croaked, then smiled at her as if being reunited after a lengthy separation.

Romilly's emotions swirled. 'Hi yourself, how are you feeling?'

'Cooler but exhausted.'

About the same as her, until he had floored her with his reaction on waking. She held his gaze for a moment, finally breaking away to place two capsules in his hand. 'Here, take these.'

'Thanks. How was the gym?' he said, rubbing his eyes.

'Okay. Well, a bit hard going, but I got it done.'

'Have a rest. Keep me company for a bit?' he said sleepily, patting the bed. 'You have to fly tomorrow, even if I'm not.'

She eyed the bed, then considered the armchair. The appeal of lying horizontally outranked. 'I'll lie next to you, but no *funny business*.' Even in his incapacitated state, she wasn't sure she entirely meant that, but she cocked a smile for good measure.

'It's all right – couldn't manage anything if I tried. Best wait for full strength.'

Pushing back against images of how their afternoon in her bedroom might look if he *was* at full strength, she kicked off her trainers and lay down on top of the covers, next to him. 'Just half an hour, though.'

'Half an hour,' he echoed.

Eyes open, hyper-aware of his breathing and the unfamiliar slope to the shared mattress, she countered her increasing attraction to him with the importance of keeping focus on her priorities. This man was not in her plan. She sighed, simply too tired to analyse her thoughts any further.

'Rest,' he murmured, 'It'll keep.' Slowly, he interlaced his fingers with hers.

Her eyelids immediately grew heavy.

She recalled stirring at some point, discovering that deep-sleeping Nathan had rolled towards her and curved an arm over her waist. For his sake, she told herself, she hadn't moved it.   Relieved to feel that his forehead was of almost normal temperature, she'd drifted off again.

Where was she? Reassuring female voices and beeping monitors. The sharp metallic tang of blood mingled with stiff, bleached sheets. Oh no, she knew this place, this sterile, windowless room. Not again. Never again. A woman scratched at her wrist, a moment's distraction from gripping pain. A man's voice? Arms around her. *It's okay,* he says, *I'm here, you'll be all right.* She really wanted to be. Her back was being rubbed. Don't leave me.

'Hey, sleepy head,' a deep rumble reverberated into her ear.

Half-asleep, she tried to orientate herself, soothed by the palm being stroked up and down her back. This musky smell, that reassuring voice. Nathan. Cocooned by his warm arms and steadied by his heartbeat beneath her ear, for the first time in as long as she could remember, she didn't want to be anywhere else. But this wasn't in the plan, she reminded herself. Again. She cleared her throat and tilted her face towards his.

'Sorry, finding me dribbling on your chest is the last thing you need,' she murmured, feeling unfathomably comfortable.

'Doesn't feel that way.'

'No?'

Nathan kissed the top of her head. 'No. Go back to sleep.' he murmured, and pulled her closer.

When Romilly awoke for the final time, twilight was yielding to a deep purple sky. Nathan lay awake on his side, facing her. She squinted at her watch.

'It's almost seven, so you need your next dose. I can't believe we've slept for nearly six hours.' She pushed herself up, but he held her sleeve.

'One more minute. Being sick feels unexpectedly good.'

A confusing mixture of vulnerability, denial, and desire pulsed through her. 'This is all ...'

'A bit scary? Not what either of us is looking for? Check and cross check.'

'I don't know what to say – or even what to think.'

'I'm not that far ahead of you. But at the moment, since my defences are down, I'll admit that the box is open. All I can do is to say I'll carry it carefully and try to do better than I've done in the past.'

She wasn't entirely sure of his meaning, but his attempt at honesty deserved some of hers in response. 'It's easier to rely on myself. Safer. There are things I can't—' She stopped. He was sick; this was not the time.

'Let's not freak ourselves out, just take small steps.' He brushed hair away from Romilly's face, then kept his hand on her cheek. 'I'll take my next antibiotics. Maybe you could fetch my phone from my jacket? I think it was vibrating.'

Romilly padded through to the living room and first collected her own phone from the coffee table, finding several texts, but with much relief, no missed calls. Removing Nathan's from his jacket pocket, the screen indicated low battery as well as showing the first line of several messages. She hadn't meant to pry, but the top one from 'Liz' read, *'ABSENT AGAIN ARSEHOLE'*. A flash of defence on Nathan's behalf was extinguished when, behind the notifications, his lock-screen photograph caught her off-guard. A grinning Nora, as a toddler, sat on his lap in a cockpit with her hands on a yoke. Of all the pictures.

'Here.' She passed him his phone, her hand still trembling.

'Thank you. Oh Christ, what time is it in the UK?' He fixed his eyes on his phone.

'It's … almost three am there. Didn't mean to look at your phone, but decent alliteration, has to be said.'

'Yeah, well Liz knows how to get attention. Sold me a bloody big house, needing an eye-watering mortgage, when all I wanted to view was something low maintenance. She knows her former profession well – got a couple of houses in her own portfolio and this property's doubled in value. I'll try Nora now.' He eased himself into sitting position.

'Won't she be asleep, and it's a school day?' she said, straightening the pillows where she had lain.

'What day is it?'

'That's not the point, and the fact you need to ask—'

'What day is it?' he repeated more irritably, then paused. 'Shit. Sorry.' He dropped his hands into his lap. 'I'm so sorry, I try to videocall her between the time she gets up and when she leaves for school. Partly, it's for her sake, but honestly, it's how I try to convince myself that I'm not a crap father.' He turned his face away.

Romilly had a feeling he hadn't shared those admissions before.

'Listen, my dad used to be away for days at a time when I was young, and we didn't have video calling to keep in touch; sometimes I'd speak to him on the phone when he rang Mum, but, trust me, I didn't forget him. As a child, you just accept the situation as normal.'

'I really hope so, it's just that her "normal" has changed a lot in the past year, what with me moving out.'

'But you're still seeing her regularly. I remember it being exciting when Dad came home, although Mum made sure I didn't disturb him too much in his first few days. Now I can understand why, of course.'

'When I've got Nora straight off of my long hauls, I often go to bed at the same time as her, just to keep ahead of jet lag. Seven pm bedtimes at the weekend, very exciting.'

'At least whilst she's this age, you can do that.'

He raked fingers through his hair and down his neck. 'Yeah, but she's changing so fast, though. Another reason to speak to her regularly. Last week when we were on the overnight inbound, I missed hearing on the day about her first tooth falling out.'

'You can only try your best. And her mother is giving you grief for having missed one call? She doesn't know you're ill, of course. And it's Tuesday, by the way. Best leave it four or five hours?'

'Liz knows there would be a reason; I wouldn't just forget. But I've a sense that lately she's baiting me, adding evidence to records of my "failures".' He leaned back onto the giant padded headboard, staring across the room.

There wasn't anything else Romilly could do; the pain radiating from Nathan had nothing to do with the flu.

'I know what you're thinking – maybe I didn't try hard enough,' he muttered.

'I wasn't thinking that at all.'

'Well, you should be. What was it she used to say? "You're never fully at home"? To some extent, that was true, in that I was always ready for sudden shift changes. You know what that's like.' He flashed her a look of expected sympathy.

Romilly nodded, sensing that he needed to continue uninterrupted – something at which he was so perceptive when it came to her.

'I thought she understood the demands of the pilot lifestyle. It was no different to when we first met, and even though captaincy two years ago has provided greater control over my blocks and routes, it was too late; she'd already realised that pilot life is terrible for relationships.'

Romilly sat down on the edge of the bed. Maybe it was the virus talking, but this account of himself seemed overly harsh.

'It got to the point that the duty-free perfumes or designer bags she'd requested – either out of boredom or punishment, I don't know – understandably weren't enough. She just needed someone … better … who can share, be there, open up. Not easy for us who spend our days blocking everything out except flying, eh?'

Listening as he confronted his supposed failures, Romilly felt compelled to comfort him, and rested a hand on the bedcover over his legs. He grasped it and squeezed her fingers. She might only have known Nathan for three weeks, but already she'd seen that his actions *showed* how he felt – his decency, protectiveness, and willingness to put himself out for others. He was right: blocking things out did come naturally to pilots. But maybe Liz hadn't been looking hard enough.

'I'll message Liz now and explain. When she wakes, she'll see it, and then hopefully they'll videocall before Nora goes to school.' He started to type awkwardly into his phone with one hand, the other still holding hers. She squeezed his and let it go.

'There's always after school? Four pm there is nine am here. You'll probably feel a bit better tomorrow morning, too.'

'I only keep after-school calls as back-up. Liz likes to have her own time in the afternoons at the club, which is when Nora's nanny is takes over. The new nanny, Maria, sometimes walks Nora to the park once school's finished, and there are after-school clubs – plus Maria's grip on video-call technology isn't as good as you'd expect from someone twenty years younger than us. If I wait until tomorrow to call, Nora will have missed two before-school calls, and she wouldn't be getting one from our flight home either. Lately I've been concerned at her not wanting to go to school, so speaking to her each morning feels even more important.'

She nodded her understanding. 'I'll give you some privacy, and go through my own messages from the sofa.'

19. Sharing is Caring

Dr Woods had reported that Romilly's dad showed continued improvement on the new medication, and she was hopeful that Romilly might see a difference by Friday. Crew Services confirmed that Alistair Blair would be captaining her flight back to London tomorrow afternoon, and Steph had contacted her three times, asking where she and Nathan were, accompanied by various suggestive emoji. Romilly had been about to placate her, when the rise and fall of Nathan's throaty voice interrupted her train of thought.

'What do you mean, *another* thing? …. Hold on, that was a small bump in traffic on the M25, she was in no dange— You know full well that I never drink and drive … What? She's perfectly fine at the apartment … Of course the balcony has got tall enough bars … *Yes*, I was there; I signed the custody agreement. I'm doing my best, but last night I wasn't well so … Yes, of course I'll be fine in time to have her at the weekend – it's in my diary…. Where in France are you going, by the way? … Yes, the Seine is lovely in autumn … Yes, okay, I'll videocall later … No, I didn't forget last night. As I said, I wasn't feeling … I know it's the middle of the night – that's why I texted … But you called me…. *Jesus*!'

Nobody was perfect, herself included. Romilly could easily get tetchy about her own mistakes, never mind with others who she felt might be misjudging her.

Maybe Nathan was the same. On his account of his relationship with Liz, it seemed justifiable to react the way she had just overheard. He'd contained his frustration relatively well, she thought, but it was good to vent, especially when the best part of your working life demanded control. A totally hypocritical thought, given that Romilly never vented to anyone, either. She debated how long Nathan might need alone to calm down. Under pressure at work, he seemed equipped to quickly regain focus after unexpected events; and she'd witnessed the ripple of tension along his jaw as he'd managed his emotions after their kiss on the bridge. But this evening, his body was weak from fighting the virus and he hadn't eaten for twenty-four hours. Come to think of it, save for a mouthful of croissant, nor had she.

Though Romilly had wanted to give Nathan longer than thirty minutes, she now needed her phone charger from the bedroom. She knocked, then poked her head around the door. Nathan was perched on the edge of the bed, holding her travel photo frame in his hand.

'Sorry, just need to grab something quickly. I bought some filled baguettes for lunch earlier, by the way, if you're up to eating something? Or we could order room service?'

'I'll come and sit on the sofa, try a baguette. I can't believe this photograph. This is you on your dad's lap on the flight deck of what looks like a 747?'

She nodded. 'When I fetched your phone earlier, I noticed your screensaver. My heart missed a beat.'

'It's uncanny. Mine was when Nora about three, not long after I'd made captain and before everything screwed up. She, Liz, and the previous nanny were on discounted seats, and we had just powered down at the gate in Dubai International. I had the cabin manager bring Nora up. I can't tell you how proud I was. It may be my favourite photograph.'

'I hope my dad felt the same.'

'I don't doubt it. This is a photo you take everywhere with you?'

'Yes. It's my touchstone − a career motivator, and reminder that his happiness is my responsibility.'

'He must have been proud when you achieved your wings. I can only imagine how I'd feel if Nora chose to fly one day.'

Romilly's eyes pricked, and she abruptly turned to leave the room. Running on empty, she couldn't deal with talking about the complexities of the history with her dad. 'I'll unwrap the baguettes, maybe find some plates.'

'Whoa, just wait a minute.' Nathan stood up and moved towards her.

'Please, not now.' Romilly walked through to the living room and busied herself with needlessly fluffing the fancy sofa cushions.

'Talk to me,' he said softly. 'Preferably sitting down.'

'You don't need this.' She eyed his white knuckles grasping the door handle.

'You clearly do, and I can listen well enough.' He plopped on the sofa and indicated the seat next to him.

Unconvinced, she stalled for time. 'We need food. I wasn't sure what you'd like, but remembered you'd said how good the food was at that Italian restaurant. She picked up the first of the baguettes. This one has prosciutto, mozzarella, basil, and tomato. I think there's some pesto in it … Yes, there is. Or you could have mine, a tuna salad. Happy to swap or share.'

He was staring at her in his way that made her babble.

'You can also have more paracetamol now if you want.'

'I know that, and thank you. In fact, thank you for being here for me. It's hard leaning on other people but having done so, what I want is for you to lean on me. I've said things to you these past hours that I've not wanted to … or been able to share with anyone. Now, what's hurting you, Romilly West?' Gentle eyes locked with hers, drawing a layer of past hurt from deep within her.

She swallowed. 'It's nothing, really … I just I overheard him talking about me once.'

'It's not nothing, if it upset you. Come here, sit with me.'

She took a seat next to him, hesitant to reopen any emotional wound. Opening one might lead to another.

He clasped her hand. 'Tell me.'

'It sounds simple, but it's complicated.'

'I'll keep up,' he said with a smile, 'but if not, I'll say.'

'*Romilly could never be a captain,*' she blurted out. 'Those were my dad's exact words. And then he laughed.'

'Who was he talking to?'

'I don't know, someone on the phone.'

'When?'

'Three or so years ago.'

'I'm sorry.' He tipped her chin towards him. 'Listen to me. You are going to make a fine captain someday soon.'

Her shoulders slumped, but within seconds Nathan had curved an arm around them. 'I can't do more than I already am. I'm pushing hard on the flying hours, picking up off-duty when I can. It's all right. Hopefully it won't be too long, and he'll be happy and proud, just like he was for my wings.' She plastered on the best smile she could.

Nathan nodded. 'I see … And now I understand your drive.'

'You do?' She really hoped he did, because she felt too dangerously close to tears to explain it.

'It's not just to prove it to him and whomever he was talking to wrong, nor is it to make him proud, is it?'

She shook her head.

'It's that you want him to experience the joy that you've made captain before his memory fails?'

All she could do was nod.

'Come here.' He eased her towards his chest, and she went willingly, feeling strong arms hold her close.

'But … it looks increasingly hopeless,' she said quietly.

'I've got you.'

Years of pent-up hurt from the overheard conversation, and the current worries surrounding her father's health blotched his T-shirt. She grappled with control, needing to be careful, or she'd begin telling him other things she worked so hard at to keep buried. With his astuteness, he'd likely pull it all out of her, and then where would they be? She lifted her head. 'Now you're all damp.'

He grazed her forearm back and forth with his fingertips. 'It'll dry.'

'This is ridiculous – you're sick and I'm ... wallowing.'

Nathan levelled his eyes with hers. 'Stop being so hard on yourself.'

Someone knocked at the door, making them both jolt. 'It's probably housekeeping come to change your bedding for tonight; I'd better let them in.'

'They can try again later.' He continued to stroke her arm. 'You are an amazing woman – keep remembering that. I know about the potency of father-and-daughter bonds, and I'm hardly a good example, but from where I'm sitting, it's time you lived your life for yourself, too.'

'Don't forget, he only has me.'

'No friends around to help?'

'No, learned not to rely on those.'

She stayed quiet at his questioning frown. Enough sharing today.

'You need to strengthen your team, then and open yourself to the idea of recruiting some top-flight crew.'

She loved that he could still make her smile. 'I suppose you have your eyes on one of those roles?'

'After the last twenty-four hours, yes, I might. Probably wouldn't have trusted myself again, before this.' He drew a thumb across her cheek to smear away a trickling tear. 'Of course, how successful I'd be may depend on whom I'm up against. Can't exactly put my best foot forwards in this condition.'

She grinned up at him, encouraged by his suggestion, and grateful for the levity after their emotional couple of hours. 'Don't think I'll exactly be inundated with applications, but how about I hold off on the interview process until you're better?'

A slow smile reached his eyes.

'Honestly, it's a relief to see that you're a little better. You had me worried.'

'Not much of a layover for you this week – sorry about that.'

'Despite the circumstances, right at this moment, it feels pretty good.'

'It does,' he murmured, squeezing her.

'Can I interest you in a filled baguette here on the sofa, with a bottle of Napa's finest water? Maybe find a fun film to watch?'

'Perfect, and while we're watching it, I can covertly gather advantageous research for my job application.'

'I knew you were looking at me in the Sky Bar the first time we met.'

20. Falling

Romilly's belly-laughs at a Netflix comedy were more infectious than the virus. Medicated by antibiotics but buoyed by her, Nathan felt his strength improve by the hour. Fuelled by baguettes, then later, delicious room-service quarter-pounders, they had interspersed television and conversation with quiet reading, and by taking in the Bay area views from their suite's picture windows. Though instinct told him there was plenty left to discover about her, and that some of those things might even be difficult, Nathan's attraction to Romilly had intensified. In the off-duty privacy of their suite, he'd seen other sides of Romilly West: caring and thoughtful, tender, and playful. She was as sexy when waking up as she was when returning from the gym, or deeply engrossed when reading. Most of all, there was a burgeoning trust between them, which he definitely didn't want to jeopardise.

Nathan caught himself smiling as he passed by the hallway mirror, after letting housekeeping out.

'Now that my bedding is changed, I'll sleep back in my room,' he said, returning to the living area and the woman who had given him reason to smile. 'You need to sleep before tomorrow's flight.'

'It will be weird knowing that you'll be in the passenger cabin behind me tomorrow. Are you sure you don't want to take up the airline's offer and stay a few more nights? You'd benefit from an extra day here, at least.'

'No, the fever is gone. I'm still aching, but with a lie-in tomorrow morning and regular dosing up, then sleep during the flight, I should be okay. Once back, for the rest of Thursday and most of Friday, I can stay at home before collecting Nora from school. This weekend, I have her until school on Monday morning, because Liz is going away.'

'Are you up to having Nora?'

'I've got to be, and anyway, she's at a really fun age. You can't help but smile around her, but she's young enough to need breaks, too, so that should work. If the weather's not too wet, I've promised her a trip to Hampton Court on Saturday. I think a day out somewhere may cheer her up; she's still too subdued for my liking.'

'I used to love it there when I was a girl. Have they still got the maze? I remember getting confused in it. Gosh, I haven't thought about that place for years. Dad insisted that I try to find my way to the middle before he began to suggest ideas for the route,' she said, gazing wistfully out of the suite window. The fear that her father may not remember those moments with young Romilly gave Nathan chills.

'If Nora could develop co-ordination skills as instinctive as yours, then maybe I'll try that with her, too.'

'He was good like that – having one eye on the educational as soon as I started school. The Science Museum was always fantastic, too – fun, hands-on experiments, and seeing science in action excited me. When I was Nora's age, Mum, Dad and I often spent time in South Kensington, at the various museums.

Sometimes we fed the ducks in the Serpentine at Hyde Park afterwards.' Hearing her tone falter, he came over to stand beside her at the window. Below them, ferry boats passed beneath Bay Bridge, but she didn't appear to register them.

'I think she'd love that. Wasn't sure she was old enough yet,' he said quietly, brushing his hand against hers.

Romilly rarely talked about childhood, or children, he'd noticed, though she hadn't shied away completely from conversation about Nora. Of course, just because she had all the qualities needed to be a good mother didn't mean she necessarily wanted to become one. That was her choice, but Nathan would need to handle their more-than-friends relationship carefully if and when it came to she and Nora meeting.

Romilly stepped away from the window and busied herself with stacking their empty crockery onto the room service trays. 'By the way, Senior Captain Alistair Blair is covering you tomorrow. I flew here with him two weeks ago – he mentioned then that he has a place here.'

'I know him from the Seniors list, but haven't come across him on my former routes. How was he as a captain?' he said, stifling a ridiculous squirm of jealousy.

'Excellent. Why? Are you hoping for a favourable comparison?'

He mirrored her smirk. 'Just guarding my position. What does he look like?'

'More grey hair, a little shorter than you, maybe. Kind of distinguished looking. Capable and quite funny.' Funny? Unfortunately, her frank response seemed like she wasn't joking.

He whistled. 'Might have to play my trump card then.'

'Oh? And what's that?'

'I have it on good authority that I'm a really *really* good kisser.' He winked at her.

'I really hoped you'd forgotten that.'

Her glorious chuckle made his spirits soar. 'You'll find out when I've recovered.'

'Captain Reed, we hope you're feeling better now,' the hotel receptionist enquired, when Nathan checked out the following lunchtime, a couple of hours after Romilly had left.

'Better than I was, thank you.'

'Your airline's crew transportation has already departed, I'm afraid,' she said, passing him a folded printout of his stay's invoice.

'That's all right, I'm dead-heading on their flight anyway – that is, I have a seat in the passenger cabin; the airline's repositioning me.'

'Concierge will call you a cab if you need one.' She smiled, eyeing the golden wings badge on his jacket.

'Thank you. See you next week.'

'Yes, and of course we have the Sky Bar reserved for your private party on Monday, eight-thirty pm to midnight.'

'Sorry, would you remind me what that's for?'

'Yes,' she consulted her terminal, 'booked under the name of Stephanie Hoffman, a fortieth birthday celebration. Up to sixty people, although we can hold more. Arrangements for a cake, balloons, and savouries, per Ms Hoffman's request are all in hand. As we've advised her, you can hook up to the sound system to play your own choice of music, and we could open up one of the smaller dancefloor covers, if your party want to dance.'

'Excellent.' Thank God that she'd mentioned it. 'That's a timely reminder, thank you.'

'No problem, safe journey home.'

Nathan checked his watch. Three hours until take-off plus an eleven-hour flight. Plenty of thinking time.

'Good afternoon, ladies and gentlemen, and welcome aboard Sterling Air's Boeing 777 flight to London Heathrow. I'm Alistair Blair, your captain, and here on the flight deck I am ably supported by pilots First Officer Romilly West and Second Officer Max Krüger. Our journey will take approximately eleven hours and twenty minutes, and we should push back from the stand in ten minutes' time. I'll check in with you all again during the flight, but in the meantime, will leave you in the capable hands of our friendly cabin manager, Steph and her fantastic team who will look after you throughout the journey. Even if you are a frequent traveller, please listen carefully to their safety briefings. Thank you.'

Sat in his window seat, Nathan quashed a churlish reaction; Blair did sound 'distinguished and capable'. He admired the confident patter, and use of superlatives when introducing his crew. No doubt Blair was cross-checking the usual procedures and routing plans with Romilly now. Another pang of jealousy wormed through Nathan's stomach, and he had to remind himself of her laser-focused professionalism, even in the unlikeliest possibility that Blair might waiver from his.

'Romilly … that's not a woman's name, is it?' the sinewy businessman beside him muttered. 'Let's hope she's not suffering with PMT, or turbulence will be the least of our worries. Can't you step in and fly us?' he said, gesturing at the lapels on Nathan's jumper. There were occasions when the airline's policy for deadheading in uniform did pilots a disservice; this looked set to be one of them.

Nathan shook his head and breathed deeply. No, he couldn't stop himself. 'Actually, I know her and she's an excellent pilot.'

'All right, mate, no offence.' The man rolled his eyes and angled himself away from him.

Steph came towards his row, smart and efficient in her welcome uniform. 'Captain, happy to have you aboard. Anything you need?'

'No, but thank you. I may sleep most of the way, but perhaps you'd wake me for meals, though?'

'Of course,' she said with a nod, closing some overhead storage bins.

'Cabin crew seats for departure please, cabin crew seats for departure, thank you,' Blair's voice bounced through the cabin.

'See you in a bit. I'll bring you an extra blanket once we're cruising.'

'Thank you. Have a good service.'

Nathan connected his earphones and peered through the window as the plane trundled through the taxiways and onto the runway. With only a partial view of the right-hand wing, he challenged himself to identify whether it was Blair or Romilly at the controls for take-off. Though techniques were fundamentally the same, each pilot's decisions spoke of their 'way' of flying. Romilly, he'd noticed, tended towards last-moment instinctive adjustments, allowing the plane just enough time to react to the subtle alterations she commanded through the yoke and flaps.

As the plane accelerated down runway 21R and up into a steep left-hand bank out over the Pacific coast, the wing flaps feathered, keeping the passengers' ride smooth. Within seconds, grinding mechanical hydraulics sounded the wheels' retraction, from Romilly or Blair's seeking of fuel-efficient aerodynamic flight as quickly as possible. Whoever was flying, they were certainly doing it well. He closed his eyes, frustrated that pilots were mostly judged on their landings; take-offs with full fuel-tanks held far greater risk. He melted into sleep, imagining Romilly at the controls.

'Captain Reed,' a distant voice murmured. 'Do you want some dinner?'

Nathan straightened himself and acknowledged a smiling Steph with a brief nod.

'Chicken or vegetarian pasta?'

'Pasta, thank you.'

She returned swiftly with a meal, setting it down on his tray-table.

'Thanks. Erm, is Max on duty?' he asked, in a roundabout way of seeking confirmation that Romilly would therefore be on her break.

'Yes, and I'm headed to crew quarters for my rest period after meal service. If there are any messages, I'd be happy to pass them along,' she said, accompanied by a small wink.

Nathan allowed himself a half-smile at her. Steph was nothing if not discreet. 'Perhaps my thanks for a smooth departure.'

'Of course.'

'And Steph? Well done on making arrangements for Romilly's birthday at the hotel. She knows about it?'

'That we're getting together, but not much else. The best news is I managed to get Senior Captain Blair aside in the crew room before we boarded, and he's offered to say a few words and raise a toast. He's also generously providing a case of a Napa champagne called Domaine Chandon. Owned by Moët & Chandon apparently. Going to be a great night – just what the crew needs, too.'

Well, Captain Blair, how very attentive. 'That's kind of him. So, he'll be back in San Francisco next week, then?'

'Yes, Crew Services have him covering Saturday's red eye. Apparently, he has a large condo in San Francisco as well as in Lon—'

'London. Yes, I heard. Well, that is excellent news,' Nathan forced. Steph's eyes levelled with his; perhaps his response had been a little cool.

'By the way, just in case you weren't aware, Romilly's birthday is on the Tuesday, the sixteenth.'

That would be easy to remember, being just two days before Nora's.

'Thank you. See you lat—'

'Excuse me lady, where is our food?' the delightful passenger next to him interrupted.

'It'll be along shortly,' Steph said with a smile, then headed for the other end of the plane.

Jesus, the cabin crew were saints putting up with this sort of flack. Nathan tucked into his meal, feeding his Blair-triggered green ogre, countered by a small sense of satisfaction in seeing the cabin crew inching their food trolleys far away up the aisle.

Nathan had been adding further thoughts to a list on his phone for next week's layover, when a message pinged via inflight Wi-Fi from Romilly.

'Thanks for your message :) Hope you're feeling okay? Back to flight deck shortly. Unless weather turns, will be landing us too. No scoring! Have fun in the maze. See you Monday. R'

With Thursday's golden dawn emerging from darkness, Monday lunchtime seemed an awfully long time to wait. Pace, not haste, Nathan cautioned himself, but after re-reading her message twenty times, couldn't prevent himself from typing an invitation for her to join Nora and him at Hampton Court. He hovered his thumb over the send button, suspecting it might be too soon, but he wanted her company. Needed it. He pressed send, wishing he were on duty and could legitimately visit the crew quarters just to see her face. Then it hit him. Never mind the flying – he was falling.

21. Highlights

'You see, even blonde hair can benefit from highlights. Look at the platinum pieces framing this girl's face.' Steph passed her phone across the crew bunks for Romilly to study.

'You've got a whole Pinterest board called "Romilly 40"? Steph! I see what you mean about the highlights, but what are all these other pictures?'

'Oh, yeah … Sorry, they're just dresses I thought might look amazing on you. Really, they were for my own use – kind of a hobby really, looking at styling for body shapes, that sort of thing. Those are ones I'd thought would go well with the new hair.' Steph smiled at her admission.

Romilly stared at one of the silky sheath dresses that clung in every place possible. 'I've never worn anything like that.'

'Yeah, I'm probably overstepping, especially as we haven't known each other long. Ignore those. If we do nothing else at mine on Saturday, at least let me chop in a few face-framing layers, and a few simple highlights will make you sparkle, ready for your big four-oh.'

Romilly scrolled through the pictures of shoes, drop earrings, and bags. She was out of practice on how to be friends. 'All right, after the hair, maybe we could look at a dress, but we're running out of time now and I wouldn't want to wear anything too … you know.'

'Roger that.' Steph clapped her hands. 'How about these then?' She leaned over and swiped to a second page of dresses. 'You're a size twelve, I'm guessing, same as me?'

'Yes, and those with the sleeves are better. I'm not big on being the centre of attention. Maybe we can avoid anything too … bright?' Romilly handed back Steph's phone and noticed a message on her own.

'Deleting anything rainbow-coloured …. Done; skim not cling … done.'

'Thank y——' Romilly replied, distracted by a message from Nathan, who had invited her to join him at the weekend with his daughter. A chill seeped through her. This was partly her own fault. Hadn't she, after all, suggested activities for Nathan to try with his daughter? A small knot formed in her stomach; watching Nathan on daddy duty with his daughter might be more than she could withstand. Suddenly she remembered that, of course, she had a genuine 'out', and typed back brief but polite apologies, explaining that she already had plans. Relief, however, proved elusive – her ever-tightening knot a reminder that if things progressed with Nathan, she would have to deal with it. That, or she could just call a halt to things right now. No new hair or dresses, let alone the prospective heartache from complications with Nathan, even if they only dated on his child-free weekends. Yes, this could all just go away. Avoid the hurt. Revert to life as normal.

'Ordered!' announced Steph, clearly pleased with herself.

'Ordered what?'

'Some bleach from the wholesalers and a mini-haul of wardrobe options – they'll be with me in time for when you arrive at mine on Saturday. On Sunday I'll just send anything back we don't want to keep. Can't wait!'

'Right, well, in that case, thanks. Sorry, I've got to get back to flight deck.'

Romilly hadn't the heart to say anything. Genuine friends were hard to come by, and Steph was there for her. Onwards, with a new member of her 'crew'.

Sitting in the kitchen at Steph's mid-terraced house on Saturday morning, Romilly was feeling relaxed, despite bearing a dozen pieces of antenna-like foil folded into her hair while highlights 'took'. Her new friend's kind-heartedness in getting to know her had encouraged Romilly to open up about her dad's situation. After a brief summary of his present medical situation, she admitted to feeling afraid for his future, and overwhelmed by the task ahead of her.

'Still, he was a little improved yesterday – that's something. In another week or two, he'll be moving to a care home, which I've got to organise.'

Steph brushed some more product onto a few strands of Romilly's hair, then deftly folded them into a neat foil envelope. 'You poor thing. Why didn't you tell me about him? You'd just said he was unwell …'

'It's not an easy subject to bring up. I can't just drop into casual conversation … *Hi, did I mention my dad's so ill he mostly doesn't recognise me, and by the way I've already lost my mum, my friends, and most of the time I'm working not just for the hours but … I don't know, maybe I'm hiding from life, keep moving so I don't stop and feel alone.*'

Steph dropped her comb. Retrieving it, she squeezed a hand on Romilly's shoulder. 'Well … maybe not all in one go like that, but you've got a friend here who would listen.'

'I manage. Blocking things out is easy once you've got the hang of it. Once my uniform is on, there's nothing that interferes with the job,' she said and shrugged.

'For flying, I see that's important, but, babe, you've got to let your emotions out in your personal life. Lean on people.'

Romilly thought of Nathan, the same words he'd used and the calm strength he'd shown when she had cried on his chest, despite feeling unwell himself. 'I'm trying. It's not easy for me.'

'I see that, but it'll get easier with practice, I promise. Maybe finding someone who understands your situation would help – perhaps another flier who usually keeps himself just as composed, at work at least, but who also might be needing to … offload and relax.'

Romilly snorted. 'Subtle, and no comment.'

'All right, but I do have a useful observation about him, if you're interested.'

'Go on, then.'

'Well, he doesn't much like to hear the name Blair. I swear he flinched when I mentioned the condos in San Francisco and London.'

Romilly saw herself frown in Steph's large mirror. 'But Nathan doesn't even know Alistair.'

'Maybe he was being, I don't know, territorial – not just guarding his work seat but keen not to have his favourite first officer's head turned by another captain – Blair's or anyone else?'

'Really?' She shook her head, then remembered: 'Come to think of it, he did ask me what Alistair looked like.'

'See! Interesting, eh?'

Why would Nathan think that Alistair could be interested in her? Romilly swigged the last of her coffee, lost in thought.

Using small pads of cotton wool, Steph wiped away errant spots of bleach on Romilly's hairline. Efficient but gentle, Steph exuded confidence in her own ability, an essential trait for handling passengers in the cabins, too. Romilly felt awkward at knowing little else about Steph's personal life, especially when she was sharing her own.

'Tell me about you – is there someone special?' Perhaps their conversation might allow the subject of Max to evolve organically.

'I wish. Been through a couple of longer-term boyfriends, but they fizzled out. One of them turned out to be not so nice and the last one took a load of my girlfriends with him, as they were partners of his friends.'

Romilly's empathetic heart missed a beat.

'I'm sorry … So, no one's catching your eye, at all?'

'A few flirtatious moments at work sometimes, nothing more than that.'

'Mm, hmm.' Romilly studied Steph as she clipped together the foil parcels. Yesterday, Max had humorously stopped mid-conversation with Romilly in San Francisco's pre-flight Crew Room when Steph had passed beside him. Unable to take his eyes off Steph, Max had blushed and lost his trail of thought.

'Honestly, I'm just living my life as it comes. That's my mantra these days. You have to take risks, remain open to the possibilities of someone new and go with things if they feel right, you know?'

No, Romilly didn't. Or at least, she hadn't. A flashback to the foggy cycle ride on the bridge and the sensation of Nathan's mouth on her jaw and neck as he'd trailed kisses from her mouth made her prickle. That, and his openness and patience while sick had proven unsettling, to say the least.

Romilly cleared her throat, dragging herself back to the conversation with Steph, but steering away from the topic of men. 'And you've got the aim of a hairdressing salon on the horizon. I'm looking forward to seeing what's under here, by the way.'

'So am I. Okay, let's have some fun and unpack one or two of these parcels before I take the foils out. Those are dresses, the boxes are shoes and bags, and this packet here has some new make-up and costume jewellery inside.'

'Steph!' The delivery van must have been half-full with her orders.

'I know, I know – I might actually be more excited than you.'

Romilly had to admit, it was like having a personal shopper show up with suggestions for outfits you'd never pick yourself.

An hour later, with hair bouncing in miraculously soft waves on her shoulders and the palest of blonde segments around her face, she was amazed at the transformation. Still her, but … sunnier.

'See – knew that would suit you. Plus, it's still easy to tie back into a ponytail for work straight from the shower – all you need to do for the waves is to wrap pieces around the straighteners like I've just showed you.'

'It's lovely, Steph, thank you,' Romilly choked out.

'Aw, my pleasure. Right, before you try dresses on, shall I open a cheeky prosecco?'

How anyone could hurt this woman amazed Romilly. 'Yes, go on then, but just the one, though, as I'm driving later.'

'Brill. While I'm pouring it, have a look to see which dress you would like to try on first, then we'll look at accessories, and after that try some make-up?'

Half a glass later, Romilly felt braver at controlling the parameters of Steph's well-intentioned 'revamp'. 'You know, I'm really not big into costume jewellery; I prefer finer, simple pieces. And I literally only ever wear mascara. I don't want to be unrecognisable – still want to look and feel like me.'

'Natural look and use your own fine jewellery – got it. So, how about this elegant, navy velvet Bardot dress, or the long-sleeved stretchy bronze one with a high neck and plunge back,' said Steph, apparently undeterred.

Romilly eyed the dresses. They all somehow seemed too much for 'quiet' drinks in the Sky Bar. 'That one's got a deep slit up the side.'

'So you can walk, yes.' Steph grinned. 'And dance.'

'What do you mean dance? When are we dancing?' Romilly faced her friend, whose cheeks had turned beetroot. 'Steph?'

'Right, I may as well tell you now – the hotel has said that if we like, you can have a dance at your party.'

'My *party*?'

Steph began waving a dismissive hand. 'No, no, not *party* as such, more of a drinks celebration, with sandwiches and a fruit platter. And it'll be exclusive, just our airline crews, maybe one or two others from the earlier flights. Fifty or so at the most.'

Fifty or so. At the most. At her party. Romilly breathed deeply, surveying the rack of items hung for her perusal, then to the look of encouragement on Steph's face. Suddenly, Nathan's words on the importance of 'celebrating the big ones' came to mind. That both he and Steph had encouraged her, helped to make the decision. 'Okay then, I'd better try all of those, and pick something special.'

'Fantastic!'

'Oh, and, Steph? Can you make sure there are no strawberries in the fruit platter? Nathan's allergic.'

'No problem,' Steph said, giving Romilly a knowing smile.

'What?'

'Nothing.'

The ensuing hour of outfit try-ons would have served a nineties film montage well. Steph used her own scarves, belts, and bags to 'customise' looks, some legitimately, others in jest. Romilly hadn't laughed as much for a very long time. When it came time to leave, she hugged Steph tight.

'You know, I don't have that many friends, but this has been a special day. Thanks so much.'

'You're welcome,' Steph murmured. 'See you on Monday in the crew room, my friend.'

Just as Romilly reached the car, her phone vibrated. Nathan had sent a photograph of the centre stone at the middle of Hampton Court Maze, with a message saying, '*Found it!*' That he was thinking of her when they were apart felt equally reassuring and scary. Their chemistry was not in doubt, she fancied the pants, and every other part of his uniform off him, but it was still early days, and their relationship was precarious. She caught a glimpse of her newly blonder hair in her rear-view mirror and thought of Steph's optimistic 'just go with things' attitude. Perhaps she should adopt a new mantra, herself – 'Be more Steph'?

22. Marion

'Yes, hello, I'd like to see some of the charms on pad fourteen please,' said Nathan, gesturing towards the jewellery shop's glass display case.

'Sure, won't be a minute,' said the teenaged shop assistant, unclipping a sizeable ring of jangling keys from his belt chain. He barely looked old enough to work there, let alone 'assist' Nathan. 'Here you are. This row is silver-plated, those are solid silver, and obviously these are gold.'

'Let me see, Daddy.'

Nathan tilted the tray towards Nora. 'What do you think?'

'Is it for Mummy's birthday?'

'No, it's for a friend's birthday.' Nathan ran his eyes along the options: butterflies, flowers, shoes, stars, handbags … Handbags – that could work; didn't Romilly own a designer bag? He squirmed, haunted by Liz's fixation on designer goods. Initial letters, champagne bottles, no, no. Then he saw it. Perfect. 'This one, please.'

'Would you like a chain for it? We have a selection in the next case, here …' Before Nathan responded, the assistant retrieved another tray and pushed it towards him. 'There are figaro chains with the ovals and circles, smooth cobra chains that lie flat, and these regular, lightweight or stronger belcher styles.'

Nathan visualised each of the necklaces on Romilly. Something delicate, and fine quality. She wasn't one for ostentatious bling. His mind cast back to an awful Christmas with Liz, when she'd pouted over a bracelet he'd chosen, saying that she'd wanted 'diamonds, not silver'. Romilly couldn't be more different.

'This smooth one, please.' He imagined grazing his fingers around Romilly's neck as he fastened it. Just as his mind wandered back to the intimacy of their revealing conversations a few days earlier, the assistant sought another decision.

'There are two lengths in this, the sixteen-inch sits at choker level, in the dip at the base of the throat, eighteen-inch falls just below the collarbone.'

Either of them would have lain beautifully against her skin, but Nathan suspected that Romilly would wear something less eye-catching, more frequently.

'The eighteen-inch please.'

'I'll thread the charm onto it for you. It comes in a standard box, but for an extra three pounds, there's this blue velvet case.'

'Yes, the blue case, please.' He imagined her opening the unexpected box on her birthday, hopefully delighted with the contents.

'Look at these!' cried Nora, pointing at some children's watches in a glass case that the store had astutely displayed at child eye-level. 'Abby has got the blue Cinderella one, so no one is allowed to copy her, but the Belle one is red and Belle's got dark hair.'

'I see … Well, we can tell Grandma and Grandpa about that tomorrow, can't we? As it's only few days until your birthday, perhaps something like that should go on your list.'

Nora nodded, pressing her nose longingly against the display case.

The young assistant discretely motioned to him that he had one of the Belle watches in stock near to the till. Nathan nodded, and had to smile. For all that he'd chastised Romilly for making overly quick assumptions about people, he stood corrected himself. Wasn't he about to hand over his credit card to the young assistant, to pay for four items, when he'd only gone into the shop for one?

Late on Saturday evening, after Nora had gone to bed, Nathan re-read Romilly's reply to his text from the centre of Hampton Court. Yesterday's concern that he might have somehow misread his radar after she declined the invitation to join him and Nora on for their day out was calmed.

'Congratulations, hope you didn't get lost too many times. Are you fully recovered from flu now? Dad has improved a little. Dreading visiting two further care homes tomorrow. Had a fun afternoon with Steph. Now a quiet night, to avoid further drunk messaging! Till Monday, Rx'

Everything he loved about Romilly was in that text. Liked about her, Nathan corrected himself. Caring, humorous, prepared to admit vulnerability, trying to move forwards with friendships, responsible, and now flirtatious. He also noticed she'd signed off with '*Rx*'.

Nathan settled down on the sofa with a large whisky to watch the highlights on TV of his cousin Dan's rugby match. After ten minutes he abandoned it, unable to concentrate on anything but Romilly. He picked up his phone and sent a reply to her message.

'*Shame, was hoping for another special message tonight. Thinking of you. Nx*'.

He willed the three dots of an incoming message being prepared to appear.

Yes! She was typing a reply.

'*Thinking of you too. Hashtag foggy bridges, hashtag foggy showers. Rx*'

'*Chokes on whisky. Did I mention you're a really good kisser? Nx*'

'*A whole new meaning, flying to S, F, Oh Rx*'

'*You're killing me Nx*'

'*Roger that. Message tomorrow? Rx*'

'*Am at parents for lunch with Nora. Will ask Mum about how she chose care home for her sister. Maybe we could call you? Nx*'

'*If she has time, thank you. Night, off for a bath now. Rx*'

'*Imagination in overdrive. Night-night, enjoy. Nx*'

Nathan slid his phone onto the coffee table, grinning at their sexy banter. Another thing he loved about her, he thought, this time without correction.

'Mum, I have a favour to ask,' Nathan said, peeling carrots at his parents' kitchen table the following day. 'A friend is struggling with choosing a care home for her father, whose dementia is rapidly worsening. Some of the time, he's lucid; at others, apparently his medication is keeping him dopey, so he can't always engage particularly well.'

'This friend – she hasn't got any support to help her with this?'

'No, she's managing it alone. The plan is to relocate him from an owned sheltered accommodation flat where she's organised additional care support, to a room in a specialist place. She's capable of all of that, and more, it's just … I don't want to see her grappling with it, when something could be done to help her.' He stood up to scoop carrot peelings into the swing bin.

His mother stopped whipping the batter mixture she was preparing for Yorkshire puddings. 'That's a lot, son. Well, I'm happy to speak to her about how we approached it for Laura, if you think that will help.'

'Thanks. Her dad was an airline captain. It must be awful.' He shook his head, then gestured at the pile of potatoes on the table. His mother nodded, so he started to peel one.

'There's a lot of evidence to say dementia sufferers aren't aware of the situation they're in,' she said, with a pained glance at him.

'I was thinking of her.'

'I see. So, this would be Romilly you're speaking of?'

Nathan chopped the potato into chunks. As usual, his mother didn't miss much. 'It would.'

'I understand. Leave it with me – maybe we could try later this afternoon while you're still here.'

After roast chicken and blackberry crumble, then a long walk in the crunchy autumn leaves strewn over Bedford Park, Nathan settled Nora down with his dad to watch *Mulan* while he and his mum retreated to the small study. They dialled Romilly's number.

'Hello?'

His heart rate increased. 'Hi, it's Nathan, I've got my mum here with me. Are you okay to talk?'

'Yes, now is good, just home from the supermarket to stock up the freezer with stacks of … well, never mind. Hi, Mrs Reed, nice to speak to you.'

'And you, dear. You're on loudspeaker in our study, but it's just us. I'm sorry to hear you've rather a tricky decision ahead of you.'

'Yes, I've visited several care homes now, don't really know what's for the best.'

'All right, tell me a bit about each of them – the best and worst aspects – and we'll break them down.' Bless his mother, who had a pen poised on pad ready, to write everything down.

'Okay, well the first one was Meadow View, a special—'

'Dad, can I have a drink please.' Nora had sneaked in and was tugging at Nathan's sleeve. Frustratingly, she hadn't wanted anything when he checked with her before the phone conversation started, but duty called.

'Sorry, Romilly, I'll be back in a moment, carry on.'

'Okay, well the second was called Beeches, that one is in Tolworth …'

Nathan closed the door behind him and took Nora to the kitchen.

'Water?' he said, reaching for a plastic mermaid beaker.

'Could I have a hot chocolate?'

His daughter's big brown eyes won him over. 'Coming up. Rainbow mug or stripes?'

'Rainbow.'

Ten minutes later, Nathan returned to the study. His mother was frowning as she listened to Romilly speak. She scribbled something on her pad and swivelled it to him. *I think she's upset.* Feeling protective, Nathan scowled at the phone, focused on Romilly's tone.

'So I don't know whether I'm doing the right … sorry … thing, if he'll be happy there and … sorry,' Romilly said in staccato. Enough.

'Romilly, I'm back now, sweetheart. Just breathe a minute.' Nathan noted his mother's glance at his endearment. Though spontaneously said, the word had felt right.

'Okay,' she sniffed. 'Don't worry. Is everything all right your end?'

'Yes, just fulfilling a hot-chocolate request.'

'Good idea. I could do with some myself – think there's a freebie instant packet somewhere in one of the kitchen drawers.' Nathan nodded at his mother to continue.

'When you're ready, tell me a bit about your family home, or where you think your dad might have had his happiest days,' said Nathan's mum.

'Well, my mum was a nurse, always helping out with community events, often cheering up staff at the surgery by baking. My dad loved to sit in the kitchen while she was icing cakes. Obviously, I missed that gene – can't cook beyond oven-ready meals. Anyway, we had a garden full of fruit trees and bushes and when Dad was off-duty, he'd tend to those. He especially loved the soft fruits, the plums, and gooseberries. Mum made fantastic jams and chutneys – he used to say how happy coming home to that kitchen and garden made him. Not the chutney-making actually, because the kitchen stank. Even though he was away with work, when I was younger, they were so close. I think when she died, it broke him. I'm no substitute.'

Nathan blinked away emotion pricking at his eyes; Romilly's heartfelt words were poignant, the ache of her loss palpable. His mother dabbed a tissue on her face, took a deep breath, and carried on.

'Right, so perhaps rule out any of the care homes without gardens, preferably look for one that has fruit trees. Are there kitchens on-site, or is food pre-cooked and brought in? Afternoon tea and cake may be comforting to him, and however vulnerable he becomes, I know that carers can assist patients with time spent outdoors in gardens when weather allows.'

'There are two that offer that, but one's really expensive and stretches the funds my dad had earmarked for his future care.'

'There are some grants available once funds are depleted, but have you thought about renting out his flat instead of selling it? You're in an affluent area; I expect you'd raise several hundred a month from it. That may postpone needing to sort out what to do with his furniture, too, if someone wants a furnished place.

'No, I hadn't – that's a really good idea. I'll look into the financial implications of that after we've spoken.'

As Romilly's voice brightened, Nathan put a grateful arm around his mother's shoulders.

'Do you think he's well enough to understand the relocation, dear?'

'Some days, yes; others, I think it would be distressing all round.'

'Another thought is to ask if you can take a couple of pieces of furniture to the new place – a favourite chair or some pictures for the walls. I'll send you a link to the website we found useful; it breaks down the steps recommended to ease a patient into the change.' His mother was already making a list for herself on the pad.

'Thank you so much, Mrs Reed.'

'Call me Marion, dear.'

'Thank you, Marion. I'll let you both go – there's not much left of the day, and I know Nathan's … got to get Nora back ready for school tomorrow.'

Nathan exchanged glances with his mother at the obvious hitch in Romilly's voice.

'All right, if you'll excuse me, dear, I need to go and wake my husband up – no doubt he's fast asleep in front of the telly and he won't sleep tonight otherwise.'

'Thank you again.'

'You're most welcome. Call me on this number if there's anything you think I can help with.'

'I will, hope you enjoy the rest of your weekend.'

Nathan's mum patted his shoulder and left the room, closing the door behind her. Nathan switched the phone back to handset.

'It's just me now. That sounded like it helped a bit.'

'She's lovely, Nathan – you're very lucky.'

'I know. You'll be okay tonight? I can call again once I'm back in Battersea?'

'No, you're on … Daddy duty. I'll see you tomorrow lunchtime; I need to organise some extra packing for this trip.'

'Why, anything special happening this week by any chance?'

'Yes … Steph mentioned something's in the offing.' The light tinkle to her words told him she was smiling down the phone.

'Right, so I may pack a suit and tie then. Just in case …'

23. Waves

Marion Reed had been as good as her word. Early on Monday morning, Romilly received links to charities and organisations offering financial guidance for families of dementia sufferers. After reading and studying their advice, Romilly made appointments for the upcoming Friday with her solicitor to sign the papers for release of her father's funds, and telephoned Cranes Park Care Home to confirm an en-suite bedroom for her father's care, moving in just a week's time.

She had been flabbergasted during a discussion with the local estate agent to discover that the potential monthly rental revenue of her dad's place could cover as much as a third of Cranes Park's bill, making a stay there affordable in the long-term. The administration of these elements, while complex and time consuming, were manageable. Romilly was aware that explaining the move to her dad could pose the greater challenge, so she had earmarked several pieces for reading while she was away this week, to help her tackle the initial approach to him when she'd see him on Saturday morning.

Despite the trepidation for that discussion, having a more organised stack of responsibilities on her shoulders made for an easier, less guilty transition to work mode as she packed the last of her flight bags, scraped her new-look hair back into the ponytail Steph had promised the lengths would enable, and changed into her uniform. Leaving her house, she'd caught herself smiling as she passed by her hall mirror. The next couple of days might even be fun. Maybe even be more than that.

'Morning everyone,' Romilly chimed, entering the crew room at Heathrow ahead of the usual flight. She poured herself some filter coffee and caught up with Max and Steph, who stood with a few women from the cabin crew.

'I hear birthday drinks are in order later. Is it the big day today?' Max said, while wiping a lint roller over his uniform.

'Thanks, it's not until tomorrow, but best to celebrate tonight – I think Steph has allowed for additional recovery time tomorrow for this one.'

Her friend grinned. 'Yes, I have – we've got the Sky Bar exclusively until midnight, but there's a club two blocks away open until three am if we're all up for that.'

Several of the crew nodded, but Romilly was noncommittal. Every time the door opened, her pulse jumped. 'Do they sell hair straighteners in duty free at the airport, does anyone know?' she asked, trying to distract herself.

'There's an electrical section, I think, but don't worry, I've got a pair with me you can borrow,' said Steph.

'Aren't you and the cabin crew staying at The Excelsior as usual, though?'

'No, it seems that Crew Services have booked the whole crew on layover into The Beaumont this time – I think we're using their suites. How lucky is that?'

'Phew,' whistled Max, 'Crew Services are putting their hands in their pockets deeper than usual.' Frowning to herself, Romilly puzzled at the inexplicability.

The door opened, and the moment Romilly connected with Nathan's eyes, there was no one else in the room. His hair was trimmed, newly shorter on the sides with twinkles of grey catching at his temples.

'Morning all, are we all ready for a cracking few days in Fog City?' he said, wheeling a larger flight case next to hers and Max's.

The assembled crew murmured their enthusiasm.

'As long as it's not actually foggy again – the bridge was a huge disappointment,' said Max.

'I didn't think so,' Nathan countered.

To avoid drawing attention to her warming cheeks, Romilly drifted across the room, pretending to consider which piece of fruit to choose from the courtesy food shelf.

'Either you've miraculously found time to catch a few hours in the Canarian sunshine since last Thursday, or you've been to the hairdresser,' Nathan murmured softly behind her, reaching for a banana from the fruit basket. 'Now I see why you couldn't make it to Hampton Court. You were missed, by the way, but we can always introduce you to Nora via a videocall sometime.'

Romilly twisted around to him and in 'just going with things' mode chose to ignore the second part, an idea he might hopefully suspend for a while. 'Straight from the barbers yourself, I see?'

He looked around the room, then gave her a subtle wink. 'It's to go with the suit, later.'

Romilly lost herself for a few seconds, imagining how she might run her fingers through his hair. A delicious twist of desire rippled through her - there was no suit in the image. She really must get a grip; there was a flight briefing to prepare for, let alone guiding a wide-bodied jet across the pond.

'Max, are you ready to go through the briefing?' Nathan called across the room, taking a seat at the round table in the corner. Romilly joined him, grateful to be focusing on their usual procedures.

Nathan's request to San Francisco Air Traffic Control to land on Runway 28L, nearest to the arrivals terminal gates, plus the good fortune of optimal weather conditions, and ground crew efficiencies all contributed to the crew being able to clamber into a crew van for a transfer to the hotel in record time.

'Okay, let's get this party started!' called Steph, sliding the van's door closed. 'Crew juice everyone?'

Paper cups were sloshed with the potent concoction of spirits 'secured' from spare unopened drinks in the galleys throughout the flight.

'Happy birthday, Romilly!' she cheered, and everyone knocked back their drinks.

Across the seats and amid the coughs and remarks about the juice's potency, Nathan's eyes glittered at hers, reading 'Desperate to be off-duty' in ways that the rest of the crew would not have expected. Romilly fizzed with anticipation, she too relishing the imminent release of a rigidly maintained public persona over the past eighteen hours.

'I'll give you those straighteners now, hold on a sec,' said Steph as they passed through the Beaumont's doors. 'Just ping me a message and I'll come and get them afterwards. I realise we only have thirty minutes to shower and change, but it won't take me long to smooth out my kinks when you're done.'

Romilly gestured for Steph to go ahead of her in the queue. 'Thanks, I'll be as quick as I can with them.'

After a brief discussion over with Bill, Nathan joined them. With the usual efficiency, the receptionist issued Steph with a room's card key, but spoke over Romilly to address Nathan with a wide smile.

'Captain Reed, welcome back! You're in good health now?'

'Thankfully, yes. Fully recovered.' He flicked his eyes at Romilly. 'Ms West is before me.'

Romilly smiled as the slightest of pressure into the small of her back nudged her forwards.

'Apologies, Ms West. In fact, yes, you're both in the same suite as before, floor eighteen, Bay Suite, is that all right?'

Romilly nodded, without looking at him. In a matter of minutes, she would be alone with this handsome, amazing man.

'Perfectly,' said Nathan, playing it cool.

'Ms West, here's your card.'

'Thank you.' Romilly croaked, then turned to Steph. 'Which floor are you?'

'Eight – seems that some of us have our own rooms, most are in shared suites. Crew Services really are feeling generous this week.'

'Yes, I've just double-checked, for some of your other crew,' the receptionist confirmed. 'Your airline made specific arrangements for this week's stay.'

As Nathan picked up his card key from the marble desk, Romilly noticed a private smile lift the corner of his mouth.

Steph left Romilly, Nathan, and several other people in the lift when she exited on her floor.

'Did you have something to do with the room arrangements?' Romilly whispered to Nathan as the doors closed.

'Couldn't possibly say.'

'Nathan!'

'Okay, maybe I called in a few favours,' he said, his poker face creasing into a smile.

Nathan's eyes held hers as she scanned his face, noticing the attractive stubble along his jaw, then lingering on his mouth. The urge to kiss him was almost unbearable, but there was no blanket of fog to ensure their privacy from other guests.

'See where that look gets you in approximately two minutes' time,' he murmured in her ear.

Romilly swallowed, giddy with pooling heat. As the lift arrived at their floor, she checked her watch. Twenty-five minutes until they would need to be up at the Sky Bar. Nathan swiped his card at their suite door, and as they entered, she motioned that they allocate the rooms as before. He nodded, eyes blazing, air thick with unspoken desire. The second after the door clunked behind them, they flung their hats onto the sofa and abandoned their bags on the living room rug. A millisecond's pause, then they fell into each other's arms, satisfying a desperate need for close contact, for intimacy. He kissed her thoroughly, emitting a low moan. Long minutes passed as pent-up craving crashed over them, kisses deepening, fingers raking through each other's hair. Then his hands were on her shoulders, pausing their reunion.

'Hello … I missed you,' he breathed in between soft kisses to her forehead and nose.

'You, too.' Wanting more, she angled her mouth up towards his, but he gently held her back.

'Trust me, it's taking everything I've got, but we need to stop so we can get ready.'

'Let's give it a miss,' she tried, leaning into his chest.

His jaw flinched and he straightened his arms, increasing the distance between them. 'Don't think that's really an option. Rendezvous here in twenty?'

She groaned, picked up her bags, and headed to her room.

Freshly showered and wearing the best underwear she owned, Romilly swore at herself in her bedroom's dressing table mirror. How the hell had Steph curled her hair on Saturday with these evil straighteners? All she could manage now were some odd-looking bends and a livid burn behind her ear. She tipped her hair upside down, aimed hairspray into the roots, and flicked back. Marginally better. Outside, there was a knock on the suite's door and mercifully, she heard Nathan speaking to Steph, then came a tap on her bedroom door.

'Romilly, you good?' said Steph.

'If I was going to a beach, maybe,' Romilly muttered, opening the door sufficiently to let Steph, in a black strappy gown, slip inside. 'Love your dress – you look amazing.'

'Thank you. Suited and booted Captain Clooney out there is living up to his namesake, by the way.'

Steph fanned herself in mock swoon. 'Well, look, your hair's not too bad.' She ushered Romilly back to the dressing table. 'You just need a few waves twisting away from your face, like this.'

In seconds, the remedial work had improved matters greatly. From nowhere, Steph produced a small bag of makeup.

'Now, a little bronzer – I know, nothing heavy … a nice eye-flick … use some of your mascara …' Steph narrated as she swiftly applied the small amount of make-up Romilly had previously conceded might be wise, given the dress she'd decided on. 'And this here is the new lip gloss to put on last thing. Romilly gazed at the modern miracle in the mirror: the new hair and barely-there make up somehow made her look – dare she even think it – sexy? 'You're okay if I nip off with the straighteners now?'

'Thank you, yes.' Romilly squeezed Steph's arm as she let her out of the bedroom door.

Butterflies danced in Romilly's stomach as she slid into the bronze dress and completed the outfit with matching heels, some dainty earrings, and her vintage Saint Laurent clutch, a gift from her by her parents on her twenty-first birthday. After checking her front view in the long mirror by her door, she threw a look over her shoulder for the rear. Taking a deep, confidence-building breath, and applying a slick of gloss to her lips, Romilly was ready for departure.

24. Toast

Nathan stared out of the suite windows at the glittering traffic that trailed across Bay Bridge, his belly full of anticipation. That Romilly enjoyed her party was important to him, as was the crew's opportunity to their hair down after a tough season. But he was still their captain off-duty too, and while among them, must counsel himself to keep his affection for Romilly discreet, however challenging.

'Nice suit, Captain.'

Nathan turned to her and felt his jaw drop. The rest of his body responded with a throb of heat. 'Christ, you look ... gorgeous. Utterly gorgeous.'

The metallic dress skimmed her outline and her hair was tousled as if he'd just run his fingers through it. Her pale eyes batted at his, her lips slick and kissable. His resolve was weakening; if she suggested once more to skip the party, he'd compromise and agree they could turn up an hour late. Attempting to steady himself, he took note of her earrings and the absence of a necklace. Perhaps he could give her his gift now instead of tomorrow? Yes, that would be perfect. Nathan had been about to ask her to sit down for a moment when there was another knock at the door. Romilly turned towards it, exposing her rear view. His eyes traced the creamy expanse of skin from her nape to the base of her spine, where it was finally covered by swishing folds of fabric that accentuated the dip and curves. He visualised tracing every vertebra with his mouth. God only knew how he'd get through the evening in company.

'I'll get it, maybe it's Steph again,' he heard, beyond the blood rushing through his ears.

'Okay,' was all he could manage and forced his legs across the living area towards his room for her gift.

'Alistair!'

'Hello, young lady, I thought I'd escort you to your birthday gathering, it being a special one.'

The man who entered their suite, without invitation, must be Alistair Blair. Immaculately tailored, though surely with fifteen years on her, he offered Romilly his arm.   'You look incredible. Are you ready?' Blair asked Romilly.

'Well, I was just …' She turned towards Nathan, awkward indecision on her face.

'Go, I'll see you up there,' Nathan murmured from the doorway of his room.

'Oh, hello, my apologies, I didn't see you there. I don't think we've met. I'm Alistair Blair.' The man stretched out his hand.

'Jonathan Reed. Captain.' He shook it with strength, and brevity.

'Ah – I know the name. Sick, weren't you? Recovered now?'

'Thank you, yes.'

'*Senior* Captain privilege, being able to accept or decline routes. Not wanting to rain on the misfortune of your illness, but the opportunity to fly with this one again was too hard to pass up,' Blair oozed at Romilly, who blushed.

Nathan constrained himself to say nothing.

'Let's all go up together,' said Romilly, a tinny but conciliatory brightness to her tone.

'Lead the way,' said Blair. 'We're right behind you and that fabulous dress.'

Nathan monitored Blair's direction of gaze as they made their way to the bank of lifts. To his relief, it remained appropriately settled on the end of the corridor. At least the task had stopped Nathan's mind racing ahead to when Romilly and he were once again alone.

The Sky Bar's tinkling pianist added to the convivial atmosphere of low-lit drinks tables festooned with clusters of helium filled golden balloons. After greeting everyone personally, but becoming separated from Romilly and Blair, Nathan eventually made it to the bar.

'Hello again, sir,' said Carter. 'What'll it be? We have free-flowing margaritas, courtesy of the hotel, and Domaine Chandon will be served shortly. The gentleman has pre-ordered a case to be chilled, ready for toasts.' Carter indicated to Blair, who was holding court among a group of giggling cabin crew, and Romilly. Someone had already put a drink in her hand.

'Vodka tonic, please.' Nathan debated taking a stool to stay at the bar, but Steph appeared at his shoulder, cradling an empty cocktail saucer.

'Having fun?' She winked at him, eyes already shimmering.

'A refill?' he offered.

'Yes, another Margarita please. Why not?'

Nathan grinned at his cabin manager enjoying herself, then flicked his eyes at Carter.

'On it, sir.'

'She looks a-ma-zing, doesn't she?'

Nathan followed Steph's line of sight, to where Romilly was throwing her head back at something amusing. God, her happiness made him happy. Blair, on the other hand, not so much.

'Nothing to worry about there,' Steph mumbled.

'I don't know what you—'

'Yeah, right.' She slapped his arm. 'Men. I'll tell you this much: looks are deceiving. For a woman like that to feel so alone in the world is a crime – truth is, all we ever need is to find that one special person who'll walk beside us.' Steph picked up her new glass and slurped a first sip.

'One vodka tonic,' said Carter, helping to rein back Nathan's mind from galloping fields ahead, and thinking about finding 'special' people.

'On the Bay Suite room tab, please.'

'Will do.' Carter nodded and sought out the next person to be served.

Max approached them, wearing a sharp, burgundy dinner suit, an open-necked dress shirt, and a wide smile. 'Evening both of you. Steph, you look lovely tonight.'

'Back at you; the girls will be swarming, I'm sure. By the way, I might hook up my phone to the sound system later, maybe tap you both up for a dance, unless my "special someone" suddenly makes himself known to me.' Steph giggled. 'Anyway, see you in a bit – I need to ensure that the cake and food is coming when it should,' she added, then headed back to the main group.

Max took position on one of the bar stools, with a frustrated shake of the head.

'You okay?' Nathan asked him.

'Sure. Yeah, of course. So, what's everyone drinking?'

As Max pasted on a smile, Nathan wondered at the truth.

An hour later, the sound of champagne corks being released filtered through the increasingly noisy gathering. From where Nathan was standing by the side windows with Max, it seemed that Steph and Blair were in cahoots, ushering people into particular positions, bringing Romilly to the front.

'Everyone, may I have your attention, please.' Blair raised his hands as Steph wheeled in a trolley bearing a rectangular butter-creamed red, white, and blue birthday cake ablaze with candles. Carter and two other bartenders meanwhile offered around flutes of bubbly from trays.

'Thank you,' said Nathan, taking a glass. The contents smelled of apples and spice, instantly recognisable hallmarks of a sparkling wine worth drinking. Damn the man.

Carter raised a thumbs-up to Blair, who cleared his throat and raised his hand for quiet. After some targeted 'shushing' by Steph, eventually everyone settled.

'Right, well, I thought this occasion warrants a few words. So, before we let the birthday girl blow out her candles, I'll just say this. In my career I've had the good fortune to fly with two generations of Wests – Romilly's father, retired Captain Charlie West, as well as these past weeks, with her. There are pilots, and there are *pilots* – both Romilly and her father are the latter. Intuitive, focused, and great company.'

At mention of her father, Romilly stared at the floor, shifting her weight. Nathan sensed she was grappling with her composure.

'Here with you this evening, we substitute your own family with work family, and we all want to wish you a fortieth birthday to remember. May you fly high, live life to the full, and be happy. To Romilly!'

Everyone echoed 'To Romilly' and sipped their drinks.

A loud cheer erupted as Romilly approached the flickering birthday candles. Nathan grinned as she feigned meeting a wall of heat, then exhaustion from the task of blowing the candles out.

'Speech!' Max hollered, beside Nathan.

Blushing adorably, Romilly cast her eyes around the room, smiling, and paused for a heartbeat as they met Nathan's. 'Gosh, I feel choked. Thank you, Alistair, for your kind words and for providing this delicious champagne, and to all of you for being here. It really means a lot. Steph, thank you for organising the drinks, balloons – everything. It's a little overwhelming to be truthful, so I'll stop there, but I'm sure you're all wanting a slice of this amazing-looking cake.'

'They'll cut it up for us,' said Steph. 'And there are some savouries coming.'

'Wonderful. Thank you, and thanks again, everyone. You've made me feel very special.'

Alistair was back at her side. Nathan couldn't fault the man's taste, nor his sentiment.

After more circulating, eating, and drinking, and occasional exchanges of fleeting but increasingly loaded looks with Romilly, it was almost ten pm. Back at the bar, he and Max were chatting to a couple of first-year male cabin crew, who were making the most of their long-haul layovers. 'Excuse me for a moment,' Nathan said to them. 'Popping downstairs – I'll be back.' He glanced over to ensure Romilly didn't see him get into the lift.

Ten minutes later, he returned to the Sky Bar, where Max, now alone, hadn't moved from his spot on a stool.

'Don't tell me you're a secret smoker,' muttered Max, staring grim-faced, out at the party.

'God, no. No, I was just … organising something,' Nathan said, noting Max's subdued demeanour. 'You haven't moved much from the bar tonight – I thought you'd be more … social.'

'Usually I am.'

Nathan hopped onto the stool next to him and swivelled it in the same direction, to where Romilly was standing with Steph and some others. Something in the way Romilly smiled mesmerised Nathan, as if he'd never seen one so alluring. He hoped that the surprise he'd organised meant it stayed on her face for the rest of the party.

'Carter?' he said over his shoulder.

'Yes, sir?'

'Would you call down to Concierge and say that we are ready. They're expecting the signal.'

'Certainly.'

Happy birthday, sweetheart, Nathan said to himself. *From me to you.*

25. Exit

After several margaritas then two glasses of champagne, Romilly's limit was nearing. She sipped slowly on her third flute, eager to remember the evening; after all, occasions like this were a rarity. Alistair had been sweet and generous; Steph had proven herself a solid, willing friend; but Nathan had stayed in the background, circumspect with their reputations and privacy. Of all the well-groomed men in the room, his were the only eyes she sought. A brief charge of electricity sizzled through her each time their eyes locked.

In the corner of her eye, her attention was drawn to the pianist, who had stopped playing and was talking to one of two leather-jacketed older men who had appeared, the first of whom was connecting leads to two microphones on stands and to some amps. He pulled the nearest microphone to his lips. 'Check, one, two,' he said, did the same with the other, then took a seat at the piano. The other man removed a shiny black guitar from its case, connected a lead to an amp, and slung its strap over his shoulder. Standing behind one of the microphones, he strummed a couple of loud chords, adjusted some knobs on the amp, and nodded. Chatter in the room dropped as guests turned their attention to something unexpected happening.

'What's going on?' Romilly said to Steph.

'No idea, nothing to do with me,' she replied, similarly casting her eyes around the room for clues.

Suddenly, the two men began to play, strumming and keying through chords to get a toe-tapping rhythm going that was immediately approved of by everyone around her.

'Oh, wow, didn't know we were having live music,' said someone behind Romilly.

'No, and they're good,' said another.

The guitarist pulled the mic to his lips. 'Ladies and gentlemen, we're here for a few songs tonight for a special celebration.'

Romilly grinned as cheers and whistles rang around the Sky Bar.

'But of course, we need a singer. Please put your hands together for the greatest tribute artiste, "Just Robbie".'

To the sound of appreciative clapping, a man the astonishing doppelgänger of Robbie Williams swaggered from the lift towards the musicians. He saluted at everyone, curled a hand around the free microphone and smiled straight at her.

She smiled back, hardly able to believe what she was seeing.

'Happy birthday, Romilly, and hello to all you hard-working folk from Sterling. This is for you. One, two, a one-two-three-four.'

The musicians pounded into action, and before she knew it, 'Robbie' had launched into 'Let Me Entertain You'. Carter and other barmen hastily lifted the carpet cover from the dancefloor in front of the band and everyone poured on. With the room's energy escalating fast, 'Robbie' segued into 'Millennium'. Crew faces were pink, singing, and sweaty around her as they danced. Romilly had never seen so many happy people. Everyone's eyes were on 'Robbie' as he and his band began 'No Regrets'. Everyone's, she realised, except for Nathan's. His were beaming only at her, from where he sat at the bar. This man. She mouthed a 'thank you', and he lifted his glass.

After a thumping rendition of 'Road to Mandalay', 'Robbie' pulled back the tempo. 'All right, let's slow it down a little for a couple of songs,' he rasped, and began an acapella of 'Feel.'

People began to pair up and sway. To her left, Alistair was weaving through the couples towards her.

'May I have this dance?' came Nathan's deep voice from behind.

Romilly turned to find his arms ready for her, and she instantly took position in their frame.

'This is … unbelievable!' she murmured into his ear as he gently rocked her.

A warm hand supported her bare back. His musky cologne added more chemicals to the ones already swirling inside her. She was hyper-aware of every point of contact, their fingers, elbows, the skim of his smart suit jacket against her breasts, and though he maintained an appropriate 'work colleague' gap between them, it was all she could do not to press her body fully into it.

'This is such a beautiful song,' she said, as 'Robbie' began her favourite ballad, 'Angels'.

'And you're beautiful – you know that, don't you?' Nathan said, barely loud enough to hear.

'I feel it, with you,' she whispered, 'and I know you don't dance, so thank you.'

'This is holding you, while there's music playing. I can manage that.'

As the song finished, couples separated and began to spontaneously applaud as 'Robbie' thanked his two musicians and talked a little of his work as a tribute artist. Romilly separated herself away from Nathan, who steadied her at the elbow before releasing her.

'More!' shouted people around her.

'Goodnight, folks, we'll leave you with this. Sing along, everyone, and get ready to bounce.'

Everyone cheered as the musicians begun the bounding introductory thump of 'Rock DJ'. Cabin and cockpit crews bounced and danced, screaming the words along with the song, revelling in the sensation of the shared group experience and pure joy.

Afterwards, 'Robbie' came over to Romilly and Nathan. He shook Nathan's hand warmly. 'Thanks for having me, it was a fun crowd – this must be the birthday girl.'

'It is, Romilly, meet Simon, aka "Robbie".'

Romilly suddenly felt a little shy; he was so like the real Robbie. 'I hardly know what to say, except that was fantastic.'

'Glad you've enjoyed it,' he said, still sweating from his performance.

'Shall we take a few pictures?' said Nathan.

Though he had Robbie's Stoke-on-Trent accent down pat during the performance, Simon turned out to be a laid-back Los Angeles native. The real Robbie's recent sell-out success at Vegas had apparently driven interest in tribute artistes Stateside. Though long-haul captains at Sterling might be earning a comfortable half a million, Romilly was relieved that Nathan hadn't actually flown the tribute band five thousand miles – instead they had travelled three hundred miles in their tour bus and were en-route to Seattle. Simon was a good sport and posed in typically Robbie fashion with groups, individuals, and her and Nathan together before he left.

'We're all up for the night club. Coming?' said Max, whom Romilly had seen little of throughout the evening, but now stood near Steph, seemed to be the self-designated spokesperson for the rest of the group.

Beside her, Romilly felt Nathan's hand brush against hers.

'That's me done for the evening, heading home,' said Alistair, appearing beside her. 'It's been a lovely evening.' He air-kissed her on both cheeks.

'Thank you for everything – especially what you said earlier.'

'I meant every word. See you soon, and please pass on my regards to your father. It would be good to catch up with him sometime.'

Nathan briefly squeezed her fingertips.

'I will.' Romilly caught, then released them, harnessing the brief comfort.

Everyone sauntered towards the lifts, chatting, and making plans for the club while they waited for their ride down to the lobby. At the back of them, Nathan stood beside her, quiet and solid, but tell-tale tension along his jaw revealed him to be as tightly wound as her.

'Jesus, these bloody lifts are taking ages,' moaned someone near the front.

'We could use the stairs,' suggested another.

'Don't be an idiot, we're over twenty floors up.'

No one moved.

'Stairs?' Romilly mouthed to Nathan, flicking her eyes at the sign marked 'Exit'. After all, it was only three floors down to their suite, probably six runs of stairs at the most.

The sexiest of smiles crossed his face as he fractionally nodded. He put a finger to his lips and inched himself and Romilly in the direction of the stairwell door. Once there, he frowned at the handle. Clearly, the noise of opening it might draw attention. Steph was focused on her phone, so Romilly quickly messaged her, asking her to discretely look up and over towards where they stood, then asked if she could please cause a distraction?

Within seconds, Steph's eyes met hers, then returned to stare at her phone. 'Oh my God!' she cried, the sound of someone discovering something mightily alarming.

'What?' said several people, turning to Steph in concern.

Inside the concrete stairwell, Romilly couldn't hear what came next. She blinked, adjusting to harsh fluorescent safety lighting, a blinding contrast to the mellow Sky Bar. They descended the first flight as quickly as they dared without making any sound, then paused to see whether anyone was following. Silence. 'It's like waiting to see if we're caught.' Romilly giggled.

Nathan chuckled, then, just as quickly, his face turned serious. 'God, I've been wanting for hours to have you alone like this.' He caught her at the waist and pulled her with him as he stumbled backwards into the breeze-block wall.

Nothing except an earthquake could have stopped Romilly as they melted into a deep kiss. She twisted her arms up and around his neck and ensured that, this time, there were no gaps between them. On they kissed, mouths, faces, and necks, breathlessly unlocking erogenous zones.

'Sh, sh stop,' said Nathan, holding them still. 'Someone's below us.' The sound of male voices chatting echoed up the deep stairwell from a floor far below. Moments later, another door slammed closed. Alone again. 'Maybe we should get to the room,' he said gruffly.

'We should.' She slipped her hand into his, every step downwards somehow fuelling desire.

One flight further and their room still seemed so far. She tugged at his arm, tilted her face back up to his, then sighed as they re-sought each other's lips, hot and needy. A slow moan reverberated from his mouth into hers as she slid a hand inside his jacket, down his back, and round his trousers, tracing his outline.

He kneaded her breasts through the thin, shimmering fabric, and slipped his fingers inside her bra, making her hiss and her nipples harden.

Another door several floors below creaked open, followed by two pairs of footsteps becoming louder. Romilly buried her face in Nathan's shirt, muffling her reaction to his fingers that ruthlessly continued their sensual exploration, and pressed her weight into his hand as it slowly slid up the skirt of her dress and brushed between her legs. Still, the footsteps neared. Almost losing her mind, half even considering whether to pull him down to the floor and make use of the stairs, she opened some of his shirt buttons, smoothed her fingers across his chest, then snaked lower. His strained groan into her hair spurred her on and she was fumbling across rigidness for his fly when the door from the floor only two flights below opened, then slammed shut, the shockingly close call jolting sense into them.

'Bed. Now. Go,' Nathan panted, hurriedly straightening her dress and re-tucking his shirt. He clasped her hand and urged her down the last flight of stairs to their floor. Nothing but lust read on her radar, nothing but excitement. He could have been leading her anywhere and she would have followed. He had just opened a door marked '18th floor' when she locked on to his glittering, jet black eyes. If she'd ever wanted a man more than this, then she couldn't remember it.

He shook his head, gripped her hand, and led her through. 'Our first time's not going to be in a fucking stairwell.'

Their shoes hit the mute plush of the hotel corridor's carpeting. At their door, Nathan's usual calm had deserted him as he fumbled in his pockets for the Bay Suite's card key. Romilly slipped her hands suggestively into his trouser pockets and saw his control begin to unravel. Next, she tried within his jacket and felt vibration at her fingertips.

'Your phone,' she breathed, 'I think it's ringing …' She pulled it free.

'Found it!' he exclaimed, brandishing the card key from his wallet as if it were solid gold and rammed it into the slot on the door. She felt herself being dragged inside, heard the door clunk behind them. His arms folded around her clamping her to his heated body.

'Stop,' she said, shoving the phone into his hand. 'Videocall – it's Nora.'

In the seconds it took him recognise his dilemma, one hand in her hair, the other poised to accept or decline the videocall, a sobering chill shivered through her. It was as if fate had tipped an ice-bucket on her, a reminder of his priorities, his life, and things he didn't know about hers. A sobering reality-check. 'Answer it,' she said, shrugging out of his grasp.

'Just … wait …' he pleaded.

'No, it's fine. It's late, thank you for an amazing night, truly. I'll see you in the morning.' She retreated to her bedroom, hearing him call after her, wait, then swear as he slammed the door of his own room.

A combination of unspent lust, past demons, and alcohol was making her head spin. Collapsing onto the bed, Robbie's 'No Regrets' rang in her ears. Yeah, she had a few.

26. Reconnect

At many points during the previous evening, Nathan had hoped he might have woken up this morning with Romilly in his bed, emotionally connected, and satiated by the unbelievable sex he knew they both needed. Ideally, she would be wearing nothing but the birthday necklace he'd have given her in the early hours of morning, which she would have instantly adored. Maybe she would also be wearing his captain's hat, but that was a whole other vision. As it was, he stretched out alone.   Outside his room, the suite door opened, then clunked. He'd put money on it that Romilly was headed to the gym. But it was a bad bet as to why. The interruption last night had either allowed her to realise she perhaps hadn't wanted to go this far or this quickly with him, or reminded her that he was a father. But she'd known about Nora for weeks now. Romilly wasn't a selfish person, he knew that, so sharing his time surely wasn't the issue.

'Run, then a shower,' he told himself, talking down his unexpended arousal as much as anything.

By the time he'd run the hilly blocks around The Beaumont, looped down to Fisherman's Wharf, and sprinted back, he'd formulated a plan. Or rather, he'd decided to stick to his original one. As Romilly seemed yet to have returned to the suite, he showered and changed, pleased to have reset his positive endorphins before seeing her.

'Morning,' she said from the living-room sofa as he left his room. Fresh from her own shower, wearing jeans and a flowery top, she was concentrating on something in a magazine.

'Good morning, and happy birthday!' He leaned in to kiss her, but the moment turned awkward when she politely offered him her cheek.

'Thank you. It looks beautiful outside – no fog for once,' she replied, only briefly scanning the horizon beyond the window.

'It is, from Pier 39, the view of Golden Gate was as sharp as anything.'

'Mm.' The magazine held her interest.

Down to discussing the weather, but he wasn't about to give up; she deserved more from him than that. 'Right. So, tell me, is there something special you would like to do today?'

'I don't mind, I'm a little tired – but I don't want to stay in the suite.' She flashed him a wary glance.

Loud and clear. Not alone in the suite with him. 'How about a walk over to The Palace of Fine Arts, then? The forecast is mild, so we could have a look around the historic structures, maybe follow the path around the lagoon.' Somewhere public. With their clothes on.

'I'd like that.' Her smile didn't quite meet her eyes.

'Yes, I remembered. But only if you're sure.' It was like reeling her back in while looking for clues to his unanswered questions. He wouldn't mention the party and what came afterwards. It might need to be addressed, maybe later, probably not on her birthday.

'I am, let's go.' Leaving the magazine on the sofa, she headed to her room. 'Give me five minutes, and I'll be ready.'

'One second,' he said to her, downstairs in the lobby area, veering them towards the concierge desk. 'Just need to collect something.'

'Here you go, sir. Enjoy,' said the concierge, with a knowing smile.

'Thank you, Bill.' Nathan hitched the large grey rucksack over his shoulders.

'How far are we trekking? I thought you said the weather's not due to turn.' Romilly frowned at him.

He tapped the side of his nose and grinned, coaxing her into a little playfulness. 'It isn't. Come on.' The slightest of smile on her lips gave him much needed hope.

'I could do with a coffee to go,' she said outside, pointing at the café a couple of units past the hotel.

'Me too. I'll nip in for us.' He hooked a thumb beneath one of his shoulder straps.

'No, it's fine, I'll go – have a seat outside here, give you a break from carrying whatever that is.'

'We've only gone fifty yards …'

But she had gone inside.

She emerged clutching two collared take-out cups and something in a paper bag.

'Couldn't resist these sourdough twists,' she confessed, passing him one of the cups. 'Want one?'

'Yes, been reading about the famous San Franciscan sourdough.' He helped himself to one of the warm plaited rolls and cautiously sipped the scalding coffee. What really warmed him was that she hadn't needed to ask how he took it.

Warm sunshine and amiable conversation, while sipping coffee and enjoying their tangy sour dough, made for a pleasant enough waterside stroll towards the Palace. Their shared enthusiasm for San Franciscan architectures and spotting of different coloured vintage streetcars, to Nathan's relief, kept the conversation flowing without awkwardness. So far, so good.

'It will be interesting to see how much the structures there look like Rome. Apparently, it's supposed to "evoke its decaying ruins",' he said, hoping to demonstrate his preparation.

'A lot of American architecture is influenced by Europe. I'd quite like to see Washington DC – it's supposed to be very Parisienne.'

'Apparently so, and Romilly is of course a French name.'

She flashed him one of her cheeky smirks. Side-on to her, he noticed the slightest of dimples. 'Someone has been reading.'

'Someone has.'

She nodded. 'Yes, my great-grandmother on Dad's side was French. I think he and Mum wanted to keep her legacy going.'

'French names for girls are cute – Sophie, Amelie, Chloé. You'd have lots of choice if you wanted to keep the tradition of your dad's family going one day.'

Romilly didn't respond. He felt the colour drain from her before he saw it. Damn, maybe he shouldn't have made her think about her dad. The atmosphere cooled and they walked on in silence until the entrance gate could be seen ahead. She seemed to be slipping further away from him every minute.

'Still happy to go in?' he said gently. 'We could do something else instead – there's a Cable Car Museum, or if you'd prefer time to yourself … I just want you to have a happy day.'

'No, it's okay, I guess I'm a bit hungover or something. Let's go in – I've been looking forward to seeing this for weeks,' she said flatly, and without making eye contact.

Nathan stopped on the path. 'If you're sure? Because you seem …'

'Yes, I am sure, sorry. Don't worry, I'll rally. Shall we start with the information centre? Something tells me I might be at a relative disadvantage when it comes to the history of the Panama-Pacific Exposition.'

'I haven't read that much.'

She cocked him a disbelieving smile. 'If you say so. Oh good, it looks like there's a film about to start over in that screening area – at least for those who haven't done their homework.'

Inside the darkened cine-space, Nathan and Romilly took seats on the nearest end of a curved stone bench, full of tourists. A few seconds later, the projection camera's timer set off a video, covering a brief history of the original construction, its works of art, and the key landmarks to visit since its renovation.

Having already researched most of it, Nathan's idle mind cast himself back to a Bedfordshire cinema in his early teens, and the agonising high stakes of the first time he'd held hands with the girl he was with. A gesture that engaged the single sense of touch to demonstrate feeling and intention.

Romilly's hands were in her lap. He narrowed his eyes to see whether he could make out if they were clasped, and whether he could slip his fingers beneath them. She turned her head slowly and as she blinked at him, black-and-white images from the film reflected in the whites of her eyes. She blinked again. He held her gaze and slowly, inch by hesitant inch, moved his hand towards hers. Her lids closed when their skin met and stayed shut while he explored the smooth, soft back of her hand. Her lips pursed as he gently turned it over and ran his fingertips over the creases and along each finger until his palm overlay flat on hers. She opened her eyes and Nathan held his breath, senses heightened, sending the silent wish for a sign of encouragement. Glassy eyes bore into his, then she curled her fingers up into his, squeezing their hands tight. He released his breath, flooded with an absurd degree of happiness, just as if he were fourteen again.

Stumbling into bright autumn sun afterwards, he ensured they stayed connected while navigating endless stone steps up to the first recommended landmark, a towering colonnade framing the edges of a wide lagoon. As they strolled between the columns, a pelican swooped towards the shimmering water, skimmed the surface, then flapped enormous wings to propel itself back up into the sky.

'Nice touch and go,' said Romilly. 'He'd pass his six-month go-around skills check.'

'Definitely. I actually failed mine one year. Got sent back to "refresh my knowledge". Think I'd been flying ten years or so by then – you can imagine the embarrassment.'

'I've only needed to do a handful of real-time ones since getting my licence. Been fortunate, I guess. What went wrong?'

'I think it was around the time that the 767s had updated the sensitivity on their yoke thresholds; I couldn't react quickly enough when pulling up. Only just made it over some hedges!'

'You were lucky. But when you think of all the scenarios they have us rehearsing for in the simulators, some engineering adjustments in reality can change everything. That worries me sometimes.'

'You just have to trust in your abilities. Don't forget – you're "intuitive, focused and great company".' Damned it, now he'd stupidly mentioned Blair. And the party.

'That was bravado for the gathering, I'm sure.'

'I'm sure it wasn't – he seemed in earnest to me,' he mumbled, full of his own suspicions.

'It was good to hear from him that my dad was respected in the industry. He's written a couple of books, you know?' She gestured towards a famous stone sculpture of 'weeping women' as they passed it. He nodded, but urged her onwards. Clearly, she was feeling delicate today; he redoubled his guard to ensure that only happiness filled it.

'Blair wrote them?'

'No, my dad. Stopped flying at fifty-five, then started writing about it.'

'What made him give up flying?'

'No reason in particular. Oh, look there's the big rotunda – might be good for a photograph or two?' She tugged his hand in that direction.

'Good idea,' he said, wondering why any respected captain would stop flying for 'no reason'.

After admiring and photographing the fifty-metre arch-framed rotunda, Nathan was beginning to flag, and suspected Romilly might also need a break. Behind the rotunda lay the head of a path that he knew zig-zagged down to a small, and rarely frequented sandy beach.

'Let's go down this way, I read about it – it's only a fifteen-minute walk,' he said, keen to have enough energy to reach it for lunchtime.

'Where does it lead to?' She frowned, understandably sceptic.

'Somewhere with amazing views – it'll be worth it.'

'I'm not sure, maybe we should just go—'

'Please, just for a while.' This could be the best part of her day; he wasn't above persuasion, or pleading if necessary.

'Okay. I hear you. Lead the way.'

27. Birthday Bumps

'Wow!' Romilly gasped as they dropped down to the shoreline.

To their left, and high up in the sky, lay the riveted supports of Golden Gate Bridge, and to their right, the bobbing masts of San Francisco's principal marina. Clumps of thick rye grass gave way to estuary-edged golden sand. A superb spot, and amazingly, they were alone. 'Yeah, the photography on the internet didn't even do it justice. How hungry are you, by the way?' He removed the rucksack and scanned the beach for the best place to sit. She stared at the bag, then up at him.

'I'm guessing it's not sandwiches in there.' A gentle wind was toying with some loosened hair around her temples. His fingers twitched with restraint.

'I haven't looked inside yet, but I didn't ask for sandwiches, put it that way. Maybe you could enjoy that view over there for five minutes while I unpack it?'

There was that dimple again. 'Okay, tell me when you're ready.'

Bill had interpreted the brief perfectly. Nathan laid out a small, blue-striped picnic blanket, and tubs of cold mezze ideal for snacking with the bottle of sparkling Californian rosé, that had stayed chilled, thanks to a wrap-around thermal cool pack. Plates, napkins, and the components of a special desert, kept under wraps until he needed, completed the contents.

'Ready.' He watched as she turned to his call. She'd removed her socks and trainers, and approached the blanket with a hand on her chest.

'That looks amazing. Thank you for bringing it.'

'Would Miss West like a glass of birthday bubbles?' He offered her sight of the label in his best French accent with one of the napkins over his arm.

'Miss West would, as long as you do, too.'

'Mais oui. Un moment, s'il tu plâit.'

'You do actually speak French, then,' she giggled, plugging her ears as he eased the cork upwards.

'Yes. You?' The cork released into the napkin with a gassy pop.

She shook her head. 'You'd think so, but unfortunately not – I have school-level German, but that hasn't been much help. I'd like to learn one day, though. Preferably while in France.'

'That sounds like a great plan. Have you visited Nice or Marseilles?'

'Sadly, no.'

'An hour and a half on a 737, almost guaranteed sunshine, architecture, and food to die for. Or you could find someone with a Cessna licence, and hire a two-seater for the day – there are lots of small landing strips in that region. Add it to your bucket list.'

As he poured, Romilly seemed contemplative, staring out at the water.

'Here …' He handed her a glass. 'To you. Happy birthday, may all your dreams come true.' He clinked his glass on hers and waited for her to take a sip. She didn't. 'Are you feeling okay?'

'Yes, but let's just toast to my dream of becoming a captain; I don't have other dreams. Or a bucket list. I've found it best not to.' No, even on her birthday, he couldn't let that comment slide.

'What do you mean?' He gestured towards the rug, and they sat down.

'Nothing, ignore me. Still tired from last night, and birthdays are a bit tricky for me. Since mum passed, there are always shadows, you know?'

'I understand that part. But you can still dream.'

'Why? They don't always come true – then you're worse off for having hoped.' She took a big gulp from her glass, then another. 'Mm, this is delicious. What shall we eat first?'

Nathan disliked speaking in tongues, but her birthday lunch was not the time to puzzle further over her hidden meanings. Time for a change of gear. 'I have something for you, before we eat.' He took her glass and twisted it into the sand before handing her the blue velvet box he'd carried in his jacket.

She stared at it in disbelief. 'Nathan! What's this? You've already given me enough, with Robbie and now this lunch.'

'Just open it.'

'Well, whatever it is, you've taken the care to choose it, so thank you. I sure I'll love it.'

He stifled the urge to hug her. 'Thank you, and you're welcome.'

The moment her eyes fell on the necklace, he knew he'd made a colossal mistake.

Blinking rapidly and swallowing away tears, she lifted the chain and pendant from its cushion and examined it closely. 'It's to remind me of my mum today? A pair of golden angel wings.' She gulped. 'Thank you, I wasn't expecting anything from you, especially not something so … so …' A tear brimmed, then trickled down her cheek.

'Stop. That wasn't … It isn't …. But I guess if that's what you … Oh.' He pummelled his fist into the sand. He was a fool. And so was that youngster in the jewellery shop, who if he'd been older, might have pointed out the wings-association.

'Nathan? Talk to me.' She frowned, placing a hand on his arm.

He shook his head. What an absolute idiot. And he'd made her cry on her fucking birthday. He stared at the food on the rug, then felt her hand move to his shoulder, and give it a shake.

'Say what you're thinking. I can't mind read.'

Echoes of the past, when he'd heard the exact same phrase levelled him, reminded of the need to improve and his promise to Romilly that he'd try. This woman deserved that from him, especially today. He took a deep breath. 'I thought they looked like our gold aviation wings, mimicking the gold thread version sewn into our shirts and the badges on our jackets. I thought of your hair, and how good the gold charm would look against your skin. Chose a chain that is strong, but silky smooth. Like you and the way you fly.'

She stared at him for a moment, then crawled closer towards him, making divots in the rug. 'Can you put it on me?' She unfurled his fist and tipped the necklace into his palm. Turning her back to him, she lifted her hair up so he could access her neck. How he stopped himself kissing it, he couldn't be sure.

The clasp was fiddly, but in a few seconds it was secure. She turned around and caught the wings in her fingers.

'Seriously, this is the most beautiful gift anyone has ever given me. To think I wouldn't have known any of that if you hadn't said something. Even if I attach additional meaning to it myself, the reasons you chose it for me are so thoughtful. Thank you.' She leaned in and kissed him softly on the lips, twice.

Unable to hold off for any longer, he curved an arm around her shoulders and squeezed her into a hug. 'You're welcome.' When he started to release her, she resisted.

'I know I'm sending mixed signals, but would you hold me a little longer?'

'Of course I can. Just let me lean back onto the rug. Lie against me – there's no one here.'

She tucked herself under his arm and lay alongside him. 'I just can't help it; this feels so good.' Almost indescribably so. He kissed the top of her head, relishing every second.

'It does, and I don't want you to help it.'

Nathan jolted and lifted his wrist. It might have been the alcohol, or perhaps the gentle, lapping water that lulled them to sleep. Only twenty minutes had passed, and fortunately the water was barely tidal. Romilly breathed heavily against him, twitching sporadically. It cast him back to the night when he was sick and he'd been roused by her whimpering on his chest, and when, without waking her, he'd carefully pushed away the spectre of whatever had been frightening her, reassuring her by saying everything would be okay. He really wanted it to be. Now he pulled her tighter, wanting to keep this beautiful, confusing woman safe.

She jerked awake. 'Sorry, I think I fell asleep.'

'It's all right, so did I. Won't do us any harm given this time tomorrow we'll be in the sky.'

'That's true. Oh no, the food …'

'The tubs and napkins have covered it. Hungry?'

'Famished.'

After they'd eaten stuffed vine leaves, salami-wrapped cheese, and piquant olives, he removed the final surprise from his backpack. He loved that she seemed immediately intrigued.

'A gas lantern? There's another couple of hours before sunset, surely?'

'We're just using the flame part. Here, hold these.' He handed her two rubber-handled metal skewers and set light to the gas.

'Interesting.' She cocked an eyebrow. 'I haven't been that difficult today, have I?'

He kissed her softly on the mouth. One last surprise. 'Have you heard of s'mores?'

'No. But I'm watching.'

He opened a plastic box containing rectangular biscuits in wrappers and a pack of pillowy marshmallows. 'This is an American tradition I read about. So, you toast the marshmallows, then squash them between the biscuits.'

'Right.' She threaded two marshmallows onto a skewer and passed it to him. 'Here's yours, just doing mine.'

'It's a bit Cub Scouts, but I'm told s'mores are delicious.'

'This is a great idea. And just so you know, I was a Brownie, actually. Just as well it's not dark or I'll be busting out some off-tune campfire oldies.'

Nathan used a laugh to *just* stop himself from saying how he'd like Nora to continue onto the Brownies after being a Rainbow. He wished he could have done, without fear of pushing Romilly away. While watching the edges of the marshmallows bubble and crisp, he allowed himself a few seconds to imagine his daughter's glorious face and how excited she must be ahead of her sixth birthday in two days' time. Another pang of guilt, a reminder of the failure on his part that she couldn't celebrate with both parents under the same roof.

'How was the Palace of Fine Arts, sir?' said Bill, relieving him of the rucksack, when they arrived back at the hotel, late afternoon. Romilly wandered off towards the bank of lifts.

'Excellent – the s'mores were a hit, and thanks again for your assistance in coordinating the Robbie tribute's booking and arrival.'

'I imagine Miss West was very surprised.'

'Pure amazement on her face as she watched him perform.' Nathan found himself smiling at the memory.

'Happy to hear that. You're off back to England tomorrow?'

'Indeed, and back here next Monday, as usual.'

'Ah, well, you'll be here for the Italia festival then – restaurants around the city open their doors with tasting menus; some have live singers. The hottest tickets are for evening performances of mini operas at the outdoor amphitheatre in Golden Gate Park. There are heaters around the seats, as it'll turn cool, but my wife and I go every year, wrapped up. She enjoys the romance of it all.'

Nathan smothered a smirk, appreciating Bill's well-judged recommendation.

'Might there still be tickets available for a performance on Tuesday evening?'

'I'll see what I can do.' Bill tipped his fingers at his brow.

'Thank you.' Nathan shook the man's hand, slipping him a folded bill.

Over by the lifts, the birthday girl studied some framed blueprints of the hotel's architecture, head slightly cocked. In a moment, he would be beside her, being whisked up to their suite. The relaxed end to their day had kept hands loosely entwined throughout their walk back, but the mood heated as soon as they entered the hotel, every touch and glance some early foreplay of what might happen once behind closed doors.

A punch of need propelled him forwards, shielding him from arrows of apprehension that complicated their relationship. Clearly, Romilly had more yet to share – but he could wait and would do what he could to help her. The fall-out from his past with Liz had scarred him, both as a partner and a father, though he had no choice but to live with and learn from it. He wouldn't compromise when it came to shared custody of Nora – and though Romilly seemed sensitive to mention of her, in time she would surely understand that. Then there were their jobs, and his determination that he wouldn't allow his professional responsibilities to falter. On this, he was convinced that she felt the same.

She turned and smiled at him, somehow sensing his approach. However many arrows flew his way, for this woman, he would withstand them. Whether she would remove her own armour and let him in, he was about to discover.

28. Relief

Romilly had seen Nathan's approaching reflection in the picture's glass and turned. Given that she hadn't exactly been at her best today, he'd been consistently patient and thoughtful. She fingered the necklace he'd punished himself over, feeling incredibly lucky to have met someone as caring, not to mention so attractive. His sexy smile made her tummy summersault. Without speaking or touching, they entered an empty lift and stared at each other in the mirror. Her finger trembled as she pressed the button for floor eighteen. The unmistakable heat in his eyes should have left her in no doubt as to his mind, but she sensed struggle in his rigid stance and in the way his hand flexed, instead of holding hers. Whether he was clinging to barely contained control, or grappling with indecision, she couldn't be sure. She glanced at herself; he could well be thinking the exact same thing of her. And he would be right.

With only sixteen floors left to ascend, her thinking sharpened, blocking out the still-dreadful lift muzak. For how much longer would she allow her past to complicate and crush an opportunity for happiness? And her race to become a captain her sole preoccupation? She'd met this incredible, stimulating man who showed her affection, encouraged her to re-evaluate life, and even dared her to dream. No, she hadn't told him *everything*, and yes, that could change things, but hadn't he said that she should live in the moment more?

She held her breath, suspecting the next move must be hers to make. *Take a chance, Romilly, remove your armour.* Be more Steph. Five floors to go; time was running out. Continuing to stare ahead, she slipped her hand into his and gripped it tight.

Nathan exhaled a wobble of breath. 'Christ, I'm trying not to rush things, but I want you so much.'

'Me too.'

'There are things yet to be said?' He squeezed her hand tighter, enquiring brow furrowed.

She shook her head. 'But not today.'

The lift's electronic voice announced their arrival on the eighteenth floor. In a haze of rapidly escalating desire, they walked the interminable corridor towards The Bay Suite.

'You have your key card?' was all her voice could manage.

'Yes.' He smiled, producing it from his wallet. He opened the door and followed her inside before locking it behind them. 'You're sure about this?' he said, catching her face in his hands.

Romilly dropped her bag where she stood, clasped her hands behind his back, and kissed him her answer, then squealed as Nathan scooped her into his arms and strode towards his room. 'Wait! Maybe pick up our uniform hats?'

He deviated over to the table, to where her first officer cap sat next to his braided one, tilting her so she could scoop them up. Randomly, she plonked them on their heads.

Nathan's eyes burned into hers, then flicked between the hat on her head and her mouth. 'Come with me, Captain.'

'Break-time, Romilly,' said Max, returning to the flight deck three hours through the inbound journey to Heathrow the following evening.

She sought Nathan's eyes, extra-careful not to linger any longer than necessary.

'Go,' he confirmed, behaving in kind.

The pre-flight, taxiing, take-off checks and procedures had been followed to the letter per usual. Steady and controlled as ever, Nathan had taken them up into the thick cloud over San Francisco. Mindfully separating personal from professional, she had ignored the unaccustomed soreness between her legs and slight chaffing across her breasts.

Now alone, resting on a cramped crew bed, memories of the previous evening replayed. It was a huge relief to discover that she still enjoyed sex because, dear God, he *certainly* knew how. Smiling at the intimate knowledge she'd gained of this otherwise measured man, she closed her eyes, hoping for at least a power nap. No chance. Heat gathered between her legs as she recalled him lost in the moment, remembering the ways he had acquainted himself with every part of her body while giving up his own to her. Having experienced his fevered words of craving and reverence as they chased their release, Romilly wondered again how Liz had, by his account, declared him lacking in emotion.

'Hiya,' said Steph, making her jump.

'Hi.' She cleared her throat. 'All okay back there?'

'Happy crew, at least. Been an excellent layover. Must say, I'm looking forward to my fortieth if it gives me the sparkling eyes that you've got.' She winked, and after removing her shoes, slid into a bunk opposite. 'He's impressive, your man.'

'He's not my man,' she began, very aware of how feeble her denial sounded.

'Come off it, he so is! And he's a good one. I know his choosing of the Robbie tribute was driven by your tastes, but he remembered a conversation I had with him three weeks ago, when I mentioned how exhausted the crew were from a long summer, and that we hardly had time to brace ourselves for Thanksgiving and the Christmas season. Last night was exactly what we all needed.' She yawned. 'I'm exhausted, though – mind if I get some shuteye?'

'Go ahead, it's definitely been a busy couple of days,' said Romilly, catching the yawn.

'Yeah, thought it might have been.' Steph giggled and rolled away from her. Within minutes, she was snoring softly.

Cabin crew sometimes played it lean when it came to sleep. For pilots about to fly the following day, sleep was a ritual that couldn't be tampered with. Other pilots probably switched their phones to 'Do not disturb', but on account of her dad, Romilly had made it clear to Benita that she could always be reached for emergencies, unless in the air. Nathan too, she noticed, as they eventually prepared for sleep last night, kept his phone beside him – though she had tried not to spoil their layover or her birthday by dwelling on parenthood complications. It was challenge enough that from the tangled sheets of his bed last night, she'd withstood overhearing snippets of him speaking to Nora by videocall in the living room for half an hour. The girl's giggles echoed through the suite as he made her laugh, but at least he seemed to have postponed his idea of her being introduced to Romilly.

Roused from an eventual power nap in the bunk, Romilly's phone vibrated in the bag beside her. Two appointment reminders, one for the solicitor, another to call the removal company ready for Monday's move. Then she noticed two texts that must have arrived just as they'd boarded. Benita had briefly updated on her dad's condition and confirmed that she would be there to help Romilly on Saturday when persuading and explaining to him about relocating to the new care home. She had also asked Romilly to telephone her once back, to discuss the plan of approach beforehand. It reminded her to re-read the articles she'd gathered on the subject.

The other text, surprisingly, was from Nathan. Her initial reaction, that he'd broken rules and used his mobile while on duty in the cockpit, was quickly debunked.

'Sent this just before we boarded. Knew you wouldn't see it until your break. Confident I'll be missing you on flight deck while you're resting. Dinner Saturday? Nx'

She smiled while composing her reply, knowing he'd only read it on his break after she'd returned from hers. *'Dinner would be lovely. Also thinking of you, and #whenpilotslosecontrol Rx'*. Despite the prospect of a challenging few days ahead with her dad, astonishingly, she hadn't felt this happy in a long, long time.

By Friday evening, Romilly was finding it increasingly challenging to hang onto that happiness. A day spent attending to legal paperwork, meetings with rental agents, preparatory telephone conversations with Cranes Park Care Home, and securing and briefing the last-minute removal company for Monday, was just for starters. She'd been partway through microwaved frozen spaghetti bolognaise for dinner, when Benita rang. In an awkward conversation, they had agreed that if things didn't go well with Romilly explaining the move to her dad, he might instead listen to Benita. After all, he saw her on a daily basis. Knew and trusted her. Feelings bruised and energy low, Romilly ate her dinner from the sofa. Tomorrow would be hard, and no matter how much she'd read on the subject, she felt underprepared. Sat with a mug of tea, and watching nothing of note on the television, she realised that *this* might be one of those moments to lean on someone for help. Hoping that eight-fifteen pm wasn't too late to make a call, she picked up her phone.

'Mrs Reed, sorry, Marion, hi, it's Romilly, Romilly West, you may remember me, I—'

'Of course I remember you, how has your week been?'

'Oh, well good, actually. I had a layover in San Francisco. It's not too late to call?'

'Goodness, no. Oh, so you might have seen Jonathan then?'

Yes, rather a lot of him. 'He captained, I was first officer.' Thank goodness this wasn't a video call.

'Wonderful. I imagine he's rather good at it. Always been calm and responsible – they make the best leaders. Did you see much of San Francisco, Andy and I have never been to California?'

'Yes, each week we, and by that, I mean all the crew, not Nathan and I alone, although yesterday, we –

well anyway, yes we try to visit something different. We've cycled the Golden Gate Bridge, visited the piers, ridden cable cars, and hiked to a hill-top park bordered by some beautiful painted houses. Yesterday we had a picnic on a small beach below The Palace of Fine Arts.'

'How lovely, and such a perk of the job,' Marion cooed. 'I have happy memories of layovers myself, mostly in Greece and Turkey.'

'I didn't realise you flew.'

'Nine years as cabin crew for Thomson – I stopped when Jonathan was born.'

'And after that?'

'Switched to a part-time administrational career, eventually worked my way up to manager. Not that I regretted being there for he and Andy, because I'd do the same again, but once you've flown for a living, it's in your blood isn't it?' Romilly felt herself relax at Marion's easy manner, and their shared appreciation.

'Yes, it really is. So, have you had a good week?'

'Andy worked for a couple of days, and I've been clearing the back garden ready for winter, pruning, sweeping leaves, that sort of thing. Can't say my back enjoyed it all that much, but a hot bath helps.'

'A hot bath helps me with lots of things. Especially with something chocolatey on the side.'

Marion chuckled. 'Very true, particularly a chunk of Toblerone – Jonathan brings them for me from the airport sometimes. Anyway, while it's good to know my new friend is a fellow bather, I'm guessing something's concerning you about your father?'

'I was wondering if you could talk me through the day you explained to your sister that she was moving to her specialist dementia care home.

Tomorrow morning, I have that conversation with Dad. We're moving him on Monday.'

'You made a decision on where, then?'

'Yes, it's actually not far from his current place in Surbiton; at the moment he overlooks the main park, and the dementia home is across the other side – his room will have a view across the small boating lake.'

'Sounds like something he'll enjoy watching.'

'I thought so, and the staff there seemed welcoming. There are secure gardens out the back, too.'

'I remember we talked about the fruit trees. How has he been since you last saw him?'

Romilly took a sip of tea. 'Truthfully? It varies hour to hour, which is difficult and unpredictable. Sometimes he sees me; others, he sees my mum, which confuses him.'

'And that upsets you, I'm sure, dear. It's the same for me with my sister. Are you seeing him alone tomorrow?'

'Yes, well, with his carer, Benita. She rang earlier to suggest she might have better success, as she sees him twice daily.'

'That was probably hard to hear, but she may be right. I remember with Laura, she needed the persuasion and reassurance of her regular carer when we explained it, and again on the day itself, I had very little to do except hover. I just had to tell myself that, on some level, she knew I was there.'

'I hope she did. By the way, I read that article you sent about the best language to use.'

'Each sufferer is different, Romilly, but that particular article I'd say was the most useful to me, at least. Hold on a sec ...'

Romilly could hear a keyboard being typed on.

'I could come down if you'd like? If Andy's not working, he could bring me, otherwise the trains are frequent to London, then it's across into Surbiton. The whole journey would take less than two hours.'

'I can't ask you to do that, and anyway, I'll be there at nine-thirty which is far too early a start for you. No, but thank you, that's so … kind.' Romilly's throat caught. 'It's days like these I most especially miss Mum.'

'I'm sure you do, but Romilly, if you need me, I'll be on the other end of this phone, any time. Let me know how it goes. Have you got something nice for dinner? It's important to look after yourself.'

Romilly surveyed remains of her dinner. 'It'll do. But I may have a bath in a bit.'

29. Detective

Easing herself into hot, fragrant bathwater, beneath a thick froth of bubbles, it took several minutes for Romilly's muscles relax, then for her mind to follow suit. Thoughts turned to Nathan, and she reached for her phone, to text him a quick message.

'Hope you've had a good Friday. Can I confirm lunchtime tomorrow if all okay for dinner? Rx'

Almost immediately, he telephoned her. His name lit up her screen, as well as her pulse.

'Crikey, I didn't mean you had to call me.'

'S'okay, I wanted to hear your voice. Shh, give me a break, guys.'

Romilly detected a background of male chatter. 'You're out, so we'll catch up tomorrow.'

'No, now's fine with me. How was your day?'

A sarcastic 'Ooh, how was your day?' echoed, followed by raucous laughter.

'Ignore those goons – they roped me into a game of five-a-side, and we're now drowning our humiliation with a couple of beers. Think I'm too old for this.'

'No, you're not. I'd say you're in excellent shape.'

'Back at you. Oh, give it a rest, guys. Hold on, Romilly, I'm just going outside to talk to you.'

'Don't break away from what you're doing; I was just confirming the plan for tomorrow.' She heard a door squeak, then a passing vehicle's engine.

'It's fine. They're just ribbing me after I swore I'd never get involved with someone again.'

Romilly trailed a circle in the bubbles, processing his words. 'Are you involved with someone?'

'I'd say so.' Romilly let his words hang in the air, trying not to let the statement freak her out.

Falling back on a familiar tactic, she changed the subject. 'I had a chat with your mum this evening, I hope you don't mind. She's so approachable and knows how it feels to be in my situation with Dad.'

'That's good, I'm glad you did that. And talking with her helped?'

'Yes, but by the way I didn't mention anything regarding, well, us.'

'She's like a detective, anyway, piecing together clues. I hope your dad is all right tomorrow, that there are periods when he recognises you.'

'Me too.'

'Listen, I've had a thought about him and having an opportunity for him to see you reach captaincy. Hear me out, I've had a couple of beers, and it's probably not something you'll agree to but, I don't know …'

Romilly shook her head at the phone. 'Out with it.'

'Okay, so, we both know you're capable enough to be a marvellous captain one day, probably a senior captain, and maybe even have a shot at being chief pilot. At the moment, it's the accrued flying hours and the seniority list holding you back, but you're within shot of it. You keep a uniform in your car, don't you?'

'Yes, of course?'

'How about you borrow my epaulettes, clip my four stripes onto your shoulders instead of your three? At least he'd have a chance to see you as a captain, his memory being up against time and everything.'

She almost dropped her phone into the soapy water. 'How many drinks have you had? You know full well that's not only against airline policy, but it would also be a lie. And you'd be disciplined if anyone found out.'

'Seems very low risk to me. I'd do it, though. If you wanted me to.'

'No, but thank you. That's so—' This man was just …

'Yes, all right – I'm coming back in! Yes, I said all right, I'll tell her! The guys say hello.'

She cleared her throat. 'I'll let you go, say hi back to them, and I'll text you tomorrow.'

'I'll be thinking of you. A lot.'

'You, too.'

'He's not great, this morning,' said Benita, greeting Romilly as she entered her father's flat the following morning.

'Hi, Dad, it's me, Romilly.' She laid her coat on the arm of his sofa.

He peered at her, from the small table in the corner where he sat eating breakfast, then frowned. 'I don't understand. Who are you? You're not Joanie and you're not Romilly? Benita?' Romilly held her breath, rigid.

'This is Romilly, she's all grown up now. A pilot, just like you were, Charlie.'

'No, she's not! And I was a captain, not being made to eat awful oatmeal for breakfast.' He pushed away his bowl and shot a withering scowl at Benita. Romilly had to hand it to Benita – nothing seemed to ruffle her.

'Charlie, Romilly's here with some happy news, about a place across the other side of the park.' Benita nodded at her.

'Yes, Dad. I've found a super residential home you'd like, lots of gardens, a view of the boating lake. Somewhere you can enjoy watching films, and reading. The rooms are very comfortable.'

'I like it here. My room is fine.'

'This isn't the best place for you, going forward. The other one is so much better.'

Her dad frowned and he began wringing his hands. 'Benita?'

'It's all right. Let's have a cup of tea, shall we, Charlie? I'll make us all one.'

Romilly switched to neutral conversation, biding her time, as Marion's article had suggested. 'It's cool in here. Are you warm enough, Dad?'

He turned his head away, staring at the photography collection of airplanes and sunsets they'd hung together on his wall just eighteen months ago.

'You enjoyed flying those 747s didn't you? Queen of the Skies, they're still known as.'

Nothing.

'There's something special about sunsets from the flight-deck at high altitude, isn't there? The gentle curvature and the colours are spectacular.'

'It was my favourite time to fly,' he said with a wistful air.

'I know – you've said that to me many times and it's mine, too.' She smiled back, and gently patted his hand.

'Passengers don't have the view that the crew on the flight deck do.' He recoiled his hand. 'You wouldn't know.' Romilly swallowed, still biding her time.

Benita returned. 'Kettle's on. Let's turn on the television for a bit,' she suggested, shaking her head discretely at Romilly. 'Alan Titchmarsh is on in five minutes, the programme *Ground Force* is being re-run.'

'He's a good gardener.'

'Yes, he is. Romilly, could you give me a hand with the tray?'

Romilly wandered through to the tiny kitchenette, trying not to feel defeated. 'This isn't going well, is it?' An arm curled around her shoulders.

'Let's have a cuppa, watch the programme, see how he his afterwards.'

Alan Titchmarsh worked wonders with a long narrow garden somewhere Up North.   Romilly glanced at her dad, keen for signs of his own improvement.

'Do you want the last of your tea, Charlie?' said Benita, offering him the mug.

'Tea? Oh, yes.'

'It's cold but dry outside. After we've finished our drinks, perhaps we could wrap up and walk through the courtyard for a few minutes, Dad.'

'Joan? What are you doing here?' A look of disbelief slid onto his heavily lined face.

'It's me, Romilly, I'm all grown up now. Shall we get five minutes of fresh air?'

'No! You go! Benita? Benita?'

'Shh, don't worry, everything's fine Charlie. Romilly, I'll stay for a bit longer – his sandwich lunch is in an hour anyway. I can make a few extra for us, but before that, maybe a short break might be a good idea.'

Romilly stood up, close to tears. 'Yes, all right, I'll be back in a while, then see how things are.' She scooped up her bag and closed the door behind her.

Shaky legs somehow took Romilly to the ground-floor reception, and she pressed the security buzzer to exit. Her head spun as she tried to remember where she'd parked her car. Perhaps it was around the other side of the building? As she turned the corner, she stopped in her tracks. Her car was there; she now remembered reversing it into the space beside the fence. But leaning against it was a man consulting his phone.

'Nathan? What are you doing here?'

He immediately started walking towards her. 'Thought you might need some moral support.'

'But ... how?' she stammered, searching his face.

'Jesus, Romilly, where is your coat? You're shaking.'

'Not cold, b-bad morning.'

He took off his jacket and slipped it over her shoulders. 'Come and sit in my car for a bit – it's just round there.'

She nodded, absorbing his jacket's warmth and his familiar smell. Once inside his car, he dialled up the heating.

'How did you know where I was?'

'Combination of my mum's detective work – there aren't many sheltered retirement accommodations that face onto Surbiton Park – and my own, since I knew the car you drive, from the airport a few weeks ago, so I checked the carparks in each place until I found yours.' He reached for her hands and rubbed them vigorously between his own.

'Thank you, that feels better. It hasn't gone so well this morning,' she said, staring through the windscreen.

'I'm sorry. What's the plan now?'

'To have a break, see whether something changes nearer lunchtime. The problem is, even if I can discuss the move with him today, the same challenge might recur on Monday morning when the removers arrive.'

'Who is going to take him there?' Nathan's eyes were full of concern.

'It's all organised. Benita takes him to appointments in her car quite frequently – the barber, dentist, doctor, those sorts of things. She says Monday should be all right if she takes him to the barbers for an hour, extend it with a walk around the park if the weather's dry, a longer drive if it's not.'

'Meanwhile you'll have the movers take his things across to the new place?'

'Yes. They're confident that they can do it in time, and have done this many times before. There's actually not a lot to move.'

Nathan kissed her hands and released them. 'All right then. Shall we pop round the petrol station, pick up a hot drink, maybe something to eat? Presumably there isn't food in your dad's flat for you?'

'That would be good. Benita is making a sandwich for me I think, but I'll buy a cake or something. She's giving up most of her Saturday – it's the least I can do.'

Within minutes, they were perusing the limited selection inside the petrol station's food market. Nathan dutifully carried a shopping basket, while Romilly, feeling the weight of the morning on her shoulders, wandered aimlessly in a fug of worry, anxious for the right thing to fill it.

'Mr Domesticated, eh?' He waggled the basket as she deposited some chocolate biscuits into it.

She managed a half-smile. 'A whole other side to you.'

He tugged the sleeve on his jacket that she still wore and pulled her to one side of the aisle. 'I love your smiles, especially the "almost" ones. You know why?'

'I think you're about to tell me.'

'The thing with the small, "almost" ones is, if I watch them, they slowly turn into bigger ones.' He gazed at her mouth. 'Here's one coming now. Wait for it … Wait for it …'

Her face erupted into a wide, uncontrolled grin.

'There. Complete with a sexy dimple. Beautiful.'

She kissed his cheek. 'Come on, charmer.'

Back in the carpark at her dad's retirement complex, they opened the packet of biscuits and sipped watery take-out coffee, while Romilly relayed the earlier conversations with her dad.

'So, what would happen if someone new came in with you now to speak about the move, a person whom he wouldn't confuse with someone else?'

'You, you mean?'

Nathan nodded.

'Well, I can ask Benita for her thoughts. Certainly, if Dad's lucid, he'd enjoy meeting you, especially if you mention the work connection and everything.'

'See how you get on, then. I'll wait for you here, either way. No rush – radio coverage of the early kick-off rugby is on, if you find you don't need me in there.'

'Thank you. I'd better go – and I'll text you once I'm back up in his flat and have established how things are.' She unclipped her seatbelt.

'Have you forgotten something?' He tapped his lips and grinned.

She leaned over and kissed him, feeling his hand gently run through her hair and his lips part. Senses filled with chocolate, coffee, and heat.

He pulled away and tipped her chin with his forefinger. 'You taste wonderful. Now, go, you can do this. I'll be right here.'

30. Bond

Twenty minutes after Romilly had gone, his phone pinged.

'Dad calmer and lucid. Benita thinks you coming up might help, so if you meant it, then Flat 19. Can let you in main door from a panel here. Rx'

'Be with you shortly. Nx'

Nathan debated the pros and cons of his unspoken idea and took a chance. After smiling into the entry-phone camera, and being buzzed inside the building by Romilly, he sought a cloakroom for his quick change.

A few minutes later, he'd made his way to the door of Flat 19. There was no bell, so he knocked three times. A smiley Afro-Caribbean woman answered.

'Well, no mistaking who you must be, get yourself in,' she said.

He wiped his shoes on the doormat. 'Thank you. I'm Nathan. You must be Benita, Romilly speaks warmly of you, and how grateful she is to have you looking after her dad.'

'They're my favourite clients. Knew her mother before she passed, too – a truly wonderful person. Come through. Romilly's just telling us about some of the sights in San Francisco she's seen recently.'

Three steps along the short hallway and he was into the living room. Romilly's dad, a balding, white-haired man in moccasin slippers, was engaged in conversation with Romilly, whose eyes danced with obvious adoration. Nathan thought of Nora at their recent toy's tea party, giddy with happiness.

'Charlie, we have someone here to meet you,' said Benita.

Romilly noticed him then, and though surprised at his uniform, the corner of her mouth lifted in recognition of his intention behind wearing it. She managed a quiet 'Hi'.

Nathan approached her dad, who took one look at him and hurried himself up from his recliner. He held out his hand and her dad clasped it. 'Jonathan Reed, but call me Nathan.'

'Good to meet a fellow captain, especially in uniform. Charlie West, retired. Please, have a seat.'

'Thank you.' Nathan sat down beside Romilly, took off his hat, and would have left it in his lap had she not gestured for it. After absently dusting off a small speck of something from the peak, she rested it carefully on her bag. From the corner of his eye, Nathan observed Charlie nodding to himself, perhaps registering the small intimacy.

'Okay?' Nathan murmured to Romilly, searching her face for any sign of distress. It was easy to see where she'd got her pale blue eyes from.

'Yes.' She smiled, then turned her attention back to the room. 'I was just telling Dad about The Palace of Fine Arts. Bit of a strange place really, wasn't it?' She brought Nathan into the conversation.

'It was. More of an homage to other places than something of itself. But we had a good day there and found a small beach nearby.'

'Yes, from there we could see the Golden Gate Bridge in one direction, the city marina in the other.'

'So, you two went at the same time?' Charlie cocked his head at them.

Nathan turned to Romilly, awaiting her cue.

'Yes, Nathan is the captain on this eight-week block.'

'I see. And how is my girl doing in the cockpit beside you?'

'Dad!'

'Extremely well. She's a talented pilot. I'm convinced it won't be long before she's a captain herself.'

'Time will tell, but she's certainly very special.'

'She is.' Nathan glanced at Romilly, who was almost scarlet, and suppressed the urge to slip his hand around hers. If only Charlie had said something more assured about the likelihood of her captaincy. 'But tell me about your flying years – I understand you were mainly on the South America routes?'

'Yes, and Africa – no jet lag for those which helped with balancing home life, and meant I wasn't so spun out when I was off-duty. You've flown to those countries yourself?'

Nathan nodded, simultaneously appreciating the collection of airplane photography on the wall opposite. 'Yes, once to Johannesburg, and a couple of times to Buenos Aries and Caracas, but the bulk of my career has been East Asian, mainly Thailand, Hong Kong, and Malaysia, but occasionally further, on to Australia.'

'Interesting … I've encouraged Romilly to fly East for the next block, but she's not for persuading. Must say, though, West Coast America seems to be agreeing with you, darling.'

Romilly typically ignored the compliment. 'I like it there, so I may stick with this rotation for another block or two … It depends. Maybe I'll switch to some Asian destinations one day, Dad.'

'And yourself, Nathan – any thoughts of changing destination after this block?'

'That also depends.' He glanced at Romilly. 'I have a six-year-old daughter, and need to consider her and my ongoing shared custody.' Romilly stiffened beside him, but he wasn't willing to hide something from her father as important as being a father himself. He understood the powerful bond in having a daughter.

'Benita, shall we make some tea for the sandwiches? Dad, Nathan?' Romilly said, interrupting the conversation by standing up.

'Yes, please,' both men replied, in unison.

Charlie watched the women absent themselves before he leaned in towards him.

'I understand completely. Being a husband, father, and pilot is challenging. I never regretted stopping early.'

Recalling Romilly's dismissive comment about her father's early retirement, he took his opportunity, 'Do you mind me asking, how did you know when to stop flying?'

'She needed me.'

Nathan mentally kicked himself. 'Of course, your late wife's illness – Romilly has spoken about that. I'm so sorry you've lost her.'

Charlie shook his head. 'As it turned out, I had already retired before Joan underwent treatment – she was the love of my life, you know, but we only lost her a few years ago. No, it was Romilly who really needed me. I might not have been there as much as I should have been while she was little – you know what commercial flying is like to start with, darting here there and everywhere just to keep your hours up and the money coming in. But to be there to support her when she really needed me, during her twenties, was something I've never regretted. When Kathy was on shift, I used to meet Romilly for lunch a couple of times a week at the British Museum, where she was working – she got me a pass and we'd sit and talk things through. Anyway, that's in the past and, as you have seen, she was born to fly.'

'I have indeed.' Nathan wished Romilly hadn't missed her father's words.

'I believe Sterling's Training and Development people still use "Pilots and Beyond" as part of the material for senior ranks?'

'Yes, I think we do.'

'Well, that's how I kept my hand in the business, and some consulting money coming in, writing what I had learned. Used to go to the British Library after meeting with Romilly, sit in the reading rooms there to research and write. The book didn't bring in what you're probably earning now, but there's no point being the richest person in the graveyard, is there?'

Nathan nodded, trying to interpret all the information. In truth, he hadn't ever noticed the author's name, but the contents of the materials which he'd studied for captaincy, he recalled as being excellent. Certain content of Romilly's history, however, still remained a mystery.

'Here we are,' Benita announced, 'a nice cuppa and sandwiches for everyone, and there's some lemon drizzle for afterwards, thanks to these two.'

Romilly returned to her seat beside him. 'All right?' she asked.

'I am.' He smiled, but sensed the tension in her stiff posture.

'Maybe we should broach the subject?' she said under her breath.

He nodded. 'Would you like me to start?'

'Please.'

He cleared his throat. 'Romilly tells me about this new place she'd seen for you, across the other side of the park – better equipped, good quality gardens and very respectable facilities provided. Sounds like an opportunity?'

'She hasn't mentioned it.' Charlie stifled a yawn.

'It will help to be somewhere better if your memory problems worsen, Dad – a familiar place to rest and be looked after when needed.'

Charlie turned to his carer. 'What do you think, Benita?' Nathan exchanged looks with Romilly, suspecting the deferment to Benita had stung. All he could do was give her a smile of encouragement; she was doing so well.

'Seems like the right place to be thinking of,' said Benita, on message. 'I've known several others be happy there. There's a space come up for next week, I understand, available from Monday, as it happens.'

Charlie picked up his sandwich and paused. 'And Nathan. Do you mind my asking a fellow captain – what would you do?' Again, Nathan glanced at Romilly. It seemed Charlie was happier taking advice from anyone but her. She blinked, her concerned eyes urging him on.

'If it were me in your shoes and knowing the care Romilly has taken in visiting and choosing somewhere for you of the best as she can find locally, I'd probably take it before the availability is lost. My aunt lives in a similar situation in Buckingham, and I'm told it was challenging to secure a space. Places like those are in enormous demand.'

Charlie nodded at him and sat quietly while finishing his slice of cake. Shortly afterwards, he began yawning widely. 'Sounds good, then, if you all think that's best. Crikey, I'm tired.'

'Let's leave you to it, so you can nap,' said Benita, 'It's been a busy morning and you said that you wanted to watch the rugby at three pm.' She glanced at Romilly, who acknowledged her with a slight nod.

'Absolutely,' said Romilly, then turning to Nathan. 'Is your cousin playing in that match?'

'Depends on which of the Premiership fixtures is being televised today.' He pulled out his phone.

'It's my team, Hornets versus Camford,' said Charlie. 'Should be a good one.'

Nathan scrolled down his phone. 'Yes, looks like he's the starting fly half.'

'Wait, your cousin is Camford's Danny Reed? I would never have guessed – you look nothing alike.'

'Yes, he's my cousin, adopted by my uncle and aunt. Had a tough start in life, but look at him now.'

Nathan couldn't interpret the thoughts bouncing behind Romilly's shifting glances, but something made her suddenly fiddle with the edge of a sofa cushion.

'Indeed, there's talk of him being capped,' Charlie continued, still engaged, but beginning to look drawn.

'There are complexities to be worked through, I understand.'

'Well, he'd better get a shift on, must be pushing thirty.' Charlie stretched his arms.

'Indeed.' Romilly tapped Nathan's leg with her knee, then indicated the door, perhaps also noticing her father's decline.

'All right, Dad, I think we'll be off now, but I'll come back to help out on Monday, there's no need to worry about packing or moving, it will all be taken care of.' She leaned in to kiss his cheek, emotion choking her voice. 'Love you.'

'You too, darling girl.'

'I'll just help Benita to clear the plates.' Romilly sniffed to Nathan, and began ferrying items to the kitchen.

'Nathan, before you go, did you see my cabinet of airplane models in the hallway? Antiques, some of them, proper tin and some are hand-painted.' Charlie indicated for him to follow as he walked slowly out of the room.

'Some of the Golden Age's best,' said Nathan, peering into the display. He sought the old man's face, expecting an expression of sentiment. Instead, the old man was staring straight at him, eyes serious.

'You care for my daughter, Captain?'

Nathan blinked. 'Yes, I do.'

'More than that?' said Charlie, with no let-up in his stare.

'I think so, yes.'

'Then, whatever happens, look after her. She's bravely tackled some tough times. Might seem strong and focused, especially if you're used to seeing her fly a huge bird like the triple seven, but make no mistake, even people with spines of steel are vulnerable. Metal bends, even melts. Everyone has their limit.'

'You have my word I'll never hurt her.' Nathan took Charlie's hand and shook it, looking him straight in the eye.

'That is a great comfort.' After Charlie's candour, Nathan felt compelled to add his own.

'I understand that, but I'll tell you, she is a source of strength to me – her drive and focus, but she's also caring. Helped me through a rough few hours of flu.'

'It's good that you truly see her. She might have taken up my profession, but few realise that she's also like her mother, caring and loving. It's an awful shame.'

'Very sad for her, losing her mother.'

Charlie nodded slowly, now seeming in immediate need of sleep. 'Yes, that, too.'

'I'm ready,' said Romilly, appearing in the hallway with her bag and Nathan's hat.

'Don't forget your coat,' Nathan replied. She smiled at him and ducked back into the living room for it.

Charlie patted Nathan's shoulder. 'Very pleased to meet you.'

'A privilege to be here. I hope the move goes well, and that you enjoy this afternoon's match.' Nathan opened the door in the congested hallway and stepped outside.

'Bye, Nathan,' Benita called from behind everyone.

'Thank you for the tea and sandwiches,' he replied, hoping that she heard.

In front of him, Romilly hugged her father, eyes tightly closed, prolonging their moment of connection. Again, Nathan thought of his precious bond with Nora, and how happy she was every time they reunited.

'See you on Monday, Dad. Thank you, Benita.' She closed the door behind them and managed a handful of steps along the corridor before turning her face into the padded shoulder of Nathan's uniform. 'That's the best he's been for weeks, months even.'

He kept her tucked close to him as they left the building. 'I'm pleased for you. That went well – he seemed convinced of the move.'

'Yes, fingers crossed that Monday will be as good.'

They reached a point at which their cars were in different directions, but Romilly seemed understandably wrung out. 'So, Kingston is what, fifteen minutes away?' he said. 'Would you like me to drive you home? I could drive your car, leave mine here, and get a cab back to pick it up so I can head home?'

'I'm not sure. Definitely do need some quiet time.' She gazed in the direction of her car.

'Understood. How safe are you to drive?'

As she appeared to mentally assess herself, bluish arcs beneath her eyes betrayed the toll the day was taking. 'I'm safe.'

'Could you call me when you're back home then, so I know you're okay?' he said, accepting the likelihood of abandoning their later dinner plans.

'No, that wasn't what I meant.'

'Which part, sweetheart?' he said, stroking her arm.

'Could we maybe have some quiet time *together*? I don't know, say we get the weekend papers, listen to some music or something.'

Nathan pulled her in close again and kissed her hair. 'We can definitely do that.' He pulled out his phone and consulted the booking portal for parking at his apartment block. 'How would you feel about coming up to where I'm living in Battersea? Looks like there's a visitor parking space available in the underground carpark.'

'How long did it take you to drive here this morning?'

'Forty minutes.'

'Okay, I'll drive home first, have a rest and freshen up. Can I meet you there in, say, three hours?'

'Of course, take as long as you think you need. I'll buy some papers and a few things for dinner. Honestly, a night in might do us both good. All things considered, it's been a hectic week.'

'Sounds perfect. I'll bring some wine.' She reached into her bag for her car keys, then lifted on to her toes to kiss him. 'Thank you, for everything. I mean it.'

He kissed her softly in return. 'Drive carefully – you're not on a runway now.'

It was only after she'd driven off and he'd slid into his own car, that Nathan remembered tomorrow's birthday celebration lunch for Nora at his parents' house. Romilly said she'd be bringing wine with her later, which implied she would likely be staying over. While that thought thrilled him, he also knew he'd committed to collect Nora from Liz's at eleven tomorrow. He would need to use this drive home and the trip to the shopping centre to debate his options.

31. More Wine

Romilly's intention had been a power nap on her sofa, of the sort she employed while on rest breaks in the air, and occasionally in crew-quarters at airports for essential energy boosts. Unfortunately, the whole week had taken more out of her than she'd appreciated, and her twenty-minute plan overran by almost two hours, even before she'd showered. Fading light and dense traffic made navigation through Wandsworth, Clapham, and into Battersea challenging, so it was almost four o'clock before she parked beneath Nathan's apartment.

Boiler House Square seemed to be part of Battersea Power Station's vast conversion to a wrap-around, glass-walled residential and shopping complex. Romilly couldn't imagine the lofty price tags. Opting to leave her overnight bag in the car, she slipped the bottle of Pinot Noir from home into her shoulder bag and stepped inside the carpark's lift, one no less prestigious than The Beaumont's. For once, she could have done with some jazzy razzmatazz to distract from the butterflies filling her stomach. She checked her appearance in her phone's camera. Her hair wasn't as well-styled as it had been without Steph's intervention, but it was clean, and she'd tried to add some curl around her face. If she was overdressed in a knitted jumper dress and long boots, it was too late now. At the last minute, she'd scrambled around for clean pyjamas, uncertain whether there would be any need for them. It had seemed a long four nights since Tuesday and his support earlier with her dad had strengthened her resolve to focus solely on her present happiness.

'How was the journey?' Nathan said, easing her coat from her shoulders as she walked into the sixth-floor apartment. Stood in socks, jeans, and a soft khaki hoodie on the white high-gloss tiles, he looked as sexy as he had earlier in uniform. He kissed her on the neck. 'You smell lovely.'

'Thank you. It was slow, but straightforward.' She removed her boots, revealing an embarrassing toe hole in the end of her tights.

She followed him through to an airy double aspect living space that was bathed in the metallic glow of imminent sunset. Beneath them lay a wide stretch of clay-coloured Thames that flowed beneath two ornate bridges.

'This view is amazing!' she declared, passing him the bottle of wine.

'It is. Shall we open it now? I've bought the papers. If not, we could save it for dinner.'

She eyed a sumptuous-looking pale grey L-shaped sofa atop a thick geometric shaggy rug. On some white, open shelving, soft piano and deep, smooth-voiced singing emitted from a record player, adding a relaxed vibe. 'Now works for me, especially sitting there with these views. This is my absolute favourite time of the day.'

'Mine too. I'll get some glasses.' He diverted into a white, futuristically sleek, kitchen area, devoid of anything on its polished concrete work surfaces. The scene jarred – somehow, she had depicted he might live somewhere earthier, less minimal and bachelor-pad cool.

'Cheers.' She clinked her glass against his and followed him to the sofa.

'Come, sit, but there's no need to talk unless you want to.' He carefully placed his glass on one of the coasters on a chrome and glass side table. 'I bought some olives, brown kalamatas – want some?'

'Lovely. Much prefer them to green ones.'

It warmed her to notice Nathan's knowing smile, but she puzzled as he searched every cupboard, having difficulty with some of the hidden opening mechanisms, before investigating each of the drawers.

'Not sure, there might be a serving bowl somewhere.'

This wasn't his apartment.

'Nope, can't find one. A cereal bowl will have to do.' He decanted some olives and brought them and the bottle of wine over. 'Been staying here almost a year – you'd think I would have found where everything was by now.' He glanced at her face. 'As you've no doubt deduced, this obviously isn't my place.'

'That's a relief. Doesn't fit with quite where I'd imagined you might live.'

'No, it's spectacular, but not my taste. I'm staying here while the owner is in Dubai for a couple of years. Friend from university, a futures broker. Clearly, I've made comparatively poor career choices.'

'Well, you're lucky, I don't have friends who could afford something like this, and I certainly couldn't,' she said, choosing not to add that, aside from Steph, she didn't have friends who couldn't afford it either.

'Current value is over four million, so it's not ever going to be in my lifetime either, not that I'd buy it. I'm just waiting for Liz to sell our house, hopefully it won't be much longer – she's seen something she'd like. Staying here in the meantime seemed like a good option; not far from Nora, good for Heathrow, but a complete change while I … well, put myself back together a bit, you know?'

She slipped her hand into his as they settled onto the downy sofa, recognising his effort once again to share with her how he felt.

'I can't tell you what it means to have you here,' he said quietly.

'It's nothing.'

'I'm experienced enough to know it's more than that between us.' He stroked his thumb across hers. 'You're the only woman I've brought here, for a start.'

Romilly leaned into him, absorbing his warmth and words. 'Well, I'm glad to be here.'

Sunset further mellowed the inner glow from a swift glass of wine and the close contact of Nathan, who had one of the weekend supplements open in his lap. It felt scarily good, sitting beside him. Romilly willed herself not to overthink, and to stay in the moment. All that mattered was now.

'Which article are you reading – because I can't concentrate, I'm so tired …' he murmured.

'Then close your eyes for a bit. I've had the benefit of some sleep earlier, and you've kept the same hours as me this week.'

'Just a power-nap, then might want some energy later.'

She angled her face towards his and they shared a tender kiss. 'Yes, I'd say you might.'

A scattering of lights amid the deep navy sky signalled that she'd snoozed beyond early evening. Fast asleep, Nathan's head had flopped onto hers, his chest rising and falling in a deep, steady rhythm beneath her palm. Slowly, Romilly smoothed her hand up to his shoulder, letting her fingers ripple lightly over his clothes, tracing the outline of his muscles, down his arm to his wrist and fingers. He stirred, pulling her tighter into him, then relaxed. The enticing smell of his cologne tipped her into a decision to wake him with a surprise she knew he would enjoy.

Exploring further, she tracked the curve and dip of his abdomen. Following an irresistible craving to feel his skin, she lifted the bottom of his hoody and felt her fingers meet warmth, then tangle with a trail of dark hair that led to his belt. As she ran her hands up and along the lengths of his thighs, then pressed across the front of his jeans, he began to stir, and within seconds the fabric became strained. To the sound of his low moan, she unfastened his belt, opened the button, then gradually lowered the zip.

'Christ,' he croaked, straightening up and blinking away his sleep. He placed his hand over hers. 'Wait, window blinds … Remote button.' He pointed at a remote control on the table.

Romilly clicked the button on the remote, and a coordinated unfurling of linen blinds from the ceiling commenced, leaving them in semi-darkened privacy within seconds. She angled her face towards him and they kissed, slowly, deeply. Making her way down his throat and trailing onto the skin bared by the pushed-up hoodie, his rumbling groans spurred her on.

'I want you,' he choked.

The same need burned inside her, but this was just for him.

'God,' he said, once his breathing had calmed after a long, guttural release, 'that was … Give me a second and we'll move this to the bedroom.'

'No need.' She went to stand up, but he caught her wrist.

'Hold on, that doesn't seem fair,' he said, fastening his jeans.

The afterglow on Nathan's cheeks was contagious. 'Honestly, it was exactly what I wanted. Where's your bathroom?' She winked.

'If you're sure, then there's one on the left, by the front door.'

'I'm sure.'

'I'll refill our wine if you'd like?' He picked up the bottle, poised to pour.

In the steps towards the bathroom, she debated her response. The alcohol from earlier had probably left her system; but if she had more now, she'd need to stay over. There was no doubting it – she'd never felt so attracted to or comfortable with anyone. She forced down the nagging prospect of accepting then losing this amazing man, with her new mantra. *Keep looking forward. Be more Steph.*

'Definitely.'

32. Call and Response

When Romilly returned to the lounge, Nathan had disappeared, so she retracted the blinds to head-height, revealing London's nightscape. Across the water, she could make out the coloured lights of Victoria and the vast black expanse of Hyde Park beyond; to the right, Westminster and Big Ben were flaunting their intricate base-lit glory. She'd just popped an olive into her mouth, when Nathan joined her, walking in barefoot and having swapped his jeans for a pair of joggers. He smelled of expensive body wash, and cocked her a smile that almost caused her to choke. She very much hoped he'd still have energy left for later.

'En-suite shower in my room,' he explained. 'Don't know about you, but I'm famished. How does spaghetti bolognaise sound?'

'Perfect. Can I help?'

'Maybe you could chop some mushrooms and tomatoes for the sauce?'

'What, no jar?' she joked, though she couldn't recall the last time she had chopped anything, let alone make a sauce from scratch.

'Very funny, I think we can do better than that.'

Perhaps it was wisest not to mention her previous night's freezer version. 'I like the music you were playing earlier, by the way.'

'And there you were, thinking you didn't like jazz.'

She glared at the pile of soil-speckled mushrooms he'd placed in front of her, debating whether they should be washed or peeled before chopping. And the stalks? She used their conversation to stall a decision. 'I didn't recognise that as jazz, but you're right. I just don't understand it, I suppose, too … unruly.'

Nathan chuckled. 'I used to think the same, but my dad explained how to enjoy it. He said it helped to think of it as a conversation between instrument players; one will play a rhythm or tune; the other will echo it – say a pianist and a drummer, or double base and trumpet. It meshes together. It's known as "call and response".'

'If you say so.' She grinned, watching him squash some garlic through a gadget.

'Okay, maybe think of it as being like the closed loop system for comms with air traffic towers that we use at work, then. They speak our call sign and number, and we always repeat it back.'

He wiped his hands and went over to the record player, turned the vinyl over and brought the cover sleeve back for her to see. 'This is Gregory Porter. Listen to this first track – you can hear the call and response between his voice, the pianist and drummer.'

She concentrated, and to her amazement, could hear what he'd explained. She'd been about to say so when she realised that he was gazing at her again. He was probably wondering why she hadn't started on the mushrooms.

'Your smile makes me happy,' he said.

God, this man floored her. 'Your smile makes *me* happy, which, if I'm not mistaken, is call and response?'

Eyes shining, he returned to the kitchen area, curved his arms around her waist and squeezed her to him. 'Yes, it absolutely is.'

She tipped her face up towards his for a brief kiss. 'I like this sort of jazz, I'll admit.'

'That's the thing, finding whether you like blues, swing, supper jazz, hotel jazz—'

She raised a hand, halting the list. 'Wait, hotel jazz?' She sniggered. 'Seriously?'

'It's played in the background in reception at The Beaumont, and in their—'

'Lifts, yes, I've noticed.' She smothered a laugh. Whatever next – kitchen jazz?

'By the way, Gregory Porter is touring again soon, including the Royal Albert Hall during Christmas week. Maybe we could go?' He darted back to where his vinyls were displayed, and returned with another of Porter's albums. In a rush, humour had left her, in its place, doubt.

She studied the album's artwork, thinking through the implications of committing to future dates. It was still only October, and she'd only known Nathan for a few weeks. Anything could happen once they knew each other better. 'I'm not sure …'

'Listen, if we're doing this,' he said, gesturing at the sofa and their food preparation, 'then two hours of jazz, out in public, shouldn't pose too much of a problem.'

'Can I think about it?'

'Of course.' He passed her some kitchen roll. 'By the way, I usually just wipe mushrooms before chopping the lot, stalks included. Do you?' He busied himself, giving a light touch to the glass hob controls, to heat some olive oil in a large pan. After chopping an onion, he added it to the pan and stirred. While rinsing his hands, he studied her face. 'What's with the little crinkle between your eyes – is it the onion, the mushrooms, or something else?'

'It's nothing.' It was becoming increasingly difficult to hide from him, not that he deserved to be misled.

He added the little pile of garlic to the pan and stirred again. 'I understand how you might be feeling.'

'You do?'

'Yes, if I'm honest, I'm a little freaked out myself, barely a year past a messy break-up for which I hold myself partly to blame. Your dad mentioned something about your twenties being difficult – no, it's all right, I'm not asking about that, unless of course you want to tell me, but all I'll say is, it's not easy to trust others or ourselves again, maybe even be convinced that we deserve someone new. Am I close?'

Now was the time, her chance. 'Partly …' She spoke to the floor, tracing the outline of a glossy white floor tile with her toe.

'And the other part?'

Say it.

'The children part.'

Nathan's shoulders slumped on his exhale. 'I thought there might be something to do with Nora. It's dating a man with a child, isn't it?' He turned the heat down on the hob, then took her hands in his. 'Listen, the joys of being a parent come with the responsibility of having to put your child before everything else. I can't change that, and I wouldn't want to. But I see that for you and me, my father duties might sometimes complicate things, especially when they have to take priority. I don't expect you to understand, but you must know that, when I'm with you, just like when we're flying, I'm focused on that. It's really that the parent thing is never far away. It's the reverse, I know, but think of how often your dad's needs probably come to your mind.'

She nodded, grateful for his honesty, admiring of his love for Nora, but wishing he would let her qualify what she'd really meant. There were times when she'd swear there was a window on her forehead, such was his ability to anticipate her moves, but even he couldn't know her past if she didn't tell him. Here he stood, patient, receptive, not to mention sexy, but he didn't need a heavy evening, especially after being so wonderful this week with her birthday and helping earlier with her dad. It was cowardly reasoning, but tonight, she could live with it.

'I understand, it's all right.' She squeezed his hands, hoping to reassure him and move the conversation on.

'Good, because I'd like you to meet Nora. I know she'd love you and she's easy to have fun with, especially if you don't mind tea parties and Disney.'

'One day, that might be nice.' He smiled and released her hands, returning to stir the pan.

'It leads me to something I haven't mentioned. Really, I should have said about it earlier.'

'And that is?'

'Tomorrow I'm taking Nora to my parents for lunch. It was her birthday two days after yours, but at the time I didn't think I should say anything – didn't want to make things difficult … Anyway, we're doing presents and a cake for her. I expect to have my face painted – that sort of thing.'

Romilly froze, praying that he didn't invite her along.

'So, I'll need to be away from here before ten to pick her up, but there's no rush for you to leave, though.'

She tried not to look too relieved. 'That works for me. I have lots to catch up on tomorrow before I'm over at Dad's at nine am on Monday morning for his move, then obviously on to Heathrow for our one pm briefing.'

He added minced beef to the pan, moving it around with a wooden spoon. 'Are you sure you don't mind?'

'Completely. Right, let me sort these mushrooms.' Unable to postpone any longer, she picked up the first one and rubbed it clean with a piece of kitchen roll. The trouble was, you couldn't postpone things indefinitely.

Romilly had set the alarm on her phone for eight-thirty on Sunday morning, but when it went off, she found herself alone in Nathan's bed.

'Stupid thing,' he was uttering, from somewhere in the living area.

She pulled on the pyjamas that Nathan had so enjoyed removing as soon as they'd gone to bed. It had barely been worth packing them.

'Morning, all okay over there?' she croaked, sauntering over to him.

'Not really. Having a tussle with wrapping paper. Never been good with it. Her other presents came gift-wrapped, but this…'

Romilly observed the Disney princess watch in his hand and different-sized cuts of abandoned, pink pony wrapping paper. 'It's a simple rectangle.'

'To you, maybe. I really want this first birthday after Liz and I split to be happy for Nora.'

'I'm sure it will be, just … give it here.' Trying not to think about his daughter, and him being a parent, she cut, folded, and stuck, then handed the wrapped watch to him. 'The price is one coffee, please.'

'Cheap at half the price,' he said, and kissed her soft and long on the mouth. 'Good morning, by the way. You look beautiful all mussed up.'

'I doubt that – I really need a shower.'

One of his sexy smiles brightened his face. 'My en-suite has a double cubicle, if you're interested? First, let me organise some coffee, though.'

'Sounds very enticing, in that order.'

Fuelled by caffeine and a thirst to feel skin against skin, they stood beneath the steamy heat of a large rainfall shower. From the second Nathan began kissing her neck and working his way down her body, to the moment his skilled fingers set to work, she was lost. The rough graze of his stubble, the soapy foam of body wash, and the cool wall tiles behind her back tipped her into sensory overload. Tumbling their damp bodies onto his bed, all she could hear were his groans and her own frantic pleas until they juddered into sweet relief.

Recovering his breath, Nathan had lain with his head on her breasts, stroking the length of her body with trembling fingers. 'That was …'

'Yeah, it was.' She ran her fingers through his hear. It really, really was.

After reluctantly dressing, they headed back to the kitchen. Nathan had dropped a couple more pods into his coffee machine, and was just removing a loaf from a cupboard, when his phone started to ring.

'Chrissake,' he muttered, after seeing the identity of the caller. 'Hello … No, we agreed I'd pick her up from home … I understand, but you've got to tell me in advance something like this … Yes, but I also have a life … That's not your business … When? … Well, I don't have much choice, do I? Fine.'

For a few seconds after the call, Nathan braced his arms on the worktop. 'Right, so change of plan. Liz is bringing Nora here. There's a fifteen-minute drop-off bay she uses in the carpark.'

'Up and out early for a Sunday. When will they be here?' said Romilly, suspending her musing of taking another shower and whether to wash her hair.

'She's on her way now, ten minutes' away apparently, and has an appointment in North London somewhere, so it's convenient to call in here first to drop Nora.'

Romilly switched to 'evacuate'. 'I'd better get going then, and skip another coffee.'

Nathan closed his eyes. 'I'm sorry, this feels wrong, but I can't do much about it.'

'Genuinely, it's perfectly all right,' Romilly called over her shoulder, scanning the area for anything of hers. 'I'll just pack my stuff quickly, then make a move.'

In less than five minutes, she'd kissed Nathan goodbye and was in the lift with a full, reusable coffee cup that he had thrust into her hand. As the doors opened at the carpark level, she froze. Standing waiting was a well-groomed, expensively put-together woman, holding the hand of the curly brown-haired girl she'd seen greeting Nathan at the airport.

'Morning,' the woman purred, 'coming out?'

'Yes, sorry.'

Romilly exited in slow motion, the only thing catching her eye as they passed one another, an identical Disney watch already on Nora's wrist.

33. Metal Bends

Monday again. The eventual two-week break between blocks could not come quick enough, but until then, as with every Monday morning on this block, Nathan had loaded his flight case into the boot of his car, hung his uniform jacket onto the ever-present backseat hanger, and slid behind the wheel of his newly repaired Mercedes. But it wasn't directly to Heathrow that he set off for; he and Romilly had texted last night and said '*See you tomorrow*', and while he expected her to interpret that as meeting for flight briefing at one pm, he had decided to leave early and head for Surbiton, just in case she needed him.

At Charlie's sheltered accommodation, Nathan had parked in an obscured spot, able to observe Romilly through the corner of his windscreen, as she gestured with the removals team, who would be packing for the quick relocation to Cranes Park. Her body positioning shielded her face from his view, but as ever, her uniform looked perfect on her; he couldn't help but monitor the removal men's admiring expressions. As Romilly disappeared into the building, Nathan fired a wish into the universe that her father recognised her, today of all days.

Considering the extent to which Romilly now permeated his thoughts, and the undeniable pull to be with her, Nathan wanted this week to broach again the subject of introducing her to Nora. Without that, she missed a huge part of who he was. But if the prospect of booking concert tickets for two months in advance had spooked her, then having her over to meet his daughter might see her running for the hills. He hoped Romilly's abrupt departure yesterday hadn't messed things up. It had felt similar to the embarrassment of ejecting an illicit girlfriend from his dorm through his window at boarding school, before the matron checked the rooms.

Next weekend could be ideal. Saying goodbye as he dropped Nora off at home after an enormous lunch at his parents yesterday evening had been as bittersweet as ever, but being half term this week, he would be picking her up again on Thursday after landing back at Heathrow and have her with him right the way through to Sunday. A win-win opportunity for quality time, and to introduce her to Romilly. He thought of his daughter's newly gapped grin and pulled out his phone to glance at his lock screen. She was growing up so fast; he must cherish every moment. Yesterday she had adored her new teddy bear, especially as it came with a Disney watch of its own to wear that matched the one her mum had given her. He'd resisted the urge to feel angry with a smug-looking Liz, because, as ever, he was surely half to blame. All he had needed to do was to communicate and coordinate. At least Liz had booked a parents' evening slot with Nora's teacher for immediately after half term, for a night when he was in the country. Perhaps then they would get to the bottom of Nora falling out of love with school.

On the accommodation steps, Benita appeared, persuading an anxious-looking Charlie out through the doors. Behind them came a blotchy-faced Romilly. As Benita passed his reluctant hand to her, then set off alone with keys in her hand towards a row of cars, Nathan held his breath. Parent and child. Child and parent. A canary-yellow Toyota pulled up, and Benita jumped out. She helped Charlie into the passenger seat, then after closing the door on him, the women briefly embraced. Nathan had been about to jump out of the car, to help absorb some of Romilly's pain as the car drove away, but the removers called her over to their van. Within seconds, she had wiped her eyes, finished whatever their conversation had been about, and was leading them inside. He fired off a text, keen not to hinder the tight turnaround.

'Thinking of you. Here if you need. Nx'

Forty-five minutes' later, and yet to reply, Romilly appeared on the steps, waving off the removers in their van, blotting her eyes. Trying to imagine a life condensed into so few boxes that they fitted into a transit, Nathan was hit by an unexpected pang of longing for his old house. The yet-to-be-used greenhouse. The summerhouse he'd converted into a darkroom for his photography. Reading bedtime stories to Nora in her unicorn-themed bedroom. He sighed. There was no going back to that house, but there would somehow be another in his near future. A home. Romilly sped off in her car. She looked calmer and in control, but the hardest part was still ahead of her. Nathan started his engine and kept his distance respectable.

'Morning, everyone – good weekends?' Nathan acknowledged Max and some of the early arrivals in the crew room at Heathrow and wheeled his case to the corner. Romilly, he knew, would not be there yet.

At Cranes Park, he'd watched her direct the removers as they'd rapidly unloaded their van, then go inside with them. Just before Benita arrived with Charlie, she'd come out to the pull-in point to welcome them, smiling with what Nathan now recognised as a mask of enthusiasm. Charlie had shuffled beside Benita up the ramp towards the building's entrance doors, his frame stiff, face bewildered, then he'd angrily shook off Romilly's arm when offered. The flash of hurt passing across her face had struck Nathan as if a physical blow to his own chest. Charlie and Benita had disappeared through the doors, Romilly trailing behind. It was all he could do not to leave his car and scoop her up, to remove her from the path of the inevitable difficulty she very likely was yet to face. Instead, he'd monitored his phone. Seeing no reply, and the time, he had headed off to Heathrow.

'Max, a word.' Nathan beckoned his second officer over to the small table where the paperwork of pre-cockpit checks and crew briefing preparation would take place.

'Sure.'

'How are you feeling right now – rested?' He studied Max's tanned face for any sign of tiredness.

'I'm safe, and the cabin crew are happy that they're with us at The Beaumont again. Crew Services have booked the rest of their layovers in this block there, too, using the suites. I guess it's more economical.'

'Very good. Would you be interested in switching to first pilot duties for the outbound today? Can't promise the take-off or landing, but you can do the exterior walk-around and run comms with the towers.'

Max frowned. 'I'd bite your hand off, were it not Romilly's seat you're offering me to switch with. Is she okay?'

'Confidentially, I believe she could do with not flying until later. She'll be fine for the mid-portion shift covers.' Nathan's phone pinged, a message from Romilly to say she had just parked at the airport, and wouldn't be late. 'I'll speak to her privately, intercept her before she reaches the crew room. There's no pressure on you; I have time to call in another pilot if necessary.'

'I realise it's not my own performance giving me this opportunity, but yes, I'll make the switch.'

Nathan rested a hand on the young pilot's shoulder. 'Max, it's your capability that reassures me you'll be excellent. I wouldn't offer if I thought any different.'

'Appreciated, thank you.'

'Right, I'll be back in a few minutes, excuse me.'

Others might not have noticed anything different in Romilly as she approached the crew room, but he saw. He knew.

'Hi,' she said, trailing her case and sipping a from a large take-out.

The smile was in place, the uniform was smart. It was her eyes.

'Welcoming committee?'

'Of a sort. How did it go this morning?'

'As expected. Thanks for your text. Sorry, it was a busy few hours.' The apparent ease with which she dismissed the emotional toll she had taken didn't surprise him. He looked her straight in the eye.

'How are you feeling? Be honest.'

'Excuse me? I'm always honest. It was upsetting – Dad wasn't at his best and I've had to leave Benita to settle him. I'll speak to her as soon as we've landed. I'm all right; the double shot is kicking in.'

He tried again. 'Remember that I know you, and what this morning has likely to have taken out of you.'

'I'm safe,' she said, her tone a little testier.

Nathan hesitated, formulating a sentence of carefully chosen words.

As he did so, a steely expression wiped her smile. 'I repeat, I'm safe. I can block out and focus – you know I can.'

'For everyone's safety, I feel it's worth you delaying your cockpit duties until later in the flight. I've asked Max to switch roles with you for the outbound. You understand how fatigue affects decision-making, and perception of what's going on.'

'You'd better be joking.'

'Romilly …'

'I've been perfectly okay this morning, handled Dad, the removal men …'

'That's not true, is it? I saw you. You were upset.'

Her mouth hung open as she placed one hand on her hip. 'You were spying on me?'

'Of course not. I was there for moral support in case you needed me. I care about you.'

'As my superior, checking up on me, you mean?'

'No, that was not my main intent. I texted, said I was there for you.' A couple of passing passengers made a double-take at he and Romilly. Two officers of Sterling Air bickering must be a perfect side-show.

'You know *full well* that I'd interpret that as your being available on the other end of the phone, not actually there in person.'

'Keep your voice down. Don't make this personal, Romilly. I'm just doing my job.'

'You're the one making it personal, you … you absolute arsehole!' she spat.

He recognised that her specific choice of words mimicked a text she'd seen from Liz, and winced. 'I think you've just demonstrated that I have made the correct decision,' he levelled, maintaining an authoritative calm.

'There's no way I'm taking the jump seat, then spending hours monitoring fuel burn and babysitting the autopilot.' Her rapidly pinking face almost matched the livid rims of her eyes.

'On this flight, you will be. Or I can call in a cover,' he said, calmly and ruthlessly suppressing the parts of his brain that feared hurting her, that admired how lovely she looked even when she was angry, and how forcibly she fought her corner. 'You can have fifteen minutes to think it over.' Not wanting to watch metal bend, he left her standing on the concourse and returned to the crew room.

'Morning, everyone,' Romilly said, arriving through the door ten minutes' later.

Relieved that she seemed to have reconsidered, Nathan beckoned her over to where he and Max were already consulting the weather channel.

'Hi, Max, hear I'm going to be seeing the back of your head this flight,' she said, taking a chair between them.

'My best view,' he said with a grin. 'Don't worry, I won't let your seat get cold.'

'All right' said Nathan, 'let's start with engineer's report on maintenance checks. Romilly, are you ready?'

'Yes. As I said, I can block out and focus, Captain Reed.' She held his eyes long enough to emphasise her intention. He nodded. The back and forth in their private life, while enticing, exciting, and at times confusing, had no place interfering with how they carried out their duties – whatever the personal cost.

Max shot Nathan a wary look, then returned to reading the reports.

'Good to hear. Let's concentrate on these papers, shall we?'

Outside the Terminal at San Francisco Airport, their crew van was filling up. Romilly was one of the last to take a seat, slipping her phone into her pocket after concluding a phone call. Despite the chilly atmosphere on the flight deck, all tasks during her shift cover had been performed efficiently and professionally, true to her word. Nathan had expected no less. Nothing else had been said, though he felt her eyes stabbing into the back of his head when he decided to assign Max to land them, which he'd managed perfectly well.

Now she was avoiding anyone's eye contact, choosing instead to stare out of the van's side windows. He would just have to wait until they were in their suite. He hoped that she had received good news from home, and that she'd had time to reconcile his decision-making at Heathrow as being warranted. Per usual, he joined reception's check-in queue behind his cabin crew. Though unusual for captains, Nathan had found that his crews appreciated the gesture. Often, they were short on time, headed straight out for the evening, whereas he preferred to unpack and head to the bar at his own pace. Max and Steph were ahead of him, sharing a private laugh; in front of them was Romilly, keeping her own company. As she reached the front, she spent longer than usual with the receptionist, then, without a backward glance, headed towards the lifts.

After Max and Steph had received their keys, Nathan stepped forwards.

'Good evening, Captain Reed, welcome back to The Beaumont,' said a friendly male receptionist.

'Thank you.'

'Here is your card key, you're in room 442, fourth floor.'

Nathan frowned, confused by the man's allocation. 'The airline has reverted from sharing the suites?'

'No, it's still a combination of double rooms and suites.' The receptionist consulted his computer screen. 'It seems there's been a last-minute reshuffle after a particular telephone request was made for yourself and the pilots to be the ones allocated to the single rooms for the duration of this stay.'

Nathan sighed. 'That's probably correct. Thank you.'

'Also, I've been passed this for you – apparently there's a time-sensitive message inside.' The man slid a white envelope across the counter, bearing '*Captain JR Reed*' in a blue cursive. Nathan wracked his brain as to whether he'd ever seen Romilly's handwriting, beyond the tick boxes and numbers of the cockpit charts.

'Thank you.'

'Enjoy your stay.'

'I hope to.'

Room 442 was perfectly adequate. Quiet, facing a glass-walled office block whose workers had long since clocked-off. After his standard unpacking, Nathan sat on the edge of the bed, steadying himself for the contents of the envelope.

Dear Captain Reed,

Very pleased to confirm that I have secured two tickets on your behalf to Verdi's La Traviata *(in three acts) for tomorrow night (Tuesday 23rd) at the Golden Gate Park Amphitheatre.*

Please contact the Concierge Desk on extension 400 at your convenience, to arrange payment.

Sincerely, Bill (Concierge)

34. Viva l'Italia

Romilly's shoes lay discarded just inside the door. For once she hadn't unpacked her case the moment that she'd walked in; instead, she lay splayed out on the bed trying to regroup. On the positive side, after the emotional challenge of moving her dad, news from Benita was that, so far, he had settled well. He had enjoyed an afternoon watching *Antiques Roadshow* with a slice of fresh cherry cake, in view of Cranes Park's rear gardens.

The view of things in downtown San Francisco, however, fared worse. Nathan had texted, saying he was headed for a nightcap at the Sky Bar. He'd included an emoji waving a white flag. She'd declined. Bone tired, and still in her shirt and trousers, Romilly let her eyelids close, desperate for the sweet relief of sleep.

No. It was no use. Just as when she had stared at the bunk above her in the plane's crew quarters, Nathan's actions still riled her. His underhanded methods, his undermining of her ability, his unfair assumptions – basically everything and anything 'un' she could fire at him. She sat up, roughly repositioning pillows to prop behind her, and caught her reflection in the dressing table mirror. She halted, eyes resting on her three-striped shirt epaulettes, and thought of Nathan's four, and what the extra stripe demanded of him. Whether he liked it or not.

'You'll be a captain one day,' she said to herself. 'What would you have done in the circumstances?'

Carter acknowledged Romilly as she approached the bar.

'Sorry that we only have the pianist this evening – a bit different from your party last week.'

Was that only a week ago?

Nathan swivelled on his barstool towards her, his expression careful. 'Glad you came. Was about to up the ante on my "truce" messaging.'

'What would that have been?' she replied, with a half-smile.

He shook his head at her. 'Hopefully you'll never have to know. Drink?'

She eyed Nathan's whisky. 'One of those, please.'

Nathan picked up the crystal tumblers and slid off the stool. 'Over by the window?'

Romilly nodded, following him to a leather, button-backed sofa. She positioned herself at one end; he sat at the other. A perfunctory scan of the glittering view filled an awkward silence. Nathan turned towards her.

'What news from your dad?'

She shook her head, still aimed at the windows. 'First, tell me why you were there.'

'Does that need saying? I should hope it was obvious.'

'You should have said something,' she said, holding up her hand to stop him interrupting, 'and not via an ambiguous text.'

Nathan took a minute, and several sips of whisky. 'Yeah. I'm sorry.'

'But?'

'No buts. I messed up. Should have asked if you'd like me there. Definitely should have told you I was *actually* there. Communication is a work in progress. Ask my daughter, she of two matching Disney watches.' Looking pensive, he ran a hand through his hair, then focused heavily creased eyes on something outside in the distance. 'Clearly I'm still going to fuck up occasionally.' He grimaced, then swallowed another sip from his tumbler.

As if she were perfect. At least he had owned up to his mistakes, however miserable it made him.

She took a sip of her own drink and waited for the peaty warmth to dissipate. 'The first thing is, I'm used to doing things alone.'

'I know that, Romilly,' he said softly.

'It's not easy to ask for help, and I've reasons to avoid close relationships. It scares me a bit.'

He shuffled along the sofa a fraction closer to her. 'Whatever those reasons are, I promised your dad I wouldn't hurt you.'

'When did you say that?'

'In his hallway while looking at his model planes. We understood each other, I think. Is there a second thing?'

Romilly faltered. She'd expected he would ask about her 'reasons', but typically, he'd given her the room to speak her truth at her own pace. 'Well, the second thing is, I'm sorry, too. You absolutely made the right call to switch me with Max today. You were doing your job, and that can't have been easy. Forgive me.' She forced herself to hold his eye contact.

He cast a quick look over his shoulder for other customers at the bar and opened his hand on sofa, reaching across the space between them. 'Forgiven.'

She grasped his hand and smiled. 'Thank you … for being there, for not giving up on me and whatever this is between us.'

When she slid a little closer, he brought her hand to his lips and kissed it, briefly closing his eyes. 'Christ, you worried me on the flight deck. I imagined you strapping on your hypothetical parachute, getting ready to evacuate.'

'Not much you could have done if I had.' She smirked.

'You think so? The way I'm feeling, I'd have jumped out after you.' His eyes burned with sincerity as something raw and heartfelt passed between them. Romilly reached for her glass, shaken by the sudden depth of feeling.

Carter appeared, collecting abandoned empties from nearby tables. 'Another round, folks?'

Romilly drained the last of her drink. 'No, thank you, I should be going, long day.'

'Me neither. But thank you for checking.'

'Very good.' Carter nodded and retreated towards the bar with his tray.

'Really hope I sleep well tonight,' she said, releasing his hand and rolling her shoulders.

'Perhaps a quiet start is needed tomorrow. How about you use the hotel spa in the morning, get yourself a massage?'

'Maybe, I'll see how I feel when I wake up.'

Nathan studied the view for a moment, as if to bide some time. 'Listen, I was thinking of heading off to take some shots of the bridge tomorrow morning, but if you're up to it late afternoon, there's an Italian Festival downtown – various restaurants are offering small bites to passers-by. Might be worth a look. Obviously, won't be as good as our bolognaise, though.' He smiled.

Despite feeling tired to the point of shakiness, the punch of attraction was as powerful as ever. 'That sounds good to me. I'm sorry about the rooms as well, by the way. Kind of regret that now – not that I've got a bean of energy right at this moment.'

'You made your point. But just know that I'll be thinking of you, asleep somewhere else in this huge place.'

'I'll message you tomorrow then.' She yawned. 'Sorry, got to go.' She surveyed the bar to see whether it was still empty, then kissed him lightly. He caught the nape of her neck and in return, kissed her mouth tenderly. Sighing, she forced herself to her feet.

'Sleep wel— Oh, that's my phone … Got to take this,' he murmured.

She blew him a kiss, just as he connected to a videocall.

'How's my little princess – enjoying half term so far?'

'Mini bruschetta?' a young waitress tilted a red-checked tray towards Romilly and Nathan as they lingered outside another Italian restaurant the following afternoon.

'Thank you,' said Nathan. 'Want one?'

Romilly nodded, though she was almost full of mini pizza, individual ravioli, and antipasti that they had already indulged in during their saunter through the

Battery district of trendy warehouse conversions that were bedecked in Italian flags.

'Delicious,' she mumbled as fragrant basil oil and sweet ripe tomato burst onto her tongue.

Nathan stepped closer. 'Just, let me …' He dabbed his thumb along one corner of her mouth, an intimacy oblivious to the bustle around them. Only the slimmest ring of his brown irises remained visible as he tasted it. 'Yes, I'd say so.' Romilly swallowed as her insides responded to his unspoken need.

They moved on, the air thick with garlic and a building thirst for more than the samples of chianti they'd tried. Her energy levels restored, thanks to a good night's sleep and The Beaumont's spa, that had worked wonders for Romilly that morning, she was all for returning to the hotel with this gorgeous man. 'I don't think we'll need dinner tonight,' she groaned, waddling her bloated stomach up one of the district's steep paths. 'So … maybe we could go back to the Sky Bar, and watch the sunset?'

'We could, but there is another option,' said Nathan, cocking a cheeky eyebrow.

'That might come after the chatting part.'

'In that case, let's go.' He pretended to get ready to run, making her laugh.

She patted his chest. 'No, no, tell me your idea.'

'Okay. Do you like orchestral operatic recitals?'

Romilly couldn't help but smirk. 'Of all the things I thought you might be about to suggest, that wasn't one of them.'

'As part of the Festival, the San Francisco Symphony Orchestra is performing Verdi's *La Traviata* in the outdoor concert space at Golden Gate Park.

There are heaters and blankets – I've seen pictures of candlelit couples' seating; it looks quite romantic.'

'Captain Reed! Pulling something romantic on me …' she teased. 'And I suppose, though it's very popular, that you've somehow managed to get—'

'Tickets, yes.' He pulled two silver-edged cards from the inside of his jacket. 'But if this isn't your idea of fun, just say so and we'll find another way of amusing ourselves.'

She fixed her eye contact, aware that this could not have been a spur-of-the-moment idea. 'When does it start?'

'In forty minutes or so. A cab would get us there in ten minutes.'

Steph's mantra pricked at her conscience. 'All right, let's give it a try. Can't say I've ever heard opera live.'

'Fantastic, let's get ourselves over there then.'

A driverless taxi passed them, with two nervous-looking passengers in the back. 'But let's not use one of those,' she said. 'Can you imagine how twitchy we'd be?'

'Completely with you there. Did you see the latest article on pilot-less air-travel?'

'I did. Not in my lifetime, thank-you-very-much. Boeing autopilot is one thing, but if there's emergency flying to be done, I'd like a qualified pilot on hand.'

'Roger that. How about we try one of the streetcars? We've photographed them enough …' he said, gesturing at the queue of people at a stop ahead.

'I'd love that. You know, I realised what their circular chrome lights and fifties retro styling reminds me of? Pimped-up VW camper vans. I always fancied a weekend away camping in one of those, somewhere like the Welsh mountains.'

Nathan chuckled. 'I know what you mean, they do look like them – so let's have a retro journey to the park in one of those then – and maybe you should put a camper van holiday on your bucket list.'

She nodded and glowed inside. She actually had something on her bucket list.

Romilly had never seen so many candles, nor such a glorious, leafy setting. Hundreds of pairs of cushioned seating curved in an amphitheatre configuration were aimed at a circular stage that was set up with instruments and chairs, ready for the performance.

'Looks like blankets are available from over there, if you want them for a bit later,' said Nathan. 'Just in case the gas heaters don't keep the chill off.'

'I'll go and get us some,' she said, spying the lengthy queue.

'All right, I'll find the drinks tent. Here's your ticket.' He kissed her gently. 'See you in the seats.'

Romilly set off in the opposite direction, absorbing the atmosphere of excited anticipation among fellow concert goers. She couldn't remember feeling so happy. In the queue, she had just pulled out her phone to take a few shots of starry sky peeking through the tree canopy when she saw Max coming towards her, carrying two blankets.

'Well hello, look who's here! Didn't have you down as a culture vulture,' he said, awkwardly avoiding her eye contact.

'Nor you,' she countered, unsure whether she felt offended or might even be resenting him having flown the outbound from her seat.

'Ah, well Verdi's *Four Seasons* is the balm of the middle classes, much friendlier, mainstream audiences. Isn't this place amazing?'

'It's really quite special. We ... I mean, I can't wait for it to start.'

'Me neither, but got to get these blankets over to ...the seats. See you tomorrow lunchtime. Enjoy!' And with that, he had left her.

She took a couple of steps forward in the queue, realising that neither had asked the other whom they were there with.

Three hours later, Romilly propelled herself through dizzying revolving doors into The Beaumont's reception, soul bursting from the experience of enchanting music, bloodstream fizzing with half a bottle of sparkling wine.

'That, was a *fantastic* night,' she said, feeling Nathan's protective arm slide around the small of her back as they headed for the lifts.

'It was,' he chuckled. 'But I'm thinking perhaps we should give the bar a miss. Bottle to throttle and all that.' She caught the wink of his glittery eyes.

'Good idea. Bed's calling.'

'What's your room number?' he asked, finger hovering near the row of buttons inside the lift.

'Four-four-two, I think.'

'You're sure?'

She glanced at the cardboard sheath for her room key, then it slipped from her fingers. 'Whoops. Yep, I'm sure.'

Nathan retrieved it, then depressed the button for the fourth floor, shaking his head. 'Can't believe that.'

'The wine was strong – I was all right until we stood up to come back here.'

'No, it's not that,' he said, taking her hand as they exited the lift. Within a few seconds they were outside her room. He used her card to open the door for her.

'Sorry again about the rooms,' she murmured, stepping inside. God, her bed looked inviting and this hunky man even more so.

'Don't be, I'm only in the next room. Really wish I'd known that last night.' He cocked his head at the interconnecting door to his room.

She zig-zagged over to it and slid open the secure bolt. 'Just in case one of us needs the other. For … something.' Nathan's eyes were twinkling at her. God, this man was hot.

'I'll do the same in a minute, just need to freshen up. You'll be okay?'

'Yep.' She gave him a thumbs-up.

Nathan laughed. 'See you soon then.'

'If not before. Thank you for a wonderful time.'

He kissed her forehead and left. A few seconds later, inside her room came the click of his interconnecting bolt sliding open. She stared at the doorknob, the proxy for him having really understood and forgiven her. It didn't turn. She lay on the bed watching it, letting the battle of nerves commence.

35. Communication

There was a difference between being alone and being alone without Romilly. In the few weeks Nathan known her, she had begun to make him feel whole again: understood, desired, needed, more like his old self – better even. He lay on his bed, aching for her, emotionally and physically. The anticipation of skin against skin, of coaxing her to a peak of ecstasy and losing himself inside her was almost enough to turn the handle of their interconnecting door, but having already made the first move, earlier at the bar, it was now over to her.

Unfortunately, she might have been thinking the opposite, because the next he knew he had jolted awake to a room streaming with early morning daylight. He checked his phone, and, seeing that it was almost eight am, skimmed his emails, acknowledging a final reminder that he should have locked in his next shift block. He still had first refusal on continuing this route, but he'd held off as long as possible before discussing it with Romilly. The thought of layovers in San Francisco without her made his spirits sink. He stared at the interconnecting door again, then out at the urban sprawl. Who was he kidding? The location wasn't the problem. It was being anywhere without her. Giddy with that realisation, he finished his emails and responded gratefully to a picture from Liz. She had sent a photo of a captivated-looking Nora on her lap as they looked at photographs of some ducklings and an electric car shaped like a banana that he'd captured yesterday morning. He had sent them for Nora in lieu of the videocall he'd suspected might be impossible from the concert. From the genuine smile in the picture, his daughter seemed much happier, being on half term.

Nathan listened at the interconnecting door for any sound of activity. Silence. He pulled on his running gear and headed downstairs.

'Morning Bill,' Nathan said, pausing at the concierge desk.

'Hello, sir. Was the concert to your liking, last night?'

'Very much – it was an excellent suggestion, thank you. I hope you and your wife enjoyed it?' Nathan made a mental note to mention Bill's excellent service to the hotel management.

'We did, thank you. In three weeks' time, a winter ice-rink sets up in that space ready for a series of Thanksgiving events and eventually the popular Christmas markets. Worth a visit – the organisers create winding paths of ice that you skate on through the trees, leading to the main rink. With hot chocolates and brass bands there, it's on most people's calendars.'

He could easily imagine Romilly at those, bundled up as they took it all in together. 'Good to know, though I'm not sure of my shift block beyond this one yet.'

'If I can be of any help, just let me know.'

Nathan zipped up his running jacket. 'I will. Thank you. Off for a circuit past the Ferry Building, back in forty minutes.'

'Excellent morning for it.'

He had sprinted the final block back to the hotel, and was awaiting a lift to the fourth floor, sweat still pouring, endorphins pumping, when the nearest doors opened. Inside, Romilly gazed out at him. From the looks of her damp gym wear, and flushed face she'd just completed several rounds of cardio in the hotel's basement gym.

'Hey,' she said, smoothing hair away from her face.

He stepped in and the doors closed. 'Hey yourself. Sleep well?'

'Eventually, after I'd stopped staring at the doorknob.'

'Same.' He smirked. 'Poor communication. Please let's not do that again.'

Romilly's chuckle was swamped by thick silence when they exited on the fourth floor a few seconds later, headed for their rooms.

'Showers, then packing?' he said, clearing his throat.

'Showers, then packing.' She opened her door. 'See you later, then.'

'Yes. Later.'

Inside his room, he gulped down the last of his water bottle. Possessed by unstoppable instruction from below the waist, his feet took him to the interconnecting door. He'd been about to put a hand to the doorknob when it started to turn. Round, round it went, and then the door flicked opened towards him.

'I was just wondering, is your shower bigger than mine?' she said, eyes searing into his as she leaned casually against the door frame.

Taking her by the hand, he pulled her inside.

Romilly lay sprawled across him, slowly recovering her normal breathing rate. The most intense orgasm of his life had blown his circuits and it was taking several minutes to string together anything meaningful.

'That was incredible,' he managed, pulling her tight to him, their bodies once again slick with sweat.

'It was, I've never felt so ... connected, ever. But—'

He wiped some sweat from his eyes. 'Christ, no buts – I don't think anything else would be possible in a shower cubicle that size.'

'I was only going to say we've got to watch the time.' She kissed his chest and playfully grazed his nipples with her teeth.

He hissed, and ran his hands over her body. 'We're going to exhaust each other at this rate and fail our "I'm safe's".'

'All right, let's pause it there,' she groaned. 'We need food and another shower. What time is it?' She reached an arm over the bedside table for his phone, frowning as she handed it to him.

'It's okay, we have at least ninety minutes before meeting in the lobby for transit,' he muttered, noting a message on the front screen from Liz: '*You're welcome. x*'.

'I need to order room service and get organised. See you downstairs?' Romilly darted around the room and into his en-suite, gathering her discarded gym clothes.

'Downstairs,' he breathed, admiring her stunning figure.

'One last kiss.' She bent down to the bed. The slow, sensual sliding of her tongue against his almost snapped his willpower, and of their own accord his hands sought her head, pulling her back closer.

'No,' she muttered, with minimal conviction. 'I've got to go.'

He released her, with a final soft, kiss. 'See you in the lobby.'

The bubble of buoyant chatter among the crew in the hotel lobby signalled that they'd enjoyed their layover as much as him. Maybe not *quite* as much. Romilly would be last to arrive; he now recognised the pattern. Initially, he thought it a reflection on her timekeeping; but it was, he'd realised, borne of historical reliance on herself, and deliberately keeping others at arm's length. Avoiding personal conversations. Though he considered himself lucky to have come to know her, among many others who did not – he wouldn't take it for granted. Communication was important. Once they were home, he would somehow carve out time while having Nora, for he and Romilly to really talk, if she wanted to. Physically, she had given herself entirely, but there was still a corner behind those beautiful eyes that shuttered away something difficult. Not that there was anything she could tell him that would change how he felt, but it would be good to finally join the dots behind her father's early retirement and whatever her twenties had thrown at her.

He approached the nearest group of cabin crew, who were laughing with Steph. 'Morning, everyone, how are we all?'

'Almost ready for transit,' said Steph, who seemed even cheerier than usual. 'Just waiting for three of mine.'

'Very good. Forecast looks fine; everything's on schedule.'

The group murmured their appreciation, and someone might have said something else, but the crook of his eye locked on Romilly who walked towards them, fresh faced and immaculate. This woman.

'Hello,' she said. 'Everyone looks happy this morning.'

'As do you,' Steph replied, 'and yes, we were all just saying what a great city San Francisco is – so much to do on layover. Great sights, amazing food, the festivals. We haven't visited Alcatraz Island yet, either, but plan to next week, if anyone's interested.'

'Sounds good,' said Nathan. 'I've heard there are other concerts coming up, too.'

'Yes, they seem to perform everything from Vivaldi to hip-hop. Though Vivaldi is the balm of the middle classes, apparently.'

Romilly cocked her head at Steph. '*Interesting* expression.'

Steph shrugged. 'Heard it somewhere.'

Nathan consulted his watch. 'Quick catch up with Max before we jump in the transit?' he said to Romilly. She smiled at him. Bloody hell, he would have to work hard at blocking out the effect of it for the next fifteen hours or so.

'Excuse us,' he said, as he and Romilly turned their backs slightly to the group, to where Max stood.

'I hope you had a *really* good layover,' Romilly said to Max.

Nathan glanced at her, hearing a loaded meaning. First Steph, now Max?

'I did. Very much. And you?' Max slanted his eyes at her.

'I did very much, also, thank you.'

'Right, well if you're both finished with the weird update, I'll just confirm that we will revert to the original first and second officer positions for inbound.'

'Understood,' said Max, nodding, 'As I expected.'

'Me too. I brushed the back of my hair especially neatly for you,' said Romilly, patting her ponytail.

'Very funny.'

'Walk-around, complete,' said Romilly, climbing into her seat on the flight-deck.

'Ground checks complete,' Nathan acknowledged.

'Crystal-clear skies – for once it should be a pretty view out of here,' she said, retrieving pilot sunglasses from her flight bag.

'Yes, it will be. Are you happy to take us up?'

'Thank you.' She nodded, with enthusiasm.

Her patent adoration for flying lit her up. At least, it was probably that. Enough, he admonished himself, time to focus. Concentrating on the seventy-six-step checklist would certainly help. 'Right, let's commence the procedures. Ready?'

'Ready.'

Twenty-five minutes later, when Max was settling into his place on the jump-seat, a ring sounded from the cabin manager intercom.

'Flight-deck,' said Nathan.

'Passenger boarding complete, Captain.'

'Thank you, Steph.'

He switched his headset channel. 'Tower, Sterling 299 boarding complete, ready for push back.'

'Sterling 299 standby for pushback.'
'Standing by, Sterling 299.'

36. Gear Up

Romilly guided the plane along the yellow lines of the prescribed taxiways and awaited clearance from tower to turn onto the runway. In the queue, she rechecked her instruments, anticipation building. On a regular day at the controls, adrenaline would be pumping, but today, fresh from a layover that had seen her relationship with Nathan reboot and deepen, she felt almost dual-fuelled. She hadn't expected that anything could compare with the prospect of flying three hundred and thirty tonnes of plane into the sky at a speed F1 drivers only dreamed of.

'Sterling 299, you are cleared for take-off.'

'Cleared for take-off, Sterling 299,' confirmed Nathan. He reached across to the central throttles and rested his hand behind hers. 'Take us home.'

Channelling everything into her task, she eased the controls forwards and turned the yoke to line up with Runway 28R's bright green lights. Soon, they were roaring past queues of planes on the taxiways.

'Eighty knots, hold,' said Nathan.

'Cross checks.'

She waited the final few seconds for his instruction to pull back on the yoke.

'Rotate.'

Up she took them in a steep climb, not a cloud anywhere.

'Positive rate.'

'Positive rate checks. Gear up,' she requested.

Nathan pushed the lever to retract the wheels.

Below their feet, the expected rumble of the nose wheel being lifted inside its flap was instead replaced by the grinding squeal of metal against metal, then a loud bang. She glanced at him.

'Negative, switching to manual retraction.' He pressed the button of the back-up option.

Silence screamed at them.

'What's happened?' said Max, over Nathan's shoulder.

Nathan frowned. 'Not sure – I think the rear wheels are up, nose wheel uncertain. Just checking the exterior cameras. Standby.'

Still hand-flying, she felt his eyes on her and turned. 'What?'

'Looks like the nose wheel has somehow twisted. I'll try again, standby.'

Romilly focused on her instruments, while Nathan retried both options, in vain. Immediately, he contacted the airport. 'Tower Sterling 299 pan pan pan, we have an emergency, request circle west, emergency route 1.'

'Sterling 299 confirmed, take route 1, state nature of emergency.'

Nathan turned to Romilly. 'Follow Emergency route 1.'

'Emergency route 1, Roger,' she confirmed.

'Tower, standby, nose wheel un-retractable, possible damage. Will advise, Sterling 299.'

'Sterling 299 acknowledged, switch to dedicated coms channel 7.5.'

'Switching to coms channel 7.5, confirmed, Sterling 299.'

Romilly diverted the plane onto the emergency route out across the Pacific and trailed a pre-prescribed wide circle while a plan was decided.

'I can't see from the video link because the camera has slipped out of position, but it looks as if the nose wheel is pointing sideways,' said Nathan.

'Eyes on the ground need to verify,' she offered, 'obviously without getting anywhere near to the runway.'

'Not that we can land like this anyway,' said Max. 'Not without making an awful mess of the runway with the nose of the plane, at least.'

Nathan glanced over his shoulder. 'Hold it together, Max, we've just got to work through the problem. Romilly, keep us circling, maintain altitude.'

'Roger.'

'Tower, I think a low pass is necessary to verify the condition of our nose-wheel, Sterling 299.'

'Confirmed, Sterling 299 standby, will clear a slot in traffic.'

'Standing by, Sterling 299.'

'Passengers are going to be wondering why we keep banking back towards San Francisco,' said Romilly.

'Yep, just waiting for Tower.'

'Don't think I've covered this in the simulator,' muttered Max.

'Sterling 299 you are cleared for a low pass at a hundred feet, approach runway 28R from the south.'

'Tower, confirmed, thank you, Sterling 299.'

Nathan cleared his throat. His contained manner belied the enormous responsibility for the situation they were in. Romilly offered him a small smile of reassurance, which he returned. He took a breath, then switched his headset to the cabin PA.

'Ladies and gentlemen, this is Captain Reed again. You've probably noticed that we haven't reached altitude, and instead have been circling out over the Pacific at around fourteen thousand feet. We have an unusual technical issue with our nose wheel that will necessitate a brief fly past of the control tower back at San Francisco Airport for observation. After we have spoken to them, I will come back to you with an update. Please remain seated, with your seatbelts on. Thank you.'

Romilly rolled her shoulders. She hadn't carried out a real-life low pass like this in a 777 before, but she was confident in her ability, even in these circumstances.

'I can take her through if you need,' said Nathan, attuned as ever, 'then we'll have to circle to burn off fuel so you can have her back for that, and engage autopilot. If the engineers and mechanics can't suggest something, our only option is going to be a bumpy emergency landing back at San Francisco.'

'Roger. But I can manage the low pass – leaves you free for all the comms.'

'Roger, so I'll also run the calculations for fuel-burn. Max, pull out the emergency landing checklists, be ready to read them through to us.'

'Roger,' confirmed Max, a little less panicked, and no doubt relieved to have a task to focus on.

The next few minutes passed in an ultra-focused state, monitoring her instruments, watching the horizon, and flying low past the tower. Back out over the sea, and drilling holes in the sky on autopilot, Romilly swallowed hard when Tower confirmed that the nose wheel was indeed presenting at an angle of ninety degrees. Her stomach clenched when engineers on the ground admitted to Nathan that they couldn't be certain of the result on impact.

The airline agreed with Nathan's calculation that two hours of flying was required to burn off sufficient fuel to minimise risk on landing. Relaying this information to Tower, Nathan was informed that, meanwhile, air traffic would be redirected, departures rescheduled, and alerts created for sufficient fire and multiple ambulance vehicles in preparation for the high-risk landing. Romilly could only imagine the extent of chaos their emergency was causing.

'Cabin Manager to flight-deck please, thank you,' said Nathan on the PA.

Moments later came a knock on the door and Steph appeared, heightened colour on her cheeks. 'Tell me some good news.'

Nathan updated her, before saying, 'So, bearing all that in mind, what we need is to ensure your team are revising the brace position with passengers ready for an impact landing and possible rapid evacuation down the escape chutes. Let me know if you have any issues.'

'Will do.' Steph briefly squeezed Max's shoulder on her way out.

'Okay,' said Nathan, 'let me update the passengers, then, Max, we'll start the emergency landing checklist.'

'Roger.'

They were most of the way through the list when a blur of motion caught Romilly's attention in the side windscreen.

'What the hell?' she blurted out as a helicopter drew alongside to within two hundred feet of them and shadowed their route. She automatically returned her hands to the yoke, in readiness to disengage autopilot.

'It's got a camera slung underneath it,' said Max

'Media or emergency services?' Nathan frowned.

'Media, er … Channel KPR.'

'Tower, be advised we have a media helicopter trailing in close vicinity, Sterling 299,' Said Nathan

'Sterling 299, we are aware. Your airline has given permission – the pictures are valuable.'

'Understood, Sterling 299,' Nathan confirmed, then turned to Romilly. 'We'd better not hit it, then.' His fraction of a smile slightly eased her tension.

'Pity they didn't arrive sooner – wouldn't have had to go for the low pass,' muttered Max behind them.

There was a knock on the door again, and Steph reappeared. 'Passengers need some reassurance, Captain. Clusters of them are freaking out. We are a live story on the news channel.'

'What?' He switched the flight-deck's small screen from the exterior camera view to the news channel and turned up the volume.

'*What we know so far is that the nose wheel on Sterling Air's flight ST299 bound for London's Heathrow from San Francisco International is stuck pointing sideways, making any usual landing impossible. An ex-military pilot predicts that chances of survival depend on whether the landing gear completely collapses backwards, causing the nose of the fuselage to hit the runway with force and skid uncontrollably, and whether heat generated from metal scraping on the ground could see pieces of hot metal puncture a fuel tank which could then ignite a fire.*'

'For fuck's sake. Cut television transmission to the passenger cabin.'

'Roger,' said Romilly, deselecting the switches on her panel.

A roar of passenger panic pummelled the door.

'Okay, Steph, I'll speak to them.'

'Thank you, Captain, and good luck all of you,' Steph said, leaving the deck swiftly.

'Twenty minutes until optimal fuel level,' said Romilly, having carefully monitored the readings from the tanks in the wings and fuselage.

'Cross-checked,' Nathan said, then depressed the cabin PA button. 'Ladies and gentlemen, this is Captain Reed once again. As you can see, we have disabled the aircraft's entertainment system, as we will be returning to San Francisco International in a few minutes. The airport has a long runway, giving us plenty of room to land. Please listen carefully to your cabin crew for instruction as to how to adopt the correct brace positions. Once we have come to a stop, it is vital that you follow their directions and any other announcements immediately and calmly. Thank you.'

Romilly could only imagine the task underway for Steph and her team, preparing three hundred and sixteen nervous adults and four infants.

37. Messages

'Last items on the emergency checklist,' said Max, 'passengers and cabin crew safety briefings—'

'Checked.'

'And finally, personal voice messages into the black box from cockpit crew.'

'They'll be playing the recording over during investigation, checking our procedures,' Nathan counselled, swivelling his eyes between hers and Max's. 'Take a minute.'

Romilly and Max nodded. Silence hung heavily.

'Max, do you want to record anything?'

'No. I don't.'

'Fifteen minutes till optimums. We'll be ready to begin our approach at the end of this circuit,' said Romilly, then wondered at Max's resolute response.

'Fifteen minutes, checked,' said Nathan, 'Understood, Max, Rom—'

'Sorry, I've changed my mind – I would like to leave a message and then to take a brief moment in the galley,' interrupted Max.

Romilly nodded at a puzzled-looking Nathan.

'Okay, Max, leave your message, then you can have two minutes.'

'Thank you.' He cleared his throat. 'Vater, wie schon gesagt, komm ich nicht zurück.'

The door clicked shut as he left.

Romilly swallowed and looked at Nathan, who was frowning.

'What was that?' he said.

'Something about not coming home, I think. Maybe there was an "already" in there, I'm not sure.'

'Jesus. I'll have a word when he's back. Do you want to leave a message?'

'Don't know if I can,' she said quietly. How had life come to this moment? It was almost surreal. What words could she say for her dad, who'd already lost the love of his life? Would it cause him more pain than comfort to hear it, even confusion?

Nathan reached his hand across the thrust levers and slipped it over hers, warm and strong. He stroked her fingers. 'Only if you want to.'

She stared at the horizon, then took a deep breath. 'Dad, thank you for everything. I love you very much. Benita, thank you for taking such good care of him.' That was all she could manage, without breaking. She still had a job to do.

Continuing to hold her hand, Nathan nodded, then inhaled. 'Mum, Dad, thank you for a wonderful life, I love you very much. Nora, Daddy loves you, be happy. Liz, thank you for raising our beautiful daughter. To the magnificent crew of Sterling 299, thank you for your service and friendship.' He suddenly gripped her hand very tightly and turned to face her. 'And to First Officer Romilly West, my co-pilot whom I'm certain will one day be in charge of us all, thank you for everything.' Swallowing hard, he brought her hand to his lips, then released it.

The door swung open, making them both jump. Max took his place on his seat. 'How long til landing?' he asked, gruffly.

'Ten minutes. We're on the approach,' said Romilly, snapping her focus back.

Nathan turned in his seat. 'Max, we've been trained and tested for nose-wheel failures in the simulators. Hold your nerve.'

'Roger that. Lots to live for.'

'Exactly,' said Nathan, cracking his fingers and buckling down his shoulder harnesses. 'All right, let's bring this girl back safely. We can do this. Disengage autopilot.'

'Autopilot off, checked,' Romilly confirmed.

'I have control.' He slid his hands onto his yoke.

'You have control, checked,' said Romilly, hovering both hands near her set, as per protocol. 'Good luck.' A trickle of sweat wriggled down her back. She breathed deeply a few times. Hold. Your. Nerve.

For five minutes as the ground came ever nearer, they were silent, time simultaneously dragging and hurtling. Romilly checked everything she could think of, re-fixed her shoulder harnesses, and pulled her ponytail tighter. She cast a glance at Nathan, but his view was fixed on his approach towards the airport markers. She peered over her left shoulder at Max, who winked and nodded. They were all as ready as they'd ever be.

With two minutes to touchdown, Nathan had the plane lined up perfectly. 'Brace for impact,' he ordered.

'Roger,' said Romilly, then pressed the passenger cabin PA button. 'Brace for impact. Brace for impact.'

Behind the door, Steph and her crew begin to shout, 'Head down, hands over your head; head down, hands over your head.'

One hundred and thirty-five knots felt more like five hundred when the rear landing gear hit the runway. By adjusting flaps and engaging degrees of air brakes, Nathan skilfully kept the nose gear off the ground for as long as possible as they rolled along on the rear wheels. Romilly monitored the news channel's live feed view, as well as her instruments and Nathan's face, which was set rigid in supreme concentration as he precisely flared the nose of the plane downwards.

Within seconds of the stricken wheel connecting with the runway, an intense smell of thick burning rubber filled the cockpit, accompanied by violent screeching of metal as the tyres burnt away and its axel sawed along the tarmac. Romilly gripped her yoke to help Nathan absorb vibration so vigorous that his whole body was being shaken.

'Wheel fire,' she called, seeing the news channel zoom in on sparks that had ignited remnants of hot tyre rubber. She prayed that no parts of it would shoot off into the engines or fuel tanks.

'Almost there,' said Nathan, hyper focused. 'Almost … there.'

Either side of the aircraft, fire engines raced alongside them, ready to intercept the moment the plane came to a halt.

A piercing alarm sounded in the cockpit, accompanied by a warning light that all pilots dreaded, flashing red. 'Fire in Engine 1,' Romilly called out, teeth chattering through the vibrations from her yoke.

Per their training, as second officer, Max double-checked her. 'Confirm, Fire in Engine 1.'

'Shutting off fuel tank valve,' Romilly stated, closing off electrics and hydraulics in the engine as well as other fire ignition sources.

'Shut down 1 checked,' said Max.

As Nathan grappled with the lack of steering while fully applying the air brakes needed to bring the plane to a gradual stop, Romilly continued with her ingrained procedures to handle the engine fire.

'Tower, Sterling 299, we have fire in Engine 1, shut off procedures followed.'

'Sterling 299, Fire Services ready.'

Finally, in the middle of the runway 28R, that they had taken off from just over two hours earlier, they came to a creaking halt.

Nathan switched his headset to the Cabin PA. 'Cabin crew at your stations. Cabin Manager, report.'

Steph was quick to call through, coughing. 'Smoke in the cabin, Captain.'

'Roger. Evacuate right. Evacuate right.'

'Evacuate right, roger,' she spluttered.

Nathan immediately flicked his headset to the passenger cabins. 'This is the captain. Evacuate, evacuate. This is an emergency, evacuate.'

'Tower, Sterling 299, mayday, mayday we are evacuating right side onto the runway. Repeat: mayday, mayday, we are evacuating right side onto the runway,' said Romilly.

'Sterling 299 evacuation right side to runway, confirm, transportation approaching.'

'Tower, acknowledged, Sterling 299, thank you.'

Nathan turned to Max. 'Commence evacuation checklists.'

'Roger.'

On automatic, Nathan and Romilly responded to Max's clear but rapid-fire instructions, whipping through the list of switches and power-downs required before donning oxygen face masks to leave the cockpit.

In the main cabin, the last of the passenger evacuation was still underway, and, per protocol, Romilly, Nathan, and Max took up their places at the open doors on the right of the plane, away from the last of tall flames and smoke pouring from engine one, and three fire engine crews hosing plumes of water. As second officer, Max went to assist cabin crew at the rear slides, while Romilly positioned herself to the front. Astonishingly, some passengers were still raking through bags for belongings, and ignoring instruction to leave. Romilly insisted they left, giving clear authoritative direction. The only thing that mattered was people. If ever there was a time to realise that, surely this was it? Nathan covered the length of the aisles, back and forth, supporting cabin crew's efforts to effect as quick and safe an evacuation as possible by keeping passengers calm but focused, ushering them to the relevant doors and slides, and ensuring heeled shoes were removed as they adopted the correct position to jump onto the escape chutes. Down, down, down, the passengers slid, their wrists grabbed at the bottom by other cabin crew and firemen to leave the area as quickly as possible.

After Nathan confirmed the plane was clear, it was the flight crew's turn to exit. Romilly removed her mask but a quick look back at him earned her a sharp 'Go!', then she flung herself onto the chute, her speed at the bottom halted abruptly by the clever friction tape designed to tilt evacuees forwards and onto their feet. She stumbled onto the tarmac, scuffing the heels of her hands, but was quickly helped up and directed to join others in one of the waiting buses. As it pulled away with a jerk, Romilly clutched a seat-back to steady herself, acknowledging thanks from a few euphoric passengers but watching others cough, cry, and sit on the floor with bloodied noses or cradling limp wrists.

Two men on the seat next to where she stood were exchanging how they'd each left voicemail messages for their families before the landing. The younger of the two still had his phone with him, and hearing that the older man had lost his during the evacuation, offered use of it. Romilly's eyes filled at the older man's gruff gratitude, and at how he'd dissolved into quiet sobs as he left yet another voicemail, saying they'd all survived. That he loved them all so much, and couldn't wait to be home. Nathan. She peered out of the window and back towards the stricken plane, hoping to see him clamber off the chute, or step into another bus, but she was now too far away.

Outside the terminal, people were funnelled by security towards makeshift emergency areas within an unused departure lounge – one section for passengers, another for crew. Inside, paramedic teams were circulating, checking everyone over, treating grazes and cuts, soothing burns from the escape slides to elbows and bare arms, and offering oxygen to those affected by smoke inhalation. Several people seemed to be wearing arm slings. Many were ghostly pale, though perhaps it was Romilly's own light-headedness making them seem that way. Her insides, already flooded with adrenaline, were slowly catching up with the reality that the outcome of the landing might not have been so successful. Her arms and legs began to tremble as she wandered around, looking for anyone she recognised. She vaguely acknowledged the grateful faces of passengers who thanked her for 'an amazing job', all the while she swallowed ominously rancid bile.

Somewhere behind her, male voices were calling her name. She recognised them as belonging to Max and Nathan, but for some reason she had begun to feel woozy, as if waking from general anaesthetic.

'Romilly!' They were beckoning her over to where they stood by some empty chairs.

In a scarily shaky daze, she took herself towards them.

'Balls of steel,' Max was saying to Nathan as she neared.

'Not quite like the simulator, I'll admit. Which by the way, Max, we have all done.'

'I know, wasn't thinking, sorry. Going to request extra practice after seeing you do this. Erm, might just go and check on the cabin crew, okay?'

'Go.'

Romilly sat down heavily on the seat next to where Nathan stood. Everything seemed muffled and numb, like being submerged beneath cold water. Where were they? She didn't recognise this building. Perhaps they should head back to The Beaumont? She liked it there. Safe. Maybe she could see Alcatraz after all. Not the night visit, though. She shivered. Perhaps she ought to speak to someone to be sure that ground crew had unloaded her flight-bags.

'Romilly, are you okay?' said Nathan, clutching her shoulder. 'Romilly?'

38. Safe

'It's shock,' said a young female paramedic to Nathan. 'But nothing more. Reassurance, keep her warm and comfortable, and she should recover in a few hours. The grazes on her palms will heal in a week or so.'

The diagnosis hadn't surprised him. Self-reliant, Romilly naturally internalised everything, so this would of course be no different. What bothered him most was her silence and his being unable to relieve her of the effects she was suffering through conversation. She sat shivering on the chair next to him, with a thin foil blanket around her uniform. All he wanted was to comfort her, but the area was teeming with security and emergency services staff. To his left and right, crew were chatting in small groups, some calling home, some had begun reuniting the baggage which fire crew had retrieved, and others were dispensing hot drinks. Nathan was still their ranked superior, still in uniform. Romilly stared wide-eyed into the distance, and she crossed her arms over her stomach to hug herself. He reached his limit.

'Fuck it,' he muttered, and pulled her onto his lap, into the circle of his arms. 'Sweetheart, you're going to be okay. We're all safe. A hundred per cent safe.' He kissed the top of her head and rocked her slowly.

Gaping seconds passed before her arms slowly curled around his chest, inside his jacket. He breathed a sigh of relief. 'You'll be okay. I've got you.' He closed his eyes and held her tight. If anything would ever happen to her …

By early evening, the cabin crew, admirably overseen by Steph, had been given the all-clear, bar a few scrapes. Nathan had agreed that Max should accompany them back to The Beaumont and see that they had everything they needed. Tomorrow morning would bring the airline's initial investigative video-link interviews and he wanted them well rested.

'Transit has arrived for you two, Captain,' said one of the ground agents. 'But just so you know, there is media interest. Security have cleared a path through.'

'Thank you. Our bags?'

The agent made an enquiry into his walkie talkie, before responding. 'Apparently they are with the earlier transit. Should be waiting for you at The Beaumont.'

'Very good, thanks for everything.'

'I think it's you who deserves the thanks. Good job, sir.'

'Thank you.'

'I'll let security know you're on your way.'

Nathan gently lifted Romilly's chin. 'Ready to head back to the hotel?'

She nodded and stood up. He clasped her hand tightly, vowing to himself not to let go of it.

'Captain Reed! Captain Reed! How does it feel to be a hero?'

Someone jostled against his shoulder, which made Romilly bump against him, so Nathan flung out his arm to keep other media representatives at bay.

'Channel 23 News. Can you say how you felt when you landed? Your quick actions staved off a disaster.'

Digital flashes dazzled, reporters yelled, but briefed earlier on the phone by Sterling's press officer, Nathan said nothing and led Romilly into the waiting van.

'Twenty minutes, and we'll be there,' he murmured into her hair after clicking her seatbelt into place.

She nodded silently, tucked in beside him.

More reporters and photographers awaited them at the hotel entrance. Nathan slid open the transit door to find Bill attempting to keep several of the more determined ones at bay.

'Sir, head straight through to the elevators, floor twenty. A member of staff will be up there to take you to the Presidio Suite.'

'Thank you, Bill.'

Still gripping Romilly's hand, he urged her forwards. 'Last bit. We'll be in the room in no time.'

Finally, after lingering fractionally too long, the duty manager left them to it. As the suite door clicked shut, Romilly dashed to the nearest cloakroom. Nathan found a well-stocked drinks fridge in the spacious kitchen-dining area and poured them both a glass of sparkling water. The sound of echoey vomiting subsided, and he was relieved to see a weak smile on Romilly's face as she joined him on one of the sofas.

'Thank you,' she said, sipping the water. 'I do feel better for that.'

'Is there anything I can get you?' he said, noting that her eyes were the only hint of colour left on her face.

'My bags? That cloakroom had disposable toothbrushes and mouthwash, but still …'

'I think they're in the bedrooms. Hold on, I'll check. Not sure how big this Presidio Suite is.'

'Presidio? That's an ex-military base over by the Golden Gate, isn't it? I was reading about it in a coffee table magazine.'

'We'll add it to our list of places still to explore.' He smiled, relieved at least to see some sign of recovery and engagement, before investigating the suite's layout. If this wasn't the hotel's most expensive one, he'd be surprised. The first two bedrooms, each with their own unique bathroom, faced the Bay Bridge, already bulb-lit against the night sky. Romilly's bags had been deposited in the first of those. The third bedroom he found, where his own bags had been deposited, was clearly the master. A corner room, the central four-poster bed in spiralled dark oak, was impressive, but it was after seeing the adjoining bathroom that made him take action.

'You're going to want that room; I'll move your things,' he said passing her as she came to tentatively investigate his reasoning. If she wanted, he'd take another of the bedrooms.

'Oh my god!' he heard her whistle.

He chuckled, returning to the master suite with her bags. 'Thought so.' She was standing in its bathroom, that overlooked Alcatraz Island and beyond, to the Golden Gate Bridge. But he knew she wasn't admiring the view.

'That has got my name on it,' she said, running her hands along an enormous, double-ended copper bath. She turned on the taps and investigated the selection of oils and bathing products displayed on a marble tray.

'I'll leave you to it. Might order some food, though – you feeling hungry?'

'Could go for something plain-ish.' Though pale, she was nonetheless considerably improved from even thirty minutes earlier. He nodded, and carefully kissed her forehead.

'Enjoy your bath.'

Despite the airline advising that they would leave Nathan to rest until morning, when he, Romilly, and Max would be dead heading on the eleven am inbound to Heathrow, his in-box contained several 'important' emails. Engineers, flight mechanics, representatives from the aircraft manufacturer, human resources, the press office, and the chief pilot all requested his response. Battersea Health Clinic had sent a reminder of his flu vaccination tomorrow afternoon, and Crew Services, while confirming his ticket, had issued an urgent final reminder to lock-in his next block. That still needed discussion with Romilly, which wasn't going to happen tonight. His hand shook slightly as he poured himself some Glenfiddich from the mini-bar, then he stood at the window, decompressing, gazing at nothing in particular. This hadn't been the first air incident of his career, but it had been the worst. Who knew if it would be his last. The job wasn't without risk. He *was* certain that days like these tested more than flying skill, leadership, or nerve; it shed light on what was important. And who.

Nathan was midway through typing out a draft statement of 299's malfunction and the evacuation, when a text arrived from Liz, asking if he was okay. News of the event had reached the UK, on account of Sterling being a British airline, and of course the nature of international media. During the unpleasant period that he and Liz were separating, if a text like this had arrived, it might have sparked his cynical suspicion that all she'd been worried about was his income stream. But tonight, he was too wrung-out to second-guess her mood, so he briefly reassured her and advised uncertainty as to exactly when he would be able to have Nora once home, due to the requirement of meeting with airline investigating officials. For transparency's sake, he acknowledged that it might also impact his prior agreement for the second part of the half-term holidays. Liz must have been feeling charitable, and dismissed any potential inconvenience to her, for once not waving dual custody legalities in his face. They agreed he would videocall Nora in an hour. The prospect of seeing his daughter's face made his heart swell.

Seconds into resuming the incident statement, his phone rang. It was Steph, and being unusual for her to ring him, he answered immediately.

'Is everything alright?'

'Yes, apart from Alex and Sarah, who are resting after smoke inhalation, and Jim who hurt his wrist on the evac, most of the cabin crew had a couple of drinks, then went to their rooms. Others are still at it – whatever they need, really.'

'Quite. And yourself?' he said, detecting her weariness.

'I'll be okay once I've slept. I heard from Crew Services that all our cabin crew are dead-heading tomorrow afternoon. Gives us almost a twenty-four-hour recovery layover here, which is probably for the best. Then the airline has put us all on a week's rest, after our individual investigative interviews. I hear that I'll be representing them at the main review with you, too?'

'Yes, that's correct, but I haven't had confirmation when that will be. Let me know if anything's needed for the crew between now and then. Romilly and I will be away from here at eight tomorrow morning for the eleven am inbound, but have the mandatory post-incident week off afterwards, too.'

The line went quiet.

'I'm guessing that wasn't the only reason why you were ringing?'

'No. This is a bit delicate, really …'

Perhaps this was something to do with Max, who had messaged him earlier to advise he wanted to fly back with the cabin crew, instead of with him and Romilly. Thinking about it, now Max's dash to the galley after his recording his black box message made more sense. He must have gone to speak with one of them, or even to Steph herself.

'It's all right, how can I help?'

'I'm trying to help you, to be honest. Have you seen any media coverage yet?'

'No, why?'

'There are some *pictures*.' Nathan felt his shoulders relax. The media was an area in which he could at least delegate.

'That's fine, don't worry – the airline's Press Officer will liaise with the news channel.'

Silence.

'Steph?'

'They aren't just of the plane and the evacuation. Some are of you … with Romilly.'

He digested the information. 'I'll have a look, thanks for letting me know.'

'Start with the *National Enquirer*, maybe. The story isn't a surprise to the crew, by the way. We're all for it. Been saying so for weeks.'

'Right.' There was a *story*?

'Just before I go – I realise this is awkward to ask, but how's Romilly doing?'

For Steph, he suspended the relationship pretence. 'Better. Enjoying a bath.'

'That's a relief. Pass her my best wishes.'

'I will.'

'Till I see you at Heathrow, then.'

'Thank you, Steph, I appreciate everything you did today. You were excellent, a credit to yourself.'

She sniffed.

'Make sure you're looking after each other, too,' he said, ambiguous in his choice of words, given the potential that Max might be there with her.

'We will. Goodnight.'

Nathan tapped *National Enquirer* into his browser. 'WINGS OF LOVE' said the bold headline on its website, accompanied by dramatic stills from the news footage of their landing and evacuation, then three pictures of him and Romilly. The largest was one of him kissing her head with his eyes closed as he hugged her on his lap. Others were of them holding hands, including a close-up of his white-knuckled grip on her as they entered the transit to the hotel. He studied the pictures carefully, but didn't bother reading far. There was no need. No doubt the airline would also have seen it, and there would be additional questions for him in the morning. He stuffed the phone in his pocket. Better to focus on what really mattered.

39. Bath Talk

Nathan tapped on the bathroom door. 'Are you feeling okay in there?'

'Yes, it's wonderful. Come and talk to me.'

Romilly had piled her hair loosely on top of her head and was gazing out of the window, submerged in bubbles up to her neck. Her face was glistening, the copper bath reflecting an amber tint. On any other day, and despite never understanding the popularity of bathing over showering, he'd be hovering for an invite to lie at the other end – or possibly behind her – but there'd be no doubting where that would lead. 'You look relaxed. And so beautiful. Do you need anything? There are sandwiches out there.'

'No, this is perfect, especially after the day we've had. The metal has kept the water warm for ages. Did I hear you on the phone just now?'

He settled for taking a seat on the stool beside the bath. 'Steph was just checking in. I'll speak to Nora in a bit.'

She swirled some patterns in the bubbles, preoccupied.

'Still thinking about it?' He immediately chided himself at his ridiculous question; how could they not be?

'You know the thing that keeps going around my head? The black box, and what I chose to say.'

He shook his head, keen to allay any regret. 'You did perfectly well.'

The water sloshed as she turned onto her side to face him, clasping wrinkled fingers onto the bath's curved rim. 'No, I didn't say what I should have. You mentioned everyone. And what you said about me was generous.' The stool scraped on the tile as he shifted himself close enough to take her hand.

'We were under pressure. It was difficult, expecting that officials might hear it. But ... what I said wasn't really what I wanted to say, either. The part about you, I mean.'

'No?'

'No.' He locked his eyes on hers, pausing.

She raised an eyebrow at him. 'Nathan?'

'I wanted to say that I'm in love with you, Romilly West, but I was damned if some accident investigator heard it before I had the chance to say it to you in private.'

Now she gawped at him.

'Surely you must know. I'm certain others see, however discreet we've tried to be.'

'Perhaps you're suffering a bit of shock, yourself. The stress of it all,' she whispered.

'No, I've been thinking this way for a while.'

She slipped her hand back into the water. 'I ... don't ...'

'It's all right, I maybe shouldn't have said anything tonight, except that ...'

'Except what?'

He passed her his phone.

'Oh.' She stared at the pictures and scrolled through the article. 'Is there other media coverage?'

'Apparently, but it'll be old news in a day or two,' he said, aiming to dismiss any concern offhand. Enough, today.

She tapped in a search. 'How did they even get these photographs?'

'No idea – a ground worker, emergency service personnel, who knows. Would like to think it wasn't one of the crew.'

'Me either. So, you're not angry about the implication made in these articles?'

'Why? For once they've reported fact.'

Romilly shook her head. 'I think head office might have something to say about this, PR at least. You won't be in trouble, for us being in uniform in the pictures?'

Sensing her increase in tension might undo all the good her bath had achieved, Nathan crouched on the floor, beside the bath, so that his head was level with hers. Softly and slowly, he kissed her, until he felt her relax. 'I'd do the same again, and take whatever comes my way. Things could have turned out very different for us all today – management know that as well as anyone.'

'I know, and thank you, for being there for me.'

'Shock can happen to anyone – could just as easily have been me.'

'Might have struggled getting you onto my lap, though.' She cocked him a rosy-cheeked smile. 'But I'd have tried something. Once I was between your arms, I somehow felt safe.'

'You are safe. And loved.'

'Please …'

'Okay, okay, forget about that at the moment.'

Romilly twisted onto her back again. 'Was Steph all right, when she rang?'

'She will be, and I've a feeling Max was with her.'

'Thought there was a relationships brewing there, especially when she came into the cockpit. Something personal passed between them, you know?'

'I didn't see that, but then there was his black box message. Obviously, I'm aware his surname is German, but there's no detectible accent, is there? He must have been raised or educated in the UK. He sounds more Bristolian than anything.'

'Yeah, I've been thinking about his message, trying to remember my school German. I think what he said was "Father, as I have already said, or maybe as I have already told you, I am not coming home." So perhaps it wasn't quite the "dramatic-doom" that we thought at the time.'

'Some history behind it, by the sound of things. Must have felt strongly enough about it to record those words, though.' Nathan shook his head, feeling thankful for the strong relationship with his own father, then concern for how the woman he loved was coping with hers.

'I wonder … mind if I search for something?' She waggled his phone.

He nodded.

After a minute or two of rapid thumb-typing, reading and more typing, she handed his phone back. 'Maybe it's something to do with this?'

Nathan read aloud: '*Successful charter airline Krügerair is in disarray after founder and CEO, the enigmatic billionaire Otto Krüger, who at 51 had announced his intention to retire at the end of the year, today admitted that his son Max may not be taking over, as originally envisaged. Sources close to the family speak of a rift between Otto and Max's English mother, Sally. It's understood that Max and Sally have refused to visit Germany from their home in Bath for five years. Max is currently a pilot for the British airline Sterling Air. Krügerair is a subsidiary of the conglomerate, Krüger Holdings GmBH, last year reporting pre-tax profits of Euros2bn.'*

Nathan whistled. 'If it's true, then it would explain a couple of things.'

'Definitely the black box message.'

'And his knowledge about luxury boats in the marina, do you remember – the day we cycled the bridge?'

'Not likely to forget that day.' She smiled at him.

Nor was he. 'And his comment about the behaviour of millionaires to Steph.'

'I wonder if she knows about it?'

'I'd hope so – it would be wrong for him to keep something big like this from her, at least not for long. It's shaped his character and is obviously still affecting his present.'

Romilly turned her head away. 'Hmm.'

'Let's keep this between us, though. It's up to them, and specifically Max, as to what he reveals or otherwise.'

They shared silence for a moment, each lost in thought. Nathan would be hugging Nora extra tightly when he got home. He didn't want her suffering from the breakdown of his relationship with Liz.

Romilly was staring at her toes, that peaked out from the bath bubbles. She looked pensive again, perhaps the day's events catching up, once more.

'I think I'll get out, maybe eat something. I need to contact Benita anyway.'

'Take your time, I'll go and videocall Nora. Then maybe we should have an early night – transit is coming at eight am for the trip home.'

'How about those sandwiches in bed, then snuggle until we fall sleep?'

'Sounds good.' Nathan kissed her again and left her to it.

Romilly lay alongside him in bed, one leg hooked over his, her fingers lazily twirling hairs on his chest. He'd have to stop her shortly; it was turning him on. Everything about her did. Though he wanted her badly, her emotional toll had taken quite enough for one day. Not that his hadn't. Were it not for the air incident, and her subsequent shock, the fact that his declaration to her hadn't been reciprocated might have hurt more. As it was, he kept her close, taking comfort from her assumption that they would automatically share a bed. The prospect of days, and nights, ahead without her, once home, filled him with gloom. He stroked her back, trying to shut out images beneath his eyelids of engine fires, evacuation slides, and her frightened face.

'Need you,' she murmured sleepily into his skin.

'Need you, too.'

'Call and resp …'

40. Revelation

At Sterling's check-in, Romilly and Nathan were advised that their seats had been upgraded to business class. She arched a brow at Nathan, but he didn't react. Whether he had exerted some influence, or the airline had felt sufficiently generous or concerned about them to make the gesture of their own accord, she was grateful. Less welcome had been the overnight message to them both from PR, reminding that the usual wearing of uniform while travelling would be required. As they waited at the departure gate to board, conspicuous and smart, she wished they had won that particular negotiation.

Within five minutes of entering the lounge, Nathan had already manfully fended off two groups of women, who showered words like 'hero' and 'life-saving'. A few moments later, an older woman, who had been lurking nearby, approached.

'Hello,' she said adjusting her cardigan, 'you're that nose-wheel captain, aren't you?'

'Yes.' Nathan nodded and smiled politely.

'And this is the one in the pictures?' The woman pointed at her.

Another courteous smile. 'She is.' He craned his neck to see the boarding agent's desk.

'Takes a jolt sometimes to realise how you feel, doesn't it?' said the woman, showing no sign of leaving.

'Yes, I believe it can.'

Romilly glanced at Nathan, careful to conceal the jumble of emotion behind her deliberately modest smile. Not only did this man love her, but he now seemed undaunted by confirming it publicly. For now, at least. Perhaps sensing her trepidation, he interlocked his fingers with hers, solid and reassuring. The woman didn't miss the moment.

'Well done, you, got yourself a brave one there,' she said to her.

Romilly risked a more gracious smile.

'As have I,' said Nathan. 'But if you'll excuse us, we'll be boarding shortly.'

'Absolutely, absolutely, I'll let you two go. Can I just have a quick picture?'

His thumb immediately stroked Romilly's fingers.

'Would you mind if we politely declined?' he said, all charm. 'I can see the ground agents about to announce boarding.'

'Absolutely, absolutely.'

'Thank you for your understanding, it's appreciated. Enjoy your flight.'

'Ladies and gentlemen, thank you for waiting, we will now be boarding rows one to seventeen.' Romilly relaxed at the much-needed tannoy announcement from the desk.

'I will. Such a lovely couple.' The woman blushed, stepping back to allow them access to the gate.

A lovely couple. The words rolled around Romilly's head as she settled into the cocoon of her business-class seat. It seemed a lifetime ago that she'd been referred to as one half of anything.

'Good morning, ladies and gentlemen. This is Senior Captain Alistair Blair, on behalf of the crew of Sterling flight 310 to London Heathrow, I would like to welcome you aboard …'

Romilly sat forwards to share a look with Nathan between their adjoining, retracted privacy shields. Caught unaware, he rapidly replaced something akin to annoyance with a warm smile for her.

'Can't believe it's Alistair!' she mouthed, delighted with the surprise.

'No, neither can I.'

'I wonder who's with him?' She wracked her mind to recall the name of the second officer she'd flown with on the first outbound of her block.

'I'd rather tune out the flight deck patter, to be honest. Do you want the papers before we're served breakfast? I know that we carry a good selection.'

'Yes, although I may skip the tabloids, unless you're wanting a souvenir edition?' She grinned.

'No need, the real thing is beside me,' he said with a wink. She smiled back, amazed at the dizzying effect on her spirits.

Well before the halfway mark of the flight, Romilly had given in and extended her seat into its lay-flat format. Uncertain how long she had been asleep, it was the sound of Nathan speaking to someone which roused her. By the time she had propped herself up, she only saw him disappearing down the aisle towards the galley, behind Alistair. She yawned and rolled over. Perhaps they would bring her back a coffee.

'Hello beautiful.' Nathan beamed an adoring gaze from his seat when she opened her eyes again.

Waking was wonderful when greeted with such tenderness; it somehow filled her with strength, and made her feel special. She no longer felt alone – for as long as this lasted, at least.

'What is it?' Nathan frowned.

'Nothing.'

He waited, as was his way.

'It's just … the way you look at me when I wake up is so … so …' She swallowed, struggling to define the feeling.

'Good, I'd like you to get used to it.'

'I'm afraid to,' she mumbled.

Nathan reached a hand between their seats, and his fingertips stroked her cheek. 'I understand, but take the leap. You know how I feel. By the way, thought you might like one of those.' He pointed at a coffee on her corner table. 'It's probably still hot.'

Grateful for the change of subject, Romilly pressed the buttons to reformat her bed into an upright seat. 'Thanks, did I see you with Alistair?'

'Yes. I admit I might have pegged him wrong.'

'What do you mean?' she said, testing a sip of coffee. Good, it was still warm.

'A few things, none worth mentioning now. Head Office hadn't informed me, but Alistair's heading the review for our incident. He's just done me a favour and agreed to move the interviews to next week. We're pencilled in for Monday morning, if that works for you. Max and Steph will both be interviewed during that session, too, but I'm sure they won't mind keeping this weekend clear either, or being delayed at the airport after their arrival home tomorrow. We all need to some space to breathe.'

'Brilliant, yes, that's good for me. I wasn't exactly enthused by the thought of off-the-plane interrogation under jetlag.' She took another sip of her coffee, which she now realised was sugared perfectly.

Nathan was grinning like the proverbial. Something other than the postponement of the investigation had clearly given him a boost.

'You seem exceedingly chipper for someone running on coffee …'

Nathan nodded. 'I feel it. Alistair's very fond of you, by the way.'

'Oh, for goodness sake, don't tell me this is what it's about? There's definitely no need for the green eye'.

'So it seems. He was telling me about his boyfriend who works on the Google campus at South Beach, back in San Francisco.'

'Yes, he mentioned Ralph at my birthday party, and offered the opportunity of a tour. Interesting place to work.'

'Really wish I'd known about that offer.'

Romilly leaned her face through their partition, simultaneously amused and flattered. 'No one has ever made me feel the way you do. You know that?'

Nathan's lips met hers with a tender kiss. 'That's good to hear.'

'There's no one else,' she stated, underlining the moment.

'Sorry, I'd just thought that maybe Alistair—'

She blinked at him, admiring his honesty. 'I see that. It's sweet.'

'I think you'll find it's protective.'

'If you say so.' Romilly kissed him again and returned to her coffee.

Nathan cleared his throat, in the way that he had something else on his mind to discuss. 'So do you think you'll extend your time on this route, commit to another San Francisco block? Seems like there is still lots to see on layover.'

'Ah, you're getting the same increasingly irate reminders from Crew Services as me, then? I was waiting to speak to you, see what you thought about flying together as well as – I don't know what to call this – our being together?'

'Me too, but we've got to log our requests by tonight. I didn't want to pressure you. Which way are you leaning?'

'Your direction.' She smiled, surprised at how easily the decision tumbled from her lips.

Nathan sighed loudly. 'Sweetheart, that's all I want. So, San Francisco for another eight weeks after our imposed rest week, the remaining two weeks of this block, and the two weeks off duty?'

'I'll lock it in tonight.'

'I think that takes us through the end of the year.'

'It seems so far away.'

'Might get to the Albert Hall at Christmas, after all, then.'

Maybe, just maybe they would.

Through passport control shortly after dawn on Friday, they were headed through customs with their luggage. 'The next few days might be complicated,' he said.

'I know, you were supposed to have Nora yesterday and you'll have her through the weekend, I remember. I need to see my dad tomorrow, then catch up at home. Could do with some time to process things.'

Nathan brushed his hand alongside hers as they walked. 'As long as you don't overthink us.'

'I'll try not to.'

'I want to see you, somehow,' he said, frowning.

'Can't sleep without me after a four-night streak, eh?' she joked.

'You know it's more than that …' he said, suddenly slowing his pace.

'Yes, I do. Sorry.' She stroked his sleeve. 'Catch up by phone?'

'Let's try to sort something out for you and me before then; it's just, juggling things with Liz and Nora …'

Romilly seemed to realise before him that their weekends were already complicated enough. 'We'll see each other on Monday for the investigation.'

'That's work. And three days away. At least we might have time during next week's recovery period. It's probably too cool for a camper van trip, but we could head into town on one of the days, have lunch in Covent Garden, visit a museum or something.'

'I don't know, I have a feeling this is all going to catch up with us this weekend. See how we feel nearer the time?'

'All right,' he said as they rolled through an empty customs hall and through the doors to the public arrivals area.

'Where are you parked? Think I'm somewhere on the top floor, of Car Park 2. I was in a rush on Monday after moving Dad. Gosh, that seems so long ago.'

'I'm Car Park 4, second floor I th—'

Sudden digital camera flashes dazzled them into a halt.

'There they are! Captain Reed, a moment for *London Today* please.' One from a small huddle of media representatives rushed towards them. Another began taking rapid fire photographs.

'Jesus,' Nathan muttered under his breath to Romilly, 'PR didn't expect any interest at this hour – it's one of the reasons they deadheaded us on such an early arrival.'

'Welcome home, Captain,' someone called.

'Thank you,' said Nathan, having snapped back into work mode.

'First Officer West, welcome home with your hero of the hour – is he also the captain of your heart?' crowed a sweaty-looking journalist, extending his phone close to her face.

'Er, no comment.'

Someone behind them impatiently jostled Romilly sideways, separating her from Nathan.

A woman and child pushed towards them, insistent against the tide of exiting bleary-eyed passengers. Romilly immediately them recognised as Liz and a sleepy-looking Nora.

'Nathan! Oh, Nathan!' Liz flung her arms around his neck, causing him to stagger backwards to within Romilly's line of sight. He steadied himself and seemed about to say something when Nora stirred into action, pure joy lighting her innocent face.

'Daddy!'

He lifted her up, transferred her onto his hip, and shielded her face from the cameras. As the photographers flashed away, another journalist approached.

'This is your family, Captain Reed?'

'Yes, I'm his fiancée, Elizabeth,' Liz piped up, posing herself next to him with her left hand lying flat over his uniformed chest, next to Nora's head. 'Welcome home! We love you, and are so proud of you,' she said with a dramatic sniff.

Romilly couldn't take her eyes of the enormous square-cut diamond on her ring finger, shimmering under the flashes.

'Er, Ms West, can we have a moment for *The Standard*?'

'No, I … No comment.'

'Let's get you home,' said Liz to Nathan, smiling. 'I have a car and driver, we'll come back for yours tomorrow.'

'Just, hold on a minute,' he replied, his jaw muscle twitching.

Romilly watched in dismay as Nathan sought her face, lips pursed to speak, only for his attention to be drawn back to his family.

'Daddy, we've made you some cakes!'

'Have you? Thank you.' He kissed his daughter's head.

41. The Driver

Romilly had been in this movie before, but the sequel had delivered an unexpected plot twist. Nathan and Liz were engaged? In a haze of self-preservation, she passed the family reunion, weaving between rubber-necking tourists and crochety business travellers attempting to locate their onward transportation.

'Follow her!' shouted one of the journalists, to her left.

'Yep, I'll shadow; I have her address,' another replied.

One voice pierced her determination to block herself from the mêlée. 'Romilly, that driver,' Nathan called out from behind her.

She turned to see him pointing over her shoulder, then back at the usual row of chauffeurs and drivers of pre-booked cars. She stopped. Was that a sign saying *Reed/West*? She retraced her steps.

'For us?'

'Yes,' the man confirmed.

Romilly turned towards Nathan, who was making slow progress along the concourse with Liz and Nora both clinging to him. For a fleeting moment, their eyes met. Romilly pointed at the driver and shrugged. This guy could be a journalist for all she knew.

With a difficult-to-read expression, Nathan nodded vigorously. 'Yes. Go,' he mouthed.

'Okay, let's go.'

The driver took in the scene, presumably seeking the other half of his ride.

'Sorry, it'll just be me. Need to get out of here.'

'This way.' The driver grasped her flight bags and led them out of the terminal at pace.

Romilly said nothing to the journalist trailing behind, who fired questions about the 'unexpected turn of events'.

'Through here,' said the driver, holding open the door to one of the carpark levels. She kept her head down and walked through.

'Did you know he was engaged and had a family?' said the journalist, still in tow.

The driver slotted himself between her and the persistent questioning. 'Leave her alone, please.'

'Are you in a relationship with Captain Reed?'

'Almost there, it's the black one on the end of that row.' The driver stretched out his arm and unlocked a shiny saloon with a remote. 'Jump in.'

Fragrant leather seats squeaked as Romilly slid into the blessed sanctuary of the car's tinted windows. The journalist turned on his heels, presumably headed for his own transportation.

'Seat belt, Miss West,' said the driver, turning on the engine. 'To Surbiton?'

Surbiton? No, she wasn't going to visit her dad. 'Next town along, Kingston. I can direct you once we're there.'

'Certainly.'

As the driver pulled out of Heathrow and merged the car with the anonymous traffic of London's orbital, the emotional toll of all the week's events caught up with Romilly. Moving her dad into his new home, the emergency landing, Nathan declaring that he loved her, and now, seeing his ex or whatever she claimed to be all over him had … had, what? She swallowed hard, staring out of the window. It had cut her to the core, that's what. An enormous Singapore Airlines A380 roared overhead, wheels yet to retract. How she wished she were on it.

Right until the moment they had walked into arrivals, Nathan had made his feelings clear. He loved her. She believed him, but had given him very little assurance in return. Until he knew all there was to know, she had held back, trying to prevent herself from feeling. Or falling. She'd failed on both counts. Now Liz, placing herself back in the picture, and with his much-loved daughter making them a family, looked poised to pick up the slack.

I should have told him. One miserable tear trickled into another.

'There are tissues inside the central armrest,' said the driver into the rear-view mirror.

'Sorry,' she said, helping herself to several. 'It's just that I might have lost a wonderful man. There are things I should have said to him and haven't. Now it's too late.' She buried her face in her hands.

'Well, I—'

'Sorry, ignore me. Hell of a week, but you don't need a passenger bawling her eyes out at this time of the morning,' she sniffed, trying to contain herself, but she was too tired to stem the outpouring of regret. 'It's just that he told me he loves me. As if I didn't already know, from the way he considers and supports me, surprises me, makes me laugh. Reads me. Just the way he looks at me, melts me. But then there's his young daughter, who deserves happy parents. She has a mum and dad who I had no idea have been or still are engaged to be married. Maybe it's best for her that I disappear back to my own life.' Romilly dabbed at her face, trying to pull herself together. The traffic slowed, bringing the car to a cruel halt beside a family in their four-by-four.

'Just—'

'No, it's okay. I'm all right on my own,' she said, eyes fixed on the family's back window that was stuffed with toys. 'I'll get back on track, pick up extra flights. Keep moving. It's a big planet to fly around; I can easily avoid seeing him.'

'I don't think you should do that,' said the driver. 'If you don't mind my saying.'

Romilly sought the driver's eyes in his mirror. 'You don't?'

'No. As far as I know, he doesn't go around telling women he loves them. When he met Liz, they had a fun few months, but then she got pregnant with Nora. He asked her to marry him because he's a decent man. Thankfully, she said no, as it turned out she already had her eye on someone else who would lavish more of his salary on designer clothes and bags, even back then. Someone who was in the country more of the time to give her the attention she needs.'

'Oh.' Clearly this driver wasn't Liz's greatest fan. And must have driven Nathan many times to know his personal business this well.

'And by the way, you're right about Nora – she would be best off with happy parents, but that doesn't necessarily mean her mum and dad should be together. Liz has probably caught wind of you in the media, and though she didn't want him, she doesn't want anyone else having him either.'

Romilly frowned. 'How do you know all of this?'

'I wanted to say something before, but was too busy getting you away from Heathrow. I'm Andy Reed, his dad. Didn't have a driving job today, so I came to the airport to surprise him. I had a feeling the media might be interested after the news story crossed the Pond.'

Now it made sense that Nathan had wanted her to get in the car. Romilly mentally rewound everything she'd said. 'Sorry I blurted all that out – I'm embarrassed now.'

'Don't be. Gives me hope to hear that Jonathan has found someone he cares about, and by the sounds of it, who cares about him, too.'

Romilly tidied the used tissues into her pocket. 'It's not that simple, Mr Reed – there are things I need to talk to him about.'

'It's Andy, and you know, nothing's insurmountable. If it's meant to be, it's meant to be.'

'I'm not sure I share that view. Life has taught me otherwise.'

'I'm sorry to hear that,' he replied, then paused before adding, 'I won't go into the details, but Marion and I have faced many obstacles. Still, it's our fiftieth wedding anniversary next February.'

'That's lovely,' Romilly said, sharing a smile with him. 'She's been so helpful to me. Will you pass on my best wishes?'

'Of course, though I'm sure she'd like to hear from you herself. Right, so we're at the exit for Kingston. Which way?'

Romilly directed Andy Reed to her modern housing development and through the warren of roads into the cul-de-sac, where her house stood quiet and empty.

'Here you are, then. Doesn't look like anyone's followed, at least. Need a hand with your bags? Or I can come in if you need?' She shook her head, but smiled, recognising his influence on Nathan's considerate nature.

'Thank you, but I'll be okay. The neighbourhood gossip network here is Rolls-Royce standard – need to keep things simple.'

'Understood. I'll flip the latch on the boot and leave you to it then.'

'Thank you for the lift, I really appreciate it. You're off on a job now?'

'No, only take on a few part-time ones here and there. Traffic permitting, I'll be back in Bedford for a mid-morning coffee with Marion.'

Romilly nodded and pulled her house keys from her bag. 'Go steady on the way home then.'

'I will, thank you. Give him some time to sort things out, and look after yourself.'

Romilly closed the front door, beyond exhausted, but clinging to Andy's words. Maybe, just maybe there was hope. She had only been inside for ten minutes, busy relighting the boiler and opening windows to freshen the air, when the doorbell rang. Thinking only that she might have left something in Andy's car, she opened the door. Instead, a face from the airport, wrapped up against the cold in a thick jacket and striped football beanie, held out his phone.

'Darren Alcock, *Express News* – do you have a few moments to talk to me about the emergency landing in San Francisco?'

'No, I'm sorry.' She started to close the door on the cold air streaming in.

'Perhaps you could confirm your romantic involvement with the captain?'

'Please leave. I have no comment. Goodbye.' Romilly closed the door, and locked and chained it, desperate not to cause a scene on her doorstep.

42. Voicemail

The spinning plates of life were in danger of smashing around his ears. A private driver whom Liz had organised to bring her and Nora to greet him was now taking them all back home. Nathan endured the journey in the back seat, wearing a masquerade of joviality to spare Nora from witnessing the anger pulsing through him. His phone buzzed in his jacket pocket. He would check it when he was alone, but he hoped more than anything that it was a message from Romilly. By now, his dad would be delivering her home safely.

Walking through the solid wood front door of his sizeably mortgaged former home, did nothing to improve Nathan's mood, but he held off from venting until Nora had gone upstairs to her bedroom. He stalked into the deluxe kitchen, beckoning Liz.

'What the *hell* are you playing at?'

'I've been thinking – maybe I made some wrong decisions.' She extracted a bottle of sauvignon blanc from a wardrobe-sized fridge-freezer, and poured two generous glasses.

'You definitely did, but that's in the past. You moved on, and now I'm doing the same. What was that performance in front of the cameras for?'

'I never actually said I wouldn't marry you,' she said, sliding a full glass towards him.

'Yes, you actually did.' He slid it back. 'Apart from the fact you know I never drink and drive, it's

341

only ten fucking am, Liz. And what gives you the right to dust off that ring and spring this on me. In public. And in front of Nora!'

Liz wafted her ring hand in the air, dismissing his words. 'Let's just have a drink – then you can stay here overnight after we go out into town for lunch, do a little shopping, like old times.'

'You can't be serious?' He paced the room, running hands through his hair. Then the truth became clear. 'You realised Romilly would be with me, didn't you?'

'She doesn't deserve you,' Liz muttered, taking a sip of wine.

'You know *nothing* about her, and she is *none* of your business,' he hissed, managing to keep his frustration at low volume for Nora's sake.

Another buzz from his phone. This time he went into the living room to investigate, desperate for confirmation that Romilly was okay. Just two messages from his dad.

'*Delivered Romilly home safely. Was upset in the car but okay when I left her. Ring me when you can.*'

And a second, '*By the way, she loves you, son.*'

A sensation akin to breathing pure oxygen filled his body with fresh hope, that this incident hadn't ruined things. She loved him. She *loved* him. He fired off thanks to his dad, then a quick message to Romilly, asking if she was all right and wanting to speak later. Next, he made a phone call.

'What are you doing?' said Liz, wandering through with their wine glasses.

'Ordering a cab.'

'Stay here, I've cancelled my plans – we can have the day together, and a family night later.'

Using their daughter as a pawn in her game was the final straw. Nathan angrily shook his head at her, just as his phone call connected. He paced into the dining room and back, while making the booking.

'There's a taxi coming in ten minutes. Please pack Nora's bag; she's coming with me until Sunday as planned.' Liz sat down on one of the sofas and crossed her arms.

'No, she's staying here.'

'We agreed to share school holidays.'

'As ever, you weren't around.'

Nathan gritted his teeth. 'You know what just happened in San Francisco. Being only twenty-four hours late collecting her is frankly a miracle. Please get her things. I'll bring her back on Sunday, or Maria can come and pick her up.'

'Fine.' She pouted, but didn't get up.

Seconds later Nora walked in. He desperately hoped she hadn't overheard their discussion.

'Daddy, can we have some of the cakes I made now?' She sloped against his leg. He knelt to her level.

'We are going to take them with us to my apartment, princess. Let's pack some of your toys for the weekend.' Her little hand clasped his fingers as they headed upstairs.

Nathan waited for the taxi with Nora and their bags in the hallway. Aside from a series of his photographs on the wall, he was relieved to realise that he didn't miss this house as much as he'd thought. Maybe the garden. He thought of Romilly's dad, hoping he'd discovered the grounds at his new care home. Nathan lingered over a favourite framed shot on the wall that he had taken of the Emerald Temple in Thailand, childishly tempted to leave Liz with a gap on the wall. No, he had the digital version; he'd find his own wall somewhere once this house was sold.

'Can we have a cake as soon as we are there, Daddy?' He smiled at her sweet voice and crouched to her height.

'Yes, we'll have one with a drink and you can tell me about your half term so far – I haven't heard if you've been to play with your friends.'

'I wanted to be here with my toys.'

'Really? But what about—' A car's tyres crunching up the in-out driveway interrupted his conversation. Nathan stood up and gathered the bags. 'We're off,' he called out. Not a second too soon.

Liz appeared, wearing a different outfit, and reeking of a heady perfume. 'Bye, see you Sunday, sweetie.' She kissed Nora's cheek and pointedly ignored him. That suited him just fine; he had very little energy, and nothing more to say.

He had just secured Nora onto a booster seat in the back of the taxi next to him when a man appeared through the driveway's entrance, walking shiftily towards the front door. The man briefly eye-balled him as he passed by. Liz's next victim was even younger than the previous one. A striped football beanie, for Chrissakes.

Reflecting his depleted capacity to think, Battersea was shrouded by a cloying river fog, when the taxi drew up at Boiler House Square, shortly before noon. En route, Nathan had asked the driver to pull in at a food store. At least he and Nora would have supplies to get them through to morning.

Even by the time Nora was tucked in bed, Romilly hadn't replied to his text. He tried not to worry, and instead took a shower before heading to bed himself. No doubt she felt as exhausted as him. His dad deserved a phone call, but the only voice he really needed to hear was hers. He pinged off a holding text to his dad and lay back against his pillows to call Romilly. Voicemail.

'Sweetheart, it's me. I expect you're asleep, which is probably for the best. Wanted to say that nothing has changed for me. There was no truth in what happened at the airport, I promise. I have Nora with me in Battersea until Sunday evening. I know you're seeing your dad tomorrow, but ring me when you can, and I'll make time to talk. Love you.'

Eggs, by the order of Nora Reed, were Nathan's start to Saturday morning. Modern triple glazing and underfloor heating kept the apartment in a toasty bubble, but outside, London shivered. They enjoyed a lazy start, with puzzles, hide-and seek with Teddy, and a Disney princess film. Bundled up, they then headed out for a visit to Battersea Park. He relished the precious father-daughter time as he rowed Nora around the boating lake and took some photographs of the Japanese-style Peace Pagoda that overlooked the Thames, so that they could draw pictures of it later.

'What shall we have for dinner?' he asked her as they entered the supermarket on the way home. 'How about perskitti?' When Nora was a toddler, she'd begun calling spaghetti 'persketti' and it had stuck.

'No. That's what they call me at school – "Persketti head".'

'What? Why? Not because of your gorgeous curls, surely?'

'They go "boing, boing, boing" and laugh.'

Nathan drew his daughter to the side, near a tower of boxed crisps and crouched down to her. 'Who says that to you?'

'Abby, so everyone copies her.'

Somewhere in his memory, he'd heard Nora mention that name before. 'Hold on, isn't that the girl with the Cinderella watch, too?'

Nora nodded, tearing up.

'Listen to me, your hair is so beautiful, they're probably jealous. Is this why you haven't wanted to go to school?'

Nora nodded. 'They don't like me anymore.'

'Don't worry, Mummy and I are going to sort this out with your teacher. We'll ring the school on Monday morning, I'm here all next week, and we've got parent's evening on Thursday, too.' He hugged his daughter tight as she slipped her small arms around his neck. Her suffering was also his. 'If anything like this happens, you must tell us, okay?'

'Okay, but I still don't want persketti for dinner.'

'How about pizza?'

'Yes, but not with olives on.' Relieved that Nora had visibly cheered, Nathan stood up.

'Sounds good, and I'll eat yours if there are.' Thinking of olives flashed a memory from the Italian Festival in San Francisco with Romilly. God, he was missing her. He distracted himself by guiding Nora towards the magazine section. At least he was getting to the bottom of the school problem.

'Do you want to choose a comic? I'm going to buy a newspaper.'

'Yes please.' Nora skipped over to the children's section and started to flick through one called *My Sparkle World*.

Nearby, Nathan popped his usual broadsheet into the shopping basket, but one of the red-top tabloids caught his eye. Jesus - was that a picture of him and Romilly from Heathrow's arrivals hall in the corner? '*COCKPIT CUCKOO*', the strap-line read, then below it, '*Rejected fiancée of hero captain fears custody of daughter after First Officer love-interest tragically lost her own child. See page 5.*'

'Daddy, this one.' Nora placed her comic into the basket.

Distinctly nauseous, Nathan scanned the ceiling for signage to the supermarket's toilets.

'Daddy?'

'Yes, right, let's go and pay.' He added the tabloid to the basket.

'But we haven't got the pizza.'

'No, right. Of course, let's go and choose one.'

Numb, and consumed with utter dread at whatever 'page 5' might elaborate on, he went through the motions of choosing, paying for, and packing up their items. Nora chatted happily as they walked back to the apartment. Something about tiaras and the free bottle of bubbles on her comic. Once home, he made them both a hot chocolate, postponing for an agonising few minutes the moment he could sit on the sofa to read the article.

'*Neighbours of Ms West remember the sorry events of fifteen years ago, when new to the cul-de-sac, West and her then boyfriend Anthony Davies, arrived. Almost immediately it seemed they were expecting and had prepared the smallest room in their three-bedroomed semi with Winnie the Pooh nursery decoration. Their daughter, whom they named Chloé, was stillborn at 24 weeks and Ms West suffered a devastating haemorrhage. A year later, after two upsetting miscarriages, tests revealed irrecoverable gynae damage. Their relationship broke down when Davies, who it's understood is now married with three children, declared his need to become a father was more important than his relationship with her...'*

Nathan had to stop reading. 'Back in a minute,' he mumbled to Nora, and made it to the bathroom just in time.

Slumped on the bathroom floor, he weighed the prick of hurt that Romilly hadn't told him any of this, against feelings of guilt as he replayed every moment that she had perhaps tried to talk to him. The hesitancy she showed when discovering he was a father wasn't jealousy; it was pain. Now, her dad's references made sense. He unpicked Romilly's reluctance to commit emotionally to him – was it any wonder, having been let down by this other man who, yes, wanted children, but who should have stood beside her, nevertheless. An awful suspicion bubbled – surely she wasn't thinking he would do the same if she'd told him? Hadn't he proven himself trustworthy? He closed his eyes, fighting the cramping in his stomach. Oh dear God … Hadn't he suggested that Chloé was a good name?

He splashed water on his face and returned to Nora, who was lying on her tummy colouring in a picture from her comic. 'Fabulous,' he said stroking her bouncing curls. 'I'm just going to make a phone call from my bedroom – won't be long.'

Nathan's usually steady hands deserted him as he called Romilly's number. Bloody voicemail again.

'Romilly, please can you call me as soon as you get this …' Damn, his voice sounded equally as shaky. 'Look, I've just seen the newspaper. I really don't know what to say, or how much of it is true, but just … call me.' He hung up, fearing his message was woefully inadequate. If it weren't for having Nora with him, he'd ask his dad for Romilly's address and book a taxi to take him straight there. He toggled up the volume on his phone to the maximum, so as not to miss it when she rung back.

43. Chicken Dinners

Romilly had wound down the taxi's passenger window during her ride to Cranes Park Care Home, late on Saturday morning, hoping the cold blast of late October air might be fortifying, and help her to process yesterday's events. While Nathan had followed up his unanswered text with a reassuring voicemail yesterday, reminding her that he loved her and saying he wanted to talk, Romilly was in a quandary. She could sense the truth of his feelings – and for a man who supposedly didn't communicate well, he was certainly trying. The problem was, while he might be ready to talk, she wasn't. As the taxi drew beneath the care home's portico, she was grateful for the prospect of an hour or two of thinking only about quality time with her dad.

'Dad, it's me,' she said, tentatively taking a seat next to him in the corner of the airy resident's conservatory. This was always the worst part. She just never knew.

'Hello, love. How was your last trip?' he said, with his gentle lop-sided smile.

'Went to San Francisco again.'

'I've flown there many times.'

'Yes, I recall you telling me. I came back with Alistair Blair this time – remember him?' It was a slight bending of the facts, but Benita had ensured that he'd had no exposure to news of the emergency landing.

'I do remember him. Yes, nice lad, charming too. Popular with the cabin crews.'

'He's a senior captain now, works part-time out of San Francisco.'

'Really? How so?' Her dad frowned.

'Well, he's mid-fifties now, I'd say.'

Her dad picked at a thumb nail, lost in thought. A sad sight. Romilly changed the subject.

'How are you settling in here?'

'I like it. My room is comfortable, and the garden is beautiful – see all those colours?'

She followed his finger to a palate of autumnal hues that graced a deep shrubbery and a tree-lined walk towards an arbour over several tables and chairs.

'Stunning.' She couldn't help but think how to frame the scene into thirds to photograph the spectacle, just as Nathan had shown her at Alamo. It reminded her of plans they had discussed for their repeat block to San Francisco, which she still hadn't locked in. Crew Services would taking matters into their own hands at this rate. 'Shall we have a walk outside? I can pop up to your room and fetch your coat for you?'

'Yes, let's do that,' he said with a wan smile.

'I'll be back in a moment.' As she took the stairs to the corridor of private rooms, passing other visitors and residents, she thought of Marion Reed and whether she too was perhaps somewhere visiting her sister. Lingering at a window that overlooked the gardens, Romilly pulled out her phone to take a photograph, then tapped out a brief message to her. *'Hi Marion, am with my dad today at his new place. About to have a walk in this garden, that he seems to so enjoy. Thank you again for your advice. You'll know I met your husband yesterday, too. I'm grateful for both of your help. I hope you are well, best wishes,*

Romilly.' As she pressed send, a notification of another voicemail from Nathan arrived. Now wasn't the time to be listening to it; she would call him when she got home and was able to think clearly.

Inside her dad's room, she sat in his easy chair for a moment, glad of Marion's advice about bringing favourite furniture with the move. She reconciled the sight of his condensed collections of books, model airplanes, and photographs of her and her mum, with the peace of knowing he had his most treasured items around him. His life in one room. She stood up to look at a framed photograph of him receiving his wings. His curtailed career still weighed on her conscience, but other than becoming a captain herself, which would also prove her capable, there seemed little else to be done that would make up for his not reaching his flying potential. Then the thought struck her that perhaps she could aim to achieve what he had not? Nathan seemed to think she could attain beyond captaincy, after all. She picked up her dad's coat and scarf, mind whirring.

The rate at which the injection of motivation fuelled her unfortunately mirrored the speed at which her dad's attention and energy levels depleted. She had imagined they might share lunch, but it was clear that for today, a limited visit was best. Given her mandatory week of rest ahead, she would be able to visit again frequently, perhaps after Monday's investigation, but on Tuesday at the latest. Shorter visits might be the answer going forwards, in which case, having almost a week between visits while on long-haul blocks simply wouldn't work.

After a brief walk around the gardens, Romilly pulled out her phone to book a return taxi home and noticed that Steph had texted her. After saying goodbye to her dad, she headed past the kitchen that wafted what smelt like a chicken casserole in the making, and perched on one of the sofas in the reception area to read the text.

'*Hi, are you okay? Just arrived LHR, seen the article in* Express News. *Call me asap, can come round if you need x*'

Expecting to find something similar to *The National Enquirer*'s feature, Romilly opened her web-browser and searched for the newspaper's site. She scrolled down, looking for anything that might have prompted Steph's concern. Wham. Hardly able to accept what she was seeing, the brutal revelation socked her between the eyes, tightening her throat, gripping her chest. Her gossipy neighbours; the spite of Liz; that dreadful journalist. She dared not listen to Nathan's voicemail now, not until she was safely behind closed doors.

Sitting at her pine kitchen table, she heard his palpable, stuttering shock. The words might not be there, but ultimately, it was just as she'd feared. Someone wonderful like him, who enjoyed fatherhood, could never want someone like her, a woman unable to give him another child. It was clear now that she had been a selfish fool and should never have allowed their relationship to get this far. She'd fallen for him, but even worse, he loved her. She deserved the pain; he didn't.

Romilly stared at the knots in the wooden table, mind plummeting into a tailspin from which she frantically tried to pull out. Think. Quick, take back control. Hadn't she only today realised extensions to her career aims? Never mind the solitary item on her bucket list, work was the answer, just as before. Nathan would find someone else. She had to do right by him. Clinging to those basic decisions, she picked up her phone. After a conversation with an administrator at Crew Services, she typed out two text messages. The first was for Steph.

'Thanks, yes am okay, don't worry. Painful past life that I don't talk about, sorry. Best to move on, keep busy. See you Monday for investigation interviews. Have a good rest of your weekend.'

The second was to Nathan. *'I'm sorry, truly. Shouldn't have started this. There is someone better for you. Will keep things professional at Monday's investigation. Have requested alternative destination for next block. Sorry again. R.'*

She hovered her finger over the send button, then pressed it. He deserved a phone call, but there was nothing else she would or could say. It was cowardly, but to protect her brittle emotions, she then blocked his number.

Romilly pulled up the notes app on her phone to assemble a list of household tasks that would keep her occupied. There must be no time for regret, self-pity, or double-thinking; instead there was laundry to process, finances to update, and cleaning to do. After fishing out a chicken tikka ready meal for later from her iced-up freezer, she added 'defrost freezer' to the list. Maybe she should learn to cook? Bolognaise hadn't been that hard, had it? She smothered images of a sexily barefoot Nathan standing in his kitchen shortly after she'd unravelled him on his sofa, by emptying the tumble drier. While folding her clothes, she grimaced at the pine-replica kitchen units around her. She rarely spent any time in the house and had never liked the decor of this room; it reminded her of a sauna. Investigating replacement doors was her next thought, but in a rush, she realised the answer to life's 'what next' was obvious. A sizeable project which would take up most of her spare time when not visiting her dad. And it meant she'd leave these appalling neighbours behind. Nathan would be pleased that she had an exciting, new non-work goal. Except that, of course he wouldn't know about it. He was no longer be part of her life. She swallowed back tears and redoubled her attention to tasks from the list. Whether she was spiralling upwards or downwards, she couldn't tell, but neither direction was stopping. At least she could avoid thinking.

Waking up on Sunday morning after a fitful night's sleep, Romilly planned a mammoth attack on her checklist of tasks. She had just opened a black bin-bag, ready to tidy her narrow back garden of fallen leaves, when Steph texted, seemingly needing further reassurance that Romilly was genuinely all right. Back and forth texts ensued, confirming that yes, she was eating, and yes, had briefly seen her dad. Then Steph rang her, still clearly unconvinced.

'Steph, I'm fine, honestly – just get on with your own Sunday and I'll see you tomorrow.'

'Hello to you too,' Steph retorted. 'Excuse me for caring …'

'Sorry.' Romilly dropped the bin-bag, appalled with herself. 'How are you? Was the flight home okay?'

'Yes, pretty standard. I was wondering if you'd like to come over? I'm cooking a roast.'

'Tempting, but I've got things to do and want to get my head clear before—'

'Seeing Nathan?'

'No, I meant the investigation interviews.' And yes, a gnawing trepidation for facing Nathan.

'Right. He'll be there, though.'

'Obviously.' Romilly didn't want to talk about this. She picked up her bin bag and gave it a little shake. 'I'm in the middle of some gardening, actually.'

'Maybe you should clear the air before that, ring him and talk things through,' Steph replied, paying no attention to Romilly's words.

She sighed.

'I might have done that already.'

'The thing is, I know that you haven't. He's texted me to see if I'd been in touch with you. It's all right – I just said I would contact you, that's all.'

'I know you mean well, but he deserves someone better. I've thought it through and made my decisions. I'll be all right on my own. I've asked not to renew my next block to San Francisco, and when I'm at Head Office tomorrow, I've got to drop into Crew Services to discuss my plans for the rest of this block.'

'What? You'll end up manning jump seats to Liberia switching this late.'

Romilly squirmed at the thought.

'You really want to avoid him that much?'

'He needs to avoid me, Steph, and move on. Listen, I've really got to get on, I'm sweeping leaves and they're scattering again.'

'What if he doesn't want to avoid you, though? Have you even asked him?'

Romilly hesitated, preparing herself for Steph's reaction. 'I've blocked him – I'm doing him a favour, trust me.'

'Right, well for the record, I think blocking him was a bit childish. This isn't college; you have to face situations, not hide from them. I'm sorry, but you're kidding yourself if you think that was about doing him a favour. The man's in love with you. Please call him. You owe him that.' Her friend's speaking from the heart forced Romilly's precariously suppressed emotions to the surface.

'Honestly, I really couldn't cope hearing his voi—' The raw truth caught in her throat.

'Oh, hun, don't, you'll start me off.'

'Anyway,' Romilly said, reminding herself that she'd survived harder times than this, 'He had been so looking forward to having time with Nora.'

'Surely a man as capable as him can find a way to manage both?' Steph replied, softly.

Romilly didn't know what to think anymore. 'Listen, I need to go, leaves are waiting, keeping me busy, you know?'

'Yes, okay. But I'm here if you need, and so is the roast chicken.'

'I know. Thank you, for caring, but I'll see you in the morning.'

44. Investigation

Steph had risen even further in Nathan's estimations. At work, a demon cabin manager, and off-duty a solid friend for Romilly, who in trying to help her, was willing to relay news from texts and conversation to him. Having a colleague being privy to his love life wasn't ideal, but having a better idea of Romilly's mind had at least stopped him from losing his own.

Suited and well-prepared, he signed in at Head Office reception on Monday morning, noting that, against her usual form, Romilly had arrived early. He hurriedly entered his own details – if he could get her alone before the investigation started, he knew exactly what he wanted to say.

'Hi there,' said a male voice behind him as he waited for the lift to the third-floor meeting rooms.

'Max, how are you?' He nodded at his second officer, who looked as pristine as ever, despite only having his feet on the ground for twenty-four hours.

'Good, Steph is just signing in.'

'We're all here then.' He tried not to sound disappointed.

On behalf of the three of them, Nathan knocked on the door of Meeting Room 1.

'Come in.' Alistair's voice. Nathan let the other two in before him, leaving him the sole option – after shaking the hands of Alistair, two management representatives, and an administrator – of taking a seat at the rectangular meeting table directly opposite Romilly.

'Morning,' he said to her, softly.

'Morning,' she replied curtly, flicking her eyes very briefly is his direction. One look at her face was enough to tell him that she had seen every hour of the night.

Alistair shuffled his papers. 'Right, let's get on with it shall we? The format will be to hear the report from Engineering; then we'll play the relevant extracts of black-box recordings. After those, we will call you in individually for your recollections of the procedures and events. Just to be clear, though this is a formal meeting, we do not anticipate anything punitive to arise from the actions taken by any of you. As you may know, the faulty component of the wheel suspension has been identified, causing the retraction of the nose gear to fail after take-off, which in turn led to the emergency situation. Of the injuries sustained by passengers, other than smoke inhalation, all were incurred on the inflatable slides or on the runway tarmac during evacuation. Are you all ready?'

Everyone including Nathan confirmed, nodding to one another. Romilly looked at everyone except him, face posed in professional attention. Back to the habit of internalising and control of old. He thought of her other faces – joy, arousal, and hope all of which he'd experienced this past last week, as well as those of fear and shock, that he hoped never to see again.

When the moment came to play the black box recording, the meeting room fell silent. Alistair and Management ticked off items on sheets in front of them, presumably when they heard each of the correct procedures being followed by the flight deck's crew. Alistair paused the recording after Max's message had played.

'Second Officer Krüger, perhaps you would translate the message you left?'

Max sat up a little straighter. 'Certainly. More or less, it said, "As I have already told you, I'm not coming home."'

Nathan glanced at Steph, who was focused on Max, then at Romilly, who now avoided anyone's eye contact.

'I see. Pessimistic, for someone with responsibility on the flight deck,' said Alistair, exchanging looks with management.

'I assure you, it was not to do with the flight or the emergency; it was a personal message for my father. A point of principle, if you will.'

'I see, well we'll draw a line under that.' Management nodded their consensus. 'Let's continue.'

When Nathan heard himself leave messages for his family, and refer to Romilly, he studied her, hoping for some acknowledgement. Still, she resolutely focused elsewhere. He peered sideways at Steph, who shrugged and shook her head.

'All right everyone, if you'd kindly step outside and leave us to it for a moment, then we'll ask each of you in. Captain Reed, you'll be called first.'

Outside the room, Romilly immediately button-holed an unlikely choice of Max for a conversation over at the corridor's window, that apparently excluded Nathan and Steph.

'Quick word?' Steph muttered.

Nathan followed her a short distance along the corridor.

'I've a feeling it may be difficult for you and Romilly to have any privacy,' she said, reaching the same conclusion as he had done already.

'Unfortunately, it looks that way.'

'Maybe I could make sure that Max and I aren't here when you come out of your interview?'

'Captain Reed, we're ready for you.'

Nathan raised his hand to acknowledge the administrator's request, then smiled at Steph's tenacity.

'Thank you, that's a good idea. I appreciate it.'

'Captain Reed?'

'Yes, coming.' He strode past Romilly and Max, neither of whom seemed to notice.

Just forty minutes later, after a thorough grilling but officially recorded praise, Nathan was back outside the room again. He stopped short, finding Romilly sitting alone on the row of hard plastic chairs.

'They'll call you in shortly.'

'Okay.' A brief nod of acknowledgement, nothing more.

'Where are Max and Steph?'

'Gone in search of a coffee machine.'

'Don't blame them. You'd think the airline would lay on refreshments for this.'

The timing and location for speaking to her was far from ideal, but this might be his final opportunity to communicate face to face. He wasn't about to give it up. 'May I sit for a moment?'

'I'll be going in any second.' She said, needlessly straightening her tie.

'Then I'll wait for you, so we can talk afterwards. Maybe we could have a coffee somewhere?'

'I'm seeing Crew Services, then visiting my dad straight after this,' she said, in a matter-of-fact tone, clearly meant to dissuade.

He took a seat beside her and chose the easier of the two subjects to extend their conversation. 'How is he?'

'Don't, Nathan.' She closed her eyes, head bowed.

The need to comfort her was overwhelming. The scuffed heels of her hands had scabbed over; almost of its own accord, his nearest hand moved towards them, but when she opened her eyes, she flinched from it.

'Please, this is hard enough.'

'It doesn't have to be. Meet me after this, before you go to Crew Services or to see your dad. We need to talk.'

'I can't.' She stood up, headed for the meeting room door.

'You can – if you want to.'

'First Officer West, they're ready for you.' The administrator poked his head around the door.

'Thanks, I'm coming right now.'

'Romilly …'

She didn't even turn back to look at him.

'Hello, how long have you been sitting here?'

Nathan snapped to attention at the sound of Steph's voice. He must have been staring into space. 'Not sure, ten minutes or so.'

She murmured something to Max, who retraced his steps back in the direction from which they'd come.

'Changed my mind about having some biscuits,' she smirked. 'May I?' She pointed at the seats.

'Please.'

Steph adopted the same position as him, leaning forwards, hands clamped together. 'I'm sensing you didn't get past the walls.'

'Erected to keep sound and sight of me out.'

'Sorry to hear that. Is it worth one last try, because if so, I have an idea? Maybe leave her a voicemail instead.'

He shook his head. 'You know that I'm blocked.'

'Yes … but I've discovered that voicemails from blocked contacts can still be left – and more importantly, accessed, if someone tells a person where to look for them.'

'And that someone would be …' He cast a sideways look at Steph's nodding head.

'Yes, it would. I could just mention it somehow.'

'I'll consider it. May be my only option, but either way, thank you for your discretion and how you've helped us. I won't forget it.'

'Open tab at the Sky Bar for the rest of this block?' She winked.

'I'll organise it, and will let you know if I do leave a voicemail.'

'Roger that. See you next week for the Monday outbound to San Francisco?'

'Not sure yet, and beyond that I don't know either – it may depend on Romilly. I'm liaising with Crew Services at the moment, but I missed the bidding window for the next block, and being all out of favours with them, who knows where I'll end up.'

'Liberia?' she said, her attention caught by something further up the corridor.

'God, I hope not.'

'Max is almost back,' she muttered. 'Well, I've successfully bid for another block to San Francisco after this. We've still got so much to see there on layovers.'

Nathan noted the 'we', but simply nodded a half-smile. Presumably Max had also been successful in securing a second block. The man in question arrived, bearing mini packs of biscuits.

'Found you the shortbread you like,' he said to Steph, who smiled up at him as he handed them to her.

'You're returning home now for the rest of the week, Captain Reed?' she said, blushing.

'No, I'm headed directly from here to my parents for a few days. In fact, I'd better be off.' As he stood up, Max took his seat. 'Good luck in there, both of you, not that you need it.'

45. Unblocked

'Come in, First Officer West, take a seat.'

'Thank you.' She could do this. Block out. Focus.

'Captain Reed has provided a detailed account of the events of 24 October, which are corroborated by the black box and witness statements from air traffic controllers at San Francisco International Airport's Tower. Perhaps you'd like to begin your own recollections from the point at which you were on taxiway Charlie One, ahead of entry onto Runway 28R for take-off?'

Romilly spoke of the steps and checks she had taken, the communication with Tower, and answered questions about the decisions and actions of Nathan, Max, and Steph. Reliving the event for the second time that morning hadn't changed her opinion that they had all performed to the high standards the airline expected.

'All right, I think we have everything. As with Captain Reed, we would like to commend you on your skilled flying and handling of the emergency.'

'Thank you.'

'And finally, one more thing, and then we'll let you go. You're aware of the mental health support available to you, should you feel it necessary?'

'I am. At the time of the incident, I suffered some post-shock effects, but not since then.' The rest of her life, meanwhile, had imploded. Romilly pushed her chair back, ready to leave.

'Might someone fetch some coffee before we see the final two?' Alistair suggested to the management team.

Agreement all-round saw a ten-minute break inserted into the timetable.

Alistair beckoned Romilly to the corner of the room. 'Before you go, I just wanted to see how you are.'

'It was a little nerve-wracking, but, as I said, no lasting problems,' she assured him, with an appreciative smile.

'I meant the weekend's newspaper.'

'Oh.' She felt her body stiffen, immediately on guard.

'Obviously I was aware that your father had retired early due to family circumstance, but not of the precise details. I'm sorry if what I read was accurate.'

She swallowed slowly, wishing he hadn't raised the issue. 'Mostly, it was.'

'Don't let this stop you from reaching your potential. By others' accounts, and my own observations, you have what it takes,' he said, his tone distressingly paternal.

'Thank you. I'll try not to. And that means a lot coming from you.'

'How is your father, by the way? I haven't heard from him in a couple of years. We used to telephone each other from time to time – I considered him as being one of my mentors.'

Romilly chose her words carefully. 'He still sometimes speaks of you, but suffers with memory problems lately. I'm visiting him directly after this, actually.'

'I'm sorry to hear that. Would you please pass on my regards?' He waited for Romilly to nod. 'You know, I was just a second officer on the South America routes when I first met him, and we got on famously. Years later, I was grinding away trying to accrue the hours needed to apply for captaincy, but he kept in touch, ever supportive and encouraging.'

'That's lovely.'

'He's always been proud of you, that's for sure. I recall a conversation with him one evening, a few years back. I was on layover in Caracas, or somewhere like that, and though he was of course retired, he'd always make time for out-of-hours catch-ups. I'd hear snippets over the years, about your progress; learning to fly; getting your licence; and then being hired by Sterling. Anyway, this particular conversation comes to mind because he repeated something he'd overheard at the annual get-together of retired pilots that had really fired him up – that in being female, "Romilly could never be more than a pilot". I remember saying to him, "You wait, she'll be the chief pilot at the airline before she hangs her wings up", and he laughed. He already knew that you were destined to make it to the top one day. And I'm certain he still does.' He placed a hand on her shoulder.

Romilly could barely breathe. 'That's … unbelievably good to hear.'

'Are you all right? Sit down a moment – there's coffee coming.' She stared at the chair, head spinning. All these years, she'd been mistaken about what her dad really thought. With a flash of dismay, she realised that there was only one person she would have shared this revelation with – and was certain that he would have been just as happy to hear it.

'I'm fine, must get to Crew Services, about my routes before visiting Dad.'

'You don't need to worry about working with Captain Reed, if that's your concern.'

'Sorry?' she said, her focus snapping back. 'What do you mean?'

'It came up in his interview when he was questioned about his black box message remark about you. He was discrete, as you'd expect because he's a decent chap, and seemingly well respected for it. Captaincy is all about making good decisions, and from his interview today, it's clear he wears his stripes well. Off the record, if the barely contained affection I saw in him at your birthday party was anything to go by, I'd also say he's rather fond of you – not that it's my business. Plenty of couples first meet at work, and pilots are no different. Lots in common, both appreciate the demands of the flying lifestyle. Anyway, just so you're aware, he's offered to switch out the remainder of this block himself so that you can continue unaffected, if that's what you wish.'

'I didn't realise he'd done that.'

'I expect your father would like him, by the way.'

Yes, he had liked him. She smiled at the memory of Nathan turning up in uniform, handsome and willing to help her that day. Showing that he loved her.

Alistair kissed her on the cheek. 'I'd better go and have coffee with the others. Well done today. Might see you in San Francisco sometime? Come for dinner with Ralph and me one night – on your own or bring someone.' She didn't miss the quick wink of his implication.

'Thank you. That would be good.'

Romilly left the room, mind whirring at a thousand knots.

'Jesus, that took ages,' said Max, brushing down his jacket in readiness. 'What's that look for? Was it that bad?'

'No, not at all,' she murmured, slumping onto a chair.

'Are you okay?' said Steph, who was frowning at her.

'Yes. No. It's just … I discovered I've been wrong about something, made an assumption too quickly without checking. It's not the first time I've done that lately, so it's good to be called on it.' The meeting room door cracked open.

'Second Officer Krüger, we're ready for you.'

'Wish me luck.'

'You'll be fine, fly boy.' Steph threw him a smile, then, just as the door closed behind Max, her phone pinged. She fumbled in her jacket pocket to read whatever had arrived.

Romilly only then realised that they were alone. 'Where's Nathan?' Perhaps he had gone to fetch some coffee? She peered up the corridor, but there was no sign of him.

'He's gone.'

'Gone?'

'Something about needing to get away for a few days – to his parents, I think. Had a face on him that looked like the sky had fallen in.'

Romilly quickly pulled her phone out of her bag to check for a message from him, then let it slip to her lap when she remembered that there couldn't possibly be one. She closed her eyes, hiding from the awful prospect that she'd lost him, with nobody to blame except herself.

Steph sat down, briefly patting Romilly's leg. 'Had a friend who discovered this thing about smartphones; apparently they automatically reject text messages from blocked contacts but keep voicemails from them in a separate folder – shockingly called "Blocked Voicemails". Also, in case you didn't already know, blocking is a one-way situation. Nothing to stop you contacting the person you've blocked.'

She stared at her friend. 'Are you trying to tell me something?'

'I suppose it depends if you're listening, this time. And might genuinely give him a chance.'

'I'm listening, I promise,' she said solemnly, shifting to face her.

'Then check your phone. There's a vending machine up the corridor, I won't be long.'

Romilly held her breath, hoping with every fibre of her soul that there was a message in her blocked voicemails folder. Her fingers trembled as she sought the correct menu. *Voicemail Nathan Reed, fifteen minutes ago.* She hovered her thumb over the play button. What if it was a goodbye message?

'Hi, it's me. I hope you hear this message. I wish you'd told me about all of this, because I would have said that it couldn't affect how I feel. Just to be sure this communication is clear, I still love you, Romilly West. We have something special here. If you feel it too, call me back. I've gone to my parents for a few days, but remember, you aren't alone.'

She slotted the phone into her pocket in a daze. *He still loves me?* Despite knowing the secret scars inside her, he still wanted to be with her? Despite the way she had ended things, blocked him, and today given him no chance to say what he'd wanted? She had to speak to him, and let him speak, too. While he was driving? No, this had to be in person. That decided it. She could visit her dad tomorrow, and dial into Crew Services from the car. Nothing was more important than seeing Nathan. Nothing.

She set off down the corridor, walking at first, jogging by the time she passed Steph at the vending machine. 'See you next week!' she called over her shoulder, then came back and hugged her. 'Thank you for being a wonderful friend.'

'Happy to help. Off to Crew Services?'

'Not unless they're in Bedfordshire.'

'Good luck!'

'Thanks. First, I have to find my car that I parked a week ago.'

46. Synchronise

The heavy motorway traffic had been agony. Almost three hours later, with afternoon light fading fast, Romilly pulled into a lay-by just outside Bedford's town centre. She switched off the engine and used her phone to search for 'The Old Post Office, Bedford'.

Five minutes later, coasting slowly past the handsome slate-roofed building with its neatly restored sash windows, she'd seen no sign of Nathan's car. After successfully circling side roads of very brown Victorian terraces for a parking space, she slipped her uniform jacket back on, and set off on foot to the house. Standing outside its imposing, black-gloss front door, with her phone in hand, she unblocked Nathan's contact details, then sent him a text.

'Heard your voicemail. Can we talk in person?'

Seconds later, his response arrived. *'London tomorrow?'*

'Can you see me now?'

The three dots of his response-in-progress flickered for a few seconds, then disappeared, followed by the sound of footsteps behind the front door, and keys being turned in its lock. The door opened, revealing Nathan, mouth agape. With his rolled-up uniform shirtsleeves and loosened tie, he looked weary – and so desirable.

'How?'

'I listened – about the old Bedford post office, and to your voicemail.'

Dark, blazing eyes bore into her as he pulled her into the hallway. As the door clinked shut, he held out his arms and she went willingly between them, sighing as he folded her tightly into his chest. She reached her arms around him and they held each other close, swaying slightly in silent connection.

'Good to see you,' he murmured into her hair.

She tilted her face up. 'I missed you.'

He bent his neck and kissed her gently. 'Me too,' he said gruffly. As he squeezed her tight again, Romilly closed her eyes, revelling in his unique smell.

Time stood still.

'Oh, sorry, do excuse me,' said a woman's voice from further down the hallway.

Nathan released Romilly, but clasped her hand. 'Mum, this is Romilly.'

'Yes, the uniform might have given her away, son.' She smiled. 'Hello, Romilly, lovely to put a face to the voice – I'm Marion.'

Romilly wasn't sure why, but she felt compelled to step forward and hug the woman, in whose dark eyes she read genuine warmth.

Marion hugged her back. 'We were just having some tea in the kitchen, before Andy and I go to the cinema. Would you like a mug?'

'Yes, I would – seems a long time since breakfast.'

'Please tell me you didn't miss lunch, dear,' Marion said, in the mildly chastising tone of someone who cares.

'Mum …'

'I didn't really plan to come, I just … realised I wanted to see Nathan and left immediately.'

Marion nodded and shared a small smile with her son. 'I see, well, come on through – maybe you'd like some fruitcake to go with your tea?'

'I'd love that.'

As Marion led the way, Nathan drew Romilly's hands upwards, kissed her sore palms, and gently interlocked his fingers with hers.

'Can't tell you how relieved I am to see you,' he murmured.

'Me too.'

The kitchen oozed homeliness from every quarry tile and scrubbed oak surface. The aroma of something simmering on the hotplate of a dark green range cooker made Romilly's stomach rumble, so the sight of a large slab of cake being slid by Marion across the farmhouse table towards her couldn't have been more welcome.

'Maybe we ought to be serving ice cream, eh, son, now that you've sold another photograph?'

'Oh?' said Romilly, savouring her first mouthful of cinnamon heaven.

'A tour company in San Francisco picked up my ice-cream and Painted Ladies shot.'

'That's brilliant,' she said, 'And so is this cake, by the way.'

Marion smiled.

'I was inspired that day,' he said, pouring her a mug of tea with his free hand, and sugaring it.

'Ready, Marion? Oh, hello again,' said Nathan's dad, arriving in the kitchen with his coat on.

'Hello, Mr Reed, how are you?'

'Do call me Andy, and I'm well, thank you,' although we are going to hit traffic unless we get going.' He cocked a knowing look at his wife.

'I'll get my bag. You two, help yourselves to some casserole later. Fortunately I'd prepared double, ready for the freezer.'

'Thank you,' Romilly and Nathan said in unison and smiled.

'Tempting as it is to have you in my arms, we should probably talk,' said Nathan as soon as his parents had left.

Romilly swallowed. 'I know, though I'm looking forward to that part, very much.'

Nathan hesitated, mug halfway to his mouth. 'You've no idea.'

She stroked his cheek. 'Hold that thought.'

'God, Romilly—' Nathan growled, putting his mug down to curve his hand around her head and bring her lips to his. The way he kissed her, slowly and tenderly, made her heart pound. But they did need to talk.

'Go on, you go first – soonest started,' she murmured, putting some distance between them.

Nathan groaned, collecting himself. 'Right. I've hashed things out with Liz. Though she hadn't realised the journalist would skew the story in that way, she should never have spoken to him. She has secured a buyer for the house, and after we split the proceeds, she'll buy something for her and Nora. Also, I got to the bottom of Nora's school problem, and had a telephone conversation this morning with her teacher, while I was on my way in for the airline investigation.'

'I'm glad to hear that. Are you going to stay in Battersea after the house sale?'

Nathan took both of her hands in his. 'So, I've asked Crew Services to switch me to short-haul routes, at least for the time being. I should have done it years ago. The shift patterns will mean I can go and see Nora sometimes during the week and maintain alternate weekends without feeling jet-lagged. How do you feel about that?'

'I understand that you're trying to be there for your daughter. That's what good fathers do. No challenging time-zone videocalls, either.'

'I'd like you to meet her, without it hurting either of you. I want to make things work for you and me, which won't be easy with you being away on long-haul layovers and me at home every night, but … Why the wide smile?'

'It's just that I'd come to the conclusion my dad needs shorter but more frequent visits, and I really want to be there for him. So, I've also switched to short-haul.'

'I can't believe that,' he said, his smile crinkling tired but loving eyes.

'It might delay captaincy while I build up the hours, but I'll explain later about something Alistair told me, that gives me confidence Dad has known all along I'm headed for it. I'd like to see how far I can get.'

'I'm right beside you.'

'I know. It's being with you that gives me strength to believe that, and one of the reasons why … why … I've fallen in love with you.' Emotion stifled her words.

Nathan pushed his chair back from the table and tugged her chair towards him. 'I love you, too. So much.'

'I thought maybe flying was all I was, and my past has meant I'd become reliant solely on myself. Meeting you and beginning to have friends again has been like switching my life from black-and-white to colour.'

Nathan took her face in his hands and kissed her lovingly. 'That's so great to hear – I wasn't sure that anyone would be interested in a relationship with someone like me, especially someone as amazing as you.' Romilly frowned at him, puzzled.

'What do you mean, "someone like me"?'

'You know, being someone who doesn't share emotion and is difficult to understand.'

'Darling, I understand you perfectly. It's my baggage that's more likely to cause a problem.'

Nathan jiggled the teapot and gestured at her half-empty mug. She nodded.

'Do you want to talk about what was in the papers?' he said, topping up their drinks.

Romilly eased back into her chair, and took a deep breath, summoning the courage needed to explain her behaviour and to share the hurt of her past. 'It's not something I've wanted to discuss with anyone. I decided it was best buried and ignored and that flying would fill the entirety of my life. But it's been on my mind since I met you, fearing that if and when you knew, and assuming that you wanted more children, I'd be … well, basically broken and rejected again.'

Nathan wrapped his arms around her shoulders and held her for a moment. 'It must have been difficult when I was talking about Nora.'

She nodded against the stiff epaulettes on his shirt.

'How much of the article was accurate, sweetheart?'

'Enough. It was an awful time, losing Chloé, the miscarriages … I'd just begun looking into adoption when Tony walked out.'

'God, I'm so sorry.'

'Yep, handed me the keys to the house, left me with the mortgage. But that's just money. Shortly afterwards, my friendships fizzled out, as I'd met them through him.' She swallowed hard, then forced herself to look him in the eye. 'There's no sugar-coating it, Nathan – I can't have children, so if you do want—'

'Stop. I have Nora and I want *you*.'

'Even though—'

'Yes.' He kissed her head.

'It won't be easy, meeting Nora. The truth is, the desire to have a child never goes away, much that I try to suppress it, and as much as I adore flying. Sometimes it catches me unaware, like if I overhear a child calling out "Mummy". It hits me – because I know that'll never be for me.'

'Couldn't you look into adoption again if you wanted? You're only just forty, after all.'

'I hadn't thought so, with the long haul and Dad. I'll see how things go.'

'You're brave, Romilly West, just as your dad said to me.'

Romilly took a moment to finish her cake. Wanting to be sure that Nathan understood one of her biggest regrets, she continued.

'The thing is, he gave up flying for me, I'll never be able to repay that.'

'Fathers don't need repaying, Romilly. We share our child's happiness.'

'You think so?'

'I know so.'

While they drank the last of their tea, Romilly felt lighter and more content than she could remember. 'You make me have dreams again,' she said, gazing into his warm eyes. 'I think I'm going to sell my house – it's time to leave that place behind, start something new.'

'If that's what you want to do, then I'm glad.'

Their phones pinged simultaneously. 'Ah, must be the Crew Services notifications coming in for the next block allocations,' she said, scrolling through the information. 'I'm routed to Marseilles, Nice, and Paris.'

'I have Paris, Nice and Toulouse,' he read, 'so we may even have a few flights together.' His smile said it all. Romilly couldn't believe their luck, and wondered privately whether management had intervened, following the investigation's commendations.

'If we're lucky. There's still two weeks of the San Francisco block to fulfil. I heard you'd offered to switch out.'

He shrugged, as if it were nothing, despite knowing the consequence of late changes. 'Knew you still wanted to see Alcatraz, have a dim-sum dinner, and do other things on your list.'

She smiled at the man whose love and support had transformed her life in six weeks. 'Not without you, I wouldn't.'

He reached for her fingers and squeezed. With his free hand, he tapped a message into his phone. 'In that case, I'm messaging Bill at The Beaumont. On next week's layover, I'm going to spend my photography commission on upgrading us to The Presidio Suite. We can lay in that copper bath with a wicked view of the Bay.

'As long as it's together, I'd love that, thank you.'

'Enough talking for now?'

'Roger that.'

They pushed back their chairs and stood up, in synch.

Epilogue

'If all baths were like this, I'd want one every night,' said Nathan, fixing his sexy gaze on her.

'You see!'

'Yes, I do see. I'm a lucky man.'

'I'm the lucky one.' Romilly reached a bubbled arm over the copper rim and took a sip of her Domaine Chandon.

Nathan swept a hand through his wet hair. 'It's been a great day. Good of Alistair and Ralph to invite Steph and Max along on the Google Campus tour with us.'

'It was. Did you hear Max say that he and Steph were going to the Berlin Christmas markets next month?'

'Yes, so perhaps things are improving with his family. He and Steph seem happy.'

'They do. Time will tell.' Romilly hoped her friend felt as content as she did.

'Nora is excited to meet you at the weekend. I've mentioned "my friend Romilly" enough times now and especially held off from going to The Science Museum, in case we could all visit it together.'

'I'd like that, even though I'm a little apprehensive.'

'I understand that – only small steps, I promise.' Nathan topped up their flutes and lay back. The best panorama of San Francisco was right beside them, but they only stared at each other, all heat, lust, and longing, a mini conversation with their eyes.

'Can you tell how much you mean to me?' he said, an unmistakable husk in his voice.

'Yes.' Water sloshed up the sides of the bath as she crawled the short distance, then straddled him.

He slipped his finger beneath her gold necklace and gently guided her lips to his. 'I love you.'

'I love you.'

'Call and response,' they said, in unison.

Acknowledgements

To my beta readers who made time in their busy lives to review early drafts of *Fall & Fly*, thank you. Your valuable feedback was crucial to its development. Claire Strombeck, thank you for your editorial services, I am grateful for your patient guidance and look forward to working with you again.

Writing can be joyous in its free-flowing highs, challenging in its self-doubting lows and every emotion in between. I am fortunate to receive the ongoing support of my wonderful children, dad, and siblings, and of friends, including my oldest friend Lynn and the wonderful women of 'Where to Next?', but heartfelt thanks are owed to four special people. To Mum and Sarah, for always believing in my journey and to my dear friend Beccie, for cheering me on, and whose treasured childhood photograph with her late, airline captain father fired my imagination for some of *Fall & Fly's* concepts.

Lastly, to my darling Gary, thank you for reviewing copious assignments during my MA, for being *Fall & Fly's* alpha reader and for the steadfast encouragement of my long-held dream to publish a novel. Our own foggy cycle ride across Golden Gate Bridge was unforgettable. I love you. Px

Coming soon –

Red, White & Cue

Meet sports journalist, Cassie, and Nathan's rugby player cousin, Danny, as the brutally seductive worlds of Planet Rugby and broadcast journalism collide.

For Polly's latest news visit:

www.thetownhousewriter.co.uk

and follow her on:

Facebook.com/pollymeekwriter
Instagram.com/pollymeek_thetownhousewriter
Twitter.com/pollymeekwriter
Tiktok.com/@pollymeekwriter

Printed in Great Britain
by Amazon

56901655R00219